DATE DUE

HIGHSMITH   45231

ONE NIGHT STAND

Books by Ben Tyler

TRICKS OF THE TRADE

HUNK HOUSE

GAY BLADES

ONE NIGHT STAND

SUMMER SHARE
(with William J. Mann, Chris Kenry and Andy Schell)

ALL I WANT FOR CHRISTMAS
(with William J. Mann, Chris Kenry and Jon Jeffrey)

MAN OF MY DREAMS
(with Dave Benbow, Jon Jeffrey and Sean Wolfe)

Published by Kensington Publishing Corporation

ONE NIGHT STAND

BEN TYLER

KENSINGTON BOOKS
http://www.kensingtonbooks.com

KENSINGTON BOOKS are published by

Kensington Publishing Corp.
850 Third Avenue
New York, NY 10022

Copyright © 2004 by Richard Tyler Jordan

All Kensington titles, imprints and distributed lines are available at special quantity discounts for bulk purchases for sales promotion, premiums, fund-raising, educational or institutional use.

Special book excerpts or customized printings can also be created to fit specific needs. For details, write or phone the office of the Kensington Special Sales Manager: Kensington Publishing Corp., 850 Third Avenue, New York, NY 10022. Attn. Special Sales Department. Phone: 1-800-221-2647.

Kensington and the K logo Reg. U.S. Pat. & TM Off.

Library of Congress Card Catalogue Number: 2004105349
ISBN 0-7582-0683-6

First Printing: December 2004
10 9 8 7 6 5 4 3 2 1

Printed in the United States of America

For John Scognamiglio
("Thank you" is not enough.)

ACKNOWLEDGMENTS

The creation of this story would not have been possible without the guidance, trust, and most especially, the revelation of experiences from a number of remarkable men who have worked as escorts in the sex industry. Most of them have requested anonymity. I respect their privacy, and this writer sincerely appreciates their generous contributions of time and memories and, above all, their unflinching candor. I particularly owe a deep debt of gratitude to James Jarod for recounting his personal experiences. Also thanks to Chance Caldwell, and to "Carlos," "C.J." and "Craig," for their suggestions and observations.

As always, I am grateful for my gifted editor, John Scognamiglio. Also, Jenny Bent, and (alphabetically) Michael Archer, Billy Barnes, Tyler J. Barnes, Andrew W.M. Beierle, Robin Blakely, Amy Cooper, Kevin Howell, Al Kramer, Rick Lorentz, Chris O'Brien, Julia Oliver, Michael Peirolo, Muriel Pollia, Ph.D., Mark Reinhart, William Relling Jr. (I miss you so much, and I thank you for leaving me with the legacy of your talent and friendship), Rene Reuegg, Steve Sanders, Mark Stroginis, J. Randy Taraborrelli, Steve Trombetti, and Jim West.

Gypsies, tramps, and thieves
We'd hear it from the people of the town
They'd call us gypsies, tramps, and thieves
But every night all the men would come around
And lay their money down.

"Gypsies, Tramps, and Thieves"
—Robert Stone

Love for sale.
Appetizing, young love for sale.
Love that's fresh and still unspoiled.
Love that's only slightly soiled.
Love for sale.

"Love for Sale"
—Cole Porter

PROLOGUE

Dow is not his real name. Twenty-one is not his actual age. Little about this man is authentic. The exceptions are his blue eyes, his thick black hair which tapers into a widow's peak to frame the ruddy complexion of his beard-stubble face, his sullen attitude, and his nine-inch dick. His Abercrombie & Fitch–model body is the sum total of steroids, precision-contouring liposculpture, laser hair removal, Botox, and collagen. Even his career trade, for which he claims to be licensed, is false. He advertises himself to be a massage therapist. In reality he is an escort. In less refined circles, a hustler.

Yet he will tell you that the word "escort" is *not* a synonym for a hustler, hooker or prostitute. His arrogance elevates him above that station of the sex trade. In fact, he believes that hustlers who give twenty-dollar blow jobs to roadside clients are devoid of class.

At a table for two, at the bustling and cacophonous Onyx restaurant in West Hollywood, Dow sits down for a prearranged lunch meeting with a man he knows only as Chuck. During the weeklong ritual of courting Dow by telephone for an in-person interview, Chuck has presented himself as a journalist with *People* magazine. He has said that he is writing an exposé about gay celebrities. Although the mainstream media would likely never commission such a potentially libelous article, Dow is both desperate enough for money and reckless for self-aggrandizement that he allows himself to be easily deceived.

Chuck is as duplicitous as his interview subject. He can effortlessly match Dow's prowess at manipulation. That trait is essential to his occupation too. He is not a writer for *People* magazine. He is Detective Chuck Grant of the Los Angeles Police Department. Vice division.

Although Dow comes with dubious and self-styled credentials (he is, after all, a hustler) he has been recommended by another informant whom the LAPD often uses to ferret out what the American religious right considers acts of abomination against nature, committed by heroes among the glitterati. Until recently, he was one of dozens of prodigiously endowed for-rent boys employed by a man simply known as Fraker. Dow has agreed, for a fee of one thousand dollars, to discuss his relationship with the notorious panderer who, over the past three years, has sent him out to sexually service Hollywood's A-List of machismo cocksuckers, power bottoms and "versatile" tops.

"I want that fucker to pay for victimizing me into a life of degradation," Dow says, condemning the notorious sex merchant whom he holds completely responsible for the fact that his life has not turned out as he envisioned.

His *bête noire* matches sexual partners for the rich and famous. "He has access to a hundred boys," Dow says of his former employer. "Out of every two hundred guys he'd meet in a week, maybe one would be acceptable for him to hire. He has the best selection of porn stars too."

But that was then. Now, Dow is practically on the street. He has been reduced to accepting a ten-minute pump-and-dump rape from any man who will offer fifty dollars. In his heyday, Dow would insist on condoms. Now he doesn't even demand extra money if a client wants to bareback him.

The captain of Administrative Vice for the LAPD would have paid five times what Dow demanded in exchange for information about Fraker. But Dow will never know this. He is not accustomed to negotiating for his services. One flat fee usually covers everything. And he now needs the cash exchange because he is no longer desirable, or in ultra-demand to Hollywood's upper echelon of clients. By merely speaking of his work outside his trade he has sinned. His decline will only accelerate.

Dow scans the room for eavesdroppers. He then speaks almost in a whisper as he takes Chuck into his confidence. He nods at the tape recorder. "Because of my career goals, it's important to me that this tape will be destroyed," he says, with a mixture of fear and self-importance.

"Absolutely," Chuck says. Chuck's response to Dow gives the impression that he and *People* magazine are equally vested in ensuring privacy. Nothing is farther from the truth. As a matter of fact, Chuck plans to make a copy of the tape as a backup. The police department will make numerous duplicates, sealing the original in a vault for legal purposes. From Dow's testimony, Chuck will blueprint the foundation for a sting operation to secure an indictment against Fraker for violation of Penal Code 266i, which prohibits procuring another person for the purpose of prostitution.

It is absurd that Dow fears exposure. Although the Velvet Mafia has made exceptions among certain favored boys, it can be predicted with the accuracy of an actuary that Dow will never have the recording or acting (he vacillates) career he claims to pursue. Perhaps if Dow had focused his attention on befriending one studio head or film star client—as truly successful boys do—then he may have had an opportunity for entertainment career advancement, or any showbiz path.

But Dow has sexually serviced too wide a variety of industry CEOs, creative executives, agents and publicists, all of whom would be loath to risk publicly associating with him outside of private hotel suites, Malibu hideaways or Palm Springs weekend homes. Also, the tight-knit and notoriously fickle Hollywood community will not forgive this act of betrayal that he is perpetrating against them. Leasing his body to the sexually ravenous elite is acceptable. Selling out their names and sexual perversions and fetishes to a journalist for cash is not.

"I've blocked out most of the horrible memories I have of specific incidents that may have occurred throughout my years of work," Dow cautions, with great dramatic flourish. It is a means of maintaining a degree of guardianship over his treasury of potentially defamatory information.

However, Chuck is not interested in prosecuting the famous clients—the actors, singers, writers and producers with whom Dow has been marketed for cash. Unlike illegal narcotics transactions, where the apprehension of buyers *and* sellers is endorsed, Chuck has been instructed by his task force only to pursue those with intent to influence another to be a prostitute, or procure another for the purpose of prostitution. Law enforcement concentrates its efforts on the profiteer rather than the customer of commercial vice. In fact, if Dow is cooperative, Chuck will ensure that he is granted immunity from prosecution in exchange for grand jury testimony.

"I don't escort anymore," Dow insists. "I'm out of the scene. I wanted to go legit. That life, for me, is in the past. I'm better than that."

Chuck is unconcerned with Dow's caution that he might not provide essential facts for this investigation. Chuck is the Barbara Walters of vice interrogation. He says to himself, *How often have I heard a subject say they don't have any information? Then they proceed to spill their guts.* "As you're no longer escorting, what is your present occupation?" he asks.

"Massage. Mostly."

"That's a typical gateway into male prostitution," Chuck says. "Isn't it?"

Dow barely nods his head. "My foray into that occupation was brief," he says. "I fucked the biggest names in the business, but I left at the top of my game," he lies. He begins to explain what he presumes Chuck does not know. "It's not glamorous or happily-ever-after like *Pretty Woman*," he says. "I never got paid to go to dinner with anybody. Only sex. There are lots of ads for massage therapists, and some of them are legitimate. I am one," he insists. "But most of the ads are from guys who don't have a regular job. A lot of students. A lot of guys washed up in porn. Or drug addicts. Damaged goods. Those are the escorts."

Chuck is an expert at exposing an alibi. He begins to peel away at the surface of Dow's life. "Tell me when and how you began as a prostitute."

Dow does not look directly at Chuck. He ponders the question for a long moment. "The first time I ever got paid for sex?" he says. "Um, I was sixteen. Still living at home in San Francisco. I had a friend in school who hustled for extra money. High school teachers, mainly. They're an easy mark. I guess because they face hot, horny teens all day. I never considered doing anything like that. I thought that if I ever sold my body, that I would have sunk as low as a man could go. Then this guy, a pilot with Delta, our next door neighbor, said he'd give me a hundred bucks if I'd let him suck my dick. I didn't have to work all summer because every time his wife left the house he'd suck me off in my folks' garage. He worshipped me. When I wanted to charge more he always paid whatever my price. I loved the attention. And I loved the power."

There is a moment of silence. Dow wants to mete out his currency of salacious information in increments.

"You're a hot fantasy for a lot of gay men." Chuck is attempting to flatter his subject into revealing more.

"I was born to be fucked," Dow agrees. "I'm a very sexual person. I jack off three or four times a day. I attract certain men. But it's still perverse. The whole intimidation thing I project is just an image. Clients don't want me. They want the fantasy of what I sell them." He considers Chuck's affirmation that he is a fantasy man. "Yeah. Friends tell me that I should capitalize on my persona."

Chuck notes Dow's vocabulary. *Persona.*

"When I moved down here to L.A., I put an ad for massage therapy in *Encounters,*" Dow says. "The calls to me began right away. I went to the guys' homes. I encouraged them to become sexual as quickly as possible so that I could get the client off, get out, and move on to the next one. I hated it when they just wanted a massage, or a massage first. I didn't want to do all that work."

"Volume," Chuck says.

Dow chuckles. "Profitable. I made like twenty thousand dollars in just the first couple of weeks. I just wanted to get some quick cash and then leave the business.

"I tried different careers," Dow says. "I got a job waiting tables. But I had to work ten or fifteen hours a day and take all this shit from obnoxious people who might or might not even leave me a tip. As an escort, I made two hundred dollars an hour, a lot of times having sex with really attractive guys. Of course I never told them, but I would have had sex with a lot of them for free, if I'd met them in a club. But some people get off paying for sex."

Although Chuck is eager for more information, his face reveals nothing of his intrigue. There is power in silence. He pays attention—not only to Dow's words, but also his tone of voice and body language. Chuck's eyes encourage his interview subject to proceed with his revelations.

"Sex for hire," Dow continues. "It was more lucrative than waiting tables. Buying sex is the way a lot of rich people spend their money. They're too lazy to go out and look for sex. Believe it or not, a lot of married men came to me because I was a venue for them to get what they really needed, which was to have another man touch them in a sexual way. But I thought that was very bad karma."

Dow stops and considers what he has said. Chuck writes the words *venue* and *karma* in his notebook.

"I thought it was wrong to enable people to be dishonest and cheat on their own relationships," Dow continues. "I didn't want that coming back on me, because eventually I want to date again. You know, find a husband of my own, maybe adopt kids."

Dow hesitates for a moment. "But then I decided that I was providing a real service. I was helping conflicted heterosexuals come to terms with who they really are. I figured it was sort of a spiritual activity I was doing. I was always compassionate with the people I fucked, or who fucked me."

With a raised eyebrow, Chuck prods Dow to explain further how he thought that he was being a hero. "I'm basically a very kind and nurturing person," Dow says, looking into Chuck's eyes. Dow attempts to transmit sincerity. "But then I was forced by my employer into degrading situations. I verbally and physically abused famous people. Tough studio executives who paid big money for me to do that to them. But I never hurt anybody. Not on purpose. I wouldn't do that. But sometimes I did take my anger out on them. These men had everything. Money. Power. Success. They wanted me, but they dismissed me like a servant when they were done with me."

"Some people pay for sex with a hustler because they want to be humiliated or abused, physically or verbally," Chuck says.

"I was an escort. I was a professional," Dow firmly corrects. "But it's true. Some guys have a fantasy that they accidentally crash into a police cruiser and Jeff Stryker in a CHP uniform steps out of the patrol car. After he checks the damage and pretends to take a report, he punishes them by letting them suck his dick and fucks them up the ass."

"Guys actually pay for that kind of mind trip?" Chuck says, feigning ignorance. He needs to make headway with the interview before the subject realizes that he is revealing too much. "I suppose even big name celebrities have their wish lists for depravity."

"I've heard a lot of disgusting sexual requests that I wish I'd never heard from stars I used to admire," Dow admits. "I've created a plethora of justifications to be able to stomach some of the things I've had to do. Now I'm scarred for life. And those men have no idea what they've done to me."

Plethora. Chuck writes down the word.

"There's one star who I used to get sent out to a lot," Dow says. "He insisted that I wear heavy-duty work boots. The kind with the steel in the toe. Before my first time with him, the boss let me know that the star wanted me to treat him rough. I was supposed to break into his house and rape him. He wanted me to kick the crap out of him for real with those boots, and then tie him up and fuck the shit out of him. He was willing to pay anything for me to do it. I was horrified at first. I could have killed him. But I was in such an angry place emotionally I thought, fuck, why not? It's his sick trip, not mine."

Chuck asks for the name of the star. *Jack Lodge,* he writes as Dow speaks. This is not news. The former professional football quarterback-turned-actor has been featured numerous times in the *National Enquirer* for being the victim of unsolved violent crimes. The truth that he is gay and pays for sex with south-of-the-border boys and day workers is a secret well kept within the industry's code of silence.

"One guy, a big producer of action films, had me tie him up and slowly, ever so slowly and delicately, slice down the center of his chest with a razor-sharp bowie knife. He wanted to jack off with his own blood. I did it, but it was only to further my career. At the time I wanted to be an actor. I wanted him to notice me."

"Jack Lunderberg?" Chuck asks, knowing this producer's reputation. "Any film work as a result?"

"One porn video. That's where I got my name, Dow. I'm really trying not to do that stuff anymore. The most I'll do, as part of a massage, is give somebody a hand job or a blow job, if the pay is good enough."

Chuck knows that he has drawn Dow into his confidence. Dow's façade of being a legitimate masseur has been stripped away. Regardless of what he tells anyone, or himself, it is clear that he is still a prostitute. And thinks of himself as one.

"But I only do it nowadays if I'm attracted to them," Dow insists. "And I would never make a client pay for more than the massage. Usually."

"Ethics?" There is a hint of sarcasm in Chuck's voice.

"I'd just rather do a legitimate massage and pursue my singing career. And I'm still hoping to get into the sheriff's academy. That's why I would be very concerned if my name was used in *People* magazine."

The waiter makes an appearance to take their lunch order. Chuck turns off the tape recorder. Dow orders a glass of iced tea, then selects the prime rib. After all, he is not paying the bill. Chuck, whose attention is focused on his work, orders a chopped salad.

After the waiter has departed, Chuck pushes the record button on his tape machine. Dow, without prompting from Chuck, continues his autobiography. "I know you'd never know it by looking at me, but I'm desperately lonely. I want a man to love me, for me. Not just for my dick. Although I've never had any complaints about my cock and how

I use it. But right now, I can't begin to pursue the kind of relationship that I would like because nobody can handle what I do for a living. And I can't give a massage without sex being a part of it. I just get so horny. And it's expected of me.

"I feel imprisoned by money," Dow continues. "The lack of it. And by my circumstances. I don't feel good about what I've done. I should be famous. I could be a singer like Clay Aiken. Or an actor. Anything. I have what it takes. I have personality plus." He smirks.

Chuck remains silent.

"I don't drink or do crystal anymore," Dow says. "When I was an escort, I spent a lot of the money I made on steroids and clothes and tons of drugs. Just to maintain, you know? I blew the money as fast as I could get it. I didn't put any of it away, or do anything productive with it. I felt so ashamed about the way I was getting paid that I just had to spend it. It was dirty money. A lot of the guys I know who hook spend the money on crystal or K or G—to numb themselves against what they're forced to do. I'm not into the whole PNP scene anymore."

"The P and what?" Again Chuck feigns ignorance.

"Party and Play," Dow explains. "Party—meaning drugs. Play—meaning sex on drugs. There's a whole vocabulary when you're in this business and trying to score. WS means water sports. Meaning sex with piss—urine. FF means fist fucking. Bb means bareback. BB in capital letters means body builder. It's confusing when you meet a body builder who is into barebacking. Then he's a BBBb."

Chuck does not require a lesson in the vocabulary of vice. "You said before that this is your nature. So why are you repulsed by your activities?"

"Guys—and women—who are hookers are looked at as lowlifes by society," Dow explains. "They think that we have so little value of ourselves that we sell our bodies just for money. It made me feel like trash to do that work. I have a lot of shame about it. I wish I never had to do it."

Dow is silent for a long moment. It is easy to read what is going on behind his eyes. He is watching himself engaged in a thousand variations on the same theme: sex for cash. Beautiful men. Ugly men. Well-endowed men. Black men. White men. Brown men. Asian men. Men in wheelchairs. Old men. Pathetically ill-equipped men. White collar. Dog collar. All these images clash in Dow's memory.

"Some would say that you serve a real purpose," Chuck says, attempting to urge him to reveal move.

Dow composes himself. "Maggots serve a purpose too," he says. "What I do is perpetuate a neurosis in men's psyches. If you had to pay somebody to have sex with you, wouldn't that be totally demeaning and a straight up insult?" he asks. "If I had to pay somebody to have sex with me, I would feel shitty about myself. Worthless. Ugly. A troll. Giving your body for sex with another person should be an expression of passion. Not a barter for cash. The human body shouldn't be easily given away, much less sold."

Dow accepts his iced tea from the waiter and stirs the drink with a straw. He continues. "Eventually, when I get together with somebody who I love, I wanted to be able to say, 'Here is my body. It is a covenant of my passion and my respect for you. I have kept it clean and pure and I've held it in great value for all these years—waiting for you. And I give it to you only.'"

Chuck controls an involuntary roll of his eyes. He nearly screams out, *Holy Christ! You're a fucking whore!* He has become impatient with Dow's moralistic self-pity. He needs to hear more about the celebrities who have had sex with Dow.

"You're very sensitive," Chuck says in mock appreciation for Dow's sham of virtue. "When was the last time you fucked Les Reynolds?"

The query, referencing Hollywood's most politically vocal conservative Christian and former TV sitcom star, is intended to push the interview toward the main objective. That goal is to fill an audiocassette tape with a veritable black book of celebrity names and their weaknesses of the flesh, all of which will be used to indict the most notorious male panderer in Hollywood.

"Okay," Dow relents. "The guy I used to work for, the one who sent me to the Beverly Hills hotshots, made us—me and the other guys—swear we'd never discuss our clients. But he'll never know about this, right?"

"I can't imagine how," Chuck says.

"Reynolds. That hateful, nelly old queen. I've fucked him with his own Oscar. I knocked over his fuckin' Emmys and People's Choice Awards as he chased me around his estate. I sacrificed myself to that man. I engaged in behaviors that are repulsive to me. I tried to turn my mind off and say, 'Don't think about what he's doing to you, this'll be over soon.' The only way for me to self-medicate was to count the money and take a lot of party drugs. And at the end of a weekend of debauchery, looking at a stack of hundreds amounting to three or four thousand dollars spread out on my bed, I'd say, 'Okay, it was worth it.' But I can't ever get my innocence back, or kiss somebody without thinking of that old freak."

"Explain," Chuck says.

"I have this belief that you absorb someone's energy when you have sex with them," Dow says. "You mix energy with people when you fuck them. His energy was just toxic. I mean, you can't be in a room with him for five minutes without it getting all over you. It's disgusting and depressing. I had to take a lot of showers after our meetings. And a ton of drugs."

The waiter has served lunch. Dow and Chuck spend the next few minutes sampling their food. Dow is ravenous. He hasn't afforded prime rib in a long time. Chuck moves his salad around with his fork. Chuck only wants to convince Dow to nail his former boss.

After tasting his salad, Chuck continues his interrogation. "William Harsh pays for escorts, doesn't he?"

Dow takes a sip of iced tea. "He was one of the first celebrities I was thrown to," Dow says, nodding. "He just wanted me to pose in the nude. I have a great body. He's a little guy, so I guess he got off on how well built I am. He never took his jeans or T-shirt off. I think he was hiding a puny physique. And a thumbnail dick. I heard he only has an inch and a half. I never saw it. He always climaxed in his underwear, without touching himself. Just the sight of me made him cum. I have that effect on men. It's my DNA."

Chuck throws out another name. "Dwayne Stone?"

"That pig? I was always told not to shave or wash for a few days before seeing him," Dow says. "He wanted guys who are extra thick and uncut, like me. The idea of my cock being rank and cheesy and barebacking on other men was a head trip turn-on for him. Shit, he's probably the hottest celebrity I ever had sex with. He is hung like a horse. He lived a totally heterosexual life—outside of our weekly meetings, that is."

Chuck nods in understanding. Dwayne Stone was every father's dream son and every queer boy and straight girl's fantasy. "I also want to hear about Linaisa and Bob. The Morrisons. They're an older couple. Well-respected writers. Part of Hollywood establishment. It's common knowledge that they were part of your club."

"Big time," Dow confirms. "At first, Bob wanted me to fuck Linaisa, while he watched. Then he wanted me to fuck her while I put a dildo up his ass. But then we switched and I started just fucking Bob while Linaisa watched and got herself off."

Chuck hears the almost imperceptible sound of the audiotape cassette automatically switching over to record on side B. He can't waste any more time on the B-List celebrities who have thus far been offered up as proof of Dow's connection to the Hollywood gay elite. He must now focus on the prize.

"Fraker," Chuck says.

The name sends a shiver through Dow, and threatens to derail their conversation. It is a look that Chuck remembers from when he worked on another undercover drug sting and asked a certain drug-addled singing diva if the rumors were true that she was born with both male and female genitals. He suspects that Dow may terminate the interview as that crackhead diva did, and storm out of the restaurant.

"Fraker is a name I keep hearing a lot as I research this story," Chuck says. "He's not a star or celebrity so how does he fit in?"

Dow hesitates. He looks at Chuck with eyes that plead *Don't ask me about him.* He glances around the restaurant. "Not here. Not in public," he says. He reaches over and pushes the stop button on Chuck's tape recorder.

"You're getting paid a lot of money, stud," Chuck says. "Answer the questions or say good-bye to the cash."

There is an unsettling silence between the two men. Chuck has trapped Dow. Chuck suggests, "Let's call him Joe." He turns the tape recorder back on.

Dow is uncertain. The name of the man now referred to as Joe has been the dominant presence in the Hollywood pornography and prostitution scene for a decade.

"Your survival money is on the line," Chuck reminds his interview subject.

"He was horrible. He was disgusting. That's all I'm saying about 'Joe.' "

"I don't believe you," Chuck insists.

"Write down this name: Derek Bracken," Dow says. "Pay the check. You'll have to come to my place to get what little shit I know. It's Derek's story that you really want. Not mine. And it leads right from this very restaurant to 'Joe.' "

ONE

Kid, you've got a load of uranium in your pants. Boys like you don't exist in the real world. You could make a freakin' fortune peddling your rod and selling your seed. I'd bet my Rolex that men—and women—would give a year's pay for a piece of you. You're in freaky horny Hollywood. With a horse dick like yours, you can get anything you want. For Christ's sake, who or what are you saving it for? Your value depreciates every time you jerk off and give up a load some sucker would pay for.

Derek Bracken divided his concentration between his duties waiting tables at Onyx, and the playback in his head of Marshall Topper's pitch that Derek should seriously consider alternative work: cock for cash.

Derek wasn't your typical six-foot-tall, blond-haired, green-eyed, killer-smile-with-dimples, muscled, waiter/wannabe actor/wet dream fantasy. Although he was all that, he had an indefinable something extra, the "It" factor which made people of both genders—queer, straight, bi, trans—unconsciously respond to him. It was as if he was followed around by a cartoon dialogue bubble floating over his head announcing: *Erotic twenty-four y/o, silky lashes, full lips, ripped bod, veiny uncut meat, big balls, smooth chest, horny sex pig, fuck machine. No reasonable offer refused.*

Derek wasn't ignorant of his charms. Marshall Topper, on the other hand, was a repulsive reptile. However, he also defined the term *cocksure*, which made some people overlook his Brillo-pad hair, pug nose, blubber lips and lewd demeanor. The fact that he drove a Hummer and lived at the glitzy La Talmadge Apartments made showbiz climbers and class conscious–types take notice of him. His dialogue bubble read: *Drug charges, DUI, felonies, misdemeanors, body odor.*

"I'm fabulously rich," he once explained the unaccountable reason for his incredible success getting laid by hot boys. "I discovered early on that I could get all the attention I wanted by bankrolling porn videos. Hot guys can't get enough of fat cat millionaires like me."

The hair on Derek's ball sack itched as he recalled Marshall's interest in pursuing him to join Marshall's coterie of for-rent boys. As the din of laughter, conversation, and cutlery bruising the plates in the busy restaurant faded into white noise, Derek's thoughts wandered to imaginary sex scenes, in which he was paid to participate. *I choose the guys I fuck,* Derek said to himself. *Not someone with a string attached to my dick.*

Marshall's voice was still demanding attention inside Derek's head. *I can instantly evaluate a stud's moneymaking potential,* the raspy voice echoed. *It's a gift I have. I'd say you could make ten K a month. More if you service the right clientele.*

Derek absently nodded his head to himself in agreement. Marshall's "voice" was louder than usual tonight; a result of a table of particularly irritating customers. Their rude treatment of him made Derek long for a new job. Or better yet, financial independence.

Marshall had been on target when he suggested that the idea of a financial payoff for sex was not an original notion to Derek. From time to time, customers at Onyx—and at dance clubs—offered to pay for play. The overtures were usually from men who were used to waving a hundred-dollar bill under a pretty boy's nose, knowing that cold cash spoke an international language.

Derek had made the trade a few times. Although it was more out of curiosity and an elevated level of horniness than for the money. Derek didn't attach any stigma to the sex trade business. In fact, he advocated prostitution as one of several billion basic human rights. "Hell, its been going on forever," he said more than once, arguing in defense of a friend who had often sold himself along Santa Monica Boulevard to pay for law school. "It's ridiculous that prostitution is illegal anywhere," Derek said. "The healthiest, most disease-free, drug-free prostitutes or street hustlers are in the countries where it is legal. The government in Holland is smart. They just tax it. May as well, since they're never going to get rid of it anyway."

But Derek had always been selective of the guys he dated, and he did not want to have to work hard to please some guy just because the guy was paying him. He had enough of that as a waiter at Onyx.

You're more of a stud than most of my boys, Marshall's voice purred. *If you're ever interested in hanging up your waiter's apron and snaking a drain for real bucks . . .*

Derek's recollection of Marshall's offer was abruptly shattered when his boss, Jet Paterson, the restaurant's female manager, suddenly tugged on Derek's shirtsleeve and led him to the side of the room. "Table seven has been seated for five minutes and they don't have menus," Jet snapped. "The guys on three need their check. The single on seventeen has been waiting since the end of Prohibition for you to return her credit card. What's your fucking problem tonight?"

Derek put on his most seductive smile, then hurried back into the dining room with the Visa card belonging to the woman on seventeen. Immediately he was back in cordial waiter mode. The woman seated at the table addressed Derek as she signed her copy of the restaurant's dinner bill. "My girlfriend's a cow," she said.

Derek smiled as he tried to connect a thread of a statement he may have made that jump-started the weird comment. He mentally ran down a list of possible links to livestock. *Steak? No, she had the salmon.*

"She's one of those happy cows," the woman added, her speech slurred. "Or is it contented? I get my animal adjectives mixed up."

Milk? No, she definitely had wine. Chardonnay. Three glasses, in fact.

The woman blushed, as if realizing that she sounded utterly vapid as she offered the unappealing bovine description of her friend. "What I mean," she said, "is that my friend's an actress. She does the voice-over for that commercial about California cheese. That's where the cow part comes in. You two would be cute together."

"I see." Derek nodded his head. *Hell, Debra Messing was just in here. I'm supposed to get excited about some voice-over actor in a TV ad?* But Derek was an artful politician who would not risk the possibility of offending any constituents, or in this case, a customer with the potential for leaving a substantial tip. "Fun commercials. The talking cows, I mean," he said.

Derek was used to men and women blatantly hitting on him. Often, cocktail napkins left on the table contained scribbled telephone numbers written on impulse, or a dare, or a state of inebriation. Derek enjoyed the flirtations. However, he usually passed the propositions on to his best pal Juan, an oversexed busboy.

Derek had learned that when Juan wasn't to be found in the dining room, he was probably in the men's room jerking off. Whenever an urge for sex occurred to Juan he had to gratify it. "I just go in there, squirt it down the drain and come back to touching all the glasses and silverware. They think it's the blue cheese dressing on my fingers," Juan joked. He eagerly accepted Derek's cast-off paramours.

Derek wasn't necessarily uninterested in the men who desired him, but he never wanted to be referred to as, "That waiter from Onyx that I fucked." The few times that he had accepted a date from a customer, he was paranoid for days afterward, concerned that patrons who chuckled conspiratorially or abruptly suspended their conversations as he approached their table were discussing whatever some friend-of-a-friend may have had to say about him.

This encounter with the cow lady seemed too much like one of Derek's nonsensical improv acting classes where ridiculous situations required equally ludicrous banter. But Derek didn't have the time or the inclination to play along with what he supposed this woman was getting at—a date. He smiled. "I'm, um, seeing someone at the moment," he lied. "It's only been a few months, but we're trying to make it work."

The woman looked into Derek's eyes and smiled. "Gay, huh?"

Derek shrugged and nodded. "Mostly."

The woman had spent the evening looking at her wristwatch, glancing expectantly at the front door and scanning the dining room. She had studied Derek and observed his striking physical features. And his voice—deep and rich. And his irresistible southern accent. It suggested to her that he had a pair of large, heavy testicles and that he would be a hard-driving and demanding lover. She once again looked at him with sexual longing. But the fantasy of Derek being possible fuckable material for her friend—or perhaps for herself—had now vanished.

"Your guy is lucky," the woman said, gathering her purse. "You've been a marvelous waiter. God knows I've had plenty of opportunity to watch you." She sighed, then pushed her chair away from the table. She brought herself to her feet. She came up to Derek's collar. "Did I just embarrass you?" she said.

"No, I'm completely flattered," Derek said. "And I'm sure that your cow friend is nice. Tell her that if I ate dairy, I'd buy her cheese."

The woman grinned. "It's not actually *her* cheese, but . . ."

Derek was a practiced master at turning around potentially awkward social situations and making others feel at ease. "Have a wonderful evening, Miss Charles," he said with a genuine smile, shrewdly remembering the name on the woman's platinum American Express card. "Come back and see us soon."

"Count on it, Derek." She had obviously mentally recorded the name on his badge. "And good luck with your career. I presume you're an actor. You've got the looks. You're bound to go far."

Derek smiled. "Yeah. All the way to the kitchen," he joked.

"Patience. Your time will come," she said. "I'll keep my eye on the screen for you."

Derek watched as the woman walked across the room past the restaurant's host. He turned away feeling cheerful and uplifted.

He then rushed to another table where two attractive and slightly built but successful-looking men of twentysomething age, held hands and stared into each other's eyes. *Junior studio executives . . . third date . . . it'll last six weeks,* Derek decided. But a pang of envy for their obvious lust and happiness washed over him. He was reluctant to interrupt their preoccupation with each other, but he wanted to make certain that they felt as though they were the most important men in the restaurant. A satisfactory tip depended on Derek's convincing them that there were no other customers who meant more to him.

"Everything acceptable, gentlemen?" he asked. Both men came out of their reveries and looked up at Derek's wide smile, anchored on either side by deep dimples. Although it was obvious from their lack of attention to their *pescado a la sal* that neither had much of an appetite for food. They said in unison that their dinners were fine.

Speaking low, as if to take them into his confidence, Derek said, "I'd like very much to bring you both another glass of wine, with my compliments."

"You're precious," one of them gushed.

"That would be lovely," said the other.

Derek need not have been so generous. He knew that customers in love tended to leave larger gratuities. The liberal tippers wanted to impress a paramour, or their endorphin levels were so high that their brains temporarily blocked their ability to add less than twenty percent of the check.

As Derek retreated from the table he heard the men agreeing that their waiter was "a stunner." He felt like whistling as he wended his way through the vast space of tables and diners and proceeded toward the bar. When he returned and placed two glasses of Merlot before them, the men each looked at Derek's badge and thanked him by name. This time as he left the table, he heard one say to the other, "If I were running the fucking network, he'd have a series so fast . . ."

From your lips . . . Derek silently mouthed, as he moved toward the kitchen. He needed to pressure the chef to expedite the chicken curry and penne with veal Bolognese for the two middle-aged men at table sixteen. They had just asked about the possibility of their meals arriving before the next snowfall in West Hollywood.

En route to the kitchen, he overheard snippets of conversation. ". . . I told him, it's easy to fuck a fool, that's why I married you! . . .", ". . . The idiot thought Clytemnestra was an STD! . . .", ". . . Whatever happened to Loni Anderson? . . ."

Derek stopped at the thankfully now-deserted *table from hell* to retrieve the plastic tray on which the dinner bill receipt rested. He frowned. "Christ," Derek muttered, as he saw that an engraved business card had been laid on top of the check, which was placed facedown. Thinking that one of the jerks from the party of four had taken an interest in him, Derek grimaced and shook his head as he read the card: SMILE. JESUS LOVES YOU.

Juan was at the table clearing the place settings. He sang, "Bringing in the sheets. Bringing in the sheets. We shall come rejoicing . . . Why would anyone write a religious song about doing laundry?"

"I think it's sheep," Derek corrected. "Bringing in the sheep."

"*Sheaves,* you dorks," another waiter said as he passed by. "Not sheets. Not sheep."

"Well, Hail Mary, full of grace, to you too. Cocksucker," Juan added in Spanish.

Derek returned to thinking about the hypocrisy of the pious smiley-Jesus sentiment, coming as it did from the most hostile patrons he'd had in months. Derek shook his head as he turned the dinner bill faceup. His eyes immediately went to the line on the receipt that was reserved for entering a tip: Ø.

Derek whirled around looking for the customers. They had disappeared. "Smile my Jesus freakin' ass!" he muttered. "They stiffed me," he said to Juan.

The patrons—two men and two women—had been difficult from the moment Derek first greeted them with his winning smile. They were dismissive of him, as though he was an impediment to their enjoyment of a satisfying evening. The first bottle of wine that Derek opened and poured for them had been rejected because it was, "Too bitter!" One of the men acted as though Derek was personally responsible for the botched fermentation process.

The onion soup gratin was, "Made by a culinary school dropout who doesn't understand gastronomic subtleties," the other man in the party claimed. Yet they consumed every spoonful. The skirt steaks, while ordered medium rare, were sent back for being *too* medium rare. Even the dinner rolls were unacceptable. Not warm enough. Not fresh enough.

"Who recommended this Calcutta dung heap to us," said one of the four, as if Derek was not standing beside their table. He may as well have been a hologram. Already Derek suspected that their harassment was a set up, an excuse to defend leaving a small tip. Derek had been prepared for a meager ten percent. But to receive nothing, that was a slap in his face.

Derek crumpled the Jesus card in his hand. He dropped the insulting gratuity onto one of the plates that Juan was collecting along with the other detritus of the slovenly diners. "The Lord giveth, and the Lord taketh away," Derek grunted, recalling the gracious customer who had the cow friend who had exalted him and his service.

"Lookie," said Juan, pointing under the table. "Somebody dropped their cell phone. Lost and found?"

"Let your conscience be your guide." Derek smirked as Juan retrieved the phone and furtively stashed it among the rolls in the breadbasket, which were bound for the garbage Dumpster in the alley.

As Juan lifted his tray and rested it on his strong shoulder, he exchanged a knowing grin with Derek and moved toward the kitchen.

Seething with resentment over the affront of not receiving a well-earned tip, Derek pushed the swinging door to the kitchen a little too hard. On the other side, Jet Paterson jumped backward in the nick of time. "Put the breaks on for the old boss lady, would you, please?" she said.

Jet was *not* old. She was just twenty-three. But she had a maturity, authority and work ethic that had catapulted her from cashier to waitress to manager in less than six months' time. She was a taskmaster and tonight she was in a grumpier than usual mood. She scolded Derek. "Find that smiley face I saw you wearing to hustle those two cuties on number seven. You're not paid to give attitude."

"My smile left in a doggie bag by that four-top on number twelve, along with my goddamn tip," Derek said.

One of the dishwashers, a beady-eyed parolee from a prison work/ release program, was loading plates and glasses onto the conveyor belt of the dishwashing machine. He overheard the complaint. "If those dudes come back, they can have one of my sneeze salads."

Jet looked aghast and covered her ears. "That's so wrong!" she said. "Spare me the vivid details. I can't take another 'eat at your own risk' story. Used condoms must not end up in the cucumber soup!"

"I can't wait to get out of this place for good," Derek said. He was once again thinking about what it would be like to have a job where he just had to get sucked off a few times a day, at a couple hundred bucks per mouth. Ten clients a weekend would be more lucrative than what he made over a forty-hour workweek at the restaurant. And a lot less time working on his feet.

"Careful what you wish for, stud." Jet locked eyes with Derek. She moved to reenter the dining room, then turned back to face Derek and held the door ajar. "By the by, Marty and Felicia have a reservation," she said. "It's her seventieth, so drinks are on the house." She smiled devilishly as she turned and left the kitchen. The door swung in her wake.

"Oh, man." Juan sniggered. "We got Marty and Felicia. He'll be on the prowl again. I'll cover your ass if you cover mine." He followed after Jet, before Derek could punch at his arm in mock reprisal.

Derek's malice toward the party who had withheld a tip faded with the news of the imminent arrival of the two regulars. Marty was in his mid-thirties, balding, already showing signs of gravity-challenged shape-shifting. He pretended to be as dense as the proverbial mud fence. His thick tongue and monosyllabic responses to questions usually belied intelligence. And Felicia was celebrating the big *seven-oh* tonight. And she was rich. Her dead first husband's business of shrink-wrapping the sides of office buildings with movie and product advertising kept her ensconced in a Larchmont mansion with Marty, her chauffeur-turned-boyfriend. "Driving Miss Crazy." For every day that DreamWorks or Mercedes-Benz rented the space outside the windows of hundreds of buildings around the world, the numerical figures in Felicia's checking account skyrocketed.

Derek actually appreciated the couple's relationship. On the surface it seemed an odd arrangement. It was the other restaurant staffers who couldn't make the leap over the hurdle of knowing that, as a condition of financial support, Marty was required to have sex with Felicia twice a week.

"Hey, it ain't that hard to do," Marty had confided to Derek one night while waiting for Felicia to shuffle out of the ladies' room. "The titties are saggy, but she's still got a pretty nice ass. Turn out the lights. Put on the porn. Bend her over and voila! I can fantasize about anything—even a guy like you—if I want to." Marty gave Derek a lascivious look.

"He makes her hot," Derek had said to Juan one evening. "And when Felicia's hot, he gets a Lamborghini. Everybody wins."

"But she's ancient!" Juan had cried.

"Money's a great aphrodisiac," Derek stated. "Try getting it up when you have the pressure of worrying about rent and food."

Suddenly, the chef's spring-loaded bell chimed in three staccato strikes. Derek's attention snapped back to his duties. "Shit! Table sixteen!" he groused.

He raced for the steam table to collect the dinners. He grabbed a pot holder, gingerly picked up the hot plates, and set them on a tray. He hoisted the load onto his shoulder and cautiously backed against the kitchen door.

As Derek arrived to serve his ravenous, pouty customers he apologized profusely for the unusually long delay. As a gesture of appreciation for their indulgence he offered to comp both men another glass of wine. "You guys are the most patient men I've ever had the privilege of serving," he cooed.

At another table, Juan sidled up to him and begged, sotto voce, "Colt model at table three. Please, please, *please,* use your charm for thirty-percent of the check for you and a phone number for me!"

Derek surreptitiously looked in the direction of the man whom Juan appeared eager to seduce. "Heck, I'd bend over for that one myself," Derek said, deflating Juan's spirit. "I'm joking," he added quickly. "He's all yours. An early Pride Day present."

* * *

As the night wore on, Derek circulated from station to station, working on overdrive to address the needs of his customers. Marty and Felicia were in a particularly festive mood, and when Derek brought two slices of cheese cake dripping with a thick cherry sauce, and a candle on one, Marty withdrew a one hundred dollar bill from his money clip and palmed it to Derek. After Derek instigated a rousing a cappella rendition of "Happy Birthday to You," he got a pat on his butt from Marty.

At eleven-thirty, Jet spread the word that she was calling a staff meeting. It would commence the moment the restaurant was empty and the doors were locked. The entire service staff was summoned, including the busboys, as well as the chefs and dishwashers. Attendance was mandatory.

"Fuck! It's Saturday night, for Christ's sake!" moaned one of the waiters.

"I've got a hot fuck waiting for me at two-thirty!" said another.

"I'm doing the early Sunday shift! I'll be a wreck tomorrow!" whined yet another.

Rumors about the reason for the assembly ran the gamut from a crackdown on food pilfering to customer complaints to a change in menu to Jet announcing she was moving on to another restaurant. "That would suit me," one waiter said to another.

"Good riddance to the bitch," another waiter snapped.

"Yeah, but the next one could be worse," someone else offered.

When the final patrons had been ushered out of Onyx, Jet locked the front door and walked back toward the banquet room where thirty employees were waiting for her. The Onyx staff was scattered in cliques, seated on the floor, leaning against the walls, perched on tabletops. All at once, everyone became silent. Jet withdrew a Marlboro box from her pants pocket. She tapped out a cigarette, then retrieved a disposable lighter from her other pocket. "Any objections?" she said, flicking her thumb over the rolling flint of the lighter and bringing the flame to her cigarette. She inhaled the smoke, held it in her lungs for a moment, then exhaled. "This is going to hurt me more than it's going to hurt you," she said as a noxious cloud swirled around her.

"You're the one who's courting lung cancer," a voice said from the back of the room. A small ripple of laughter rolled through the crowd.

"This is serious," Jet interrupted. "We're all canned."

For a moment, no one made a sound. Perhaps what Jet had just said was a joke. Maybe they hadn't heard her correctly. "This is our last night," she went on, "Onyx won't be open tomorrow."

Derek spoke up. "What are you saying, Jet?"

"Are you deaf?" She looked irritated. "I'll repeat for Derek and all the ESLs. Go home tonight. Wake up tomorrow. Get up. Then start looking for another job, 'cause you ain't got one here. *Comprendo?*"

The room erupted with dozens of questions posed simultaneously. Jet took another inhalation of smoke. "Onyx has been sold. The new owners plan to renovate the place," she said.

"How long?" Derek asked.

Jet shrugged. "Look, this is a shock to me, too. I just found out this afternoon. The owners called me at home."

The room grew silent as Jet explained that the Barton brothers had sold Onyx to the owners of a popular restaurant in San Francisco who wanted a slice of the West Hollywood money pie. They planned to re-model the dining room to duplicate their success in the Bay Area. The good news was that they would consider rehiring as many of the Onyx staff as possible.

"But that's bound to be months away and there aren't any guaran-tees." Derek frowned with dissatisfaction. "None of us can afford to be unemployed."

His words were met with a roar of agreement. "What did you say to them?" Derek spoke up again. "What about your job?"

"This is my last night, too," Jet said. "They've sent a team of security officers to collect my keys, count the money and escort me—and all of you—off the property. It sucks. The ungrateful shits are too scared to come down here and tell you this themselves. I know how you all feel. Trust me, I've got rent and bills to pay too!"

"So what are we supposed to do?" Derek spoke for everyone pre-sent. "Decent waiting jobs are almost impossible to get in this town. Are we eligible for unemployment benefits?"

"The full-timers will get an extra week's straight time. Everybody else . . ." Jet's words trailed off. But the message was clear. Those who needed help most—busboys and dishwashers—would get nothing, except the possibility of being rehired when the restaurant reopened.

"I'll stick around and try to answer any other questions," Jet said, "but I've told you exactly what they told me. One thing I'll add, and I know it doesn't mean much, but I've loved working with all of you. There isn't a single one of you I didn't think was a terrific employee. I wouldn't have kept you on just because you're cute."

Slowly, with the lethargy of a sports team that had been defeated in a hard-fought championship, the former employees of Onyx began to move into the main dining room. There they saw that, indeed, Jet was right about the security crew. Men in blue uniforms bearing the insignia of STAT SECURITY, were posted at the doors, at the cash register, and at the entrance to the restaurant's office.

"Leave your aprons and name badges over here," said a burly black man with a drill instructor's voice. "Anyone who has keys to any of the doors or locked cabinets, turn them in to me. Members of my staff are in the employee locker room. If you have personal items there you'll have to sign to get them out. Let's go, people," he ordered.

As if they were automatons programmed to accept commands, each of the waiters, busboys, kitchen staff and host converged into a single file line and began depositing onto a tabletop all items that belonged to the restaurant. Then, one by one, they gathered at the front door where another uniformed, frozen faced guard acted as sentry.

Juan joined Derek in the crowd. When the entire staff, minus Jet, was assembled at the exit, the head of the security contingent signaled the guard at the door who turned the key in the lock. He held the door open as the employees walked out for the last time.

TWO

Early morning sunlight filtered through the roll-down bamboo shade covering the window in Derek's one-room apartment. Lying in bed, on his back, the top sheet draped to his bare waist, he studied the Rorschach water stains on the ceiling. A toilet flushed next door. The sound of a screeching blow dryer in another unit penetrated the wall. The scent of coffee percolating in still another apartment filtered in through the open window along with cool, damp air.

Derek became vaguely aware of the shorter intervals between the sounds of automobile traffic passing in front of his apartment building. *Fuck life,* he was too tired to say aloud. But the thought counted.

On any other morning, Derek would, by now, be in his jogging togs, preparing for his ritual five-mile course through the hills and flats of West Hollywood. But the impact of his layoff from Onyx made him immobile. He felt utterly defeated.

Too morose to do much more than blink his eyelids, Derek lay in bed calculating his meager net worth. He thought about his monthly expenses: rent, utilities, car insurance, cell phone, minimum payment on the enormous balance on his Citibank credit card, gym membership, acting and tap dance classes, his expensive hair stylist at Diamond Salon. He came to a sobering conclusion: financially he was fucked.

Although Derek estimated that he had enough cash in his savings account to cover his rent for a month, he realized that it would be impossible to meet *all* his expenses. Until now he hadn't considered that most of his meals were at Onyx, and therefore free. As of this morning, even scrambled egg whites were a luxury item.

Cross-referencing his anxiety with the awareness that he had no marketable real-world skills, Derek knew that he wasn't qualified to do anything besides perform as an actor and serve food at restaurants. His experience with the latter far exceeded the former. His theatrical credits consisted entirely of equity waiver roles in experimental one-act plays written by friends, and presented, also by friends, in store-front theaters along Melrose Avenue in Hollywood. A professional director in a legit show had never cast him. And, other than the mind-numbing monthlong temp job as a file clerk in the insurance claims department of Executive Indemnity when he first moved to Los Angeles, his resume included just one employer: Onyx. The fact that he seldom networked with waiters at other restaurants would make soliciting peers for assistance to help find a position at The Ivy or even the Olive Garden difficult. There was no one to whom he could turn to rescue him from his dire situation.

These thoughts made staying in bed his activity of choice so as to avoid a face-to-face with reality.

For a while longer he lay thinking about his priorities in life. Rising to the surface of his thoughts was the fact that he could no longer de-lude himself into thinking that fate would soon throw a film or televi-sion role to him. Thus far, neither of the Stevens—Spielberg or Soderbergh—had discovered him. And he realized that to put any ex-pectation into believing that such a thing might suddenly occur was as stupid as waiting for the Prize Patrol to arrive with balloons, and cham-pagne, and a five-foot-long check.

The daylight permeating the room became more pronounced. Derek decided that he could not give up and accept the hand that fate had dealt to him. Reluctantly, he raised himself up and pushed away his bedsheet. He swung his legs over the side of the mattress. "I've sur-vived a lot of crap," he said out loud. "I can survive another bump in the road. Yeah," he agreed, "that's what Oprah calls it. 'A bump in the road.' " Then, all he could think about was how rich Oprah was.

Derek finger-combed his hair, then stepped naked to stand before the mirror that hung on the wall above his chest of drawers. He stud-ied his well-defined physique and grimaced with the thought of his gym membership about to expire and being unable to pay for another year. "Muscle memory," he whispered. "A couple of weeks off from training won't be impossible to reverse."

The idea of losing even a hint of his hard-earned musculature made his resolve to find a job this day all the more intense. "I'll find something," he pledged to himself as he padded to the bathroom to shave, shower and prepare to meet potential employers.

It was a Sunday afternoon. The air was hot and unusually humid, drifting through the Los Angeles Basin, settling there, too heavy to move. The warm day had coaxed the tank-top boys of West Hollywood out en masse, to exhibit pumped and 'roided physiques that they diligently worked year-round to achieve.

Street traffic, as always, was congested and seemed to move at parade float pace. Derek drove his ancient, badly dented, faded brown Honda Accord along Santa Monica Boulevard. He stopped in at every restaurant: The French Quarter, Numbers, Hugo's, Marco's Trattoria, even the odious Barney's Beanery, which had, until only a few years ago, displayed a sign that barked: "No Fags Allowed." At each restaurant, smiling seductively, and asking about employment opportunities for a well-qualified waiter, Derek heard variations on the same theme. "The full-time manager is off today. Come back Tuesday. But don't count on anything. We've been cutting back."

He then drove up to Sunset Boulevard and checked out Gaucho Grill, Endive, Kate's Kitchen and the Mondrien Hotel. The same response greeted him at establishments along the Strip.

Finally, late that afternoon, dejected and becoming more pessimistic by the restaurant, Derek returned to his apartment. He unlocked the door and stepped into the stifling hot space. Los Angeles's old bungalow apartments, of which his was a classic early twentieth-century version, were built long before the invention of air-conditioning. The archaic electrical outlets could not even support the required outlay of wattage from a modern Kenmore window unit. Hence Derek's discomfort throughout the summer.

He removed his black slacks and his wrinkled white dress shirt, which was diaphanous with perspiration. He separated his body from his white briefs, and dropped everything onto the floor beside his unmade bed.

At that moment, from his peripheral vision, Derek caught the red blinking light on his answering machine. Three blinks followed by a momentary pause meant the possibility of three job interviews. He pushed the machine's play button.

Juan's voice issued through the speaker. He lamented that although he had already started searching for another busboy job, the establishments at which he inquired were not only not hiring, they were as rude as if he had been a homeless man begging for a handout. "Which I'll soon be, if I can't get something right away." Juan choked back a tear. "Boss, if you hear of anything, please let me know. I don't want to have to go back to my gringo ex-boyfriend."

Voice number two on the machine was Derek's playwright friend, Roberto. "How's it hangin' bud?" he said. "Don't tease me with the truth. Hey, I'm casting a show." Derek perked up. "Know anyone with a decent Irish brogue who can play an ambivalent priest? Ya see, he's torn between his divine calling and his conflict with a weekly Saturday night ritual of sodomizing runaway twink prostitutes in his church's sanctuary. I'm reading from the casting sheet. 'Must be willing to perform wearing only a crucifix and a clerical collar . . .' "

Derek nodded, smiling.

" 'Has to urinate on cue into the confessional chalice . . .' "

Derek grimaced.

" 'Charles Durning look-alike. Sexual endowment not important.' Hope you can help. Love ya. Mean it."

The answering machine beeped again. "Hey, hon! It's Cath. What's up at Onyx? Dropped by for brunch and the place was shut tighter than . . . Need I say more? Call me. Let me know where you're working. Miss ya."

Of all Derek's friends, Cathy Taylor appeared to lead a charmed life. She was the wife of the president in charge of daytime programming for Link Media. Attractive, rich, intelligent, articulate, well traveled, and respected for her philanthropic and political endeavors, Cathy and her husband Andrew were a poster pair for heterosexual domestic partnerships in Hollywood. Although Derek knew that the marriage was based on mutual convenience, the couple was physically stunning together. "I'm a damn good photo op," Cathy said to Derek one evening. "Andrew needs a trophy wife, and I need him to help court celebrities for my AIDS, breast cancer, and women empowerment charities."

Cathy was one of those rare individuals who moved with ease and grace among both the Hollywood and Washington social elite, as well as the lowest order of service people. In the same breath she could discuss the most up-to-the-minute dish about J. Lo., then immediately switch to offer pointed and loquacious observations about the latest calamities on Capitol Hill, the Supreme Court, and her favorite topic, the White House.

Despite her rise from inner-city schoolteacher to city council member, then onto her marriage to Andrew and life among the aristocracy, she seldom forgot a friend. Her many chums—of which Derek had become one as a result of often serving Cathy and her guests at Onyx—all had her private telephone number and E-mail address. Her loyalty to friends was as legendary as her public row with Senator Rick Santorum after she persuaded Andrew not to obtain a VIP pass for the Republican's wife when she wanted to attend a taping of her favorite daytime drama. In retrospect, Cathy said that she regretted meddling in that situation. "I probably deprived the poor dear of a real man to fantasize about. Gracious! Do you think she can actually play tonsil hockey with that old goat?"

Derek adored Cathy. However, he would never ask her for a favor, especially when it came to his acting career. Still, he felt confident that if his back were ever completely against the wall, Cathy would go out of her way to help him.

"End of messages," the answering machine's digital voice announced.

Derek resolved to return the telephone calls when he was feeling less melancholy. "Like when I'm dead," he said, flopping down on his bed. He was debating whether or not to call Marshall Topper and let some asshole suck his dick for a few bucks. *Or,* he thought, *maybe I could call the Colt model, the one that Juan wanted so badly. A fuck might put me in a better frame of mind.*

Derek considered a dozen guys who he knew would drop whatever plans they had for an opportunity to be humped by him. Images of bodies flashed through his mind's eye, and he realized that he was already hard and in need to shoot a load or two.

Unconsciously, Derek began to stroke himself. Slowly, caressing his torso with one hand and clutching his weighty cock with the other, he immersed himself in a trance of being the cum-pig in a hot bareback gang bang fantasy. The men of his cum-soaked fantasies were always strangers with whom he had held eye contact once, or persons he'd waited on at one time or another. They were anonymous, possessing all the physical characteristics of every hot guy Derek had ever seduced or worshipped. Men with the lust of a muscle-bound tattooed felon serving a prison sentence of life without a bitch of the female persuasion.

Derek's hobby was memorizing people's faces and bodies. This had often come in handy when he greeted, by name, a second-time visitor to Onyx. It rarely failed to generate a large tip. Now, as he focused on climaxing he recalled one stud who had recently come into the restaurant. Their eyes had locked on each other's for a moment longer than necessary. Derek recalled that the man had worn a small silver earring, rimless glasses and a three-day beard stubble. The V of his open-collar oxford cloth shirt hinted at a high level of testosterone evidenced by a massive amount of dark chest hair. Derek imagined a seductive ape in heat with a lean body under the clothes.

Now, Derek raised his arm and turned his nose to his own hairy underarm pit. He inhaled deeply, then groaned with satisfaction from the intoxicating scent of perspiration. It was as potent as that of the woolly football player with whom he had fallen in love in high school, and who had remained the benchmark against which all other conquests had since been measured.

Derek's eyes involuntarily squeezed tightly closed, his face contorted, and he breathed in short rapid cries until he finally shot a thick load of milky cum in two rapid-fire, groan-inducing bursts. Holding his cock still firmly, if less determinedly, his adrenaline dissolved. His body relaxed. He allowed himself to float into a state of momentary satisfaction.

Then slowly all worries that had been set aside started demanding his attention again—that and the mess he'd made all over his body.

Derek reached over the side of the bed and onto the floor to pick up a box of tissues. One, two, three—he pulled out the sheets and laid them over the thick puddles of semen. He listlessly blotted and swabbed himself, then dropped the sopping ball of Kleenex over the side of the bed.

Derek now became aware that the apartment was growing darker. The thundering sound from a passenger jet crossing the sky overhead en route to LAX made the walls vibrate. He heard the obnoxious, eardrum-blasting bass reverberation from a car stereo approaching from several blocks away. Then, as the car passed by Derek's building, the thumping syncopation faded and moved on toward Crescent Heights Boulevard.

Derek stared into the encroaching blackness thinking that although he had appreciated the security of steady employment, he should have spent more time concentrating on his acting career. He had lost three years. Three years of his now fleeting youth. *By now, I should be driving a BMW and starring in a television series,* he thought.

Derek realized that the weekly paycheck from his job at Onyx had allowed him to acquire a feeling of indifference about the future. But now, Derek was terrified. He knew that he should never have been so stupid as to depend on anyone but himself for financial security. He'd given too much power to Onyx. He'd made the presumption that as long as he kept his part of the bargain—to show up on time and do the required work—that he could wait patiently for his big break as an actor.

Ha! Your big break! Derek would have laughed at the absurdity, but he was too weary. The truth—that he hadn't tried very hard to fulfill his dream of being a working actor—was suddenly agonizing.

He silently berated himself for not placing his ambitions first on his list of life's priorities. "Look out for number one!" he said out loud. In order of importance, a job should have been second, third or fourth. He realized that he had done what most every loser on the planet did—sold his soul for a steady paycheck.

What the hell have I done with these past three years? he asked himself. He had nothing to show for all his work. He tried to think of what his original goal had been. *The same as everyone else's goal in this freakin' town,* he thought. *But I wasn't ferocious enough in my quest for acting work. Damien was ruthless,* he decided, recalling a former Onyx waiter who now starred on the Showtime series *Sex, Inc. He's made his dreams come true. His new house was featured in* Architectural Digest. *And where am I? Not even a fucking waiter anymore.*

As Derek lay in bed, unconsciously massaging gluey leftover cum into his skin, he became vaguely aware of a drop in temperature in the room. He wriggled himself under the bedsheet. *It was easier to bust my ass working for strangers, than to bust my ass fully committing myself to working toward me,* he thought.

Like most people who find ease and security in a day-to-day occupation, Derek had become complacent working and picking up a paycheck every week. There was always *tomorrow* to focus on what he claimed he really wanted.

You're a fucking idiot, Derek chastised himself. *You just put off doing the real work.*

Another voice in his head tried to argue. *You were being practical. You don't quit a steady paying job and rush off and pursue a dream that probably won't come true anyway. You had to survive in this town.*

Finally, exhausted from the debate and a day of frustration, Derek allowed his eyes to close. *Everything's okay,* he coddled himself and hugged his pillow. *I won't make the same mistakes. From now on I'm going to work very responsibly. All the money I make is going to go toward paying off bills and making myself independent. No one will ever hold all the strings to my life again. The next job I get will just be a means to an end. From now on, I come first.*

THREE

"**R**ead my lips. '*Le-git-i-mate* massage!' "
Standing in his small apartment with Juan, Derek exaggerated
his enunciation. He protested Juan's overwrought, motherly notion
that by hanging out a shingle as a massage therapist Derek was one
step up from street hustler. It would lead to personal calamities of epic
proportions.

"If you'd ever learn to *habla Inglés,* you'd see that my ad definitely
includes the all-important word 'legit.' Is there anything so difficult to
understand about that, señor?"

Juan managed a flaccid smile. "Don't insult my comprehension of
your native tongue," he said. "Let me offer you a lesson in cultural anthropology. *Gay* anthropology. You are here. West Hollywood." Juan
drew an invisible line through the shag rug carpet fibers with the heel
of his shoe. "Guys who live in West Hollywood and its outlying communities, who pick up *Encounters* or go online to find a sex date, expect guys who place ads in this rag, and who look like you, to offer a
service."

"A hundred bucks doesn't buy as much as it used to," Derek said.
While trying to convince Juan of his guilelessness, Derek was also
working to sway himself toward believing that he wasn't making a
colossal mistake by entering into a business that involved body to
body contact and suggested sex for hire. He agreed with Juan that for
some this was an outright open door to the sex trade. "But what *I'm*
offering is a therapeutic and healing experience for body, mind and
spirit," Derek recited from a proof page of his ad as it would appear in
the "Massage/Escort" section of the classifieds. "I provide background

music with soothing sounds of spring rains, summer evening cicadas, autumn hooting owls and winter arctic winds. And a full-size massage table, scented oils and candles."

"An additional *service*," Juan continued his harangue. "These customers will expect something above and beyond what is tolerated at Burke/Williams. Boss, you're not an idiot. You know exactly what I'm talking about. *I'm* the one who should be taking an ad. Caucasians like you can get a real job in an office or as a ride operator at Disneyland."

"This is all about not being able to find a so-called real job," Derek said. "I've been searching for a month. We're in a horrible economy, and I don't have a degree in anything. I have to use my entrepreneurial imagination. I'm just offering back rubs."

"Then explain the need for your picture in the ad. Nude. I swear I can see your pubes." Juan squinted at the image.

"Bait. I might . . . maybe . . . perhaps . . . work without a shirt. Now and then. For a bigger tip. Like when I used to give free drinks at Onyx. But no touching by the clients." He sighed. "It's just an idea."

"And the caption: 'Well endowed.' What does that have to do with—"

"I'm endowed with large, strong hands. See." Derek held out his hands for inspection, then made meaty fists. "No one wants tentative, sissy, cat paws rubbing 'em down."

Juan continued reading. "VGL. Hung. Fit. Gym bunny. Tight ass. In or out. Serious only."

"There," Derek insisted. "I definitely used the word 'serious.' That will cut out the perverts. Potential clients will know that I'm on the up and up. If it's in print, it has to be the truth."

Juan scowled. "'Full release?'" He looked up at Derek in judgmental silence.

"What?" Derek implored. "The guy in the *Encounters* advertising department helped me write that. He said that the objective is to seduce customers."

"Seduction! You admit it!"

"Yes! No!" Derek fumed. "And the ad guy was right about quick responses. Hell, the paper hasn't hit the stands yet, but it's posted online. I've already booked two appointments for later."

Juan shook his head. "Boss, you're not even licensed. This is a come-on seeking nothing but guys who'll pay you to let them suck you dry or to have you fuck their sloppy butt holes. You're getting into a very twisted business. You'll be rubbing more than rose-scented oils into your so-called 'clients' bodies when they get a look at your . . . what did you call it?" Juan paused to once again study the mock-up for the ad. "Oh, yeah, here it is: your 'AbFab.' "

Juan shoved the proof page back into Derek's hands, then looked at his friend with sad eyes. "I just don't want you getting into something that will make you feel degraded. The real world is rough. Getting into the so-called massage business will make it worse."

"Or better." Derek put a hand on Juan's shoulder. "We're both practically destitute." He sighed. "I'm sneaking in and out of this place because the rent is past due. I can't afford gas for my car. My membership at Equinox expires this month. And I'm reduced to eating mac and cheese from a freakin' blue box! The carbs are taking away my six-pack! Hell, I can't even afford quarters for the laundry! Smell my shirt."

Juan turned away from a wrinkled T-shirt that Derek picked up off the floor. "I won't let my life go any farther down the drain than it has already," Derek said. "I'm doing this to survive. Not to mention I'm doing something positive for humanity. A public service. I'm a healer."

"Oh, spare me!" Juan said. "You're not doing this for any humanitarian mission."

"Whatever," Derek conceded. "But I still have to survive."

Juan paused, then said matter-of-factly, "Look. You can definitely make a few bucks feeling guys' bodies or letting 'em grope you. Truth be told—and I never thought I would tell you, or anybody—I've worked the streets."

Derek blinked. "When? And why?"

Juan explained, "After we first crossed the border. Down around Alvardo. Between Sunset Boulevard and the 101 freeway. They call it The Beanfield. I guess 'cause a lot of migrant day pickers work the bushes there. They can pick up a few extra bucks giving quick blow jobs to frustrated closet-case married men leaving their downtown offices on their way to their three-bedroom homes with backyard pools in the Valley."

"It's nothing to be embarrassed about." Derek hoped that he sounded supportive. "It's all in the past. A nonissue. I don't judge you, you don't judge me."

"I'm not embarrassed," Juan defended. "I did what I had to do. But tell me it's a nonissue after some guy you don't know and who thinks you're a piece-of-shit-loser spic shoves his dick down your throat and expects you to suck him off until you clean out his load."

Derek grunted. "Join the club."

Juan gave him a blank look.

"I turned down so many offers in my life that I finally decided to see what cock for cash was all about. I figured that if somebody wanted to pay a hundred bucks for me to fuck them, I shouldn't diss it until I tried it," Derek said. "In the end it was just sex. The guys weren't at all disgusting. Of course, I had my pick. It wasn't something I needed to do. But it's a different story now."

Derek forced a smile. "Look Juan," he said, "I know what I'm doing. The ad guy at *Encounters* said that some massage therapists rake in a couple of thou a week, tax-free. When I have enough, I'll quit."

"Enough what? Cash or chancres?" Juan said. "There's no such thing as enough money, Boss." He shrugged his shoulders in resignation. "Just promise me that you'll play safe. No stupid-ass macho shit, even if someone promises a big tip in exchange for anything more than you feel absolutely comfortable about doing."

Derek touched Juan's shoulder to turn him around, then guided him backward until he was standing next to the massage table, which Derek had borrowed, from Cathy Taylor's personal masseur. "I'm not planning on doing anything except making money. I promise. You'll see. I'll get a reputation for being a fun and friendly legit massage guy who does quality work and makes his clients feel great. They'll come begging for more."

"They'll *cum,* all right," Juan said.

"Maybe I'll even get a few regulars who have high-pressure jobs and who need a release of tension." Derek faced Juan. He put his hands on his friend's chest and began to unbutton his shirt. "You'll whistle a different tune after enjoying a free sample of my work. I've had a few massages in my day, so I'm practically an expert."

"Through correspondence school?" Juan joked.

Derek shrugged. "Since I've never actually given a massage, I'll leave it to you to tell me what feels good and what I might need to pay more attention to. Now, lie down on the table and shut up." He smiled. "I need to practice. After all those trays you've hauled over the years, you definitely need some satisfying stroking."

Juan grinned, then methodically finished taking off his shirt. As he kicked off his Nike trainers, he simultaneously unfastened the buttons on his jeans, pulled down his pants, and stepped out of the legs.

Derek was aroused with the contrast of Juan's dark skin against the white of his Jockey underpants. Juan's chest and arms too, were more pumped than Derek expected. His blowsy busboy uniform had concealed a chiseled, compact body.

Derek discovered that, as he admired Juan's ripped torso, he was quickly growing hard. *What if I respond this way with my real customers?* he thought. He was practically salivating over Juan's body. He reacted to the treasure trail of straight black hair that ran from Juan's sternum down over his tight stomach and into the waist of his underpants.

But the cargo in Juan's underpants was the real revelation. Looking at the large if still-flaccid volume that strained the fibers of the cotton sack, Derek figured that Juan could probably match him inch for inch. He swallowed hard. "Impressive," Derek said. "Now, I'll show you just how much restraint I have."

"Or *don't* have." Juan smiled.

FOUR

Derek had spent much of the day cleaning his apartment, and he was now expecting his first client in just moments. He nervously scrambled to make last minute adjustments to the ambiance of the room. He corrected picture frames that were slightly askew on the walls. He righted a lamp shade tilted too far in one direction. He fluffed the pillows on his bed. He smoothed out the comforter. He lit three votive candles, then he went through his CD collection. Among the discs of Beyoncé, Metallica, Twiztid, and Led Zeppelin, he found an Ella Fitzgerald collection. Someone had given it to him as a birthday present, and it was still shrink-wrapped.

He cursed at the plastic packaging, which, under any circumstance, was difficult to tear open but seemed more so when he was in a hurry. Derek retrieved a steak knife from a kitchen drawer and weaseled the tip of the blade into the clear wrapping. When he got to the jewel case he nearly broke the lid releasing the disc, which he then placed on the CD carousel. He turned the volume to barely audible.

Derek stood in the center of the room and scanned his small living space. "It ain't Neverland Ranch," he said out loud as he played with turning a light on and off trying to choreograph the environment.

There was a knock on his door.

"Fuck! Okay, just be calm," Derek muttered. "This is your business. Be professional. He's just a client."

He took one last look in the mirror. His hair looked professionally tangled. His tank top was filled out seductively. He walked to the door and tentatively placed his hand on the knob. *Smile, baby!* he heard a voice inside himself remind. With that he pulled open the door.

Derek's heart plummeted as his eyes took in the physical form of a man who had to be in his late sixties. It had always been difficult for Derek to assess someone's age on the phone. But this man was clearly in the twilight of his allotted time on earth. He stood at about five feet seven inches, and he weighed over two hundred pounds. His bulbous features included heavy bags under bloodshot eyes, aquiline nose, jowls, thick wet lips and at least a double chin. His meager crop of shoe-polish black dyed hair was a comb-over.

"Derek?" the visitor said, visually taking in the stud before him. Derek stood dumbstruck. The man reminded, "We have an appointment."

Derek immediately returned to the moment. He forced a smile and welcomed the man into the apartment. He apologized for seeming distracted, and for the size and lack of décor in his residence. "But it's clean," he quickly added.

"I see you even have a massage table," the man said as he made himself at home, slipping off his shoes and unbuttoning his shirt. "That's cute."

Within seconds the man was naked. His back was hairy and spotted with moles the size of plump raisins. His butt flesh hung like gray-colored bread dough. He had a boner.

Oh, Christ, what do I do now? Derek screamed in his head.

The man leaned against the table to face Derek with his fleshy dick pointing straight out and his ball sack dangling. He folded his arms across his sagging chest. His bitch breasts were covered in gray hair. He lasciviously cocked his head suggesting that Derek move closer to him.

"Just relax on the table while I heat the oil," Derek instructed.

"I don't really have a lot of time, kid," the man said. "Why don't we skip the formalities. Just take off your clothes. Or do you want me to take 'em off for you?"

Derek panicked. "Ah, sir, aren't you here for a massage?"

"If that's what you want to call it," the man said.

"Then please make yourself comfortable on the table and we'll begin."

"No, that's not all right." The man suddenly had a hostile edge in his voice. "I'm horny as hell and I'm paying you a hell of a lot to pop my load. Get to it."

Derek was mortified. "Sir," he said, "I'm a professional. Perhaps you confused my ad with one of the others in *Encounters*. I'm strictly a legitimate masseur."

The man sighed and shook his head. "I get it. I'm an old troll so it'll cost me more. How much? Hundred and fifty? Two hundred? You're a hot piece of ass so I'm willing to pay. So take off your pants and let me lick your nuts."

Derek blinked at the man. For an instant he almost felt sorry for the guy. He wanted to find a way to satisfy him in some way other than with sex. Derek thought it must be painful for the man to know that nobody except a nurse in ER would voluntarily touch him. Regardless of the guy's age, he still had sexual needs. It must have been humiliating to be horned up every day by the sight of hot young studs, whether on television or on the street, or in his porn collection who probably reminded this man that his days of true intimacy were over.

The guy barked, "Okay, three hundred. Just take off your shirt and I'll play with my nipples, jack off and leave."

Shit, three hundred bucks to let some old man jack off in front of me? Derek thought. *For that kind of dough he ought to be able to get into bed and slobber all over some cute hustler.*

With as much sensitivity as he could muster, Derek said, "It's not that your offer isn't incredibly generous . . ."

"Generous my ass!" the man barked. "You asshole hustlers are all alike. You advertise one thing then make us pay through the nose for something else. I oughta call the cops. You probably don't even have a license to practice massage!"

By now, the man had lost his erection and began gathering his clothes. Derek tried to disappear as he leaned against the wall next to his bed. He watched the man quickly step into his pants, pull on his socks and slip his arms into his shirt. He put his feet into his loafers and buckled his belt. As he buttoned his shirt he said, "I'm filing a complaint with *Encounters!* I'll make sure they retract your ad, you fucking cockteaser! In fact, I'm going to spread the word that you're a diseased piece of ass. You won't be hustling guys for much longer. You're not getting a dime out of me!"

"I'm sorry this didn't work out the way either of us expected," Derek apologized. He was not really feeling any remorse, except for the fact that he wasn't getting paid.

The man opened the door and slammed it shut behind him as he stormed out.

* * *

Derek was at once furious that he'd wasted his time with the jerk and afraid that all future encounters might be similar. *Christ, he didn't come here for a massage! He expected sex!* Derek choked back a tear that had as much to do with feelings of failure as it did with being frightened of meeting his next customer.

Then his mind turned to the three hundred dollars the man had offered him. *What would have been the harm?* he thought. He filed away the idea for the future when he might give more serious consideration to such an offer.

Pushing himself away from the wall where he'd been leaning for the past full minute, Derek walked around the room and snuffed out the candles. He changed the CD to Metallica and took a can of low-carb beer out of the refrigerator. Although he didn't want to be inebriated when the next client arrived, he needed something to take the edge off his anxiety. As he popped the flip top and took a long gulp, he wondered what he should do differently when the next man arrived. He thought about doing a line of crystal but decided against it. He didn't want to be a male hustler *and* a drug addict.

His answering machine clicked on. He walked over and turned the volume up. It was an unfamiliar voice. "Um. Hi. I'm leaving a message for Derek. I'm responding to your ad in *Encounters.* Would you please call if you have an available appointment tonight?" The man provided his telephone number. "Ah, okay. Hope to hear from you. I'm Tom." Click. Buzz.

Derek looked at his watch. He calculated the time between now, and his next appointment, factoring in a full hour for the massage. He padded the time by half an hour and decided that he could squeeze Tom in at eight-thirty. He picked up the telephone and dialed the number.

With a voice as friendly as he could achieve, considering his recent confrontation, Derek spoke to Tom. They agreed on a time to meet. Derek gave the client his apartment address.

"That's two blocks west of Fairfax," he said. "But I should tell you something before you decide if you want to come over or not. I'm legit. If you're looking for more, try someone else."

A brief silence came from the other end of the line. "Ah, that's cool, I guess," Tom finally said, his voice registering vague disappointment.

"I just thought I'd better explain because it seems that my ad is being misinterpreted," Derek said.

"Are you surprised?" Tom asked. "I mean, your picture is incredibly hot. And the way you describe yourself . . . it spells sex."

"To you?" Derek asked.

"Well, yeah," Tom said. "But as a matter of fact, I'm sore as hell from playing racquetball. I could use a good deep tissue massage. See you at eight-thirty?"

"Cool," Derek said. He hung up the phone, smiling to himself.

Then a knock on the door brought him out of his reverie. This time instead of candles and music, Derek switched on a light. He reached for the door handle, telling himself not to be surprised by what form of creature occupied the space beyond the door.

He turned the knob and pulled. The man standing before him was younger than the previous client, but perhaps at the most only by about ten years. "Hey, stud," the man said and scooted past Derek before he could be invited in. The man took a quick look around as Derek closed the door. "Nice place," the man said sarcastically. "You like old movies? Older is the best kind. Like men, you agree?" It was less a question than an observation of the reproductions of posters from *Charlie Chan in Egypt, The Treasure of the Sierra Madre,* and *Gold-diggers of 1933* which were taped to the walls. Derek didn't have an opportunity to reply before the man faced him, cupped his hands around Derek's face and kissed him.

With lightning speed, Derek broke away. He pushed the man as hard as he could, sending him crashing against the massage table, up-turning it. "What the fuck!" the man cried. "You stupid freak! You ass-hole, fuckin' freak! You hurt me! I think you broke my fuckin' ribs!"

Derek was immediately contrite. "Look, I'm sorry. But that was completely out of bounds! I didn't say you could touch me!"

"I'm paying for your goddamn ass, kid. You're a whore, baby. I can do any fuckin' thing I want. You're a toy."

Derek was still stunned—dazed by what he considered an attack and confused by the way it had been presumed that for the price of a massage that he was willing to give it up. "You touch me again, and you'll end up on life support," Derek snapped.

The man pulled himself up to a standing position. His anger sub-sided slightly. "Come on, bro," he said. "Let's forget that happened and just do the nasty. You want my money and I want you to pound my ass with that sweet dick of yours. It's a simple trade agreement."

Derek was not certain what the man was capable of doing to him. "Money?" he said absently.

The man nodded knowingly. "So we're gonna play that game are we?"

"Game?" Derek said.

"Don't play 'Daddy, what's beer?' with me, kiddo. Or are you really as green as you pretend to be?" Then the man smiled. "Let me fill you in, boy," he said.

"I'm not your boy!" Derek countered.

"No. You're certainly a man."

Derek hadn't counted on men being so raw with desire to have sex with him that they'd do almost anything to get it. Just then, his answering machine clicked on. Derek had neglected to turn the volume down, and a voice came through the speaker explaining that he'd read Derek's ad and wanted an appointment. "Hey, man. Ya like to party? Your ad doesn't say. Are you chem friendly? I got favors for both of us. Ring me back."

As the caller left his telephone number, the second client gave Derek an *I told you so* grin. "Here's the deal," the man said. "I've got two hundred bucks in my pocket." He reached into his jeans and pulled out a money clip. He extended his hand toward Derek. "It's yours. But I don't want to shit right for a week. I want you to shove your load up my ass. Fifty dollars extra if you bareback me. Now, take off your clothes. I suck your dick until you're stiff, then you fuck my asshole. What could be simpler? Two hundred. Take it or leave it."

The two men stood facing each other in a stand off, like Wyatt Earp and the Clanton brothers at the OK Corral. "Look," the man said with a heavy sigh, "you sell yourself 'cause you need cash. I'm ready to pay a small fortune for your load."

Derek was still angry, seething at the predicament he had created. "As a matter of fact, the last guy offered me three hundred," he said.

"Fuck!" the man said. He started toward the door. "I don't care how big your cock is, I ain't paying three hundred bucks to take it up the ass!"

"Okay. Hold on a minute." Derek reconsidered. "I have rules," he said.

The man turned. With a cocky smile he began to unbutton his shirt. "Rules?" he asked. "What kind of game did you have in mind?"

Derek could see the man's pants begin to bulge where his eager cock pressed against the fabric of his jeans. "Rules like, I don't kiss. Don't expect romance. I'll fuck you until I cum, then it's out whether you cum or not!"

"Control freak issues, eh?" the man said. "I'm supposed to get an hour for my money. I cum when I'm ready, not when you or anybody else tells me to. It's my dime, not yours."

Derek abruptly changed his mind again. "No," he said. "I'm worth three hundred. Fuck off."

"Fuck you," the client said. "You so-called escorts all think you're some goddamned fucking Adonises. Well, you're not. You're a dime a dozen, and not one of you is worth the price you charge, you two-bit whore!"

With that the man gave Derek a long, withering look of contempt and turned again toward the door. He said over his shoulder, "The next time you jerk off, think about the bundle that you could have made unloading yourself in my ass." The man opened the door and left the apartment.

All at once Derek felt emptiness, depression, rage and fear. He had always been able to delude himself into believing that he was special and talented, that he could be successful at anything he truly wanted to do. Now, he was faltering. The truth punched him in the gut as he realized that he was just the opposite of what he pretended to be. He was unemployed, deep in debt, living in the same studio apartment that he rented when he first moved to Los Angeles, and he was turning down men who could buy him out of his financial troubles. The sum of his parts equaled loser.

The answering machine clicked again. Derek listened to a man state in a condescending tone that he wanted Derek to be at his address at ten o'clock. The man could have been ordering a pizza.

When the phone call ended and the machine went back to sleeping, Derek became aware of the faint, ambient sensations of neighbors in other apartments. He inhaled the scent of dinners being cooked. He felt the vibrations from traffic along the street outside. But Derek was too absorbed in his own thoughts to be completely conscious of the fact that life went on all around him.

The phone rang again and the answering machine clicked on. It was another male voice leaving his pager and cell phone numbers.

This time, Derek flopped onto the bed and put a pillow over his ears. He took another swig of his beer.

There came a knock at the door, and Derek awoke with a start. It was precisely 8:30, by the numbers on his digital alarm clock. He sat up on his bed, weighing his options. He had two: answer the door, or not answer the door.

He sat in silence until another tentative knock on the door convinced him to get up and answer. He moved lethargically, telling himself he had to get a peephole for the door. Being surprised every time he answered a visitor was something he had at least some authority to change.

Derek placed his hand on the knob and slowly pulled open the door. There, dressed in a tan-colored button-down shirt, black slacks and black pointed-toe half boots, stood a man as handsome as a Brooks Brothers model, with a wide white smile.

"Derek? I'm Tom," the man said. Politely he extended his hand.

A smile grew across Derek's face as he accepted the gesture of introduction. "Great. Come in," he said. "Hope you found the place without any problems."

"Your directions were very good," Tom said. He briefly looked around the apartment but his eyes quickly settled back on Derek. Each man studied the other for an awkward moment. Neither seemed confident enough to verbally offer his thoughts of attraction and sexual lust.

"Why don't we get started," Derek said, breaking the delicate moment. "You can hang your clothes on the back of this." He pointed toward the chair next to his makeshift desk. "I'll step into the other room while you disrobe. Get comfortable on the table and just call me when you're ready."

The only other room was the bathroom. As Derek walked backwards the few steps it took to reach the loo, he felt slightly off center by Tom's smile. "Just make yourself comfortable," Derek repeated. "I'll be in here."

Derek flipped on the light in the bathroom and closed the door behind him. "Fuck! I'm already hard!" he berated himself. "How am I supposed to touch him without making a move on him?" Derek looked in the mirror and tried to calm himself. "Okay. Be cool. You were pissed off before and now you're upset because Mr. Stud Muffin is on the other side of this door, and you've already given advance notice that there's no sex. Just wash your hands and get on with the job."

Over the sound of water rushing from the spigot into the cracked porcelain sink, Derek heard Tom's voice. "I'm ready."

Derek turned off the water, dried his hands and opened the bathroom door. He took a deep breath and walked back into the room.

Lying on his stomach, Tom was stretched out on the table. A white cotton sheet with which Derek had shrouded the table was tossed to the edge of the massage table, revealing Tom's impressive body in its entire splendor. Tom's muscled arms were dangling over each side of the table. His head was placed facedown on the head support extension.

Derek walked first to the CD player. *This deserves some mood music,* he said to himself as he switched discs and pushed a button. Ella began to softly sing, "Long ago and far away, I dreamed a dream one day, and now, that dream is here beside me . . ."

"Hmm, love her." Tom's voice sounded sleepy and relaxed. He readjusted his body on the table, preparing for Derek's soothing touch.

Derek took another long look at Tom's muscled back, picked up a plastic bottle filled with scented oil that Cathy's masseur had given to him, and poured a liberal amount into the palm of his left hand. He placed the bottle back on the bookshelf beside the table and rubbed his hands together. Then he placed them on Tom's body.

As Derek kneaded Tom's skin with his strong thumbs he heard intermittent sighs. "Hmm. Amazing," Tom moaned. "Mmm. Yeah. Jeez. Great thumbs."

Firmly caressing Tom's neck, shoulders, back and arms, Derek forced Tom's neck muscles to yield to the knowing touch of his hands. Derek intuitively knew where to spend his time and energy, and he found himself slipping into a mental zone not unlike that which he experienced while jogging. He could tell that Tom was blissfully content. Derek realized that he was excited touching his client and taking pleasure from the service he was providing. Occasionally distracted by the erection in his pants, he repeatedly adjusted himself.

After nearly thirty minutes working on Tom's backside, Derek whispered, "Okay. It's time to turn over."

As if in a trance, Tom slowly moved onto his side, then rolled over the rest of the way. Derek was delightfully taken aback, not only by the sight of Tom's chiseled chest, but by the sheet which had been forced into a tent by Tom's large, hard cock. "Sorry," Tom said. "That always happens when I'm relaxed."

"It's a good sign," Derek said. "Means you're comfortable with me."

"Mmm," Tom moaned in satisfaction. "Very comfortable. And we're only half done."

Derek was silent but thought to himself, *With just the massage, I'm as hard as you are.*

For the remainder of the hour Derek squeezed and pressed Tom's pectoral muscles, petted his sternum and abs with long strokes, and drew each arm, from shoulder to fingers, through his hands. Finally, with his fingers, as light as feathers, gently tracing the taut skin over Tom's chest stomach and legs, the massage was over.

"Don't move for a few moments," Derek said.

Ella was singing, "You smile, a song begins. You speak, and I hear violins. It's magic . . ."

Derek walked away from the table and returned to the bathroom. After running the water in the basin and washing his hands he returned to the room. Tom, his hard-on unabated, was raising himself up to a sitting position. He was upright, his legs hanging over the side of the table. A portion of the sheet covered his massive equipment, and he looked as though he'd just roused from a dream.

Stepping onto the floor, Tom reached for his underwear. Modestly, he turned his back to Derek. Derek was as hypnotized by Tom's firm ass, as he was by the long, thick dick he was hiding. Tom slipped into his underpants and turned around. The cotton fabric strained with the fullness of his cock.

"Wow," Tom said in a groggy voice. "Wow," he repeated. Then he retrieved his slacks from where he had draped them over Derek's chair back. Balancing precariously, he stepped into his pants. "Mind if I splash some cold water on my face?"

"Not at all," Derek said, pointing toward the bathroom. "Would you like something to drink? Some juice? A beer?"

"I'm so relaxed that if I had a beer I'd probably collapse on your bed," Tom said. "But thanks anyway."

A moment of disappointment raced through Derek's head. He silently cursed the fact that he could do no more than massage Tom's body. He felt agonizing frustration. *What would be so terrible about inviting him to stay? He's obviously ready to shoot a load. And I'm available,* Derek thought as he heard the water in the sink run for a few seconds then stop.

Tom emerged from the bathroom with a wet face. He finger-combed his hair. A few drops of water had beaded on the skin of his chest, and he used his hands to move the moisture around to speed the evaporation. As he pulled his shirt over his shoulders he said, "You're amazing."

"Glad you liked it," Derek said. "I hope you'll come again."

"Absolutely. Do you have a card? I'll tell my friends that they have to have you." Tom smiled. "I mean, that they should make an appointment."

"Cards?" Derek hesitated. "They're being printed," he lied. "But by all means, tell your friends. Especially if they're as special as you are."

Tom smiled as he reached into his pocket. He withdrew a neatly folded wad of twenty-dollar bills. "You're a hundred, right?" he asked.

Derek was silent. For a moment he considered waiving his fee. He could explain that this was an introductory offer. But Derek desperately needed cash. "Yeah, thanks," he said, accepting the money.

"Worth every cent," Tom repeated. He pushed the bills into Derek's hands. "I'll need your touch again soon."

"Me, too," Derek uttered. "I mean, any time."

Tom smiled again as he stepped into his half boots. Then he straightened and looked into Derek's eyes.

"I really do mean any time," Derek said. "This is what I do, and I'm happy that it was satisfying to you."

Tom paused for a moment, looking Derek up and down. "Okay. Great. I'll give you a call."

With that, he opened the door and disappeared into the night.

FIVE

Derek's apartment suddenly seemed a very lonely place. Although he occasionally entertained tricks and one night stands here, their departures were usually a relief. He valued his independence. But he did not like the feeling he experienced after Tom's departure. He wasn't depressed, but he sensed that his life was now, somehow, less fulfilling and exciting.

For a long moment after Tom left, Derek stood in the center of his room staring at the door. "Professional decorum, my ass," he said. "If I ever get my hands on that body again . . ." Derek berated himself. "You had to insist that you're freakin' legit! The least you could have done was offer to give a full release!" He resigned himself to probably never seeing Tom again.

Derek busied himself moving the massage table farther against the wall next to his makeshift bookshelf. Then he picked up the white sheet on which Tom had lain. Derek held the sheet to his face and inhaled deeply, tracking the lingering scent. Derek sniffed Tom's man smells and phantom vestiges of the rose scented oil.

The hard-on that had arisen from before Derek even began touching and stroking Tom's skin became more pronounced. Derek removed his clothes and climbed into bed, pressing Tom's sheet up in his face. He inhaled deeply.

Derek visualized himself and Tom naked together. He felt himself pressed into the bed under Tom's torso. He imagined Tom's pelvis brutally grinding against him and their lips sealed together while their hands explored the planes and orifices of the other. He fantasized about Tom fucking him and kissing him while they both came at once.

His body's need for sexual release escalated. Derek's climax came sooner than he would have liked.

Then, after a few minutes of rest, he'd gathered his energy and decided that he'd better call Juan to let him know that a psychotic client hadn't murdered him. He picked up the phone and dialed.

Juan answered. "Well, la-de-dah. Boss man's a massage virgin no more. Tell me all the nasties."

Derek said, "They were just guys. Two were sort of a little older. Ancient, actually. But one, the last, was a freakin' knockout. And no sex."

"Your nose is growing, Boss. I can feel it through the fiber optics."

"Well, maybe they *wanted* sex," Derek admitted. "I think that's probably natural when someone's touching your body." He tried to make it sound as though any physical response was simply spontaneous and as incidental as every man's early morning hard-on. "Nothing out of the ordinary. That's it. Very uneventful for my first day on the job. Just didn't want you to worry. We'll talk again in the A.M."

"Bottom line. How much did you make? More than tips on Saturday night?"

Derek realized he'd had three customers but had earned less than if he'd served one table of six that had ordered several bottles of wine. "Never enough, as you said."

"Right," Juan said dubiously. "They wanted sex and you paid *them* to leave."

"All right," Derek confessed. "This business sucks. Literally. I had only one actual paying customer. But there was absolutely no sex. I'll give this job a chance until the ad runs out. But I was honest about there being one hot guy. God, I'd like him to be my husband. He was definitely boyfriend material."

"Okay, stud," Juan said. "Go jerk off—if you haven't already—and we'll talk later. I heard they're hiring at the Airport Hilton. Gotta get up early to go down and fill out an application."

"Good luck," Derek said. He hung up the telephone. Finding himself hard again, he fondled himself for a few moments, thinking of Tom. Then he turned out his light and drifted off to sleep.

Sometime in the night, Derek was wrested from unconsciousness by a male voice. It took him a moment to realize that his answering machine had activated. He'd neglected to turn the ringer on the telephone back on. "Y'there? Y'there? Pick up, man. I need a good fuck right now. Y'there?" Then the call terminated.

Derek lay in the darkness of his room. His thoughts returned to Tom, but they were quickly replaced by images of his first two "clients." He thought that if he were destined to be receiving such gross misfits for the rest of his massage career, he'd better learn to cope with them. "Or get out of the business," he said aloud. He found himself beginning to slip into an abyss of depression. He realized that Tom was probably an anomaly, and that most customers would be like the first two. Trollsville, U.S.A.

Derek lay staring at the outline of the window, through which the meager light from a street lamp spread through the blinds. He thought about the near certainty that soon he'd have to let some rotting-toothed, foul-breathed, untouchable suck his dick. Or that he'd be forced to fuck the ass of a sagging-tit Buddha-belly.

Wait a minute! Derek upbraided himself. *This is a job. It's just sex. Some guys can't get free sex because they're not good-looking or they don't have a decent body or they're just unsure of themselves. Face it. In this town, if you're not under thirty-five and good-looking or steroided out, you may as well be put through a meat grinder and made into hamburger. You're about that useful. They come to you to get off.*

Derek became resigned to the fact that he couldn't be picky and wait around only for guys who looked like Tom. Still, he decided, the next time he opened the door to Uncle Fester or Cousin It, that he would pocket the cash before stripping off his shorts.

Morning arrived. The sound of police sirens racing past his apartment building brought Derek to consciousness. Rather than spend another inactive moment conjuring up disgusting scenarios of the men who might call and visit during this day, Derek forced himself to get out of bed. He dressed in his jogging clothes, left the apartment, and hit the sidewalk running.

As much as jogging was exercise for his body, it was also therapy for his mental attitude. With endorphins surging through his brain, he felt convinced that the day would reveal surprises that would change his life. By the time Derek returned to his apartment, five messages had been added to his message machine. Four were responding to his ad, and one was from Cathy. He dutifully wrote down each of the phone numbers, then called her.

"Still not working, eh?" Cathy said. She had already made suggestions about restaurants to which he should apply. He had already checked each of them out. "Andrew's got network meetings in New York," she went on. "The fall schedule is crap, and if he doesn't find a *Queer Eye* kind of break-out hit, we'll be joining you on the unemployment line."

"Oh, hey, can you hold for a sec?" Derek asked. "Another call."

Derek pushed the call-waiting flash button on his cordless telephone. "Hello, it's Derek."

"Derek? Oh, you just said that. Sorry. It's Tom. From last night?"

Derek perked up. "Oh, right," he tried to sound calm and a bit distant. "Can you hang? I'll get off the other line." Derek switched back to Cathy and begged apologizes. He told her he had an important call he had to take.

"Hope it's about a job, hon," Cathy said.

"Sort of."

"Good luck."

Derek pushed flash and was reconnected to Tom. "Sore shoulders again?" he asked.

Tom chuckled. "Something's sore, but I don't suppose you'll want to help me out."

Derek was about to cut in and say, *Try me.* But before he could get the words out, Tom said, "I admire your professionalism. Or maybe I'm just butt ugly and I don't turn you on." He chuckled again. "Or maybe you're straight. Oh, I hadn't thought about that. I apologize if I'm being a predator here."

"Not a bit!" Derek exclaimed. "No boyfriend either," he added pointedly.

"Well, that's a crime," Tom said. "And impossible to believe. So how about another massage?"

"Absolutely," Derek said. "I'll always clear my calendar for my favorite client."

"How do I rate being your favorite so quickly? I don't think I even tipped you last night," Tom said.

"From you, a tip is hardly necessary," Derek said. "Actually, I say that to all my clients. Makes 'em feel special." He hoped that his voice made it obvious that he was teasing.

"Thought so," Tom said. "So let's say tomorrow night? Around eight, if you're available?"

"Actually, I've got an opening tonight, if you like. A last minute cancellation." He lied.

A moment of silence. Then Derek heard Tom clear his throat. "Cool." He almost sounded casual.

"Same time?"

"Same time." They hung up.

Derek's appointment with Tom made it easier for him to ignore the new messages on his machine. He was assured of another hundred bucks, so he decided that he wouldn't even bother to return the calls from the other men. "If they're that anxious they'll call back," he decided to the empty room. His confidence was growing—and so was his dick.

For the hour that Derek spent that night massaging Tom again, he was torn between wanting to seduce the man off the table and into his bed and being the "legit" masseur he swore he was. It was divine torture to rub Tom's taut skin and knead his bubble butt and see his cock rise to the occasion.

Again, when the session was over, Tom was so relaxed that he could hardly move. He said all of the right things: that Derek had strong yet sensitive hands, that he wished the massage could have gone on for hours more. But this time, after stepping into his jeans and pulling a red T-shirt over his head, Tom hesitated a moment. Finally, he asked, "I don't know what your policy is about seeing clients outside of work." He waited a beat. "But if you'd like to have dinner sometime, I think that would be great."

Derek nodded his head. "For you, I'll make an exception."

Tom smiled, relief displayed across his face. "Listen. I've got a dinner party I have to go to Saturday night. I hate to show up alone to these things. Third wheel and all. Like to be my date?"

"Sounds like fun."

"We should be there by seven," Tom said. "The host is a great guy, and his friends are all interesting. You'll probably get a ton more clients from his circle. Dress is casual. I'll pick you up around six-thirty."

"You're on," Derek said. "See you Saturday."

SIX

At precisely six-thirty Saturday evening there was a knock on Derek's door. *Punctual,* Derek thought. He opened the door.

"I thought you said casual," Derek remarked when he greeted Tom and saw that he was dressed in stylish cargo pants, and a deep blue dress shirt open at the collar and down two buttons. Derek was wearing 501s.

"No, you look fine," Tom said, reassuring. "This is just me. What you're wearing is perfect for the evening."

Derek collected his wallet and keys, and cell phone. He just as quickly returned the phone to the desk. "No business tonight," he said to Tom, not bothering to mention that he no longer could afford cellular service.

"We'll take my car," Tom said as they stepped out into the apartment courtyard and Derek closed the door to his unit. A moment later, Tom released the car alarm system with a touch of a button on his key fob.

A Mercedes C280 beeped, then flashed its lights once. Although the automobile impressed him, Derek didn't say a word. As far as he was concerned, Tom could simply think that a Mercedes was no more a novelty to him than the palm trees that lined every street in Southern California. Derek opened the passenger side door, slipped into the leather seat, reached for the seat belt, and buckled in for what he was anticipating to be a memorable night.

Tom turned the key in the ignition and pulled out onto Fountain Avenue, then made an immediate right onto Poinsettia. From there, he drove down to Santa Monica Boulevard and headed west. "I should tell you about our host," he said as he lowered the volume of the CD player. "Brent is a really nice guy, and he gives great dinners. He keeps them intimate, so it'll just be us and at most two other couples."

Derek smiled to himself. *Other couples,* he thought, enjoying the fantasy of one day being able to call a man like Tom his partner.

"But I have to warn you about something," Tom continued. "You may not be used to people like Brent or his friends. They're not your average . . ." He'd stopped at the light at La Cienega and flipped on his right-hand turn signal.

"I'm very good with people," Derek assured. "I was a waiter before I started my massage business. Trust me, I've met all kinds, and I can get along with practically anybody. Anyway, you don't strike me as someone who would associate with anyone who was barely adequate."

Tom turned to Derek and smiled.

As the car climbed the steep hill toward Sunset Boulevard, Derek was becoming more curious about where they were headed. He seldom ventured west of Fairfax. The neighborhoods became more exclusive with every block traveled toward Beverly Hills. Tom's car made its way past Doheny and the mansions along Sunset Boulevard, then beyond the Beverly Hills Hotel and maneuvered through several circuitous streets. Finally they arrived at their destination.

Valiant Drive lay in a secluded area of Beverly Hills that even some longtime residents were not aware of. The mansions were obscured from all outside view. Even the tall entrance gates were protected by solid black steel plates. Security cameras recorded the neighborhood morning maid brigade as well as every FedEx delivery and lookie-loo tourist.

Tom pulled up to an enormous, ornate gate. He pushed the button to roll down his car window, then reached out and pressed a series of buttons on the estate's security call box. Instantly, the gates began to slide horizontally, like a steel curtain along a traverse rod.

"You must come here a lot," Derek said.

"I do," said Tom.

As the car drove through the entrance and wove its way down a serpentine drive, Derek's eyes grew wide at the sight of the surrounding lush trees and gardens. "Where the heck are we, the Geffen estate or something?" Derek said, with awe.

"Davie should have it this nice," Tom chuckled. Somehow, Derek didn't think it was a joke.

As they rounded a corner, the main house came into view. Derek gasped. "Holy shit, it's Barbra Streisand's house! Or Cher's!"

"Darn! You've spoiled the surprise." Tom laughed. "Actually, an even bigger diva lives here. Ever hear of Weybridge Cottage?"

"Cottage?" Derek mocked. "A cottage is what Hansel and Gretel live in. The Seven Dwarfs have one. This is Sleeping Beauty's castle."

"You're impressed?" Tom asked.

"Now I'm really not properly dressed," Derek said.

The car park was a wide expanse of cobbled stone opposite one side of the great house. Derek opened his car door and stepped out. He watched as Tom reached into the backseat and retrieved a gift-wrapped bottle. When the two were standing together, facing the granite structure complete with towers and gargoyles, Tom said, "The only thing to be nervous about is the bitch."

"Wife or girlfriend?" Derek said.

"Neither. The very kickable little mutt that Brent dotes on."

"I'm great with animals. How do I look?" Derek asked.

"You look very handsome, my friend," Tom responded. "And I'm sorry that I couldn't tell you where we were going. Secrecy, you know."

"Who lives here?" Derek begged.

"You're about to find out," Tom said. He handed the bottle to Derek. "Here," he said, "you give this to Brent. He'll appreciate it."

Derek accepted the bottle as Tom pushed the doorbell. *Brent? What famous person is named Brent?* Derek wracked his brain.

In the background, they could hear the doorbell chimes echoing as if in a vast hall, and the reverberating sound of a dog yapping. "That's Greta. The miserable little shitzu," Tom warned. "She's small, but she's liable to take your face off if you're not careful. If she were mine, the coyotes would have—"

At that moment, the door opened, and Derek blinked in surprise and shock. The man standing in the portal was none other than two-time Academy Award–winning actor Brent Richardson. Derek recognized Brent immediately and was dumbfounded. He was surprised that this wasn't the first face that came to mind when Tom mentioned *Brent.*

"Heya, Tom!" Brent beamed, pushing open the gate. "As always, I can set my watch by you. Come in."

Tom and Derek entered the house. Brent, dressed in black slacks and a yellow silk shirt that modestly concealed his famous body, put out his hand toward Derek. "Hi, I'm Brent," he said, taking Derek's hand. Greta barked furiously, staying safely behind her master's left leg.

"Yes, you are. I mean, I know. Um, it's incredibly nice to meet you. I'm Derek." The words tumbled out in a clumsy jumble. He accepted Brent's strong hand in his. "Oh, a little something." Derek pushed the bottle into his host's hands.

"Very nice," Brent said in his familiar voice, which was famous for its aristocratic sonority and perfect enunciation. He appeared to sincerely appreciate receiving the wine offering. "Please, come," he said to the new arrivals. "Rand and Pat are filling me in on all the shows they caught in New York. What can I get for you to drink? The usual for you, Tom? And for you Derek?"

"Oh, anything," Derek said.

"We're starting with a Dom '97 that Rand brought," Brent suggested.

"Great," said Derek.

Although Derek concealed his awe for the grandeur of the home through which he was now being guided, he furtively observed the opulent interior. A wide, carpeted staircase was the central feature of an octagonal, two-story foyer. Antique picture frames held dark oil portraits, and the floor over which they walked was gray slate.

As the trio moved through a hallway and down a short corridor they entered the Great Room. A distinguished-looking middle-aged man dressed in black tie approached bearing a silver tray upon which two flutes of champagne rested. He held the tray out first to Tom, who said, "Hey, Everett. This is my friend Derek."

Everett smiled. "Always well when you're here, sir," he said. "Nice to meet you, Derek." He held the tray for Derek to accept a glass. The butler then offered a cocktail napkin to both men. "I'll be 'round in a moment with nibbles."

Tom's name was called out simultaneously by the two other men in the room. As Tom moved toward the other guests, Derek followed. Introductions were made and Derek immediately felt as though he belonged in the group. Rand and Pat were both as casually but elegantly dressed as Tom. Although they were no more than perhaps fifteen years older than he, to Derek they seemed years beyond in their manners and self-assurance.

Tom whispered into Derek's ear. "Rand's Oscar is for set decoration. Pat is the CEO of Link Media."

"My best friend's husband is the president of daytime programming for him," Derek whispered back, happy to be able to appear connected to show business.

Pat overheard and smiled. "You know Cathy Taylor? She's such a dear."

"She would have to be in order to maintain such good humor about Mr. Young," Rand added.

Brent reentered the room, with Greta following close beside him. "I'm afraid it's just the five of us tonight, guys. Matt's in emergency surgery, and Paul's rehearsal for *Spotlight* is running way behind. Says that Rachel Yarmouth can't remember her lines, poor dear. Please, God, put the public out of its misery, before that happens to me!" He held up his hand as if taking a solemn oath. "Promise?" he asked the room.

"Surgery?" Derek asked. "Is it serious?"

"Oh, very!" Brent said in a grave tone as the others looked at him with tight smiles. "It's one of the great tragedies." He waited a beat. "Travis Fimmel packed on five pounds over the long holidays and Matt's vacuuming it out."

The other men in the room sniggered as Derek sat smiling, but perplexed. "Matt's a plastic surgeon," Tom finally said. "His specialty is keeping beautiful people beautiful, even when they're well past their sell-by date."

Brent added, "In Travis's case, we want to keep that stunning piece of flesh around as long as possible. Wink wink."

Derek smiled, processing his realization that Brent Richardson was gay. The Hollywood underground rumors about him were true. Derek recalled a long-running defamation of character lawsuit that Brent had filed against a former physical fitness trainer who alleged that Brent had attempted to pay him for sex. Brent took the case all the way to trial and won. He staunchly denied the allegations, but now Derek realized they were probably true.

Brent was, foremost, a respected actor who won practically every award for which he was ever nominated. His film and theater performances were legendary, and many people in the world adored him. He was handsome in an unconventional way. Sophisticated. Articulate. A talented pianist and dancer as well. A wonderful teller of anecdotes on Leno, Oprah, and Ellen. Brent was the man whom ordinary men admired, and their girlfriends and wives fantasized about marrying. He didn't necessarily inspire thoughts of sex, but rather romance. He had many of the same attributes that made Hugh Grant a star, with a touch of Colin Firth and David Hyde Pierce.

"But seriously," Brent was saying, interrupting Derek's thoughts. "Matt's a brilliant doctor, and his partner Paul is equally renowned for doctoring troubled plays. You'll adore them when you finally meet. Just be warned. Matt will probably want a poster-size picture of you to decorate his office. His patients think that the men who adorn his walls are all products of his surgical work and da Vinci-like talent. The truth is, he just likes to surround himself with beautiful things."

Derek thought that it was amazing enough to be sitting in Brent Richardson's Beverly Hills home. But having the actor speak directly to him with such interest and graciousness, was icing on this rich cake.

"Forgive me," Brent said. "I've embarrassed you by so flagrantly discussing your physical charms. I apologize. Let me refill your glass." He lifted Derek's empty flute from his hand and stood up just as Everett appeared with another drink. Brent handed the glass to his servant and took the freshly poured champagne from the tray. He handed it to Derek and smiled. "Don't be shy about asking for more. There's a cellar full of this stuff."

In the distance, Derek heard a faint tinkling. Brent said, "Gentlemen. I do believe that dinner is served. Shall we?"

Still chatting amongst each other, they followed behind Brent, who led them out of the cavernous Great Room, down an art-filled corridor, into what appeared to be an indoor tropical rain forest with an immense rectangular table that Derek guessed would seat twenty people.

An indoor pool, designed to resemble a deep green Amazon lagoon surrounded by lush flora, dominated the room. He saw that it was raining over the foliage and algae-colored water. A sprinkler system hidden in the vaulted ceiling produced gentle drizzle. Four marble statues of male nudes were strategically placed around the lagoon.

As Brent walked to his chair at the head of the table, Tom whispered into Derek's ear. "From Windsor Castle." He indicated the upholstered chairs.

Brent suggested, "Rand, I'll put you there." He pointed to a chair with its back to the pool. "Pat, you're on the other side. Tom, why don't you take this seat?" He directed to the chair beside Rand. "And

Derek, you sit here so you can enjoy the parrots and statuary." The chair to which Derek was conducted was the place of honor, next to the host.

Everett entered the vast room and began pouring white wine into each guest's glass. An older woman in a housekeeper's uniform appeared and pushed a serving cart over the sandstone floor.

"Heya, Emma," Tom said in salutation. Emma smiled and nodded, but she did not speak. She busied herself at the cart, commencing to serve each guest. She seemed not to pay attention to the repartee that bantered back and forth amongst the men.

As Everett and Emma divided attention to the guests between them, they went about their business of removing the domes from each place setting. "In Europe they make a big to-do about choreographing the lifting of the lids simultaneously from each diner," Brent said. "But I obviously don't have the staff for that. My apologies."

As the men enjoyed their starters of pumpkin-filled ravioli in a cream and sage sauce, followed by sea bass with lemon caper sauce, the dialogue ricocheted from Hollywood to politics to a story Brent heard on NPR about gay wedding planners to the latest venom spewed forth by Pat Robertson and a naughty limerick that was going around about linking Laura Bush to Lynn Chaney to Ann Coulter. Derek listened attentively. He enjoyed being on the sidelines, taking in the quips and witticisms. But he didn't dare offer an opinion of his own or try to top anyone else's barb or anecdote. He knew that he'd learn much more by simply remaining a spectator. These gentlemen—and he felt he was assigning that word with its correct definition—were the role models he had always wanted. Interacting with them for what had only been a short period of time had already changed his attitude about how he wanted others to view him.

The dialogue segued to the book of the moment. It seemed that everybody was reading Leon James's debut novel, *Wind Up Toys.* "He almost lost me before the end of that first page-long paragraph," Rand complained. "If I hadn't heard such praise ahead of time, I would never have had the stamina to continue. But thank God I did!"

"I completely see Diane Lane in the role of Stephanie, don't you?" Brent said.

"Oh, and *you* should play Alex," Tom added. "All agree? I totally cast you as I was reading it."

"Who's directing?" Rand asked.

"My agent says they haven't even gotten that far yet," Brent said. "Please let it be Randal Kleiser. This is his kind of story. And I've been desperate to work with him."

"Leon was my neighbor when I first moved to Hollywood." Derek spoke up. He blushed when he realized that he had actually uttered a sentence. Now all eyes turned to him. "I used to hear him clacking at the keyboard all hours of the day and night. I've never known anybody as disciplined and dedicated. He totally deserves his success."

Brent sighed. "I am such an awful host. I haven't asked you one single question about yourself. Please ignore my complete lack of social graces. I'm just a self-absorbed old actor." He smiled. "Are you a member of the literati, too?" Brent seemed genuinely interested.

"Me? Ha! No." Derek shook his head. "Far from it. I'm a waiter, not a writer. That is, I *was* a waiter until Onyx closed. That was where I worked."

"So tell us more about Leon," Brent prodded. "Is he as delicious as his picture on the book jacket? And I thought Sebastian Junger was a hottie. I think the primary reason it took me so long to wade through Leon's novel was because I kept flipping to the back jacket flap just to stare at his picture. If I get to do the film adaptation, I'm going to insist that the producers negotiate to have him on the set at all times. I'll need him to help me understand all of the subs."

Brent looked across the table. "Did you guys get all that symbolism about the guy who was in a constant dream sequence, despite the fact that he seemed to have a constant stream of sex with all those carpet installation men?"

"I didn't get that it was a dream sequence," Rand said. "I thought he was just a horny real estate broker who was bored with sitting on open houses."

Paul chimed in. "Oprah explained it last Thursday. The guy was actually dying. The whole story takes place in the moment that he's being strangled and beginning to go through the tunnel of white light. It's his wasted life that's flashing before him, not a dream sequence at all."

"Oh, Lord," Tom said, swallowing a bit of pilaf. "I was certain that the guy was in detox, and going through the DTs. Now I get why he wanted to yell but no sound would come out. I thought it was a dream sequence too, 'cause I used to have that recurring nightmare where you're being chased by a big black unseen thing and you're so terrified that when you open your mouth to call for help, you're mute. Jeez. I'd better read it again."

Derek recalled his association with the now-famous novelist. "He was actually very cool to know, and yes, very hot in the looks department." Derek glanced at Brent and nodded in agreement with his assessment of Leon's picture being seductive. "On his answering machine he simply announced, 'I'm writing a novel. I'll call you back when I'm finished.' I don't think he had more than two friends. If there were more, they probably dropped him for never being available."

"Very admirable," Brent said. "Delayed gratification is underrated. I admire anyone who is disciplined enough to do the work and do it right."

"But what about his sex life?" Rand asked. "Surely a man as handsome as Leon, got out now and again."

All eyes turned back to Derek. "Not much," Derek said with a shrug. "I mean, I didn't keep his appointment book or anything, but he once told me that when his folks sent him money at Christmas or for his birthday, he called an escort because he was too busy to waste time at bars or on the Internet."

"An escort?" Rand said.

"That's someone you hire for sex. It's an uptown name for 'hustler,' or 'prostitute,'" Derek said. "Someone you can order online like a pizza, or from a rag like *Encounters.*"

"Yes, little boy, we are vaguely aware of what an escort is," Rand said.

"Sorry." Derek laughed uncomfortably. "I've just been doing some research on the subject, and I always think that because I'm learning something new, that everybody else is as much of a neophyte as I am."

Derek sighed. "I've absolutely lost track of Leon. He moved out after he sold the book and now he's probably so rich that he can buy a house somewhere around here." Derek gestured toward the elegant room to imply that his old friend was now worth a fortune. "One thing I remember most is that he was so absorbed in his work, that he'd forget to eat. I'd often bring stuff home from the restaurant and leave it at his door."

"Oh, my God, that's in the book," Brent said. "You're in the novel. He lived on leftovers of fish cakes and garlic bread, right? Did you really feed him through his mail slot?"

Derek was a bit taken aback in happy and incredulous disbelief by Brent's response to his association with Leon James. "God, no. That was all made-up stuff. I think I may have tossed a bread stick through the slot one day. But that's where the truth and fiction separate . . ."

Derek stopped talking to reflect on where he was and with whom he was in conversation. "Wait a minute," Derek said, putting down his fork. "You're Brent Richardson, and you're interested in the fact that I'm the model for a bit of atmosphere in a novel? I honestly didn't even think twice about what Leon wrote until this minute."

"A modest one," Brent said, winking at Tom. "We like that. A lot."

"But seriously," Derek said, "you've worked for your celebrity. The only reason I'm in Leon's novel is because the character he created—and perhaps Leon as well—had to rely 'on the kindness of strangers.' "

Brent took another sip of his wine. "I always enjoy hearing behind-the-scenes anecdotes about artists and how they create their work," he said. "And I'm impressed that an actual character in a novel is seated by my side. I feel as though I'm Claire Boothe Luce giving a dinner and Crystal Allen has unexpectedly crashed my party!"

By the time the dessert plates were removed the dinner had been in progress for two hours. "Oh, God, the time!" Brent sighed. "It's not a school night, so can you guys stay just a bit longer? I want to screen this film from a young director for whom I'm trying to help secure distribution. Just the first reel. I promise."

Derek gave a questioning look to Tom. He was having one of the best evenings of his life and didn't want it to end any sooner than absolutely necessary. Tom smiled and nodded.

Brent stood to lead the way out of the dining room. The assembly moved down another long hallway and down a flight of stairs into a screening room. "This was once the ballroom," Tom whispered to Derek.

"I hope that after you're seen this you'll be as excited by the wunderkind director as I am," Brent said. "Trust me when I say he is going to be huge."

SEVEN

Although Derek was exhausted, he was emotionally buoyant. The ride home, sitting next to Tom, made his euphoria all the more tangible. "Was I all right?" he asked. He needed to be reassured that he didn't make a fool of himself in front of men whom he admired and who he so much wanted to like him in return. "I didn't talk too much, did I?"

"Brent adored you." Tom smiled. "They all did. Who wouldn't? I imagine they'll be retelling your story about Kate Beckinsale at every other dinner this week. Imagine, offering to sign autographs in exchange for free meals at Onyx." He placed a hand on Derek's knee. "I just hope you had as good a time as I did."

Derek said, "I never thought that I'd have a friend who knew such incredible people."

Tom gave Derek's knee a tentative squeeze. "I'm pretty lucky to have a few really great friends," he said. He took his eyes off the nearly empty street for a moment to look at Derek. "Like you," he said. "Look, I know it's late, and I have an early meeting, but can you put your status as a 'legit' masseur on hold for just a few hours? I'd really like to reciprocate and give you a rubdown."

Derek took Tom's hand and held it. Forcing himself to be calm, he said, "I've got a really tight muscle that could use a massage."

He pulled Tom's hand over to his crotch and placed it on the bulge in his pants. Tom lightly laughed. "I've been staring at the picture in your online ad for days."

"And I shagged my pillow the other night, pretending it was you," Derek confessed.

* * *

Against all odds, Tom found a space to park the car at the curb directly in front of Derek's apartment. Tom followed as Derek led the way through the courtyard toward his unit.

"Shhh," Derek whispered. "The apartment manager's an asshole. Don't wake him."

The porch light by Derek's front door was burned out, and he cautioned Tom to watch his step. Vibrating with excitement, Derek fumbled in the darkness to find the keyhole. He inserted his key into the lock and turned the knob, but before he could push open the door himself, Tom shoved both Derek and the door simultaneously.

Willingly, Derek tumbled to the floor into the black room. He pulled Tom along with him. While lathering Derek with kisses, Tom simultaneously found the door with his foot, and slammed it shut. He quickly peeled out of his clothes. Derek just as quickly shed his clothes too.

A potent scent of virility emanated from Tom's flesh. The aroma made Derek uncharacteristically supplicant. The sounds of their urgent moans and the taste of each other's sweet saliva brought them to delirious intoxication.

Their eyes began to adjust to the darkness. The silhouettes of their body forms became abstractly visible. Tom rolled to his side and stood up. He took Derek by the hand and forced him to his unsteady feet. Tom led Derek to the bed and pushed him onto the mattress. The bedsprings groaned as Tom added his weight to the bed and onto Derek.

Derek reached out for Tom's cock, which was as hard and impressively large as Derek had known it would be. He forced himself out from under Tom's grip and moved down to the bottom edge of the bed. Then Derek knelt between Tom's legs. He pressed his face into his playmate's ball sack. One at a time, he sucked on each large testicle washing the supple skin and dense patch of hair with his tongue. He tasted Tom's scrotum and inhaled the pungent scent emanating from his pubic bush.

Derek then dragged his tongue up the side of Tom's engorged shaft and circled the helmet head. He tasted the sticky sweet of Tom's precum. Then, opening his mouth, he ravenously descended on Tom's cock, careful not to let his teeth scrape the tight, thin skin. Using his tongue, he swabbed down to the base, and felt the protruding veins.

Derek's own dick was aching from the volcanic pressure building deep within. He could feel an impressive amount of gluey emission seeping out to coat the head of his prick.

Tom proved an unselfish lover, waiting for Derek as Derek was for him. Finally, after nearly a half hour of exhausting foreplay, and getting to know every inch of each other's bodies, Tom said, "God, I can't take it anymore. I want to fuck your ass. I need to."

"Me too," Derek moaned. "Fuck me and shoot your load."

Tom roughly grabbed Derek's legs and spread them apart. Then he spat on his fingers and began massaging and lubricating Derek's hole.

"Wait," Derek said. "A condom—"

"Christ, I want you now!" Tom snapped. "Don't ruin the moment! I'm negative! I'll take a chance that you are too!"

Tops all say they're negative, Derek thought, as he extricated himself from Tom's grip. He reached under the bed and felt around the inside of an open shoe box. He touched what he knew was a Trojan, which he retrieved along with a small bottle of lube. "Here," Derek said. He was trying to ignore that Tom was somehow angry that he would not let Tom ride him bareback.

"Christ," Tom snorted. Then Derek heard the sound of the condom packaging being ripped open. Derek flipped the lid of the bottle of lube and squeezed a generous amount onto his three fingers. He slathered his hole inside and out. Then he reached out to guide Tom's huge tool into him, and at the same time confirming that the condom was in place.

They began cautiously. The head of Tom's swollen flange was huge. By degrees, willing himself to relax his sphincter, Derek could feel Tom's whole piece sliding into his most private space. Breathing in quick bursts, he dropped his legs from Tom's shoulder and settled them around his insatiable top's waist. He hooked the heels against Tom's butt cheeks and applied enough pressured to make Tom drive his cock as deeply as possible.

"You're so fucking tight," Tom murmured.

Derek was in blissful agony. And as Tom pounded into Derek's butt cheeks, Derek jacked off his own dick, careful not to stroke himself to ejaculation just yet.

Tom was consumed with lust. The tender and sensitive man with whom Derek had spent the evening had morphed into an utterly aggressive power top.

Derek had a desperate desire to remain immersed in this mind and body transforming experience. The pummeling that his ass was taking was more than what he had ever hoped for. He didn't want it to end.

"Kiss me while you fuck me!" Derek gasped. "Kiss me!"

Tom continued the piston thrusting from the tight holster of Derek's ass. He leaned down as Derek raised his face to meet Tom's lips.

As they locked their mouths and swapped tongue together, Derek reached out and cupped the back of Tom's head in one hand. He sensed that Tom was ready to blow his load. Derek began to vigorously stroke himself. As he grew closer to climax, he drove his tongue deeper into Tom's mouth.

It was a losing battle for both men. Tom, his sweat falling in droplets onto Derek's chest, thrust deeper and moaned louder. Derek, too, could not control his body or his groans of satisfaction. Pulling his lips away from Tom's he cried, "Oh, Christ! I can't . . . hold . . ."

And with that, Derek unloaded his thick stream of jizzum. He shot from his hole like rubber bands snapping into the air and landing on his face and chest.

As Tom pounded his shaft into Derek's ass, he made the sounds of a rutting animal. In the few seconds before his climax, he withdrew his cock from Derek. He yanked off the condom and his cock erupted a burst of white ropy semen.

When Tom's was released, he dropped his full body weight onto Derek. The men intertwined their legs, and held each other tightly. Soon afterwards, they fell into a deep, contented sleep.

EIGHT

The room was filling with morning light when a knock at the door snapped Derek and Tom back to consciousness.

Derek slipped out of bed, finger-combed his hair and stepped into his jeans. Shirtless, he went to the door. "Wha?" he asked.

"It's Garson," a voice answered from the other side. "We need to talk."

Derek looked over at Tom who was sitting up in bed, the sheet pulled to his waist. "Apartment manager," Derek whispered. He turned the knob and pulled open the door. Garson's eyes tarried longer than they should have on Derek's chiseled chest, biceps, pecs, and abs. Then he said at last, "Look, man. I know you're out of work and all, but your rent is two months behind. It's not me doing the talking here. Know what I mean? It's the property management company. You've gotta come up with the money pronto. I'm supposed to give you this."

He handed Derek a long manila envelope with the name and address of an attorney in the upper left-hand corner.

As Derek stood with the door ajar, opening the envelope, he was aware that Garson was looking past him into the small apartment. He saw Tom, who was rising from the bed. Garson swallowed hard as he watched Tom stepping into his white briefs, then pulling his pants over his legs, and zipping his fly.

Scanning the document, Derek's eyes fell on a line with a dollar sign and the figures $2,500.00. He looked up and caught Garson's eyes still glued to the interior of his apartment. "I can't pay this," Derek said. "I'm unemployed. I don't have this kind of money right now. What about my security deposit? Can't you use that for the month?

Garson said, "The old manager let you move in without a first and last, which is probably why he got fired. He was too generous to hot guys."

"So, according to this, I have to cough up twenty-five hundred bucks within three days, otherwise, I'll be evicted?" Derek said.

Garson was contrite. "Man, I don't make the rules. But it's my job to enforce 'em. The management people want cash or a money order within three business days. Otherwise . . ."

"Otherwise, what?" Derek asked.

"Otherwise it gets ugly. The West Hollywood Sheriff's Department sends a posse to evict you. Instead of me, they come to your door. Trust me, those dudes lose a lot of their sex appeal when they're on official business. It's not gay porn cop fantasy."

Derek was stunned. What had begun as a blissful night of passion with one of the most seductive men he'd known, had turned into a morning in which he was utterly humiliated. Especially in front of Tom. He knew that a man of Tom's means and social standing would never be interested in someone from a far more humble station. There was a distinct barrier between the classes, especially in Hollywood. They were inter-fuckable, but only older men married younger men without pedigrees.

Garson once again took his eyes away from Derek and settled on Tom, who was still shirtless and now standing beside Derek.

Tom smiled at Garson. "Sorry," Tom said, "I apologize for eavesdropping, but I couldn't help hearing that Derek, who until his unexpected and forced separation from the workforce, had never been late with a rent payment for this unit in this so-called residence. Which—no offense intended—is plainly verging on being in violation of municipal code 52972c-12, among others."

Garson blinked, but he didn't say a word.

Tom continued. "In the brief time that I've been here, I've noticed at least a dozen housing violations. But I'm sure you've pointed each of these items out to the property management company haven't you?"

Garson's jaw dropped.

Tom went on in his most gentle and pleasant tone. "As the on-site representative for the owners, you would also be held liable for fines levied by the city and its various departments that are responsible for maintaining rental property which is safe and secure. A good-looking, intelligent man such as you doesn't strike me as one who would be derelict in his duties." Tom took the envelope and letter from Derek's hands. "Derek will take into consideration your good faith efforts to help maintain a proper environment when he deliberates the various elements of the claim that he is filing against the property owners and their manager which, of course, is you."

Tom handed the material back to Garson. "By the way, thank you again for bringing to Derek's attention the fact that a certain sum of money is due in consideration of his continued residence here. He will, of course, honor his commitment just as soon as all the violations are corrected. Have a lovely day."

While Garson stood still and dumbfounded, Tom closed the door in his face. Derek turned to Tom with a look of utter incomprehension of what he'd just witnessed. "What was that?" he said. Then he started laughing. "Did you see the look on Garson's face?"

"The same look that's on yours," Tom said, smiling.

"I'm . . . I'm . . ." Derek held up his hands as if to surrender. "I'm speechless. You've got a golden tongue. I mean, I already knew that . . . You bailed out my ass."

"That's what law degrees are for," Tom said. "Stanford don't matriculate no dummies."

Derek blinked. "You're a lawyer? Sorry. You must think I'm such a self-absorbed asshole not to have at least asked about your work. I should have known. The Mercedes. The rich friends. Are you famous too? I mean, should I know who you are?"

Tom took Derek in his arms. "You know who I am. I'm the man who fucked you mercilessly last night." He laughed.

His lips met Derek's. They melded together, their tongues languidly exploring the other's, tasting the tang of sleepiness.

Their ardor became more intense, and soon Tom was guiding Derek backward toward the bed. Shedding their pants once more, the two men were as hard and eager for each other as they were the first time last night. They dropped down on to the mattress and jump-started their lovemaking from the night before with even more abandon.

Derek pushed his man down on the bed and forcefully pinned his arms over his head and against the mattress. He leaned in and placed his lips against Tom's which parted to accept Derek's tongue. Derek released his grip on Tom's wrists, and they enveloped each other in their arms. He cupped his hands around Tom's face, and the two of them reciprocated fervent kisses.

"I fucked you last night, now it's your turn to fuck me," Tom said, as his hands roamed Derek's body. "Fuck me as hard as I fucked you."

Derek ached to find Tom's hole, but he realized he was out of condoms, and said so. "Use the one that was up your ass last night," Tom said, breathless.

Derek was in a quandary. He didn't want to offend this hot man and risk spoiling the sex, as well as the possibility that this could turn into the relationship that Derek had dreamed of having.

"Wash it out, if you feel that concerned," Tom said, reading the hesitation in Derek's actions. "But hurry, because my ass is aching for you!"

But for Derek, the moment had passed. "Ya know what?" he said. "No. With me, when the pants come off, the condoms go on. I could almost make the mistake of ignoring my personal rule because I want you so much. But I have to draw the line. No used condoms. Not up your ass, and certainly not up mine. Sorry."

Tom became angry. "Christ!" he shouted. He rolled over on to his back, his dick still hard.

Derek rolled onto his back and stared up at the ceiling. The sounds of activities outside the apartment wafted in to the unit. A leaf blower. Traffic. A dog barking. But Tom was silent. Derek suddenly felt that the room was too small, inducing claustrophobia.

Then: "Will you at least let me suck you off?" Tom asked. "Or is that on the AIDS activist's sex warning label, too?"

"Swallow at your own risk," Derek said.

Tom's anger evaporated. He rolled onto Derek and began to kiss him again.

Ten minutes later, sated and still holding on to one another, Derek, in a voice husky from his moans of satisfaction, said, "Stanford, eh?"

Tom caressed Derek's chest with a hand. He grunted affirmatively.

"I'm impressed," Derek said. His eyes drifted for a moment to the clock on his desk. "I'd like to keep you chained to my cock, but I don't want to mess up your career. You've got a meeting."

"No meeting," Tom said.

Derek gave Tom a small nudge. "If we hadn't hit it off, you would have had a meeting, right?"

"You catch on quick," Tom said.

Derek chuckled. "If you weren't so fucking hot, and if you didn't rescue my ass from the clutches of that gargoyle Garson, I'd say you were just sampling the menu."

Tom said, "Mmm. Old-fashioned home cookin'. It's about time for dessert." Then he slipped down under the top sheet until his mouth once again found Derek's cock.

While Tom showered, Derek switched on his Mr. Coffee machine and prepared a light breakfast of English muffins, and orange juice. By the time Tom emerged from the bathroom, his hair wet and his dress shirt wrinkled and pasted to his still-damp torso, Derek had laid out what little food he had in the apartment.

Tom gave Derek a quick kiss on the lips, then looked at the table and smiled at the effort Derek had made. Two toasted muffins, fork-split in halves, were on a plate next to a yellow tub of margarine that was nearly empty. "Looks delish," he said. Derek wondered if Tom was being sarcastic, then dismissed the thought.

Ravenous, the two men devoured their breakfast in minutes. "I obviously didn't expect a guest," Derek explained. "I would have been better prepared. At least I'd have more food."

"I'm not usually a breakfast eater," Tom said. "Although I'd probably go through the DTs without my morning Starbucks. So this is perfect. You've hit all the right notes." He sipped his coffee, then helped himself to another cup. "Now, what's going on with the landlord situation, if you don't mind me asking?"

Derek was suddenly ashamed. "That little scene had to happen while you were here. Goddamn it. I'm so fucking embarrassed."

Tom took another sip from his coffee mug. Derek sighed, deciding that he might as well tell the truth about his financial situation. *Maybe this relationship will be over before it begins,* he said to himself. "I'm starting a new career. I was a waiter at Onyx, and the place closed a couple of months ago. I haven't been able to land another wait gig since, so I thought I'd try my hand at massage. But I have to turn down ninety-nine percent of the calls I get."

Tom nodded. "The 'No sex, I'm legit' bullshit?"

Derek said, "What was I thinking when I placed that ad? But I'm so fucking broke. I'm at a point where I'm going to have to start letting the guys who call at least get themselves off on my table. I thought I was such a talented guy, but I can't even afford the next ad in *Encounters!*"

Derek felt suddenly close to tears. Tom reached out and put a hand on his shoulder. "It's not your fault. The economy sucks. But you've got a ton of potential, so I know you'll get back on your feet. You're bright, articulate, and God knows, you're hot. Any employer should be on their knees if you'd agree to join their workforce."

Derek shook his head in dismay. "I have to be honest. I'm not really employable. I went to acting school instead of college, so I don't have a degree. I've basically only worked as a waiter. I had these big fantasies of being a star, or some damned type of celebrity."

Tom reached for the Mr. Coffee carafe and poured the remains, sharing the last with Derek. "First of all, a degree is practically worthless in this market," Tom said. "Do you know what having an academic degree means? It just proves that you're capable of showing up for classes, and that you have the capacity to finish what you start. A college degree is no measure of one's potential. And, God knows, it doesn't guarantee success."

Derek had known his share of people who graduated from prestigious schools, but who were basically incompetents.

"You can't imagine the number of people I know with graduate degrees who are in the same boat as you," Tom continued. "On the other hand, I know many who've made a fortune with only a high school diploma, if that. It's all about finding your niche. Discovering something that you do well. You make yourself into a commodity, and you trade your skills for a paycheck. And that's just what most people do, they trade their souls for a lousy paycheck. By the way, you're very good at massage. You really could make a serious go of it. You just need the right clientele."

"That's easier said than done," Derek said. "No offense, but when you've got a law degree from Stanford, you can't possibly know what it's like to be obliged to an employer, worrying every day, knowing that if you do or say one thing wrong, you could lose your job. And even when you're a good worker, it doesn't matter because employers have no allegiance anymore. One day you're working your butt off, cursing because you *have* to work in the first place, and the next thing you know, you're out, wishing you had a job to complain about. It sucks."

Tom looked away for a moment to take in the tiny apartment. The sink and kitchen counter were no bigger than a bathroom vanity. The bathroom was the size of an airplane lavatory. The carpeting had to be twenty years and a dozen tenants old. The dingy walls were cracked, the windowsills were thick with nearly a half-century's worth of paint, and the ceiling was discolored with several different shades of beige. "No offense back at you, but do you want to live this way always?" he asked.

"If I could afford Beverly Hills I'd be there," Derek said. "Of course this is *not* the way I want to live. But it's the best that I can do for the moment."

"You mean the best that you'll settle for," Tom countered.

"Nobody in their right mind would choose to live in this place," Derek said. "And trust me, after visiting your friends last night, I cringed at the thought of coming back here. If you hadn't been with me, I'd have been hugely depressed. I have to believe that this will change."

"That's at least a start," Tom offered. "You've got a positive attitude. Nothing stays the same. Everything is cyclical. You'll be employed again very soon. But . . ."

Derek waited for Tom to complete his thought. "What?"

Tom said, "You didn't ask for my opinion, but if I were to offer it, I'd say that you'll never . . . maybe not never . . . you'll *probably* never dig yourself out of your financial mess, and move up in the world if you simply place an ad in a fuck magazine offering a massage. Frankly, even if you gave your customers sex, you'd have to work long and hard—no pun intended—to afford a decent lifestyle."

"You're saying I'm fucked?"

"I'm not saying you're fucked," Tom protested. "I don't waste my time with losers and I know you're not a loser. You're just temporarily off your mark." Tom looked at his wristwatch. "Oh, I've got to run."

"That meeting is suddenly on again?" Derek asked.

Tom smiled. "It's not what you're thinking. But do me a favor?"

"What?"

"Don't answer any more calls from prospective customers. I know you need rent money, and you've got to eat, but hold off for a couple of days, if you can."

"You want me to save myself for you?" Derek asked coyly.

"Just take a couple of days to look for another job. In the meantime, I'll make a few phone calls on your behalf. But no guarantees."

Derek reached into his pocket. "This is my net worth," he said taking out a ten-dollar bill and four singles. "I figure that the dinner I had at Brent's last night will keep me from starving for a day or two. I can work this small fortune into a couple of days of peanut butter sandwiches, but after Tuesday or Wednesday . . ."

Tom looked at the money, which Derek held in his hand. Derek's eyes were glistening with fear and embarrassment. "I'm not without empathy," Tom said. "If you think I was born with a silver spoon, you're mistaken."

"Stanford," Derek said.

"Believe it or not," Tom said, "my parents had nothing to do with me going to Stanford."

"That's why there's such a thing as scholarships," Derek said.

Tom shook his head. "My grades were decent, but I wasn't exactly the type of student that a big college would actively recruit. Let's just say that I had a benefactor."

"Shades of *Great Expectations?*"

Tom nodded. "In a way," he said. "The most important thing I've discovered is that you have to trust that you'll survive. No. More than survive. You need to thrive."

Derek said, "I know you're right. I'm just going through a rough stretch. I'll try my luck at Denny's and Bob's Big Boy. I've sunk that low."

Tom smiled. "If those places don't work out, I've got a few ideas. Trust me, okay? You're very sexy, and I'm going to do whatever I can to help out. Now, give me a kiss, then get my ass out of this dump."

NINE

"Juan," said Derek over the phone, "just when I thought life was almost worthless a little spark of hope reignited. I've met someone."

Derek rattled on about his client-cum-fuck buddy-cum-potential boyfriend material, and the incredible orgasms they'd shared. Derek rambled with his exciting news about meeting a big star—whose name he didn't divulge—and the way his new friend had handled a potentially ugly scene with the apartment manager, and how Derek was temporarily saved from eviction.

After a few minutes all Derek could hear on the other end of the line was silence. "Juan?" he asked. "Are you there?"

He heard a deep exhalation of breath. "Yeah," was the one word that followed.

Derek immediately felt ashamed that he was yammering about his own good fortune, when Juan's back was still firmly against the wall of destitution. "Still no job?" Derek said.

"I called the asshole," Juan confessed.

"Your ex?" Derek asked.

"I hadn't eaten in two days. He took me to dinner."

"And you had to pay him back?"

"His weight issue has gotten worse," Juan said. "I actually had to take a couple of folds of his stomach and get them out of the way before I could get to his dick."

Derek had heard many horror stories from Juan about the way his former boyfriend had treated him. A Caucasian, the man was two decades older than Juan, and he made certain that Juan felt as demeaned and beholden to him as possible. He enjoyed taking Juan to expensive restaurants, then publicly criticizing the way that he pronounced the name of something on the menu. Juan had once made the mistake of ordering proscuitto as an appetizer, and not only mispronounced the word but didn't have the vaguest notion what he had requested. It wasn't just public humiliation that Juan had to endure, but also the fact that the man openly cheated on Juan at every opportunity.

Derek was adamant. "You're not moving back in with that prick. Things are going to change for both of us. Tom, the dude I told you about, offered to help me out. And I promise, if he has connections and can get me a wait gig, I'm bringing you along. Please don't sell yourself out to that fat bastard."

Derek could hear Juan starting to cry. "I can't afford self-worth. I can't get work and my rent's past due. My electricity is going to be turned off on Wednesday. I only have two choices. Move back with the asshole, or kill myself. Make that three choices. I got a call from Marshall Topper. You know that creep who used to come in to Onyx? Said he has a list a mile long of guys who want me. I was right. There's a big market for thick uncut Latino cocks and shaved butt holes."

Derek became angry. "Knock it off, Juan. You do so have other choices."

Juan practically shouted into the telephone, "If you, a fucking hot white boy, can't get a foot in the door for a decent job, then I'm completely fucked! I'm illegal!"

Derek took a deep breath. "Juan," he said, "I want you to hang up the telephone, grab your toothbrush, and get your illegal Mexican ass over to my apartment. Now. I am not letting you go through this alone. I've got enough money for a six-pack, and we're both going to figure something out."

"No, Boss," Juan said. "I've gotta stand up for myself."

"The hell you do," Derek countered. "Listen, we all need help from time to time. Right now I need your help as much as you need mine. Get your beautiful butt over here. Now!"

Juan gave a weak laugh. "I can't even afford the fuckin' bus fare!"

"Get that toothbrush and a salsa CD. I don't have much gas in the car, so meet me on the corner of Western and Fountain in forty minutes. I'm taking the bus and coming to get you."

Derek placed the telephone back on its cradle. He rummaged through his desk drawer for change. Among paper clips and rubber bands, he found three quarters, three dimes and two pennies. The coins, in addition to his fourteen dollars, would be enough for a round-trip bus ride for two, plus a six-pack of Corona Lite with a little left over. He picked up his leather jacket and apartment keys, headed out, and locked the door behind him.

Derek and Juan sat on the floor of the apartment, drinking beer and listening to a CD of Grupo Niche. They talked about friends from Onyx. They discussed Juan's ex-boyfriend and made jokes about how flabby and soft he was. "He's got a thing for Latino boys." Juan chuckled. "I'd love to send him some gangbanger to ream his loose butt hole."

They reminisced about their former customers, including Marty and Felicia. "Ha!" Derek chuckled. "Their names came up in conversation at a dinner I attended the other night. Who knew they were so well connected."

Derek confided to Juan that Felicia had a yearning for the Latino. "I never told you this, but remember that party I worked at their place? Marty was so pissed at me when I told him that Jet called you in to work. He had planned to have you fuck Felicia. That was before they were married."

Juan said, "You're such a naïve fuck. It wasn't Felicia that Marty wanted me to fuck. It was him. I stopped by after the restaurant closed and made two hundred off him that night."

Derek was stunned. "Wait a minute, you hypocrite," he said. "You were all over me about placing an ad that suggested sex, and you actually turned tricks with Marty? You're a freakin' fraud!"

"It was a hell of a lot better than working The Beanfield," Juan said. "And I made more in twenty minutes from that one cock, than from sucking off a dozen commuters."

Derek considered for a moment, then said, "I know this will sound horrible, but let me just say that you could make a fortune fucking white guys."

Juan started to interrupt. "Wait a second," Derek jumped in. "The thing is, I wasn't completely honest with you when I said that my first couple of clients were only interested in massage. The truth is, one of them offered me three hundred bucks. And that was just to let him jack off on me. I was completely insane to turn him down. I'm down to a pocket full of lint and gum wrappers. We're both great-looking guys.

Neither of us have particular moral views about making a buck on our backs. Why shouldn't we cash in?"

Juan drained his beer can and crushed the aluminum in his hand. "Big bad boyfriend demeaned me enough. So did those assholes at The Beanfield. I don't want to invite it in."

"You prostituted yourself with that dinner," Derek said. "You exchanged sex for food. You don't want to see it that way, but that's what you did. But my mom exchanged sex with my dad for her household allowance and a new car every few years. She hated giving him head, but I know she did it because he held the checkbook."

"Boss, you're ruining the evening. I know what I did with the asshole, and with Marty, and with a hundred other guys. Been there, done that. I've still got my dignity, for Christ's sake."

"Dignity?" Derek said testily. "Isn't that why I couldn't bring myself to let those trolls use me?" *Dignity,* he thought. *I can't afford gas for my car, food for my stomach and the rent for this run-down rat hole. But I've sure got my fucking dignity.*

The Grupo Niche CD ended. The room became silent. Juan stared at the poster for *The Treasure of the Sierra Madre.* The sound of traffic outside mingled with that of a jet passing overhead. Then the telephone rang.

Derek let the machine pick up, and a male voice spoke. "Hey, stud, do you look like your picture?" The caller sounded inebriated. "I need a dick and I want yours, if it's the size you say it is. Pick up, God damn it." There was a long moment of silence. "Okay, so call me. Three-two-three. One, two . . . ah, fuck you."

The machine clicked off. Silence once again enveloped the apartment. Then the sound of footsteps on the front porch caught their attention. A knock shattered the serene, if depressing, atmosphere. "Hey!" It was Garson's voice. "Boy! I know you're in there. And I know you're having sex with that Mexican! I'll use my master key if I have to. Open up!"

Derek simply sat staring at the door. He was half expecting it to open and reveal Garson and a cadre of West Hollywood sheriff's deputies. Garson continued. "I just want you to know that your smart-aleck friend didn't scare me this morning! I've talked to the landlords! They've got a bunch of lawyers who handle lowlifes like you! You think you can hole up in there forever? You're crazy, mister! I'm watching you! The next time I come to your door, I'll have an eviction notice!"

After one final angry blow to the door, Derek and Juan could hear Garson's footsteps as he stepped off the porch and retreated down the concrete walkway. "Maybe if you let him suck your cock . . ." Juan whispered.

"He's a greasy-haired, unshaved, blubbery excuse for a man," Derek said. "Even as a baby I'll bet he had that pointy rat-snout face. Oh, God, what am I going to do? What are *we* going to do?"

Juan stood up to fetch the last of their beers. "I'll split the can with you," he said, flipping the tab and slurping the foam. He handed the can to Derek. "You can always fuck Felicia while I fuck Marty."

Once again the telephone rang. Another male voice. "Hi, um, I've never done this before, but I was wondering, um, if, um, I could maybe make an appointment. Um, for a massage I mean."

Juan looked at Derek. "It's only a matter of time, Boss."

"Yeah," Derek agreed. "But not this time. What about you?"

Juan shook his head. "Not yet. Please, dear God, not yet."

TEN

"Gotta bleed the lizard," Juan said. He stood up and crossed the floor to the bathroom. Although he closed the door, and pushed the repeat button on the stereo for another track from the Grupo Niche CD, Derek could hear Juan's heavy stream cascading into the toilet water. *What a load*, Derek thought as he imagined the force and amount of jiz that a piece like Juan's would expel. The toilet flushed. Then Derek heard water rushing from the tap into the sink basin as Juan washed his hands.

The door reopened and Juan stepped back into the room. He had removed his shirt. "It's so hot. Can't you open a window in this place?"

A stab of lust jabbed at Derek as he took in the image of Juan's brown skin and the black chest hair that surrounded his nipples, collected at his sternum and trailed down his abs and into his pants. Derek tried not to act as if he even noticed his friend's body. Juan knelt down on to the floor and stretched out on his back, cradling his head in Derek's lap.

Derek placed a tentative hand on Juan's forehead and began petting his friend's head of rich, black hair. Juan closed his eyes. "Are you comfortable?" Derek asked. "Maybe you should just climb into bed."

Juan reached up and took hold of Derek's hand as it caressed his forehead. He brought it to his face and pressed his lips to Derek's fingers.

Then he moved Derek's hand to his chest. Derek gently began to caress Juan's pecs. He grazed Juan's nipples with the pad of his index finger. He opened his palm and stoked the warm planes of Juan's chest.

Derek was sure that Juan could feel the strong, erect cock under his neck. "Bed," Juan finally said in a sleepy voice.

"Up you go," Derek said. He extricated himself out from under Juan and helped him to his feet. Juan smiled as he removed his pants.

At first, they were back to back with each other. Derek turned out the light and stared into the blackness of the room. The phone rang two more times, and the answering machine clicked on and off with each call. Between interruptions, Juan asked in a plaintive voice, "Derek? Will you hold me?"

Without a word, Derek rolled onto his side. His face met Juan's strong back and he gently kissed the warm skin covering Juan's shoulder blades. He put an arm around his friend's torso, and Juan molded his body to fit into the serpentine shape in which Derek had arranged himself. "Sleep well, my friend," Derek whispered. "You're safe."

Although the men were hard and horny, they quickly fell into an alcohol-induced sleep. When morning arrived, Derek and Juan were still spooning. As a garbage truck made hydraulic noises outside, and traffic along the street became more pronounced, the men wrested from their sleep with groaning erections.

"Boss, I gotta pee," Juan said, extricating himself from Derek's arm.

Derek rubbed his eyes, then looked at the clock. It was nearly seven. He realized that it was the first time in recent memory that he slept with his underpants on. Stretched across his morning hard-on, the fabric felt restraining. He heard the toilet flush and turned to watch Juan come back to the bed.

Juan's Jockey shorts displayed his heavy cargo. He sleepily padded back to bed. As he looked at Derek's bare chest, his plump cock jumped involuntarily.

Derek noticed the subtle movement. "Damn, I can't pee if I'm hard," he joked.

He left the bed and made his way to the bathroom. As Juan resettled himself into the warm bed, Derek brushed his teeth. A few moments later, Derek presented himself in the room once again and slipped in beside Juan.

Juan's neck rested on Derek's arm, a bicep for his pillow. Derek's free arm surrounded Juan's waist. Derek's chest and stomach were pressed against the warm flesh of Juan's back. Derek inhaled his friend's unwashed male scent.

"When I was a little boy in Mexico, my daddy used to hold me like this in bed." Juan sighed. "I remember how he smelled. Beer and cigarettes. His body was so warm and strong. And I loved it when he cuddled with me." He paused. "Did your daddy treat you well?"

Derek thought for a moment. "He was okay, I guess. I hardly remember him. I know that he never held me like this. He was always too busy with his job. Too much responsibility. Would never say no to more work. Hardly ever even had a day off. Forget about vacations. Being stuck at home with my mom and me was his idea of a waste of time. But my first lover used to hold me. Especially right after sex. That's always been my favorite part of sex, the holding afterward."

Juan reached for Derek's hand and held it against his chest. He then moved it slowly down his torso, over the hair covering his abs, finally settling on his fully erect cock, which he had extricated from his underpants.

Derek reached down and removed his own underpants. Then he rolled Juan over and cupped his friend's face in his hands. He began to kiss his brown lips and taste Juan's slightly sour tongue. The two men wrapped each other in their arms. Their lips and tongues began exploring each other's bodies.

As Derek probed Juan's nipples, then began kissing the back of his neck, Juan reached up and felt Derek's swollen biceps. Finally, their hard dicks and pubic bushes began grinding together.

Rising up to straddle Juan between the vice of his thighs, Derek leaned his face against his partner's chest and slathered the brown skin with a ravenous tongue. He sucked on Juan's hard nipples, then buried his face in the dark pits of his underarms. As he licked the hollow of Juan's throat, his hard dick pressed against Juan's stomach. He could feel Juan's tool pressed against the crack of his ass.

Juan reached behind his head to grip the metal bars of the headboard. His chest expanded and deflated in rapid bursts. "Fuck," he whispered, tossing his head from side to side. "Fuck."

They transferred positions. Derek reached up behind and over his head to grasp the metal bars on the bed as Juan began devouring every centimeter of his neck, sternum and stomach. Juan scoured the flesh of Derek's body.

At last, facing his prize, Juan buried his face in the untrimmed thicket around Derek's cock. He inhaled the warm scent radiating from the bramble of Derek's pubic bush. Then he opened his mouth to receive the glistening dick. He moaned in satisfaction as he swallowed the thick, veined meat.

Derek's cock was absorbed then released, swallowed whole again, and then disengaged. He could feel the pressure of his semen rising to the surface. He whimpered in ecstasy. As Derek neared the point of no return, he gasped, "No condoms."

"I'm so ready myself, Boss," Juan panted. "We'll just have to jack off."

Juan straddled Derek's waist, then began to violently massage his eight-and-a-half-inch tool. "Fuck me, Boss!" Then, in a near photo finish, he and Derek climaxed together. Juan shot his ample load all over Derek's chest and stomach. Derek's load spewed forth, mixing with Juan's to form a warm puddle that spread over his skin. Juan milked his meat, then shook his shank to squeeze out the last beads of semen. Then he collapsed beside Derek.

Both men continued to breathe heavily for a few moments. Then, by increments, they regained their composure. For a while, neither said a word.

Finally Juan spoke. "How about if you and me, we get a place together. A two-bedroom place. Just to save on rent."

Derek knew that he was going to have to find a way to save on expenses. "Sure, as soon as we can afford a first and last on a place," he said. "That would be cool. Maybe in Silverlake." He didn't reveal what he was really thinking, which was that money was a serious obstacle. His car needed to be repaired. He and Juan still owed back rent on their respective apartments, and there were no jobs for either of them in the foreseeable future.

Just then, the telephone rang, and the answering machine picked up. This time it was Tom. For a moment Derek panicked. After his intimacy with Juan, he hoped that Tom would not allude to their own tryst from the previous night.

Tom was saying, "I've made a few phone calls. I might have something for you. A job. Sort of. But we should get together to discuss this seriously. The sooner the better, so call my cell the moment you get this, okay? I know it's early . . . um, seven-fifteen . . . but I wanted to head you off at the pass, so to speak, before you ended up doing something someone would regret. Okay. So call me. I'll be reachable until noon, then I have an appointment. Leave a voice mail. Um, this is kind of important, so call ASAP." Then he hung up.

"He's such a cool guy," Derek said wistfully, hoping not to spoil the bond that he had established with Juan. "He did say the word 'job,' didn't he?"

"His exact words were, '. . . A job. Sort of,' " Juan said. "He doesn't sound very certain. But hey, take anything that pays. Then you can be *my* sugar daddy. But what did he mean by 'head you off at the pass?' "

"He suspects I'm getting desperate enough to start prostituting myself," Derek said. "He's right."

"So he wants to save you from the life of a typical crystal meth–addicted street whore, eh?" Juan teased. "He must like you."

"Wait'll you meet him," Derek said. "He's incredible." Derek realized he was about to say something very flattering about a man he hardly knew, to the man with whom he had just shared an intimate morning.

"What? He's your Prince Charming?" Juan said.

"And you're my fairy tale fuck," Derek said. He rolled back onto Juan. They began kissing again with uninhibited passion.

ELEVEN

"Why so clandestine?" Derek asked as he and Tom drove along serpentine Mulholland Drive in the hills above Los Angeles. "We could have talked at Starbucks. Or over the phone."

Tom kept his eyes on the road, which seemed populated with joggers who plodded along the shoulder from one blind curve to another. Along this sometimes-treacherous route it was not enough for motorists to be cautious of rockslides and an occasional deer or coyote crossing the road. They also had to be wary of other drivers who were dividing their attention between the view of the city on one side and the traffic of shirtless runners streaming by. Here, bodies glistening with perspiration were a common, major distraction.

"It's a beautiful day," Tom explained. "I just thought we could chat and at the same time take in one of the great things about living in L.A., the hiking trails."

Tom signaled with the right-hand directional and eased his Mercedes onto the shoulder of the road. He pulled into a dusty dirt parking area and eased his car up next to a carved wooden sign announcing that they were at Runyon Canyon. He reached behind his seat and retrieved two twenty-four-ounce sports bottles of spring water. "Keep hydrated," he said, handing one to Derek.

They exited the car, and Tom locked the doors. There were no other cars in the parking area, which didn't mean that the trail might not be crowded. But it was a good indication that there would likely be fewer hikers than if they'd come on a Sunday afternoon. The bucolic surrounding was a paradise for Los Angeleans.

"You're pretty sexy in that tank," Tom said, putting his arm around Derek's waist. "And the shorts definitely work for you. Very hot."

The two walked for a short while, beginning their descent down the narrow trail. The late morning air was still fresh, although Derek could see that in the distance a dark strip of haze was already encroaching over the L.A. basin.

Derek resumed their conversation. "I'm a little curious. You were pretty coy when you said you might have a job for me. What's up with that?"

Tom did not immediately respond. He continued along the trail in silence, leading the way for Derek. "Did you have a good time at Brent's the other night?" he eventually said.

An ominous non sequitur, Derek thought. "The best. I mean, just getting to meet the man was awesome. The fact that he turned out to be so nice was a bonus. And his friends were way cool too."

"He pretty much said the same thing about you," Tom said.

Derek's jaw dropped. "Brent Richardson thought I was cool?" He beamed. "He really said that? God, that is too awesome. How did my name even come up in conversation?"

Again, Tom did not answer the direct question. "Um, what did you like best about Brent?" he finally said.

"Are you kidding?" Derek said. "He's Brent Richardson, for God's sake. He's rich and famous. Millions of people adore him. Millions would trade their lives with him in a flash, if they could."

They continued walking for a short while, then Derek spoke again. "Actually, that's just surface stuff," he said. "I'm not really star struck, and I'm not a star fucker. I don't want to sound too woo-woo California, but I got a really good vibration from him. The way he included me in conversation was like something a friend would do, and he didn't even know me. I just think that he's very special. Also, the fact that he didn't come on to me."

"You flatter yourself," Tom said.

"I don't mean to," Derek said.

"Would it have made you uncomfortable if he had made a pass?"

"I think he's very sexy. But I would have been embarrassed because I was with you," Derek said. "My policy is I leave the dance with the person I came in with."

Tom's eyes sparkled in the California sun. "You're a good guy."

"I don't want to sound boastful or anything," Derek said, "but too many times I've been out with someone, and one of their friends has tried to move in on me. I'd never do that. Even if I liked someone else's boyfriend, and it's happened, I respect the boundary."

Tom nodded. They continued walking down the path. The terrain was not arduous, but it was still a good workout for their legs. After a short while he said, "We're friends, right?"

"I hope so," Derek answered. "You know, I don't have sex with every hot-looking body that throws themselves at me."

"Although you could," Tom teased. "You must know that you make guys fucking crazy. Did I throw myself?"

Derek countered with a small laugh. "Some guys make me nuts too. Offbeat guys. Guys that my friends think I must be insane to fantasize about."

"Explain," Tom said.

"How about that doctor on *Scrubs*? Zack Braff?"

"Get serious!"

"He's hot!" Derek insisted.

"He's cute, but not hot!"

"And the black guy on that old series, *Boston Public*? The principal?"

"So you're into old black guys?"

"Young. Older. I'm just into quality. Romantic guys."

"Try younger," Tom said. "Who do you like in the eighteen to thirty demographic?"

"Derek Jeter."

"Baseball? Yankees?" Tom asked, surprised.

"Future Hall of Famer."

"Anyone else?" Tom fished.

"Nope. I don't get a boner for the Justin Timberlakes of the world, if that's what you mean. But I'd marry Treat Williams in a flash." Derek paused. "There is one real-life guy," he said. "A client."

Tom grinned. "Just admit it's me, okay?"

"I admit it." Derek laughed. "And I think it was a mutual exercise in throwing ourselves."

"No one could blame me," Tom countered. Just then, a shirtless guy with pale skin and a swimmer's build, wearing short shorts, walked around the bend. He gave Derek and Tom a wide smile as he passed by.

Once the guy was out of earshot, Tom said, "Now that was a normal, healthy, *young* stud, affirming what you should already know about your sex appeal. Guys have already wanted to throw money at you just for a taste of your dick."

"Don't spoil the morning by reminding me," Derek lamented. "But I'm resigned to taking the next offer. If someone wants to pay me for the pleasure of my cock, then why the hell not take advantage of it. Who am I to say no, when they're practically shoving their ATM cards up my ass?"

"Seriously?" Tom said.

Derek said, "If I tell the universe that I'm broke and need cash, what do I do when it's waved in my face?"

Tom said, "People pray for things, and then when they actually get what they asked for they often dismiss it because it didn't come in the expected package all wrapped up in a pretty pink bow. So they don't recognize it. I think prayers are often answered in a form that we don't identify simply because we limit ourselves to the obvious. Just because something is not exactly as we expected, we tend to reject anything new and unusual. Always keep an open mind to accepting unusual packaging. The answer to your prayers may be staring you in the face."

Derek said, "God, if selling sex is the answer to my prayers, I'm praying to the wrong god."

By now they were halfway down the canyon. Then Tom said unexpectedly, "Brent wants to have sex with you."

Derek stopped dead in his tracks. "You heard me," Tom said.

"What brought that up?" Derek asked. "I thought he wasn't the type to move in on somebody else's boyfriend?"

"You're not my boyfriend."

"But I like you. I thought you liked me, too," Derek said. "What did you tell him about us?"

"What's to tell?" Tom said.

"What's *not* to tell?" Derek crossed his arms in disbelief. "You and I are friends and we've had sex together. That doesn't make us husbands, but it makes us more than just chat room buddies."

Tom frowned. "Okay, first of all . . . oh, God, this is not easy. Do you have any idea how difficult it is for someone like Brent to get laid?"

"Fuckin' easy. Guys *and* women throw themselves at him!"

Tom shook his head. "It's not easy at all. He's a superstar and fame is a double-edged sword. He can't just open up a copy of *Encounters* and pick out some boy to fuck. He has to be the most discreet man on the planet. I know for a fact that he's only had sex with one man in seven months. It isn't that incredibly attractive guys don't come on to him. Of course they do. But that's not what he's looking for. He's on film locations around the world, and he can't take a chance that some dude isn't a mole from *The National Enquirer.*"

Derek shook his head in amazement. "Why are you telling me all this stuff about Brent's personal life? And, you're as much of a stud as you say I am. Why don't *you* fuck him?"

"I do."

"What?" Derek looked surprised and dismayed. "You fuck Brent Richardson?"

"Shhh!"

In a quieter voice Derek repeated, "You fuck Brent Richardson? But not anymore, right? You just said he hasn't had sex in seven months."

"I said that he's only had sex with one man in seven months. I'm that one man."

Derek's mind was reeling. "Wait a minute. You and I had sex yesterday morning, then you had sex with Brent Richardson last night? I hate to be territorial, but . . ."

Tom looked into Derek's eyes. "But what? Look, I think that we have something special. In fact, I'm telling you this for two reasons. One is that I don't want to keep any secrets from you. To be totally honest, Brent *pays* me to fuck him. You and I had sex because we were hot for each other. When Brent needs a release he pays me to top him. It has nothing to do with how I feel about you. And it's how I support myself, if you really want to know the truth."

Derek stared at Tom. "This is such a weird conversation," Derek said as he continued along the hiking trail. "Are you an attorney, or, like, a Bel Air escort?"

"A little of both," Tom said. "But I only practice one profession. Remember the benefactor I talked about? He was a great guy. He put me through school, in exchange for having sex with him. Rich people do that. Millionaires can get anything they want. Even if they're old and nobody else will touch them, money definitely buys happiness. It gave him pleasure to help me rise above what otherwise would have been a very limited station."

Derek stopped walking again. "Jeez. I've got a gazillion questions. How did you meet this benefactor guy? Do you still see him? Do you have sex with other guys for money? Oh, right, you already said that's how you make your living."

"He died," Tom said. "We were lovers, but because he was so well-known, we couldn't register for domestic partnership, and he procrastinated about changing his will. So I had no claim to anything from his estate, even though he would have wanted me to have it all. But the New York Stock Exchange would have felt shock waves if I'd made trouble for the corporation that his family founded."

"You shared your life with the man, and he left you with nothing?" Derek said.

Tom thought for a moment. "The truth is, I came to him with nothing but my body. But I left with a superior education, the experiences of traveling the world, dining in the finest restaurants, and becoming friends with some of the most influential people on the planet. I even met Princess Di in London. It was tough for me to give up all that luxury when he died, but what I received from that relationship was more than just what money could buy. Also, I'm not a gold digger. I would never embarrass our friends in such a way. But it all worked out."

"You're selling your body for money," Derek said. "How do you figure things have worked out so well?"

"First of all, my friend, I'm not cheap." Tom paused. "How often have you made five thousand dollars for one night of sex? And good sex at that, not the slimy and disgusting sex that the thirty-dollar blow job boys have. I'm talking about fun, universe-expanding, exhausting and fulfilling sex? Huh? Can you name even one time when that has happened to you?"

"With you," Derek said quietly.

Tom smiled shyly.

"Five thousand bucks for sex?" Derek continued. "Christ, where do I sign up?"

"You're joking," Tom said.

"Who would be insane enough to spend that kind of money when they could get someone for less than a tenth of that sum?" Derek said.

Tom said, "It happens every single minute of every day in this town. Celebrities need sex just as much as common folk. But they can't go out to a bar and pick someone up. Charlie Sheen used to have Heidi Fleiss to pander for him. The gay celebrities—and there are more in this town than you'd ever imagine—have their way of procuring the same thing. You think five grand a night is outrageous? The price is relative. If you make $25 million for a movie, and you do a lot of movies, like Brent, what's five thousand dollars? It's chump change. Disposable income takes on a whole new meaning when you're one of the Hollywood elite. And the for-rent boys are disposable.

"I've worked for more than garden variety Hollywood celebrities," Tom continued. "A lot of businessmen pay for sex when their work brings them here from out of town. They take out cash from the corporate fund, for entertainment, when they're traveling. Instead of going to dinner with clients, they hire escorts. More than a few Warner, Disney, Universal, and Sony studio executives have paid to be with me."

Derek blinked. "I'm shocked."

"This planet is crawling with very wealthy people who won't settle for less than the best of everything, be it their homes, cars, yachts, private jets, or sex partners," Tom continued. "Most people don't think they deserve anything more than mediocrity, and so that's exactly what they get. A ranch house and mortgage, a job they hate but stay with because of the paycheck and health benefits, and the false security they get from every day being the same as the predictable and trivial day before. Ordinary people don't even take two-week vacations. 'Quiet desperation,' as Thoreau said."

"That's not me," Derek said.

"I don't think it's you either," Tom agreed. "So what are you going to do about it?"

Derek was quiet for a long time. Then: "Okay, so tell me something. If Brent's got you, why is he interested in me?"

"Because I'm getting out," Tom said. "I don't want to be his aging toy boy anymore, even if I really like the guy. And I'm definitely into Brent—and the other men who are my clients."

"How many others?" Derek asked.

"Let's just say that I'm in demand."

"I'm such an idiot," Derek said. "Here I thought that maybe you were as interested in me as I was in you. I couldn't keep my freakin' dick down when I massaged you that first night. And then, when we had sex, it wasn't like the ordinary sex you have when you meet a guy and you take him home and you suck and fuck and then he leaves, or you wish he would leave. I got a whole different feeling from you. And I thought you felt something for me too."

"About being an idiot, you're way wrong," Tom chastised. "I wouldn't have taken you to Brent's house in the first place, if I didn't think you were the real deal."

"No, I'm definitely missing more than a few gray cells," Derek said. "I'm an idiot because it didn't occur to me until this very moment that you were auditioning me. You brought me up to Weybridge Cottage to let a buyer inspect the goods and to see if I fit among the décor in his home. I must have passed the test because then you took me home and tried me on for size. So to speak." He laughed bitterly.

Tom said defensively, "That's not what—"

Derek was livid. "Fuck you," he cut in. "How long have you been looking for a replacement for the job of fucking Mr. Big-Time Movie Star? Have you fucked many applicants? What qualifications do I bring to the position that the other candidates lacked? I'm only eight and a half inches. It's not that uncommon, so I'll rule out my equipment. I'm straight acting, quote unquote, so I guess that's a plus if one is expected to work for a closet case."

Tom kicked at a small stone. He was looking out over the L.A. Basin. Then he turned back to Derek. "If you were as dense as you claim to be, you wouldn't have seen through the façade so quickly. I said that I had two reasons for telling you about me and Brent."

"If you're about to tell me that I've won the Lotto to be his next plaything, keep it to yourself," Derek said. "I'm going back to the car. Take me home when you're ready."

He turned around and began retracing his steps up the steep pathway. "You're certainly an arrogant cocksucker!" Tom called out. "I never made you an offer for anything! Don't be so damn full of yourself."

Derek turned around and stopped. "First of all, I'm glad you didn't present an offer. It would have been an insult."

"You're being evicted, aren't you?"

"What's that supposed to mean?"

"The sheriffs will be serving you papers tomorrow morning at nine. I checked."

Derek complained. "Fuck you. I've got everything worked out. I'm moving in with a friend."

"Do you mean Juan, the guy who slept over last night?"

Derek was stunned. "You're spying on me?"

Tom said, "You're right. I put you through a few tests. When I discovered you were trying to be a legit masseur, I thought maybe you'd make a good candidate for this job. I tried to seduce you, but you held your ground. Points for integrity. Physically, you're a fantasy man. You ratcheted up more points for your dick size, not that Brent is a size queen. He's not. And, of course I had to make sure that Brent agreed with my initial assessment of your character and physical appearance. He did. So yeah, I took you for a test drive. I know what Brent likes. You fit the mold."

Derek said, "I'm not a piece of meat."

"Which is exactly why I want you to see Brent again. Get to know him a little better. Trust me, Derek, I like you a lot. Really, I would not subject you to anything twisted. Brent is one of the nicest, most decent men on the planet. I just know that you'll get along well." He paused for a moment. "I'm just asking that you consider your options. You and Juan—and I really don't mind that you did each other last night—"

Derek said, "You don't have any right to mind about anything that I do. I'm not in your employ."

"You're absolutely right," Tom said. "I just meant that from what I know of Juan, he's a swell guy. The two of you could find your way out of debt . . . if you really want to."

Derek stared hard at Tom. On the one hand he wanted to pummel the guy for making him feel like a commodity. On the other hand, he was desperate for a job.

Tom said, "Look, you made the point a couple of minutes ago. Remember you said that you should try to recognize when your prayers are answered? So these circumstances aren't necessarily precisely what you imagined. Just don't prejudge anything, that's all. Will you at least think about it? Will you come over to Brent's tonight? Some cocktail chatter by the pool?" Another pause.

"I like you a lot," Tom said. "Believe me, if I didn't think you were right for Brent, you wouldn't get anywhere near him."

"Is that so?" challenged Derek.

"Yes," Tom said simply. "It's so."

TWELVE

A Santa Ana wind was blowing, and the scent of night blooming jasmine permeated the air. As Derek and Brent strolled the lighted pathways, on the grounds around Weybridge Cottage, they sipped champagne from crystal flutes. They talked of favorite movies, national politics, and dreams of the future. Their rapport was as easy as it had been during the dinner party. Derek found himself enjoying the company of the famous star and was comfortable talking about everything from his years of wanting to be an actor to his new job as a massage therapist.

"I assume you already know I have an ad running in *Encounters*," Derek said.

Brent nodded. "You're more brave than I could ever be."

The path they were walking had come full circle around the grounds and they were now standing beside the swimming pool. "Sex, for me, is a luxury," Brent said to Derek as they took a seat on the sofa beside the shimmering blue water. Brent's backyard was like a vast outdoor living room. Designer furniture decorated the space. Iron knockoffs of Rodin sculptures peppered the lawn. An enormous yellow rubber duck with wide zombie eyes floated in the pool.

"I've never thought of myself as a particularly sexual person," Brent admitted. "I've been so focused on my career for the past twenty years. Funny how you work so hard to get something, and then when you have it, somehow it doesn't seem as important. Oh, don't get me wrong; I love my job. I also love sex. But I used to think I couldn't have sex with another man because if the truth about me ever got out, I'd be ruined. I could live without sex, but I couldn't live without my work."

"Audiences probably wouldn't care if they knew you were gay," Derek said.

"Don't believe that for a moment," Brent said. "There's a reason why Richard Chamberlain couldn't come out until his career was practically over. Hell, even that old queen Charles Laughton never came out. Guilgud was so famous and comfortable with himself that he didn't give a fig. But I'm no Guilgud, as that asshole Richard Roeper pointed out after the release of my remake of *Julius Caesar*." Brent gave a weak laugh. "Trust me, although I'm damn proud that I belong to an industry that is made up mostly of brilliant and successful gay people, the folks who buy our entertainment fantasies aren't nearly so understanding."

Derek sipped his champagne. He surveyed the illuminated grounds of Weybridge Cottage. "I can understand your career being more important to you than sex," he said. "Sex could never buy all of this. But what about love? Haven't you ever been in love?"

Brent took another sip from his own glass. He sighed. "Here I am, forty-eight years old. More successful than I ever imagined. But I've only been truly and deeply in love once. And it was many years ago."

"Tell me about it," Derek said.

"Maybe the first time cuts the deepest," Brent said. "There was this guy, the choreographer for a Broadway show I was lucky enough to get in to . . . just the chorus, but still . . ." He took another sip of champagne. "Simon made me believe that I was the hottest thing on the boards. And, I admit, all modesty aside, looking at old pictures now I have to agree with him, although I didn't think so at the time. Anyway, he was amazing to look at, too. And also talented. He had a Tony Award, and he was tall and authoritative, and he was the best sex I'd ever had. Long story short, we ended up living together. At the time I thought sex equaled love. It doesn't. Sex is just a temporary activity. It's little more than an animal response. The body's desire for another body. I had my real animal reaction when I found him fucking another chorus boy in our bed. There was more than one. And I still had to go on and do a show. I don't know how I ever got through those numbers."

"This guy cheated on you, and you still hung around for more?" Derek said.

"Love does strange things to a person," Brent said. "In retrospect, Simon did me a favor. I was so angry and hurt that my vulnerability came through in my acting. John Schlesinger noticed me, and . . . well, the rest is Hollywood history. I got out of theater and into films. Although I've never looked back, I still often think about Simon. Last I heard he was teaching at a dance studio in Brooklyn." Brent turned to Derek. "So who broke your heart?"

Derek waved his hand as if to dismiss the subject. "Back in Omaha, where I was raised. I thought he was so brilliant and talented, but he was the most self-absorbed man I've ever known. When he deigned to cast his attention on me, I could trip to Mars and back. Like you, I mistook sex for love. This guy wanted sex all the time, and I wanted him as well. But even when I wasn't around, he still wanted sex all the time."

"I know where this is headed," Brent guessed.

"I was so in love that I abandoned my friends and gave up my apartment. I wanted to do whatever it took to please him. Which meant leaving college. *And* my independence."

"What was your major?" Brent asked.

"Theater, of course. I gave up a scholarship for that son of a bitch! Then, after a couple of years, he found someone else and asked me to leave. So I came to California. I didn't know a soul here, but it didn't much matter. And, until recently, it seemed that my life was on an upward trajectory."

Brent looked into Derek's eyes. "Tom mentioned your present circumstances. I'm sorry. But things will turn around. Everything's cyclical. You'll find a job soon, I'm certain of it."

Derek suddenly felt as though he was flunking what he thought was an interview. Brent wasn't acting as a potential employer. Not willing to lose the chance that he had naively concluded was a done deal, Derek became emboldened. "As a matter of fact, Tom suggested that I might be of service to you," he said.

Brent was silent for a time. Then he said, "It's a little complicated. I don't really need . . . You're young and should be with someone . . . someone you like." He paused. "You're twenty-three, and I'm forty-eight. I'm usually a very sensible guy. I look at my friends and wonder why they can't date within their own age range. I see it all the time. Fortysomething men with twentysomething boyfriends. These men are asking for the heartache that happens years later. Eventually, one becomes resentful about the other's place in the universe because they're at such different levels of growth. At different ages we all have different aims for what we want out of life and careers. When the fortysomething becomes sixtysomething and is ready to retire, the twentysomething who has become fortysomething still wants to play. They're completely out of sync. The twentysomething's youth becomes irritating to the fortysomething. And, vice versa, the crotchety old man is going to be annoying to the younger guy. The age differences only work against them."

"Um, I was only thinking about sucking your dick," Derek said. "And I'm a little too old to be a NAMBLA boy."

Brent laughed. "Sorry. I guess I'm always looking way down the road, instead of living in the moment."

For what seemed to Derek a long time, the men looked at each other. "We hardly know each other," Brent finally said.

"You've already been presented with my references, Mr. Richardson," Derek said.

"Hypothetically speaking," Brent began, "if we were to, you know, engage in . . . I mean, if I were to indulge myself . . ." Brent laughed nervously. "The truth is . . . I'll come right out and say it." He stalled by pouring more champagne into his half-filled flute and into Derek's empty one. "I am looking for someone with whom I can be intimate on a regular basis. I want a man. Okay? Not a boy. Not some movie star–worshipping sycophant. I just want a man to take care of one area of my life that is out of order."

"Why was that so hard for you to say?" Derek admonished.

"Are you kidding?" Brent said. "I have a career, a reputation to think about. If it ever got out that whenever Brent Richardson is having sex, he fantasies that he's Diane Lane getting fucked by Richard Gere . . ."

"Do you often speak of yourself in the third person?" Derek asked.

"*Brent* is not who I am. Brent's a character I play every moment of every day. The big movie star. It's a great role, and I love it. But it's not all that I am."

Derek said, "So who is the *real* Brent Richardson? From what I see, and most of the world would agree, Brent is pretty special."

Brent smiled. "You're pretty special too, Derek," he said. He shifted on the sofa and tucked one leg under the other. With one hand holding his champagne flute and his other arm stretched out over the back of the couch, he heaved a deep sigh. "I have just about everything that a human being could want. This incredible house. An apartment in

Manhattan and the other house in the Berkshires. I'm buying a castle in France. I truly love my career. I'm incredibly blessed in every way."

"Except one?"

"No, my life is perfect as it is," Brent retorted. "I don't need anything."

"Then what am I doing here?" Derek asked. As far as he was concerned, Tom had misguided him. Or, Brent was gracefully trying to acknowledge that he wasn't interested in sex, let alone an *arrangement*, with Derek.

In motion pictures, the director of photography focused his lens on Brent's eyes to reveal the actor's inner thoughts. Brent's greatest talent was emoting depth of feeling without dialogue. It was a gift that would have made him a star in the era of silent films, if he had lived in that age. And now, although verbally expressing one idea to Derek, he was telepathically revealing another, and transmitting a signal of lust.

Then, without a word, Derek pulled his shirt off over his head, unbuttoned his 501s and withdrew his hard slab of meat.

Brent stared at the sight of Derek's blood-engorged cock and swallowed hard. He lifted his eyes for a moment to take in the view of Derek's strong chest and rippled stomach muscles. Brent, as if guided by instinct, slowly leaned forward and wrapped his hand around Derek's prick. He guided the glistening cock to his lips.

Holy fuck! Brent Richardson is holding my dick! Derek thought as the star's tongue slithered over the mushroom head, exploring him. Images of having watched Brent on movie screens for nearly half his life flashed through Derek's mind.

Brent slipped from the patio sofa and knelt on the grass as he sucked down Derek's sex pistol, dragging his tongue up and down the thick sausage. He ran his hands up to Derek's pecs and abs.

And after only a few minutes of Brent teasing Derek's penis with his hot tongue, and with his fingers digging into Derek's ass cheeks, Brent groaned with pleasure, as he auto-ejaculated a hot load into his own pants.

Derek withdrew his cock from Brent's mouth and, ripping away the fastened buttons from Brent's jeans, reached into the actor's cum-filled underpants. He scooped out three fingers full of semen, then slathered the thick, warm fluid onto his own saliva-slick dick and began to furiously massage his meat. Derek began hyperventilating, and a moment later, he shot his full load onto Brent's face.

Once he had released the last drop, Derek stepped back. He looked down at Brent and the splotches of white cum that dripped down his cheeks.

Brent ran his fingers through the congealing mass on his cheek and brought his fingers under his nose, as if sniffing a wine cork. Then he pushed his fingers into his mouth. He eyes closed with ecstasy, as he tasted Derek's fluid. He then licked his fingers clean.

Derek shook his now-flaccid cock one last time before carefully setting it back into his pants. He reached for Brent's hand and helped him rise to his feet. "Let's get you into a fresh pair of tighty whities," he said, and guided Brent back toward the house.

THIRTEEN

It was ten A.M. the following morning when Derek returned to his apartment. Juan was asleep in the bed, his bare body covered to the waist. One brown leg was exposed from under the sheet. The room was stifling with hot, unventilated air. As quietly as possible Derek opened the window. He then removed his tank and jeans, and lay down beside his friend.

"You smell like sex," Juan said in a sleepy voice.

"I didn't mean to wake you," Derek whispered.

"I was up late worrying about you."

"I'm fine. We'll talk about it later. Right now I'm exhausted."

Juan sidled his bare back up against Derek's chest as they had the previous morning. Although Derek was utterly sated from sex with Brent, he still found himself hard from the feel of Juan's dark, silky skin next to his own.

"Whatever you say, Boss."

In moments, both men were asleep.

During the ensuing dream-filled hours of Derek's sleep, his mind revisited Weybridge Cottage. The images that played out were variations on what he had in reality experienced with Brent. In one image Derek was on his knees in Brent's master bathroom, pulling down his host's underpants. As the star stood exposed before him, Derek buried his face in Brent's crotch and groomed his thick, hairy patch with his tongue. He inhaled the warm scent of Brent's fresh ejaculate.

In the next image they were together in an immense shower, with a dozen jets of water spraying forth from the surrounding marble tile walls. Brent was on his back on the shower floor with his arms flailing and splashing as Derek harshly kissed him.

In another image, Brent's climax was a geyser of champagne that frothed over his body and bubbled through his chest hairs. As Derek wrestled with his partner, they were oblivious to the fact that they were literally drowning in the effervescing liquid.

In the distance Derek heard the telephone ringing.

"Boss? Heya, Boss?"

Derek was wrenched back to consciousness by Juan's voice. Derek opened his eyes to see Juan holding the cordless phone. "Telephone. Your friend, Tom."

Not certain what time it was or even what day it was, he accepted the phone from Juan's outstretched hand. He cleared his throat. " 'Lo?" he said, in a deeper than usual voice. "Huh? I guess. When? Right."

Derek handed the phone back to Juan. "Christ," he said, lethargically pushing aside the bedsheet and blanket, and getting up from the bed. "He wants to see me. He said it's urgent."

The late morning sky was gray and the air chilly. Overnight, a thick marine layer had crept in from the ocean, deep into the city. The atmosphere was dull and somber.

Tom had insisted that they drive to Santa Monica for a walk on the pier. As they cruised the long stretch of San Vicente toward Ocean Avenue, Tom played Derek the latest Three Tenors CD, which instead of having a calming effect on Derek only irritated him. They all sounded alike. Derek couldn't distinguish Domingo from Carerras from Pavarotti. It annoyed him.

When they reached the edge of the California coast and found a parking space at the curb above Pacific Coast Highway, it was lunchtime. Office workers were out for their midday exercise. Joggers trotted along the palisade, weaving in and out of a parade of tourists and local residents who were undeterred by the dreary weather.

As Derek and Tom ambled along the walkway beside the cliff above the Coast Highway they made small talk about their workout regimens, the possibility of expatriating to New Zealand if the American government continued on its path toward global anarchy, and how much they both wanted to be the queen of England for a day. Then Tom handed Derek a white envelope.

Derek looked perplexed as he opened the flap. He came to an

abrupt stop as he viewed the contents. "This is five hundred dollars!" Derek exclaimed.

"Brent feels bad that it didn't work out, so he wanted you to have a little something."

Confusion played across Derek's face. Flustered, he asked, "What didn't work out? We had sex. Great sex, in fact. All night long. It worked out quite well, if you ask me."

Tom shrugged. "Brent felt otherwise," he said. "He didn't think that an arrangement between you and he would work."

Mystified, Derek knitted his eyebrows. He took a deep breath. Then he gave out a slight chuckle. "No wonder he gets the big bucks for acting. He sure had me fooled."

Tom tried to sound comforting. "All actors are liars. Brent a little more than most. Even I can't read him usually."

Derek felt dejected, unable to understand what had happened to spoil what he was certain they had both felt. "Funny thing is, I really liked him."

"Them are the breaks, eh?" Tom said. "But don't feel too disappointed. You've still got me."

"I was too intense with Brent, right?" Derek frowned. "I shouldn't have been so bold with him. But I honestly thought that's what he wanted. I know I wanted it."

"It really wasn't anything you did or said," Tom continued. "Brent has his reasons for doing things his way. But hey, you made some money, and you had fun, right?"

"I don't want his money," Derek said, handing the envelope back to Tom.

"Don't be ridiculous," Tom said. "You're in desperate straits. This is a pittance to Brent. He wants you to have it."

Derek shook his head. "Quite honestly, I couldn't have paid for a better time. I'll always remember the night Brent Richardson sucked me off."

"Seriously, Derek, you've got to take this money. It's more than just for services rendered."

"Yeah, I know what it's for," Derek said. "Hush money. It's to keep me from spilling the story to the *Enquirer.* Hell, they'd pay me ten times this amount for the scoop on Brent."

Tom's mouth dropped. "Don't be an asshole."

Derek gave Tom an evil grin. "Don't wet your pants," he said. "I don't kiss 'n' tell. The fact is, I like Brent a lot. But I won't take his money because it makes me just some *thing,* some *object* that he can buy. Well, he can use this to buy a nipple ring, or put it toward his next Botox treatment, for all I care. I had sex with the man because I wanted to have sex with him, not because of any financial gain."

Tom looked askance at Derek and said, "I'm not stupid. I see what you're doing. You're playing me. *And* Brent. You think that by turning down five hundred bucks we'll believe that you're different from every other two-bit street hustler. It's not going to work, my friend. You're not casting a line baited with your innocence, and reeling Brent in like some prized marlin."

Derek shook his head again. "I'd rather you didn't call me 'friend.' You're nothing but an aging high-class whore, and if you think I'm after Brent, you're nuts. Don't forget you're the one who solicited me! Ya know what that's called? Pandering. And, it's a felony. So don't go turning the tables and making me feel as though I'm using anybody. Just keep the fucking money. I'm outta here."

With that, Derek turned around and headed across Ocean Avenue toward Wilshire Boulevard. He still had a few dollars left in his pocket, enough to catch the bus and get home.

"Christ, I am an idiot," Derek said in agreement with Tom's assessment as the bus pulled up to the curb. "I'm broke and I keep turning down money."

FOURTEEN

The stale heat of summertime never seemed to leave Derek's apartment. Juan sat on the floor, bare-chested, perspiring, and morose. "They changed the locks. I can't even get my clothes," he lamented, close to tears. "The next call that comes in from a dude who wants you to blow him, I'm taking it."

Derek was stretched out on the bed, his fingers linked behind his head. At that moment the telephone rang. Neither Juan nor Derek reached over to pick up the receiver.

"Hi, hon. Cathy. I hope you're in town."

No, I'm doing shows in Milan this week, sweetie, Derek said to himself, annoyed by his wealthy friend's lack of awareness of his dire situation. Then he checked himself. Cathy was a sensitive and understanding woman and Derek immediately felt bad that he'd momentarily resented her.

"I know this is late notice," Cathy continued, "but is there any chance that you could serve at a cocktail thingy tonight? My place? Lance suddenly up and quit on me. Or more accurately, Andrew strongly suggested that he leave. Poor Lance. He was in tears." Cathy was rambling now. "So I'm without enough help for this evening. If you could serve, just for a few hours, that would be awesome. And if you know someone else to help out . . . Call me ASAP. Okay, hon? Thanks tons."

Derek sat up. "There's your job, Juan. We'll make some cash and eat too." Derek gazed up at the ceiling with a look of thanksgiving.

"Call her back before she hires someone else," Juan insisted. "I can't eat another slice of plain-wrap white bread and peanut butter!"

Derek reached for the telephone and dialed Cathy's private number. She came on the line immediately. "Yeah, I just missed you," he explained. They chatted for a few minutes before Juan heard Derek repeat, "Four o'clock. Cool. I'm bringing my friend Juan to work too. See you then."

Juan sighed with relief. "I thought for sure I'd be spending tonight pumping my dick into someone's pathetic lard ass," he said. "We couldn't have gone on like this for much longer. Any moment, your landlord will do the same thing that mine did to me."

"The asshole is probably watching and waiting." Derek thought for a moment longer. "When we leave the apartment this afternoon, I'll go out the front door. You exit through the window. That way he'll think one of us is still here."

"Boss," Juan said. "We may as well not even go. We can't even afford the bus fare to Beverly Hills. And forget about a taxi."

Derek reached for the phone and pushed redial. "Hey, Cathy. Me again. Can you send your car? Mine's in the shop. Great. See you in a few."

"Voila!" Derek preened for Juan. "Ask and ye shall receive. Now, did I tell you about the jerk I thought I was falling in love with?"

"All afternoon," said Juan.

At four P.M. there was a knock on the door. Derek called through the door. "Who's there?" he said, half expecting the voice to belong to Garson, or a West Hollywood sheriff.

"Mr. Bracken? I've been sent by Mrs. Young."

Derek and Juan both breathed heavy sighs of relief. Derek answered that he would be out in just a moment. Then he pushed Juan toward the window. "Out! Go on! Watch out for the spiderwebs! The bushes are crawling with 'em!"

"I'm more afraid of the INS than any stupid spiders!" Juan declared.

He sat on the windowsill and slipped one leg at a time outside. The bushes were thick oleander, and Juan had to wedge himself between the building's stucco wall and the dense shrubbery before extracting himself and stepping out onto the sidewalk.

In the meantime, Derek opened the front door. He shook hands with the driver, who introduced himself as Frank.

"The staff turnover at Mr. and Mrs. Young's is becoming heavy,"

Derek joked as he stepped outside. He closed and locked the door. "Frank, we'll be taking one more passenger."

As they rounded the building, Derek saw Juan standing on the sidewalk next to the Lincoln Town Car. He was speaking with Garson.

"Get us out of here, now!" Derek whispered to Frank. The driver wasted no time bolting for the car. He engaged the engine and unlocked the doors. Derek made his dash. He ignored Garson as he leaped for the door handle and pulled the rear door open. "In!" he yelled to Juan.

Garson smiled, waved, looked at the car and said, "Fancy schmancy!"

Safely inside the vehicle, Derek said to Juan, "We're dead. He caught us both leaving! Our stuff'll be on the street in ten minutes. We're so fucking fucked!"

"It's not the end of the world, Boss."

"The hell it isn't. Now, even if we wanted to hustle—" he caught himself and looked at the back of Frank's head. He lowered his voice to a whisper. "If we wanted to take on a few clients, not only will we have no place to receive them, we won't even have a telephone. This is absolutely the end!"

"Boss," Juan said in a calm voice, "Garson said he was happy that everything had worked out, and he was glad we were staying on. He said he knew you'd come up with the back rent."

Derek looked at Juan as though his friend was about to deliver the punchline of a joke. "Why would he think that?"

"That's what he said, Boss. It didn't seem like a set up or trap to me."

"Cathy," Derek ruminated. "Cathy's my only friend with money. I didn't think she even knew how desperate things were." Derek leaned forward and peered into the front seat. "Frank," he said, "did you stop at the building manager's apartment before you came to get me? Did Mrs. Young have you bring the manager an envelope?"

"No, sir. My only instructions were that I should pick you up and deliver you by four-thirty. Shall I call her, sir?"

Derek shook his head. "No. That's cool. Thanks." He looked again at Juan. "She's too much," he said. "She's always helping people out. I just never thought I'd have to be one of them. Now I'm totally embarrassed. She probably thought up this cocktail party—if there really is a party—just so we'd have some work. She's amazing."

Frank steered the car along Coldwater Canyon, then entered Beverly Hills and turned onto Lexington. They continued on past mansions built in the nineteen-twenties. Turning onto Benedict Canyon, the car continued the slow incline to Tower Grove Road, where the car once again turned right. Now, ascending from what residents euphemistically called "The Flats," into the most prestigious area of Beverly Hills, they passed homes that every major star of the golden age of motion pictures had occupied at one time or another. Soon, they arrived at the Taylors' house.

Juan was bug-eyed. "You have got to be shitting me, Boss," he said, gaping at the size of the three-story mansion. "This is a freakin' hotel."

"Watch your language tonight," Derek cautioned. "I don't want you using any four-letter words here. Some really famous people will probably be guests. You've got to act in a proper way. Just pretend that we're back at Onyx. Only don't hustle the cute men."

"Boss," Juan said with anxiety, "this is way too fancy for me."

"You're the Mexican help," Derek reminded. "You belong anywhere that rich white people have work they don't want to do themselves. Just relax."

Juan nodded in agreement as they stepped out of the car. "No, this way, around the back," Derek instructed as Juan started to head for the front door. "I'm the help too, and the help always enters from the servants' entrance. Just follow Frank."

Frank used his key to unlock the back gate, and the trio entered the secluded yard. The landscaping, the pool, the incredible view of Century City in the distance below seemed to mesmerize Juan. Looking to the right, he nudged Derek. "That's the beach, for Christ's sake!"

"Language!" Derek pleaded. "Yeah, that's Santa Monica. On a clear day you can see Catalina."

Just then, a woman shrieked with enthusiasm, "Derek! You're such a doll! Thank you, for dropping everything to come to my rescue! It's been a madhouse since Lance left!"

Cathy gave Derek a warm embrace, standing on her toes to kiss his cheek. Turning to Juan she smiled and said, "Surely, you're Juan. Derek said you were handsome, but I didn't expect Antonio Banderas. Thank you, too, for coming over. I'm at my wit's end. It's such a pleasure to meet you." She took Juan's hand and shook it in a way designed to immediately put him at ease.

"There're only about twenty of us tonight," Cathy went on. "We're hosting one of the new senior VP's in Andrew's office. Shouldn't be overly taxing. Some of them you already know. Then there are a few from the New York office. All of them lovely, I'm sure. Okay, I'll stop droning on now and let you work things out."

As Cathy turned to leave them to the kitchen, Derek put a hand on her shoulder. "I don't know how to thank you enough, Cathy."

She looked bewildered. "I'm the grateful one, hon."

"You know what I mean," Derek smiled. "You're the most generous person on this planet. I'll pay you back as soon as I can."

Cathy looked confused. "Pay *me* back? For the opportunity to save my Armani-covered butt?" She patted Derek on the cheek. "Socorro is in the living room giving the harpist a hard time. Maybe you can go and save him. I'll be down in a jiff."

Now it was Derek's turn to be confused. Cathy preferred to contribute her philanthropic gifts anonymously, but she was always happy to acknowledge her patronage if someone else brought up the subject. That she denied paying Derek's rent baffled him. There was no one else in his life with the graciousness, let alone the financial wherewithal, to help.

But for now he had to drop the subject. It was time to work. "I'll show you were everything is," he said to Juan, escorting him into the vast kitchen.

In less than an hour, the guests arrived. Although the women appeared to be dressed casually, anyone who read *Vogue*—and Derek at least looked at the pictures—could tell that the threads were haute couture. A handsome pianist accompanied by an equally stunning blond male harpist, played background music. As guests entered the Taylors' home, one by one and couple by couple, Derek leaned into Juan. He whispered, "Sherry Lansing. The Katzenbergs. Candace Bushnell. Anne Bancroft. I'll let you take her wrap."

Juan wandered among the guests with a tray of hors d'oeuvres, while Derek busied himself at the bar, placing champagne-filled flutes on a silver tray. Absorbed in his work, concentrating on being as cautious as possible, Derek gingerly picked up the tray by its rim and balanced it in the palm and fingers of his left hand. With his right hand he picked up a clutch of white cocktail napkins. He adjusted his posture, focusing his eyes on his precarious lading. At that very moment . . .

"Ah, champagne!" A familiar male voice spoke into his ear, startling him.

Derek's tray of drinks slipped and clinked as he reacted to the voice. There was the near embarrassing tragedy of losing control of his balanced load. He then looked into the smiling face of Brent Richardson.

"Whoa," Brent said, reaching out to help avoid the disaster of the glasses tipping completely. He took several cocktail napkins out of Derek's other hand and began blotting what had spilled onto the tray.

"I sincerely apologize, sir," Derek said.

"Sir?" Brent whispered, chiding Derek. "After last night, I think you can at least call me Mr. Richardson." He grinned at Derek's quizzical expression. "I'm joking. It's Brent, of course. And seeing you here saves me a call."

"I beg your pardon?"

"Actually, I planned to call you this evening," Brent whispered. "I wanted to say thanks again for last night. Um, any chance of seeing you again?"

Derek was confused. "Um. I thought that you . . . ?" Derek shook his head. "I have to work."

Disappointment registered in Brent's eyes. "Well, once you're settled, maybe?" he said.

Derek was about to walk away to serve the other guests. At that moment, Cathy appeared at Brent's side. "Did the big ole movie star make my friend Derek nervous?" she chided, offering her cheek for Brent to kiss. "I was afraid you'd already left for reshoots in New Zealand, Brent."

"I leave a week from tomorrow," Brent said. "By the way, it's my fault that the champagne spilled. I startled the poor guy."

"You startle everybody with that unfortunate face of yours." She sniggered. "Not to worry. Derek's the best in town. I just wish he'd find permanent employment."

"So do I," Brent said.

Eventually, the crowd thinned out. Cathy spied Derek and went to where he was collecting glasses and other cocktail party debris. "Yeah, that one's a dreamboat, isn't he?" she said.

Derek's eyes followed Cathy's until he realized she was looking at Brent. "Even Andrew gets nervous around him." She chuckled.

Derek apologized to Cathy for nearly dropping the tray of champagne. "I turned around and he practically bumped into me."

"Not to worry," Cathy assured him. "But if you're going to have an accident, please aim for that bastard in the Brooks Brothers talking to Andrew. Over by the Remington."

Derek looked over. "He's the new senior VP of programming for Link," said Cathy. "I can tell he's anxious to get his legs wrapped around Andrew's ass." Cathy showed a false smile. "I've got my spies, and if I discover that he's got any ideas about cuckolding me, I'm not above calling in a few favors."

"A glass of Merlot would complement his necktie."

"Oh, not tonight, hon," Cathy said. "And if it comes to a contract for a hit, I can think of better ways to make him crawl back to Disney or whatever den of iniquity he slithered from."

As the guests began to filter out of the house and the ambient noise of many simultaneous conversations faded, the music from the piano and harp seemed to grow louder. Derek and Juan continued to busy themselves serving the stragglers. Derek noticed that Brent was now engaged in conversation with the master of the manor, Andrew Taylor. And then Socorro, the maid, summoned Derek to the kitchen. When he returned, Brent was gone.

FIFTEEN

"All in all, not a bad night, eh?" Derek was speaking to Juan as they stepped out of the Lincoln and began walking toward the apartment.

"I handled myself rather well, I'd say," Juan boasted. "What's up with you and that movie star dude?"

Derek feigned ignorance. "Which one? There were so many."

"The one who's always getting an Oscar. Brent What's-his-name."

"Brent Richardson?" Derek said. "He was the jerk who bumped into me and almost cost me a tray of Cristal. What about you and the piano player? Huh? I saw him hand you his card."

As Derek unlocked the door and stepped into the apartment, Juan reached into Derek's pocket and withdrew their pay envelope. He hooked a finger under the sealed flap and ripped along the edge. Then: "Holy shit!" From the envelope he pulled out five one hundred-dollar bills. "Is this a mistake?"

Derek looked at Juan's fistful of cash. "No mistake," he answered. "That's Cathy. Even before she got rich, she was generous. She says this stuff has to be circulated, and the more she shells out the more it comes back to her." Juan was staring at the money as a tear rolled down his cheek.

Placing a comforting hand on Juan's shoulder, Derek said, "I told you that things were going to work out. We're going to be fine. I promise."

At that moment the telephone rang. Although Derek was still screening all calls, he automatically looked at the answering machine. He noticed three unheard messages. "I'm definitely not renewing that massage ad," he said, as the new call was recorded.

Derek recognized Tom's voice. "Thought I'd check in and see how my favorite waiter is doing."

"Asshole!" Derek spat.

"I had a call from Brent," Tom continued. "I don't want to leave a message about it here. Call me. Tonight, please."

The machine disengaged. Juan looked at Derek. "See, my gaydar isn't completely haywire," he said. "You and that Brent guy were so obvious."

"We were not," Derek corrected. "We were both just surprised to see each other again."

"Again?" Juan countered. "So the rumors are true! He's gay. *The Enquirer* is always right!"

Derek raised his hands in protest. "Tom took me on a date, and then we went up to Brent's house for dinner. That's all."

"You went to Brent Richardson's and didn't tell me?" Juan asked. "I told you about the time Madonna put her hands down my pants, didn't I? And you were dessert, right?" Juan sniggered.

"Of course not," Derek said. "But Tom's a total prick."

Derek crumpled the empty envelope and dropped it into the trash can beside the kitchenette sink. Juan refused to let the topic drop. "So what do you think it is that this Tom guy couldn't tell you over the phone? Probably that Brent wants to fuck you, or you him, but he was afraid you'd take the recording to one of the tabloid rags? Just a wild guess."

Derek scoffed. "Not every man I meet wants to fuck me."

"Just the gay ones," Juan deadpanned. "So call him back. Find out what's up."

Derek, just as curious as Juan about Tom's cryptic message, picked up the telephone and from memory dialed the number. He looked at Juan, indicating that the line was ringing. Then: "You called," he said coolly.

He eased himself onto the bed and divided his attention between watching Juan recount the money over and over, and listening to Tom.

Then: "It was you?" Derek said with incredulity. "Why? You know I can't pay you back. Of course I'm grateful. But why did you do it? Now, don't make me feel obligated to you, Tom. Yes, I know that *I am*, but I didn't ask to be." He paused. "I'm not being defensive. It was a great thing what you did for me, and yeah, I owe you big time. But . . ." Derek became silent. He nodded. "Twenty minutes? But I'm exhausted." Derek sighed. "What changed his mind about me? Yeah."

Derek hung up the phone.

"Boss, you don't have to do anything you don't want to do," Juan said. "So he paid the rent. That doesn't make you his kept boy."

"That's rather a moot point now," Derek said as he stripped and tossed his work clothes onto the bed. "If it weren't for Tom, we probably wouldn't even be in this apartment right now. We'd be living on the street."

"Fuck him," Juan said. "We've got money. We don't need him."

Derek walked into the bathroom to brush his teeth, leaving the door open to continue the conversation. "He just wants me to visit Brent again. I guess the famous movie star is lonely."

Juan walked to the bathroom and leaned against the door frame. "I'd say he was more horny than lonely. He's certainly not hard on the eyes."

"Quite frankly, he's my type—if I have a type," Derek said.

"So if he comes on to you, it won't be difficult."

Derek gave Juan a look of resignation. "I'm just saying, *if*," Juan reiterated. "But seriously, just as I tried to stop you from selling yourself to the guys who answered your ad, I'm telling you again that you don't have to do anything that's against your principles. You're a big boy. That's the only speech I'm giving."

Derek spat toothpaste into the sink's running water. He wiped his lips on a towel. "I'm not easily bagged," he said, taking a form-fitting T-shirt out of the dirty clothes hamper. "Maybe Tom just wants Brent and me to be friends."

"Boss, let's get this straight. That Tom guy is pimping. I know it, and you know it. He's picked you out, and now you're marked to have sex with Star Stud. Which is cool, as long as you don't let anyone take advantage of you. Never sell yourself short. Or cheap."

Derek pulled the shirt over his head and tucked it into his Diesels. He looked at himself in the mirror, turning one way and then another. He straightened and arched his chest. Then he smiled. "I do look fuckable, don't I?"

"I couldn't blame anyone for wanting to have sex with you," Juan said.

"Do you really think Brent wants to?"

"Don't play naïve with me." Juan smiled. "I'll put it this way: I'm not planning to wait up for you. But if you're not home in a week, I'm calling whoever tailed Scott Peterson."

Derek embraced Juan. "I really wanted to celebrate our windfall by having sex tonight with you," he said. "Maybe tomorrow?"

"I'm not easily seduced." Juan smiled. Then stepping back and checking Derek out, he laughed. "Like hell I'm not! I'm so horny right now I'm going out to Rage for a beer and a butt. But you go have fun with your old movie star. While you're licking his star-fucking ass, I'll be banging something that wasn't even born until about the time Brent made his first movie."

Derek feigned resentment. "He's only forty-eight, for crying out loud."

"Who's your daddy?" Juan joked.

The two men looked into each other's eyes, and for a moment, they were silent. Then, a knock on the door broke the spell. It was Tom, come to escort Derek back to Weybridge Cottage. "Play safe," Derek cautioned Juan as he began to move toward the door.

"And you play hard to get," Juan responded.

SIXTEEN

Derek opened the passenger door to Tom's Mercedes and slipped into the leather bucket seat. He adjusted his shoulder restraint. Both men stared out the front window. As they drove west along Fountain Avenue, k.d. lang was singing "Crying" over the CD stereo system. The vibrations from her voice filled the void of verbal communication between Derek and Tom.

Finally, Tom gambled an effective icebreaker. "That was a stupid thing I said this morning," he said. "I didn't mean to call you a two-bit street hustler. It was a cheap shot. Can we go back to being friends?"

Derek did not speak.

"Listen, I tried to make it up by paying your rent," Tom said.

"Thank you," Derek said.

Tom smiled and nodded his head. "You've gotta get over your bull-shit pride, man. People will always want to help a good-looking guy," Tom said. "Let them, if it makes 'em feel good. They hope they'll get in your pants in return."

"And you want my ass again in return for bailing me out?" Derek said.

"What I want is for you to not be angry with me," Tom said. "I want us to be cool again. I admitted to being a prick. I'm not groveling any more."

After a moment of silence between the two men, Derek relented. "We're fine," he said. "Let's just forget this morning. Just one question," Derek continued. "Why Brent's change of heart about me?"

"I told you, he's one of those moody-actor types. An artiste," Tom said.

"Maybe you just misread his signals."

"The important thing is that he asked me to bring you by again."

In that moment, Derek realized that they were driving through Beverly Hills. And soon, they were at the gates to Weybridge Cottage. "Call my cell when you're finished. I'll take you back," Tom said.

Derek blanched. "What? I'm going in alone? I thought we were all going out for drinks and to talk. A social thing."

Tom rolled his eyes. "Brent wants to speak with you. One on one."

Derek crossed his arms over his chest. "Take me home."

Over the brief course of their association, Derek had seen small indications of Tom's shifting moods. Now, suddenly, Tom's easygoing nature turned ugly. He violently put the car's transmission into park and faced Derek. "Enough of your games, you cocksucking, asshole, whore. This is how it is: You're blessed and cursed with a certain look. Certain men would think they'd died and gone to Cock Heaven if they could get a mouth full of your dick or a piece of your ass. Brent's one of them. I once played my hand the same as you're doing and it paid off. So don't think you're doing anything original with that wide-eyed innocence routine. But don't get too cocky. Brent likes a lot of men. You're just one. There'll be someone else tomorrow night."

Derek was speechless.

"So here's the deal," Tom resumed his tirade. "I'm going to open the gates and you're going to walk to the house and ring the doorbell. You'll be graciously welcomed into the house by the man himself. Brent will have a bottle of champagne chilling on the back patio. You'll politely accept his invitation to join him for a drink. After you've drained half a bottle, you'll lock eyes with him. Then you'll peel off your shirt. He'll take a deep breath, and then put down his glass. That's your cue to pull his pants down to his ankles, bend him over, take your dick, and fuck his ass. Got it? Oh, and tell him he's a worthless piece of shit while you're at it. He doesn't receive enough humiliation from the critics."

Derek made a quick vault for Tom's throat. He smashed his head against the window and held him pinned there for a long moment without saying a word. Then, with another quick shove, he disengaged his strong hand from Tom's throat and fell back onto his seat.

Tom coughed and breathed rapidly. In a moment he composed himself. "As I was saying . . . Fuck him tonight. A blow job was the right way to introduce yourself. But now he'll want that freakin' python of yours buried all the way."

Derek was completely lost for words. He was pissed off at himself for being such a poor judge of character as to be duped by Tom into trusting him. He was revolted by the memory of sleeping with Tom, and having once again confused a handsome face and sexy body with the spark of love.

Tom broke the silence. "And if you don't get out of this car in thirty seconds, I promise that I will drive down the hill and put you out on the corner of Sunset and Doheney. By the time you've walked the rest of the way to that crack den of an apartment that you call home, you'll find your precious friend Juan out on the sidewalk. He'll be crying next to a pile of your shitty jeans and CDs. Officers from the West Hollywood Sheriff's Department will be on hand to: One, serve you an eviction notice; two, fine you for vagrancy; three, ticket you for trespassing; and four, arrest you for drug possession."

"I don't use drugs!" Derek demanded.

"They'll find a stash in your apartment. I guarantee it."

Tom took another deep breath and suddenly his personality once again turned agreeable. "Ah, come on, Derek," he said with a plea in his voice. "There's really nothing to it. You get to fuck a superstar. Do you know how many millions of men, and women, would trade to be in your place?"

"How great can he be if he associates with the likes of you?" Derek retorted.

"What is so wrong with having some fun with sex, and getting paid, too. Did I mention the amount of money?"

Although Derek would not look directly at Tom, he was attentive, waiting to hear the rest of the sales pitch.

"Five hundred an hour. A two-hour guarantee. Plus tip. It's five grand if you spend the night. You will never make such easy money doing anything else. It's safe. He's not at all kinky. And you can afford to buy that pony you've always wanted."

Derek involuntarily chuckled but immediately checked himself. "Five grand will be just enough to pay you back and get you out of my life," Derek said.

Tom shrugged. "Spend it the way you like."

Derek was suddenly spinning with the thought that he could earn so much money simply by having sex.

"Twenty-five. Twenty-six. Twenty-seven. Do I have to count all the way to thirty?" Tom asked in a playful voice.

Derek reached for the door handle. Without looking at Tom or uttering another word, he pulled the handle and pushed open the door. He stepped out into the warm night and closed the door behind him. He waited for a moment and then turned and walked to the gates. He pushed the white call button and the gates began to slide open, as Tom's car peeled away.

In a moment, Derek was walking toward the house, and Brent was waiting outside the door.

In the diffused light filtering from within the foyer, Derek thought that Brent was almost more handsome than he was on a movie screen.

Brent's eyes surveyed the chiseled, buffed-out package that was Derek. He smiled. Without words, he seductively and approvingly cocked his head to invite Derek inside.

Tom had been wrong about the seduction scenario. There was no champagne, and no shy movie star waiting for a first move from Derek. The two men had recognized their mutual attraction and within seconds, both were stripped of their shirts and tasting the other's lips, tongue, and skin. Where Derek was tall and muscular with his flesh tightly pulled over his chest and biceps, Brent was shorter in height and taut enough for Derek to feel his bone structure. His body was naturally sexy, but not gym pumped. His torso boasted long dark hairs that were soon slick with perspiration.

Lost in each other's bodies, there was no mistaking the signals this time. Both were in clear need for sex. They savagely kissed and dueled with their tongues, demanding to satisfy their hunger for sex. Derek pinned Brent against the wall, knocking a painting askew. He voraciously buried his face in Brent's chest hair. He then allowed Brent to overpower him and in moments, Derek was forced onto the cold marble floor of the foyer.

The two locked fingers as Brent vacillated between sucking on Derek's lips and tongue and rooting into his armpits like a ravenous pig in a trough. Both emitted nonverbal sounds of urgency and were too completely into the other to pause for even a fraction of an instant. Their need for sex commanded their undivided attention. And when Brent began washing out Derek's navel with his tongue, while simultaneously unzipping his jeans, both knew it was time for Brent's bed.

In one swift movement, Derek was on his feet and dragged Brent with him.

Brent took his now-disheveled lover by the hand and swiftly led him toward the stairs that led up to the bedrooms. Quickly ascending the wide staircase, they entered a long second-floor corridor and raced toward French doors at the end of the hallway.

The bedroom was enormous. Derek judged it at least the size of the Great Room downstairs. Before they were halfway into the candle-lighted space, they had discarded their remaining clothes.

Brent fell onto the bed and Derek covered him with his own body. While the men passionately and ravenously continued to deluge each other with ardent kisses, their hips ground into each other as their thick, stiff cocks met and their pubic hairs meshed.

Brent readjusted his position and worked his face down the length of Derek's solid body. With his lips and tongue acting like a bottom-feeding leech he scoured every centimeter of flesh. He splayed his hands over the planes of Derek's chest and allowed his fingertips and palms to absorb the sensations. His focus was on the biggest attraction along the journey. When his nose and mouth were finally in the warm area of Derek's cock, he involuntarily spoke. "Oh, Christ, you're perfect."

As Brent fixated on the thick blue-veined meat, he slowly drew his tongue up along the side of the flange. Coating the thin sheath of skin with saliva dripping off his tongue, he simultaneously inhaled the scent of the thick and steamy rain forest briar patch of pubic hair. Brent made his fervency known with inhuman guttural sounds.

Derek raised his head and placed his hands on Brent's shoulders. He watched as the star devoured his meat from head to base. The sight of watching the performance made Derek crazy with lust. The scene could have been from one of the most erotic Falcon porn videos he'd ever watched. Too close to climax, he guided his lover back up to meet his face and once again they kissed violently.

Rolling over onto his back, Brent moaned, "Oh, God, fuck me. Take me! Fuck my hole. Do it. I can't hold off much longer."

Derek looked up and over at the bed stand. There, on a cocktail napkin, rested a bottle of lube and a wrapped condom.

"Oh, God, I want it," Brent begged, his eyes ravenously absorbing the packed chest and tight abs of Derek's body.

As Derek leaned over to pick up the condom, Brent dragged his hands over his own body, and played with his own stiff prick. "Fuck me now," he begged again in a maniacal frenzy, as if having Derek's cock pounding his ass was an emergency. With the intensity of a drug addict desperate for a fix, and watching with the impatience of a crystal freak, Brent gaped at Derek's procedure with a rubber.

As he placed his ankles around Derek's neck, Brent watched as Derek took his handful of meat and began to slowly guide it into Brent's hungry butt hole. Brent gritted his teeth and cried out in pleasure and pain. But as Derek skillfully continued to ease his cock deeper into the grateful actor, he recognized the transformation of the man's guttural noises from discomfort to utter satisfaction. "Oh, fuck!" Brent cried, verbally confirming that Derek was giving him the greatest lay of his life.

Derek had the ability to cum at will, and would hold off until Brent was sated. He moved in and out of Brent with pistonlike precision, randomly intensifying the force with which he plunged and extracted his rod.

Brent gasped with each painful thrust and moaned at each retraction. Push and pull, assail and retreat. He was soon no longer able to endure the need to climax. He began vigorously stroking himself. The faster his hand moved over his cock, the faster Derek attacked his ass. In the final moments leading up to ejaculation, Brent held one of Derek's ass cheeks in his hand and forced his middle finger to penetrate Derek's butt.

Derek drove himself even deeper into Brent. And then . . . a cry of intense pain and pleasure rose up from Brent's diaphragm. His cock erupted. His load shot first to his face, followed by a second wad of thick man juice that reached the hollow of his throat.

Derek continued to drill his way into Brent's hole until it appeared that Brent was spent and too weak to continue enjoying himself. Derek then slipped out of Brent, removed the condom and quickly pumped himself dry, mixing his cum with the puddles on Brent's throat and chest. Then he collapsed in exhaustion and lay down beside the star. He reached over and placed his hand in the gooey conflation of their fluids and scooped some of it off of Brent, and rubbed it on himself, in an act of spiritual bonding.

In a voice that was filled with satisfaction and exhaustion, Brent whispered, "I snore."

Derek began to stir when he felt a hand gently caressing his thick chest and playing with his nipples. With his eyes closed to the morning light, he smiled as he remembered where he was and with whom he was sharing a bed. "Mmmm," he said, starting to stretch his body into consciousness. He rolled over and blindly placed a hand on the chest of the body he had enjoyed the night before. His eyelids began to flutter. And as he opened his green orbs he looked directly into the eyes of . . . "What the fuck!" he yelled and suddenly vaulted to the other side of the bed.

"Morning, studly."

To Derek's surprise, it was Tom in bed beside him, covered to his waist by the silk sheet, and obviously naked. "Where's Brent?"

"Don't you mean, where's your money?" Tom said. "Don't panic. There's an envelope with your name on it in the foyer."

"Just answer my question," Derek said. "And what the fuck do you think you're doing in bed with me?"

Tom propped himself up against the headboard and placed two pillows behind him for support. "Don't get so damned pissed off all the time," he complained. "Who said I wanted to have sex with you in the first place."

"The fact that you don't have any clothes on, and you're so fucking hard that you're making a tent with the bedsheet, and you were touching me," Derek raged.

Tom reached down under the sheet and held himself. He took his swollen cock out from under cover and slowly stroked it. "Would it kill you to pound my ass the way you slammed Brent's last night? I heard all about it. After all, I did get you the best gig in Hollywood. I think you owe me."

Now, Derek was really pissed off. He got out of bed and found his jeans crumpled on the floor. He slipped into the legs and looked around for his shirt.

"It's still in the foyer," Tom said, reminding Derek of the tussle with Brent that began the moment he entered the house.

"I don't fucking owe you anything," Derek said. "You can hold the rent thing over me and you can dangle the movie star carrot. I'll have sex with you right after I bareback Pat Robertson." Derek picked up his Skechers and his socks and marched out of the room and onto the second floor landing. He descended the staircase and into the foyer. His shirt had been neatly folded on the hall table, and an envelope with his name printed in black Sharpie was placed on top of it. Derek folded the thick envelope and shoved it into his jeans pocket. He then pulled his shirt over his head and tucked it in the waistband of his pants.

Tom had put his pants and T-shirt back on and had wandered downstairs to join Derek. "If I'd known you were going to be so much trouble, I wouldn't have even fucked you for fun. You seemed like a team player."

"You haven't stopped fucking me," Derek said.

"The way I see it, paying your rent cancelled out the fucks in your apartment, and the money you made here evened out what you owe me."

Then Tom changed his disposition. He became the rueful, self-effacing man to whom Derek had once been deeply attracted. "Look, man, I'm sorry. Really, I am. I thought about you all night long. I regret the way I've acted, and especially the way I've handled things with you."

Derek took the pay envelope out of his back pocket. Angrily he counted out fifty one hundred dollars bills. "There!" he yelled, stuffing the money down the neck of Tom's shirt, "we're even!"

Tom turned away from Derek for a moment. "There's always interest due. Compounded daily." He grinned. "Severe penalty for early withdrawal."

"Don't even go there," Derek warned.

"I'm joking," Tom said, then pounded his hand against the wall. "Damn, I wanted things to turn out different with you!" he said. "I made a huge mistake when I brought you up here for dinner that night. I was trying to impress you with my friends. But then Brent said he wanted to get to know you. I've known him long enough to realize that means only one thing. I resented you both. But because he is the great Brent Richardson who gets everything and everyone he wants, I went along with helping him out. I'm sorry that you were the one in the middle who got hurt."

Derek was unmoved by what Tom was saying. "Look, the thing of it is, I genuinely care about Brent. Even if I never see him again, I had fun. He's a special man," Derek said. "As for how you felt about me at first, that's why there's such a thing as courting. Fortunately, you showed your true colors before I got too involved. You're an asshole."

"Fuck your gratitude." Tom smiled evilly. "You would never have had sex with a mega movie star if it wasn't for me."

Derek countered, "I've had sex with movie stars before. I've fucked my share of name brands too! I had a Kellogg for breakfast and a Stouffer for dinner. I have sex with men because I want to. I had sex with you for the same reason. And, believe it or not, I'd have sex with Brent Richardson for free."

"Well, then, you're really stupid," Tom said. Quickly catching himself, he shook his head. "I didn't mean that, Derek. You're actually to be commended. You've got what most men in this town don't have."

"Eight and a half inches is not that uncommon."

A third voice entered the verbal altercation. "Scruples," it said, forcing Derek to turn toward the voice.

Tom, too, turned his head and forced a dry cough.

At that moment, Brent Richardson, dressed in an untucked madras shirt opened at the collar and down three buttons, entered the room. He continued speaking. "And I want you to stay in my home. If you want to," he said, revealing himself from the darkness of an alcove of the foyer. "Pay no attention to Tom," Brent said, staring at Derek. "I don't trust him either. What's this about him paying your rent? He didn't. I did. He owes you a refund. Let's you and I go out to the patio and chat. Everett will serve breakfast. After last night, you must be as starved as I am."

Derek was confused. He looked first at Tom, who was collecting the money from under his shirt and placing the currency on the round Lalique table at the center of the foyer. "Don't I get a reward?" he asked, holding up several of the green notes.

Brent smiled at Derek and cocked his head toward the corridor that led to the Great Room, which led to the patio and pool. Without looking back at Tom, Derek walked toward Brent, who patted him on the back.

SEVENTEEN

The Southern California morning sky was powder blue, and the air temperature was warm enough to enjoy breakfast outside. Derek and Brent took their seats at the wrought-iron and glass-top table. Ornately cast silver cutlery place settings were laid before them. Everett appeared from the *cabaña* with a carafe of coffee. He poured first into Derek's cup and then into Brent's. Two pitchers of chilled juice—orange and grapefruit—were already on the table. As he deftly draped a white linen napkin onto the laps of both men, Everett asked which juice Derek preferred.

"Grapefruit, please," Derek said.

"And might that be your choice each morning?" Everett asked, making mental notes about Derek's preferences.

"I never tire of grapefruit," Derek said, as he picked up the juice glass and consumed the contents in one long thirst-quenching chug.

As Everett departed for the kitchen, Brent reached out and touched Derek's hand. "Hope you don't mind, but I usually let Everett surprise me with what I have for breakfast. After today, you can ask him for anything you want."

Everett returned and set breakfast plates before the men. On each were two poached eggs over potato pancakes, dressed with a mixture of diced carrots, onions, and spinach.

"From now on, you can have just egg whites if you like." Brent smiled. "But this morning is sort of a celebration. I'm welcoming you into my home."

A million thoughts flashed through Derek's brain as he thought of the implications to what he was getting himself into with this job, the description of which they had not even discussed. Tom had alluded to what Brent was looking for, and had, by using himself as an example, illustrated the basic elements of the arrangement. *Have sex with Brent and earn an annuity*—Derek recalled words to that effect.

"More coffee?" Everett asked Derek and Brent. He refilled both cups and then left the men to enjoy their breakfast and engage in private conversation.

Derek picked up his knife and fork and began sampling the food. He immediately pronounced the breakfast the best he'd ever tasted, which made Brent smile.

"Everett's a genius in the kitchen," Brent said. "He'll take good care of you. So will I."

Derek shook his head. "What am I doing here?" he asked. "I mean, I know what I'm here *for,* but why me? And when you're bored, am I going back to selling flowers in Covent Garden?"

Brent swallowed a forkful of food and took a sip from his coffee cup. He looked at Derek. "Good questions," he said. "I'd ask them too, if I were in your pants. I've consulted about this with a couple of friends of mine who first brought you to my attention. They actually know you, and gave a high recommendation."

Derek shrugged his shoulders. "Who?"

"Not supposed to tell," Brent said, between bites of breakfast. "They're very private people, but well connected. This sounds weird, but they actually sort of help the rich and famous get laid."

"Head hunters, eh?"

"Literally." Brent laughed.

"We should both know what we're getting ourselves into," Derek said. "You have the upper hand."

Brent pushed his plate a few inches forward and dabbed his lips with his napkin. "As a matter of fact, I've never done this before," he said.

"But Tom . . . He said that you and he . . ."

"The arrangement I've had with Tom just sort of evolved. We never discussed the finer points of service and compensation."

"You mean how much bang you get for your buck?" Derek said.

"In a manner of speaking," Brent said. "Most important, I just want us both to be okay with everything." Brent looked at Derek with sincerity. "I don't want your life to simply revolve around mine. You've been down that road with your first boyfriend."

Derek too, gave his plate a short nudge and poured another glass of juice. "Do you really want me to move in?" he asked. "Will I stay in your room, or have my own?"

"Yes, I want you here. And you'll have the tower on the other side of the house all to yourself. Decorate it any way you wish. Oh, and I have accounts at all the shops on Rodeo, so anything that catches your eye . . . What else do you need or want?"

Derek thought for a moment. "One thing I need is to borrow your car today," he said. "I've got to collect a few things from my apartment."

Brent waved away the question as if it needn't have been asked. "Of course. Take your pick. I've got six. Use them whenever. All the keys are on hooks by the kitchen door."

Derek blinked. "Then, I'm on my way." Derek pushed his chair back from the table. "What time do you want me home?"

"You're not a prisoner out on a work furlough. You don't have to answer to me for anything," Brent said. "We should just be considerate enough to consult with each other and coordinate our schedules."

"Then I'll be back here by four o'clock," Derek said, and leaned down to kiss Brent on the lips. "Anything you need while I'm out?"

"Everett takes care of everything I need. Well, almost everything." Brent smiled. "Plus I'll be reading scripts all day. We'll eat in tonight, if that's okay with you."

"Very much."

"I'll be waiting. Impatiently," Brent said with a wide smile.

As promised, six expensive cars—and one police vehicle—occupied the courtyard inside the gate of the estate. Tom had explained that the police car was a decoy meant to deter potential intruders. Derek selected the Jaguar. He pulled open the car door and slipped into the comfortable leather seat. He marveled at the interior, the highly polished wooden dashboard and the cockpit-like dials and needles and buttons and switches. He found the ignition switch slot, inserted the key and turned it to start the vehicle. He found a compartment with CDs and selected one, which was a dance remix of the *Six Feet Under* HBO program theme music. And then, with his foot on the brake, he shifted the transmission into drive. Derek smiled as he released his foot from the brake and slowly rolled out of the parking spot. The car moved over the cobblestone courtyard and down the serpentine drive toward the main gate of Weybridge Cottage. When he passed over a metal plate embedded in the ground, the two iron gates slowly parted. When they were fully separated, Derek drove off the estate.

As he practically floated east along Sunset Boulevard, Derek looked at the car phone. He pushed a button that said speaker and heard a dial tone and then pushed a series of numbers.

"Be home!" Derek said aloud, just before he heard Juan's voice. "It's me," Derek gushed. "You're never going to believe . . ."

"I was getting worried. Where are you?"

"You'll see. In twenty minutes I want you to go outside and wait by the curb. No more questions until I see you. Okay?"

"I'm not dressed," Juan said.

"You've got twenty minutes. See you then." Derek pushed the disconnect button and continued driving. At Crescent Heights he turned right and drove over to Fountain Avenue and then turned left. As he passed Fairfax, Derek started to feel a knot in his stomach. Suddenly, he began to feel uneasy, especially about how Juan would respond to the life-altering news. As he approached Poinsettia, he found a space by the curb that was just large enough to accommodate the car. And there was Juan, looking up and down the street, taking little notice of the polished gold-colored Jag, until Derek blasted the horn and rolled down the electric window.

Juan moved cautiously toward the car. Curiosity showed on his face. He peered in through the open window. "Boss?" he said.

Derek laughed. "It's not mine," he anticipated the first question that Juan would ask. "It belongs to . . ." He looked around for eavesdroppers. "Let's go into the apartment. I've got tons to tell you."

This time when they saw Garson coming out of his unit, they didn't feel that they had to hide. Derek and Juan simply walked to the doorstep and entered their single room.

Derek stopped and took a different look at his surroundings. Everything suddenly seemed cheap. The atmosphere depressed Derek. He kicked back onto the bed and realized how thin the mattress was. If he had ever before noticed that he could feel the bedsprings digging in to his back he had ignored that fact. Now, it was all too obvious.

Juan joined him on the bed. "I was right, wasn't I?"

Derek offered a guilty but satisfied smile.

Eager for the details of his friend's rendezvous, Juan said, "Spill it."

"It was fine," Derek teased. "Sex is sex. Except with you," he amended. Then he pulled Juan backward and rolled over and straddled his waist. He seductively lifted his friend's white T-shirt and put his index finder into Juan's navel.

"Don't!" Juan giggled. "God, one movie star fuck and you become Mr. Happy Pecker. It must have been more than just okay."

Derek laughed. "It was amazing!" he said. "Not only is Brent sexy and smart, all of our problems are now solved."

"Our problems?" Juan said. "We've got a roof over our heads, and enough money to buy food for a week, maybe longer, depending on how much you hauled in last night. How much?"

Rolling off of Juan, Derek reached into his pocket and withdrew the cash. He held the money high into the air and then released the currency, letting it flutter down onto Juan's body.

Juan looked at the money, which was more than he'd ever seen in his life. Then he looked up at Derek. "What did you have to do for this much loot?"

"The usual. A little light bondage. Water sports, fisting. Same ol' same ol'. He's easily trained."

Juan could tell that Derek was joking. "Boss, nobody pays this kind of money just for sex! I don't care if you're Bill Gates or Barry Manilow. And rich people are the cheapest of all! If you remember, the millionaires who slummed at Onyx were all fucking lousy tippers!"

Derek got up off the bed and went to the kitchenette. He took a drinking glass out of the sink, turned on the tap and rinsed it out. He filled the tumbler with water and then opened the freezer and collected several ice cubes. As he dropped them into the glass of water he said, "I have a job. But you wouldn't approve."

Juan sat up and looked blankly at Derek. "Hey, a job's a job, Boss," he said, collecting the cloudburst of cash around him. "If poverty has taught me one lesson, it's not to be judgmental about how anyone earns a living. Even if you have to occasionally hire out your dick, who am I to judge? I'm ready to do it again myself but I can't afford an ad."

Derek walked back to the center of the room. "This job is a little more respectable, I think."

"You think?"

"And it pays extremely well."

Juan made a noise that sounded like a chuckle. "If this is your monthly paycheck, I'd say, yeah, go for it."

"Nightly. Well, actually, that was more like an introductory offer. I'll find out tonight how much I'll really be earning."

"You said what, Boss? That you made this for one night?"

"Still no *comprender Inglés*?" Derek said. "Yeah, just one night. It's a crock of shit when they tell you this stuff doesn't grow on trees! It does! I shake the branches and this is what falls out. I'm on a cash retainer and every time I have sex with Brent, I get a fist full of dough. It's like working on commission."

Juan leaped up off the bed. He was incredulous. "Wait a fucking minute. This is too weird. This is too unbelievable. What the fuck is going on?" he said.

Derek nodded his head in agreement with Juan's assessment of the change that had taken place in his life. "Look, everything has been building to this," he said. "It's a natural progression. First I got canned from Onyx. And remember that guy Marshall Topper who came in a lot? He used to tell me that I could make a good living letting guys suck my dick. Then I placed an ad and met Tom. He obviously liked what he saw, and I passed his test.

"Turns out that Tom works for Brent," Derek continued. "It was his job to find a guy who would be sexually compatible with Brent. He tried me on for size and I fit. They both agreed that I have something, um, special. They recognized that I'm trustworthy, I guess," Derek said. "Tom and Brent liked that I was ready to walk away from all the cash they tried throwing at me a couple of times, even though I'm broke. Scruples. That's what they said I have. They tested my loyalty too. When I got all upset by the fact that Tom was naked and coming on to me in Brent's bed, that scored me a ton of points."

Juan was reeling from an overload of information. "What was Tom doing naked in bed with you in the first place?" he said. "I thought you were having sex with Brent."

"That was earlier. I was asleep. He crawled in and started to make out with me. But I controlled myself and to my surprise, Brent was in on the scheme."

"Obvious question," Juan said, playing devil's advocate. "If this Tom is such a stud, why isn't he servicing Brent? Seems like a natural."

"As a matter of fact, that was their initial arrangement," Derek said.

"Why have you been recruited for his job?"

Derek scrunched up his face. "Honestly, I'm not too clear on that. Tom says that he's tired of it and wants to opt out. I think Brent just wants some new, younger meat."

"So you're on borrowed time," Juan said. "The moment this guy tires of you, or Tom pimps him another cutie, you'll be history. Out on your ass. It'll be Onyx all over again, with nowhere for you to go, except down to a lower rung of hustler-dom."

Derek took a deep breath. The thought had crossed his mind that he was dispensable. Like any other job, there wasn't necessarily any security. And there was even less with this arrangement. "I can't think that way," Derek said. "But I won't be stupid with the money. I'm putting away as much as possible, so if and when my services are no longer required, I'll have something to fall back on."

Derek noticed that Juan suddenly looked desolate. "You've got to understand something about these people," Derek said. "Movie stars and studio executives and famous people have sexual needs just like you and me. But unlike Average Joe, they can't go online and find some stranger to fuck them. And, forget about ringing up an escort who advertises in *Encounters.*"

"Isn't that how this all started for you?" Juan said with a melancholy voice.

"Sort of. I mean, Tom was getting desperate to find someone for Brent. But it was some friends of Brent's who checked me out first. A guy as famous as Brent needs a go-between."

Juan flopped back down onto the bed. "Guess I'm history, eh? You can afford a better place to live now. This really sucks."

Derek realized that he hadn't given any thought at all to what would become of Juan. He had been so preoccupied with the sudden change in direction of his life, and thinking about moving in to Brent's mansion, that Juan's predicament hadn't occurred to him. "I neglected to mention that I'm moving to his estate. So you can have this place all to yourself."

"Swell," Juan said without emotion. "On my own again. In an apartment that I can't afford by myself."

"I'm taking care of the rent," Derek said. "Who knows when I'll have to come back to this dump."

"What you should do is fix me up with one of your rich movie star friends."

Derek was silent for a moment. Just as he was about to tell Juan that he'd help him financially until he found another restaurant job, he suddenly had an idea. "You're very hot, Juan," he said. "I'll definitely put the word out. Once I get to know Brent, and what his friends are looking for . . . Hell, you and I would make an unbeatable team."

Juan shook his head. "I've gotta find a real job, and a place to live."

"You don't think that what I'm doing is a real job?" Derek said. "I don't blame you. Everybody looks down on those in the sex-trade business. But this is different."

"Like, how is it different?" Juan said.

"It's different, because I know the person, and it's an arrangement. It's not like I'm one of the guys who takes ads out in the escort section of *Encounters.*"

"Yes it is, Boss. You did exactly that. The only difference is that you got lucky." Juan scooted himself off the bed and picked up his apartment key from the desk. "I'm going out for a while. We can talk later."

"I'm back at Brent's at four," Derek said. "Have to return the car and . . ."

"Yeah, 'and . . .' I wish you success, amigo," Juan said. And then he left the apartment.

All of the enthusiasm that accompanied Derek during the drive from Beverly Hills back to his old apartment had been slowly dissipating. Now it was entirely depleted. He began to question the integrity of what he'd agreed to do. Derek felt a physical pressure bearing down on him as he thought about why his life seemed so different from everybody else's. He wondered why he wasn't dressed in a business suit and working in an office tower. Or why he didn't have an actual house of his own in which to live, rather than a dump of an apartment. Although he realized that he would be living in a mansion, it wasn't his. And it was temporary. "But all things are temporary," he reminded himself. A nice car to drive? Sure, he'd have that too. But again, it wouldn't belong to him.

On the other hand, he reasoned, most people hate their jobs. They have mortgages that they struggle to meet each month, and car payments, and maybe child support. "It's all a trade-off," he argued aloud. "You do a job and you get compensation. Whether it's crunching numbers for an accounting firm, pulling apart engines in a gas station service bay, acting in films, or selling sex. A job is a job."

Derek looked at his wristwatch. He picked up a few CDs, several pairs of jeans, a few T-shirts and his underwear and socks. He packed them all into a canvas bag. The apartment seemed claustrophobic in its size. "I hope to God I never have to come back here again," he said.

As he was about to reach for the doorknob, he realized there was one thing left to do. He dropped the bag and went to the desk. He picked up the gas bill envelope, which was stacked on top of the cell phone bill, the Visa bill, and other bills that served as reminders of his poverty. He removed the contents, and turned the envelope over. Finding a pen in the desk drawer, he scrawled a quick note:

Juan. I love you. I'll be in touch.

He signed his name and tucked the five thousand dollars from Brent into the envelope pouch. Then, he laid it on the pillow where Juan's head would rest that night.

Then he walked out of the one-room apartment.

EIGHTEEN

Derek's job description was not detailed in any actual paperwork or stored on a computer hard drive. To create such a document would jeopardize the secretiveness of the arrangement. Instead, when Brent met up with Derek for cocktails that evening, he verbally spelled out the terms as simply as his two headhunter friends had suggested. Pouring two flutes of Cristal, Brent began by saying, "I hope you weren't misled by Tom about your compensation."

Derek didn't speak, but silently he thought, *I'm about to be fucked.*

"The way it's suggested that this should work is that each week I write you a check for five thousand dollars. Regardless of how much or how little sex we have," Brent said. "That whole five grand thing for one night was another of Tom's lame tests. He wanted to see how much you were willing to throw back in his face." Brent laughed. "So I hope you're not too disappointed."

Derek took a deep breath and a long drink of champagne. He didn't say so, but five thousand dollars a week was more money than Derek ever thought he'd earn from any job. He factored in the use of Brent's expensive cars, free gourmet cuisine, and taking up residence in a Beverly Hills mansion which was equal in its legendary status to Harold Lloyd's Green Acres and Mary Pickford and Douglas Fairbanks's Pickfair. But Derek didn't say a word. He continued to listen. And, if he had been pressed to offer his true feelings, he would have said that he would have consented to sex with Brent for a fraction of that amount.

"By the way, I go on location day after tomorrow. We'll be away for three weeks."

"We?" Derek said eagerly. "I get to travel with you?"

"Sorry. The royal 'We,' " Brent said. "You're too scene-stealing to take on a film set. Some of my friends bring their boys and call them physical fitness trainers or dialogue coaches. But I'm too big a star—in all modesty—to risk being caught by one of those horrible tabloids. Oh, sure, I've heard all the rumors." Brent shook his head. "They say I'm Hollywood's biggest closet case. Maybe it's true, if you don't count old stars like Raymond Burr and Rock Hudson. But I'm not coming out. At least not until I decide that the time is right."

Brent poured himself another glass of bubbly. "I get a couple of days off in the middle of the shoot and I'll fly home. I'll really need you after having to do scenes with Viggo. He's intense, but he's certainly seductive!"

"Three weeks? No problem," Derek said. "I'll fill my hours by catching up on reading, working out and going to the beach. A tough job, but someone . . ." he trailed off.

"Are you cool with the financial arrangement? I mean, if you need more I can try to persuade my business people, but they have to account for every dime I spend. And if, just hypothetically speaking, you want to have sex with someone else while I'm away, I understand. A boy with your, um, bottomless appetite . . ." He let the words hang in the air as his dick grew hard and he pictured Derek pumping someone else's ass. "I don't want to play games where one of us feels guilty if another intriguing body comes along. I only ask that you be discreet and careful."

Derek placed his glass on the coffee table and stood up next to Brent. They locked eyes and Derek lifted Brent's T-shirt and placed his hands on his chest. He flicked his fingers over his new employer's nipples and then leaned in for a deep kiss on his lips. "What I need more is your ass, Mr. Sexy Movie Star. And if I need to take care of business while you're away, I've got a perfectly strong hand."

Brent chuckled in the middle of their kiss and pulled Derek closer to him. "You can have all of my ass that you want," he said and helped Derek slip his tank over his head. "Fuck me before Everett calls us to dinner," Brent said.

Derek picked up the champagne bottle and the two flutes, and followed Brent out of the Great Room and into the hallway leading to the foyer and grand staircase. Together Derek and Brent ascended to the second floor, their cocks already throbbing and oozing pre-cum with expectation.

Brent was now at ease with Derek, and when they arrived in the master suite, Brent discarded his jeans with far less self-consciousness and hesitation than before.

Derek placed his thumb over the opening at the neck of the bottle and gave it a quick shake. He pointed it at Brent, released his thumb and sprayed a surprised and playful Brent.

"You bastard!" Brent exclaimed in jest. "I'm soaked!"

"I'm here to clean you up." Derek laughed. "And if you're a good boy, I'll give you a champagne enema."

The morning of Brent's departure had begun much earlier than usual. Although Brent was nervous about flying, especially about the long journey to New Zealand that lay before him, he still wanted Derek's body. After indulging in what had become their ritual morning fuck, Brent showered, dressed and was ready when the limousine arrived at the gate. Everett had packed his suitcases the night before, so he had little else to do but to provide Derek with a last minute worry list.

"You know about the security system. And there's extra cash in the safe, if you need it. Oh, and if you could let Everett have a couple of days off, I think he wants to stay at the house in Connecticut. Emma can take care of the place."

"How many times are you going to repeat all of this," Derek said, reminding Brent that there was no reason for concern.

At the last minute before opening the front door, Brent embraced Derek, lifted his tank and kissed his chest. "Fuck! I'm going to miss you," he said. "Be a darling and be good."

Derek nodded his head and felt genuine caring and, even, missing him already.

Within hours of Brent's departure for LAX and his flight to Auckland, Tom visited the house. He was again the friendly man with whom Derek had started to fall in love. He seemed to be genuinely interested in how the arrangement was working out for both Derek and Brent.

As Derek lounged by the pool in a pair of light blue Speedos, he said, as quietly as possible, "Do Everett and Emma know what I'm doing here?"

"Why? Any problems?" Tom said.

"None. They're great. But I feel a little weird being around here without Brent. I don't want them to think I'm the new prince of the manor."

"They get paid quite well for their duties and discretion," Tom said. "Anyway, they're loyal and practical. They know that you're living here, but Brent lets them put two and two together on their own. They're not idiots. You're not the first one, after all. And they'll treat you with as much respect as you show them."

Tom removed his shirt and pulled off his 501s, under which he too was wearing a pair of Speedos. He took another sip from a champagne flute that he'd brought poolside, and then pulled up a chaise beside Derek. He applied a tanning sunscreen and settled back to enjoy the warm rays and UVs. After a few moments of peaceful silence, he said, "By the way, Brent's French pal Francois Uberand is coming to L.A. for some meetings. He's staying here."

Unflinching, Derek simply said, "Cool."

"If you're not too busy, you might want to show him a good time," Tom added.

"There's Disneyland, the Getty Museum, maybe you can arrange for us to go to a premier, or a screening of something."

Tom smiled. "Francois is the biggest star in Europe. He's coming here to discuss doing an English Language film with Mel. I don't think he'd want to attend a premier. For him, that would be work." Tom paused for a moment. "Remember I told you how I made so much money from fucking friends of friends?"

"Hmm. You're hospitable, if not repetitive."

"When the cat's away . . ."

The unspoken idea lingered in the air between the two men until Derek finally sat forward and gave Tom a quizzical look. "Show him a good time? What are you suggesting?"

"What do you think I'm suggesting," Tom said.

"Not interested. I can wait a few weeks for Brent to return."

"You're not in a relationship," Tom harrumphed. "Brent always wanted me to take advantage of earning a bundle when he was away. And I did. I still liked sex best with Brent, but at a thousand dollars per butthole, who could turn that down?"

Derek's eyes popped. "A thousand dollars? Who's worth a grand? Not me!"

"You underestimate your desirability," Tom chided. "And the amount of some men's per diem," he said.

Derek remembered what Brent had said about understanding if he wanted to have sex while he was away. *I only ask that you be discreet and careful,* Derek heard Brent's words. And the idea of earning extra money for jack hammering another star's ass was suddenly intriguing. "So, what's he like? I mean, is he attractive? Is he fun. Does he speak English?" Derek asked.

"He's a huge celebrity in France. Does that tell you anything?"

"So was Gérard Depardieu, but I wouldn't plow his hole," Derek said.

"Think Ben Affleck with an accent so thick he should sue Berlitz to get his tuition refunded," Tom said. "You'd score a lot of points by memorizing a few simple French words and phrases. You know, something that will make him feel more comfortable in your home."

"*Voulez-vous coucher avec moi, ce soir?*" Derek said.

"Giuchie, giuchie, ya, ya dada," Tom responded. "You continue to amaze me!" he said.

"A thousand dollars," Derek repeated. "Christ almighty. When does he come in to town?"

"Tomorrow night. Oh, and Derek, there's one more thing. Do you remember Rand and Pat? From the first time you came to the house?"

Derek instantly recalled the two older men, both of whom seemed fun and easygoing. "Of course. I liked them a lot." He shaded his eyes and looked over at Tom whose gym pumped body was beading with perspiration.

Tom kept his eyes closed as he spoke. "And they liked you too. In fact, they have talked about nothing else but you! How attractive you are. The intelligence that shined through. Your terrific sense of humor . . ."

Derek scratched his head. "Is this leading to where I think it's leading?"

"Probably."

"Tom! They're too old for me! They were great guys to socialize with, and I'd like to be their friend. But I can't have sex with them. It's creep," Derek said.

Tom heaved a sigh. "Look, Derek, I know this job will take some getting used to. There's a learning curve."

"This is all okay with Brent?" Derek said. "I think he would have said something to me about it."

"No, he wouldn't. He's bashful enough when it comes to *having* sex; he's even shyer if he has to talk about it. Anyway, these guys aren't as famous as some others. But in their own circles, they're masters of their crafts and they can't afford to be thought of as associating with escorts. I mean, they're the geniuses behind what makes a director or actor look good. And they're very easy to please. You won't have do anything except let them appreciate you. Trust me, they don't expect reciprocation. Just get naked and let them enjoy looking at you and touching you."

Derek was losing patience. "How much?" he asked curtly. "I don't want to turn into a machine, for Christ's sake. Turn me on and turn me off. I'm not a convenience."

"Of course not," Tom purred, while thinking, *that's exactly what you are.* "They can pay five hundred each. And that should be about the extent of the work while Brent's gone. It's really only a few hours a day."

"A day?" Derek blasted back. "I have to have sex with these people every day? I can't do that!"

"I didn't mean every day," Tom backtracked. "But since Francois will be staying here, he'll undoubtedly want you a few times."

"At a thousand per?" Derek wanted to make certain of the agreement.

"Yup. You can be financially solvent by the time Brent gets home."

"What if he finds out? Someone's bound to say something."

"And risk having you cut off from them in the future?" Tom said. "I don't think so. Plus, they would never want to make Brent envious or angry."

"What other surprises are you going to throw at me?" Derek complained. "This is getting complicated."

"Hey, it's just sex. Think of all those dumpy straight people who would love to have sex even once a year. You get to have it as often as you want. And with the rich and famous. So just lie back and enjoy this new adventure." Tom looked at his wristwatch. "All this talk about other guys having sex with you has made me very horny. Can we go to bed? I want you."

Derek was whatever the opposite was of horny. *Indifferent,* he thought. Sex with Tom had been hot and fulfilling. But now, knowing the man as well as he did, he was a complete turn-off. "Not unless you've got ten grand you wanna hand over before we fuck," he said, effectively ending the conversation.

*   *   *

With Brent gone from the house, the mansion seemed too quiet and dreary.

Derek was never given a proper tour. The only rooms he had seen were the Great Room, the kitchen, and Brent's bedroom. For a few hours he occupied his time by self-guiding himself around. At first, he felt like an intruder and half expected that at any moment a Mrs. Danvers would surprise him and offer a suspicious look. But no one bothered him. In Derek's head, he heard the lyrics to an old song, ". . . I bet you couldn't imagine that I one time had a house, with so many rooms I couldn't count them all."

Derek awoke early the next morning, slipped into his jogging togs and set out around the estate, before hitting the automatic gate release and venturing onto the quiet residential streets of Beverly Hills.

When he returned, he heard activity in the kitchen, and in some distant room in the house. Everett and Emma were at work at their various activities that kept the house well maintained. Although he was hungry, Derek was still uncomfortable having the staff wait on him. He thought that he knew what they were thinking about his relationship with Brent, and he was embarrassed. "I have a job to do, just as they do," he chastised himself.

"Morning, sir," Everett said with professional decorum, as Derek entered the kitchen for a glass of Gatorade. "Egg whites, steak, and juice?" he asked.

"Don't go out of your way for me." Derek smiled. "I can make do with just a bowl of cereal and yogurt."

"Not at all, sir," Everett said. "Please sit. Breakfast will be served momentarily."

For the next half hour, the two men chatted about a wide variety of topics. Derek discovered Everett to be friendly, intelligent, funny, and with a background in film production. "When I realized that I was not cut out to be an evil prick, I left the business," the butler said.

Derek chuckled. "So how long have you been with Brent, er, Mr. Richardson?"

"Since his first picture," Everett said. "That would make it, oh, I guess twenty years."

"And you enjoy your work? I only ask because I used to be a waiter, and I really hated serving other people."

"I have the ideal job. Mr. Richardson is a faultless employer. I would do anything for him." *And have,* he thought without verbally expressing himself to the young man whom he hardly knew.

As Derek enjoyed his breakfast, he continued to interrogate Everett. "How did you get this job in the first place?" he asked.

"As often happens with employment, I simply fell into it," Everett said, evasively. "One thing led to another and, well, here we are. More juice?"

Derek drained the rest of his glass. "No, I think I'll hit the shower, then get some sun by the pool. Have to look good for our guest tonight," he added, with a touch of ambivalence. "Have you met this guy? What's he like?"

"A serious actor," Everett said. "A perfectionist, if you get my drift."

"A stick up his butt, eh?" Derek said, reading between the lines of Everett's response. "What's he look like?" Derek said.

"After your shower and sunbathing, I'll run one of his films for you," Everett suggested. "His last one was very well received. And, he takes his clothes off for a love scene with Dylan McDermott. Very instructional."

Derek smiled. "Cool," he said, and thanked Everett for breakfast. He pushed his chair away from the table, and walked to the huge shower connected to his bedroom.

Within a half hour Derek was refreshed and changed into his swimming trunks, and went out into the hot, late morning sun. He picked out a towel from the *cabaña* and laid it over a chaise longue. He slathered a bronzing sunscreen over his face, chest, shoulders, arms, and legs, then laid down to absorb the rays.

Well aware of the potentially damaging effects of too much sun on the skin, Derek was careful to allow no more than half an hour on his front and back sides. He wanted to avoid that tough, leathery look that some older men he knew who were once sun worshippers had acquired. There was a time when mothers would tell their kids to go out and play in the sunshine because it was full of vitamin D and good for them. Those were the kids who turned into the guys with masses of white spots on their faces from where skin cancers had been removed. Derek was determined never to let that happen to his face or body.

After forty minutes of absorbing the heat of the day, Derek left the chaise, walked to the pool, and dove into the water. The cold shock was bracing. He swam underwater, came up for air and stroked the length of the pool several times. He submerged once again, holding his breath as long as possible before returning to the surface for air. Treading water and loving the thought that it was only a few days ago that he was literally ripped away from a one-room apartment, to live in a Beverly Hills mansion so large that the owner had to ask his major-domo how many bedrooms and bathrooms they had. (Eight bedrooms, ten bathrooms.)

Then he heard the sound of applause, and his smile and reverie changed. Derek shook the wet hair out of his eyes and looked toward where the sound was emanating. Rand and Pat were both seated at one of the four wrought-iron glass-top tables under a wide umbrella. "Our very own Greg Louganis!" Rand called out with a large smile. "Isn't he fucking gorgeous," he said to Pat, in a voice loud enough for Derek to hear.

Christ, I thought it would be a few days before they came for me! Derek said to himself. *Okay. Be friendly. This is your job, and you'll get a big payday.* "Hey, guys," Derek called out as he stroked toward the shallow end of the pool. Then, like Bo Derek emerging from the ocean in her film *10,* and slowly ascending the submerged steps, Derek proceeded out of the pool, as water cascaded down his strong muscular chest.

Rand and Pat held their collective breaths as they watched Derek. The mental image that they had both formed of Derek at their first meeting did not compare with the near naked god who stood dripping chlorinated water before them.

Green outdoor carpeting surrounded the pool, and protected Derek's feet from the white-hot cement. He padded over to the chaise and picked up his towel.

"Oh, do let the warm air dry you!" Rand cooed.

"Yes!" Pat said. "It's far more beneficial for the skin . . . if you let things happen naturally."

Derek was a quick study. He dropped the towel back onto the chaise and walked to where the men were seated. He stood before them, his muscled body already pink from the hot sun, and posed in a manner that he knew was seductive. "Brent's on location," he said, knowing full well that they were aware of the master of the manor's absence.

Rand swallowed hard. Without taking his eyes off Derek's pumped chest he said, "He told us we could come over and play in the sand-box."

"So to speak," Pat added. "I hope he mentioned that to you."

Derek forced a smile. Although the temperature was probably ninety, he was shivering and could tell that his skin was a carpet of goose pimples. He wanted to drape a towel around himself, but he also wanted to keep the men sexually excited. *Just get it over with so they'll leave,* he thought to himself. "As a matter of fact, he did not."

Both men looked aghast and disappointed.

"But Tom did. And I've been looking forward to seeing you guys again."

"Oh, not nearly as much as we've looked forward to seeing *you!*" Pat gushed.

"You have no idea!" Rand added. "Um, can we, um, see what's under your trunks?"

Derek smiled. "What, this little thing?" he asked as he slowly rubbed the palm of his hand over his crotch and then seized his tool through the wet fabric. He was quickly hard and it clearly showed through the thin nylon of his Speedo. Teasing the men, Derek watched their fascinated faces as he lifted the hem of his bathing trunks to reveal the head of his fully erect penis. In measures he exposed his cock to the two men whose mouths were agape in stupefaction. Rand drooled.

"May I touch it?" Pat politely asked.

"Taste it too, if you like," Derek said.

Simultaneously, Rand and Pat both fell to their knees. Pat was first on the scene, his tongue, a tentacle with a billion taste sensors, danced on the helmet head of Derek's thick mushroom-head dick. He then opened his mouth as wide as possible and sheathed Derek's swollen cock almost to its base. Slowly, and with the suction of a vacuum hose, he tried to inhale Derek's large penis. He then reluctantly, but generously, offered the meat to Rand.

The intense pleasure that Derek received from having his dick sucked made him forget that he was, in reality, a rent boy. He didn't even think about the fee that Tom had promised they'd offer. He was just as horny as the two men and happy that hungry mouths were being fed.

"There's a hide-a-bed in the *cabaña,*" Rand said with urgency in his voice. Pat immediately agreed, and they both stood and took Derek by the hand and walked to a structure that was larger than Derek's old apartment.

Derek was surprised to find that the bed had already been opened, but there were no sheets over the mattress. Still he automatically stepped out of his bathing suit and flopped backwards onto the bed. Simultaneously, both men discarded their clothes and joined Derek who was more impressed with their bodies than he thought he would be. Both men needed to lose a little weight, but otherwise they were far from unattractive.

Rand had strong wide shoulders and a matte of chest hair that nearly obliterated his nipples. Pat, a choreographer, was toned in the way that a dancer often is—lean and defined. And his average-size cock was surrounded by salt-and-pepper-colored pubic hair. Both men immediately went to work to bring Derek to climax.

As Rand slathered his tongue over Derek's nipples and underarm pits, Pat tried to suck down all of Derek's cock.

Derek held back his orgasm as long as he could, but within ten minutes he bucked and groaned and shot a full geyser load, which both men greedily slathered over their respective dicks and then jacked themselves off with his cum. They simultaneously spilled their own loads over Derek's chest, while whimpering like punished children.

The fly to their spider, Derek thought of himself as he laid on his back, his chest and stomach covered in jiz. Rand and Pat lay down on either side of Derek and passed out. Derek, too, found himself beginning to drift off to sleep. After jogging, then baking in the hot sun, followed by swimming and the ordeal of sex, he was physically exhausted. He wondered how he would be able to perform again later that night, with the Frenchman. Then, Derek too, drifted into unconsciousness.

When the three men stirred once again, it was no more than ten minutes since they had climaxed. Each of them offered compliments to the others for the level of excitement they had brought to the occasion. But mostly, they praised Derek, who knew that he had done nothing more than receive their lust-filled attention. He had not kissed either man, nor had he gone down on them. His contribution had merely been to be the willing object of their desire. And Derek found that it wasn't at all hard to do.

Soon, the two visitors were off the mattress and Rand and Pat were debating whose socks were whose, and searching for their respective clothes. Derek, with congealing cum on his body, stood up from the bed but didn't bother to put his still-wet nylon bathing suit back on. Instead, he followed the men out of the *cabaña,* and when they reached the pool he dove in for a bath. As he cleaned off his body, he noticed that Rand had laid an envelope on the table and placed a glass of lemonade over a corner to prevent any breeze from absconding with the contents. Derek smiled knowingly, and then once again stepped out of the pool—this time nude. With his sex deed completed, he felt it safe to enfold himself in a large beach towel.

"Look at the time," Rand said, without actually looking at his watch. "We've got to run. But this was the most amazing afternoon I've had in ages!"

"Oh, yes!" Pat agreed effusively. "Thank you, Derek, for . . . Well, for absolutely everything!" He looked at Derek's penis, which even flaccid was long and fat.

"I'm here," Derek said, nodding his head, acknowledging that he was amenable to them dropping by again.

"We'll certainly see you before the master of the manse returns!" Rand said. Then he turned to follow Pat across the yard and into the house.

As soon as the men were out of sight, Derek walked to the table where the envelope rested. He opened the sealed flap and counted the cash. "Not bad for an afternoon of fun."

NINETEEN

The answering machine in the Fountain Avenue apartment clicked on. "Trying again to reach you, hon." It was Cathy. "Working your precious buns off, no doubt. Give a call when you have a sec. Love . . ."

Juan recognized Cathy's voice and grabbed for the telephone. "Cathy? Cathy Taylor? It's Derek's friend, Juan."

"Hi, sweetums. I hope Derek told you how pleased I was with the work you two did for me," she said.

"Oh, yeah, he did. And you were too generous with the pay envelope," Juan said.

Cathy pooh-poohed the thanks. "You guys deserved every penny. Wish it could have been more. So where is our buddy?" she said.

Juan stalled for a moment. "I guess he's been too busy to call with the good news. He got a job. No, not in a restaurant. A private home. It's a live-in position. Not sure whose house."

Cathy was excited. "Why didn't I think of him when Lance quit? What a dummy I am. If he checks in, tell him that we've got to do lunch. In the meantime, I'll check around. One of my friends is bound to know which house he's in. No secrets in Beverly Hills, you know."

Juan wanted to laugh at Cathy's assessment of the easily breached immunity from scandal to which the rich and famous thought they were invulnerable. But in a moment of desperation, and not knowing exactly what he was saying, he asked, "If Lance's position hasn't been filled, I would love to apply. You know that I'm a good worker. And I have plenty of experience."

The line was silent for a moment. Juan immediately wanted to take back his words, knowing that it was completely inappropriate to have made such a request to someone he had only met once. But desperate times called for desperate measures. He wanted nothing of the money that Derek had left and now his own funds were once again running in short supply. He was panicked. "I apologize," he said into the phone. "I didn't mean to put you in an awkward position."

"Hell, no, honey, not awkward at all," Cathy said cheerfully. "I was just thinking what my schedule was like today. Come on up to the house and we'll talk."

Juan breathed a deep sigh of relief as he said, "Yes, ma'am. When would you like to see me?"

"You know what they say, 'There's no time like the present.' My youth symphony board meeting was cancelled. I've got a few hours before my thingy with Andrew's USC alumni. Can you be here in, say, an hour?"

Juan was ecstatic and terrified at the same time. He remembered the address and said that indeed he would be there within an hour. The moment he hung up the telephone he called for a cab, brushed his teeth, changed into one of the white shirts that Derek had left, as well as a necktie. There was nothing he could do about the old jeans he wore, or the battered shoes. But he cleaned up as best he could.

In twenty minutes a white car with the insignia of Star Cabs, painted in silver on the side, arrived. The driver, who was new to L.A., had to be guided by Juan to the destination. Juan paid the fare and added a minimal tip, which he could ill afford. He stepped out of the cab and wondered if he should go around to the back of the house, as he did before, or go directly to the front door. He decided on the latter and climbed the steps to the Youngs' front entrance.

Juan rang the bell. Cathy opened the door. She smiled warmly and invited him in. The house seemed larger than Juan had remembered.

"I've made iced tea," Cathy said, leading Juan through the foyer down a long hall to the kitchen. The vast kitchen space had two center cooking islands, and a large round dining table in the breakfast nook. "Love your tie," Cathy said, trying to make him feel at ease, although it only made him realize how unkempt he was from the waist down. "Now, here's what your responsibilities are, and Andrew, Mr. Young, is sometimes particularly difficult to please. Just a warning. He's a doll, but he's got such a hideously stress-filled job and he often takes his frustrations and anxiety out on others."

For the next hour, Cathy spoke as if there was no question that Juan had the job. She gave him a tour of the house and its grounds, and was particularly pleased that he was able to communicate with the gardener and the pool man. "My Spanish sucks," she said. "Try as I do, I can't count past ten. You're a godsend!" She apologized that this was not a live-in position as Derek's new job was, but she added that there was a transportation allowance. "I noticed that you arrived by cab. Will you have any difficulty getting here every weekday morning by six?" she asked.

Juan didn't have time to consider just how he was supposed to get this far into Beverly Hills each day without a car, but he didn't let that stop him from insisting that he was never late for his job at Onyx.

"Then it's all set!" Cathy beamed. Then she frowned. "Please tell me that you can start in the next few days."

"I will be here at six o'clock tomorrow morning," Juan said. "And you will not regret hiring me."

"Oh, honey, I just hope you don't regret taking us on!" Cathy laughed and said that she would have their driver take Juan back to his apartment. The two exchanged a handshake and Juan practically skipped down the stairs to the waiting car.

As the Lincoln Town Car descended Tower Grove Drive and turned onto Benedict Canyon, Juan asked if Frank would mind dropping him off at the Beverly Center, instead of driving him all the way home.

Entering Macy's, Juan found the men's clothing department. He looked around for a few minutes before a sales clerk approached and offered assistance. "A new job," Juan announced. "I'm low on cash but I've got to have a pair of black slacks and black shoes."

The clerk looked Juan up and down in a manner that suggested that he was horny and would help the sexy Latino in any way that he could. He said, "This department is always having a sale. And I'm allowed to give special discounts if I say it's for myself or a close friend. So let's go shopping, shall we?"

Juan followed the clerk and together they selected two pairs of black slacks for the price of one. The shoes weren't Prada, but they were presentable.

"You'd look like a mill if you wore one of these!" the clerk gushed, holding up a deep blue Perry Ellis shirt.

Juan grimaced. "I'm down to my last hundred and twenty," he said. "I don't even know if I can afford the pants and the shoes."

The clerk look around, and then wiggled his finger for Juan to come closer for a private word. "If I make a suggestion, will you promise not to hit me or report me to management?" he asked, a little frightened.

"That depends," Juan said, his eyesbrows knitted in misapprehension and curiosity.

"Look, I'll let you have the slacks, shoes and half a dozen white dress shirts for a hundred bucks and . . ."

Juan suspected what was to follow but kept his mouth shut.

"I need a dick, now, and I can tell by the size of your feet that yours would be just right. What do you say, stud? Deal?"

Juan's dark eyes pierced through the clerk's blue ones. His poker face was frozen and indecipherable. After a long moment in which beads of perspiration formed on the clerk's forehead and he was almost ready to apologize for being so forward, Juan said, "Deal. Ring these up first."

The clerk, exhaling in relief, accepted Juan's one hundred dollars, and removed the electronic anti-shoplifting devices attached to each item of apparel. With his purchases bagged and in hand, the clerk said, "Go into the dressing room area. The door after the last stall. Wait for me."

Juan followed the line of sight where the clerk was pointing and began to walk toward the changing rooms. He entered the quiet back area and found the small utility room. Nervous about having sex in a semipublic place and concerned about security cameras that might be set up, he nevertheless unbuttoned and removed his shirt and laid it over a stack of boxes. In a moment, the door opened, and the young clerk stepped in.

The clerk's eyes grew wide with excitement when he saw Juan's brown flesh, and the carpet of thin black hair that laid sparsely over his well-defined chest and stomach. "Oh, God," was all the clerk could say.

"What about security cameras," Juan asked, concerned that there would be evidence of their meeting.

"None back here," the clerk panted as he placed his hands on Juan's chest and slowly explored the contours of his body. He leaned in for a deep kiss on Juan's full lips and to suck on his tongue. Then he bent down and unbuttoned the fly on Juan's 501s. He reached inside. When his hand encircled the thick warm sausage of Juan's sex he automatically inhaled in a burst of desire. "Shit, man," he said, and brought the meat to his face. He breathed deeply the scent of moist pubic bush and then opened his mouth and began nourishing himself on Juan's swollen piece. The clerk was ravenous. Juan was scared and wanted this to be over quickly. The more of Juan's penis that the clerk swallowed the closer Juan came to climaxing.

It was obvious to Juan that the clerk didn't have a gag reflex. As Juan's pelvic bone smashed against the guy's nose, the clerk kept motioning for Juan to slam harder.

Too quickly, Juan knew that he was about to explode. "Man," he whispered. "I'm coming. You want it?"

The clerk, his mouth stuffed too full to do anything but groan, nodded his head rapidly, desperate to taste Juan's load.

Trying his damndest to be quiet, Juan began hyperventilating. He didn't want to call attention to what was occurring in the back room, but he also couldn't control his fast approaching orgasm. And then he thrust and bucked deeper into the man's throat. The point of no return had been reached and whether the guy really wanted it or not, it was impossible for Juan to stop the explosion that was seconds away.

All that Juan was aware of was the sensation of his jizzum rising from his balls up through his cock and now . . . now . . . he grabbed a tuft of the clerk's hair and yanked the man's head as if he were fucking someone's asshole. His throat constricted and he made the sound of straining to lift a heavy load. And then his cock erupted. At the same time the clerk choked slightly, but continued to drain Juan dry.

In a short amount of time, Juan pulled his now sensitive piece out of the guy's mouth. Cum dripped down the corners of the clerk's lips. The guy's tongue darted out toward Juan's piece again and began lapping up the last drops of semen from its head. He wiped his mouth with the back of his hand and sat back on the floor, his own penis clearly outlined in his pants.

Juan picked up his shirt and slipped his arms into the sleeves. He buttoned up, but left the tails untucked. "You'll have to get yourself off," he said.

The clerk was dazed with satisfaction "You had a lot," he said. "Come back and see me again. You'll need more clothes."

Then Juan left him sitting on the floor. He walked out of the store with a new wardrobe, twenty bucks in his pocket, and the first sex he'd had since Derek left. It was also the first time in a while that he'd bartered his cock for anything material. It felt different than when he worked the freeway off-ramp bushes. This was empowering, and he suddenly had a new appreciation for what Derek was doing with his tool. No one was getting hurt, everybody benefited, so what had been his hang-up, he wondered as he walked home.

It was a long walk. His shoes, which he'd worn for the interview with Cathy, were not made for long treks among the hills and flats of Los Angeles. His feet were soon aching and blistered. At the pace in which Juan progressed, ever cautious of the traffic that whooshed by him, it took two hours before he reached the apartment. Finally in his unit he neatly placed his parcels on the bed. Juan stepped out of his shoes and clothes and walked to the bathroom. He turned on the shower and immersed himself in a hot, cleansing spray.

Refreshed, he towel-dried himself and padded back to the bed where he lovingly removed the garments from their bags. He carefully cut off labels with a fingernail clipper. He gingerly removed pins from the shirts, and hung the bright, white garments on hangers. In retrospect, considering all that he was able to get for little more than the price of a blow job, he thought that he should have included a new belt, black socks, and underwear.

Although it was still early in the evening, Juan calculated what time he would have to rise in order to walk to Beverly Hills in the morning. Although he had all of Derek's money hidden in among the CDs, he no longer had enough of his own to hire another cab. *I'm not complaining about having to walk,* he said to himself as he considered the journey. *By car, at that hour, we're talking twenty minutes. On foot . . . Christ, two hours at minimum. And I can't be late, so I'll plan on leaving at three.*

Juan retrieved a slice of leftover pizza from the refrigerator and made that his dinner. Then he set the alarm for two o'clock and climbed into bed. He was sure that he was giving himself more than enough time, but he was determined not to screw up his chance for success at the new job. It had been too long since he'd had a paycheck and he was not going to let Cathy—or himself—down.

Morning arrived too quickly. Then, dressed in his new slacks, shirt and a black bow tie that he found in one of Derek's drawers, he placed his new shoes in a white plastic grocery bag and set out in his old but comfortable Nikes.

The early morning was pitch-black and, being Los Angeles, it was frightening to walk the streets. From West Hollywood, he walked along

Fountain Avenue to Crescent Heights Boulevard, to Santa Monica Boulevard and into Beverly Hills. He reached Benedict Canyon, and from there it was still a long walk to Tower Grove. The eventual climb up the steep serpentine hill was arduous.

By the time he reached the Youngs' home, the morning sunlight had begun to filter through the trees. He was exhausted, and his day was just beginning. But at five thirty, it was too early to report for work. And so he sat down on the curb under a streetlight in the cool damp morning.

As a few coyotes roamed the street searching for pet cats, Juan's euphoria over landing a job turned to trepidation. Hungry and cold, loneliness began to wash over him. He thought of Derek and how, inadvertently, he had been responsible for getting him this new job. Then he thought of how much he missed Derek, and the sense of security Derek had brought to his life, even during the darkest days of their financial crisis.

The next time Juan looked at his wristwatch it was time to go to work. As instructed, Juan pushed four digits on the security keypad at the front gate and let himself in through the back area. Cathy had provided a key to the house and he easily accessed the kitchen door. He promptly pushed another security alarm pad to prevent the silent alarm from being activated and summoning the police and the Beverly Hills security patrol.

Slipping on his new black shoes, Juan placed his trainers into the plastic sack he had brought and found a nook for it in the laundry room. He then began preparing Starbucks coffee, exactly as Cathy had instructed that her husband wanted it made. Soon, he heard activity upstairs. Andrew Young, it had been reported to Juan, was up at five, and in his private gym by five-oh-five. He was showered and dressed by six forty-five. He arrived in the kitchen for his coffee at precisely six-fifty. The *Los Angeles Times* and the *New York Times* had to be folded and placed together with a rubber band around them, and ready for him to pick up as he dashed out of the house in time to make it to his office in Burbank by seven-thirty.

Juan was forewarned not to expect so much as a "good morning" acknowledgment from Andrew. The man expected his staff, at home and at the office, to do their jobs and not interrupt his thoughts with anything as trivial as social niceties. He did not care what anyone thought of him, and he certainly didn't care what anyone thought about anything that he didn't think was interesting or important.

As Juan busied himself pouring the freshly brewed coffee into an aluminum travel mug, and adding the prescribed shot of whisky, he was startled when a male voice offered, "Morning. You must be Juan."

Juan reeled around to find a handsome, tanned, well-groomed man in an expensive business suit, leaning against the Viking refrigerator. "Didn't mean to startle you, Juan." The man reached out his hand and offered a shake. "I'm Mr. Young. Andrew, that is. We're on a first name basis in this house."

"How do you do, sir," Juan replied, happily accepting Andrew's hand and returning his bright smile. "Your coffee is all ready, sir . . ."

"Andrew . . ."

"Andrew. Sir. And here are your papers. Is there anything else I can do for you this morning, sir? Andrew."

Andrew winked at Juan. "Just keep smiling and work out better than Lance and all the others before him."

"I'll certainly do my very best, s—Andrew."

"You're a quick study. I'm sure you'll be fine, Juan."

At that moment, Soccoro, the maid, opened the back door and entered the kitchen. "Good morning, Mr. Taylor," she said, wearily.

Andrew ignored her, held Juan's gaze for a fraction of a moment longer, then picked up his coffee mug and newspapers, and turned on his heels. He left the room as Soccoro began adding water to the tea kettle. "And good morning to you, too, asshole," she said under her breath.

Socorro looked at Juan and smiled. "You must be the new one," she said. "Mr. Young obviously approves. Want some friendly advice? Stay out of his way."

Juan introduced himself. "Why do you call him Mr. Young? Isn't there a house policy of speaking to each other by our first names?"

The maid laughed weakly. "I guess it's a matter of who is speaking to whom. The Mrs. is a blessed soul. Him? He's a piece of shit. Look, I don't know you, so I'm not saying anything more. It's none of my business that he treats some people one way, and a boy with a face like yours another way. You'll see. You're an adult. You can do what you have to do to take care of yourself." Soccoro threw her hands up to end the discussion.

TWENTY

Sex with Rand and Pat. It wasn't nearly as arduous for Derek as even the shortest shift at Onyx. Still, after the men departed Weybridge Cottage, Derek fell into a deep sleep in his private apartment. When he awoke late in the evening, Francois had already arrived at the house. He was sipping a Merlot and admiring the garden, when Derek finally introduced himself.

To be a sex symbol in America, one has to be gym pumped and flawlessly assembled. Francois Uberand exuded sexuality, but in a natural, confident way. He did not spend hours every day with a trainer, or limit his intake of carbs, although his body fat was eight percent. Slightly shorter than Derek, Francois was solid, beefy and rugged as a football quarterback.

Unsmiling but not unfriendly, Derek accepted Francois's hand in greeting. "*Parlez-vois Anglais?*" Derek asked.

"*Oui.* A little," Francois said modestly, then began speaking very broken but charming English. He tried to explain that he'd been studying with an American teacher, with the hope that he would be able to make the crossover to Hollywood films. "You are Brent's boyfriend?" Francois asked pointedly.

Derek smiled. "No," he said, trying to find the words to describe their association. "We have an *arrangement.*"

"*Oui.* An *arrangement.*" Francois nodded his head in understanding.

"Where did you and Brent meet?" Derek asked, trying to alter the conversation.

"I fell in love with Brent at the festival in Cannes. He won the *Palm*

D'or for *Shirtless.* He was more beautiful than Hugh Jackman. And so my agent she introduce us. We had ferocious sex."

"You and Brent, or you and your agent?" Derek mocked the Frenchman.

"Oui," Francois said, not quite understanding the question. "You have nasty sex with Brent?" he asked. "I thought we would fuck again. I am now in his American house and he is away."

"Brent is very sorry that he could not be here to fuck you," Derek said and thought, *If that's the gutter language Francois speaks, then I will too.* "Brent has asked me to take his place. If you don't mind," he said.

Francois smiled for the first time. *"Oui.* Francois is very much glad if you fuck him."

Derek took Francois's glass of Merlot from his hand and raised it to his own lips. He knocked back the red wine. Colliding with his empty stomach, the alcohol made an immediate impact on him. He set the glass down and as he straightened up, he slowly peeled off his tank top in an erotic show. Bare chested, Derek moved in closer to Francois. "I saw your movie *Cri de la Conscience* on DVD this afternoon. Shall I fuck you the way you fucked Latanya Veber?"

Francois removed his own T-shirt and enveloped Derek in his arms. Their lips quickly met and each opened his mouth eager for the other's tongue. Francois's masculine body made Derek more aroused. He loved the smell of a man's perspiration, and Francois had not showered after his long flight from Paris. Derek devoured the Frenchman's rank odor. His tongue lapped at the stud's stomach, sternum, chest and underarm pits. "Come on," he finally said, leading Francois back into the house. As they walked through the kitchen, Derek paused for a moment to retrieve the wine bottle and two glasses. He moved swiftly through the house and up the grand staircase to one of the guest bedroom suites. The wineglasses were unnecessary. When they arrived in the enormous bedchamber, each chugged from the bottle.

Derek was the first to peel off his pants. He stood posing for a moment as Francois absorbed the sight of the horse-hung American.

Francois unfastened the rubber band that gathered his hair together and shook his mane loose until it cascaded over his wide rounded shoulders. He then unbuttoned his own jeans and let them slip to the floor. He stood for a moment affecting a confident pose, as if to boast, *We French have reason to be proud, too.*

Derek ardently gazed upon Francois's dark hairy torso. He admired the Frenchman's pecs and biceps and the obvious attention he paid to maintaining a stomach, which was flat and exhibited his rippling abdominal muscles. Derek appraised Francois's cock and decided it was equal in proportion to his own.

Derek took another swig of wine and stood close to his guest. He held out the bottle and Francois accepted it. He took a long swig. He took a quick glance around the room and reaching out, he set the bottle on the top of the nightstand beside the bed.

The men stared into each other's eyes for a long moment before tentatively leaning in for a kiss. At the moment of lip contact, both men ravenously opened their mouths to devour the other's tongue. They inhaled deeply and were suddenly enveloped in unbridled passion to conquer the other. In a moment they were on the bed, firmly entwined in each other's arms and legs, while their tongues, hands and fingers explored every fiber of hair and contour of skin.

They automatically reached for each other's fully erect cocks. Francois's was long, thick and uncut, which mesmerized Derek. He held it firmly in his hand, feeling the velvety moisture of pre-cum. Francois's balls, too, were large. His sack swung like a pendulum.

Derek's upper body strength enabled him to overpower Francois, who feigned opposition. With the Frenchman pinned down on the bed, Derek forced his own face into the dark hairy pits of his underarms and cleaned out each one with his tongue. The scent was intoxicating and drove Derek to the brink of orgasm. He vacillated between burying his face in the two hair-filled caves and feasting upon Francois's chest and nipples.

At the same time, the men were grinding their pelvises into the other's and their dicks were rigid against the other.

Suddenly, Francois drew more strength than Derek expected, and flipped his assailant over and onto his stomach. As the Frenchman straddled the length of Derek's body, his hands ventured everywhere. He simultaneously dragged his tongue from the small of Derek's back, up his spine to his shoulder blades and neck.

Derek clutched a pillow and stuffed a corner of it into his mouth to mute his cries of ecstasy. But when Francois began gnawing on his butt cheeks and then forced his face into the sensitive crack between his buns, Derek could no longer maintain control of his voice and sounds. His body was responding in a way it seldom had before.

The Frenchman's long hair dragged over Derek's back tickling and stimulating him as if a million tiny insects with millions more microscopic feet were scattering over his body. In sublime tormented agitation, Derek reached down behind him to find the Frenchman's head. If the man did not soon stop his pig-like rutting into the depth of Derek's ass, Derek knew he would lose all sexual control and too-swiftly climax. He wanted this ordeal to go on for hours. He grabbed a handful of Francois's hair and yanked it.

Sensing his partner's pleasure, Francois forced Derek to roll over onto his back. He splayed his body over the American's before straddling his chest and bringing his cock to Derek's face.

Still reeling from his body awakening, Derek cupped Francois's ass and leaned his face forward to accept the thick flange. His tongue felt every swollen vein buried just below the surface of the hot and musky scented member. Derek's mouth greedily consumed as much of Francois as was humanly possible.

Francois positioned himself to bury his dick deep down into Derek's throat and he forced himself in and out of the hungry mouth.

Derek continued to cup Francois's ass in both hands to keep the man's dick aligned with the awkward position of Derek's face.

Finally, Francois extricated himself from Derek's mouth and quickly went down to his partner's cock. There he suckled for a short time before turning himself over on his back and begging, "Fuck me!"

Derek, crazed with desire, reached over to the bed stand and opened the top drawer. He withdrew a stash of condoms, a tube of lube, and a bottle of poppers. He quickly donned the condom, lubed Francois's ass and offered him the bottle of amyl, which was greedily accepted.

As Derek grabbed Francois's calves and dragged his body closer, the French movie star splayed his hands over Derek's chest and looked up longingly at his new American friend. "Fuck me," he groaned.

At two in the morning, after each had climaxed twice, Derek and Francois were both ravenous for food. Redressed in only their jeans, they padded down the staircase to the kitchen in search of something to eat.

Everett had left a note with instructions that there were two plates of lasagna in the refrigerator. As Derek took out the food and prepared to place their dinners in the microwave, Francois found another bottle of wine and a corkscrew. "French," he said, looking at the label and smiling. "I thought Americans no longer drank French wine. You re-named it something like Bush Boujolais, or Cheney Chardonnay. Ironic since that Bush maniac was alcoholic. Yes?"

Derek smiled. He liked Francois's sense of humor. More than that, he liked the way they had had intense sex. The Frenchman was sexy, and sensitive, and surprisingly needy. He was a passionate and un-selfish lover. "You're incredibly desirable, Francois," Derek said as he accepted a glass of wine from his guest. "You acted as though you hadn't had sex in a year!"

Francois took a drink from his wineglass. "The last time I had sex was more than a month ago! Fans think that I have sex three times a day. That's what they say in the magazines. In truth, I masturbate three times a day. If I'm out, I go to a nearby bathroom. I flush it down the toilet and I'm over. I make semen come out of me and I'm satisfied. It feels good. For a little while, at least. Soon I have to do it again. But I can't get fucked unless it is arranged. To be a star means that you can-not have a fuck. They don't teach that in star school." He laughed.

The microwave timer dinged, and Derek carefully removed the plates. He placed them on the kitchen's center island countertop and indicated for Francois to take a seat in one of the high bar chairs. "Until I met Brent, I thought that stars were sex magnets," Derek said. "But it's not true. That's why I'm here. I never thought I'd make a living doing this kind of work, but so far it seems to be working out."

Francois looked perplexed. "Who else do you screw?"

"Besides Brent? Well, a couple of his friends stopped by today. I've been very lucky. Brent is very handsome. And you are *tres extraordi-naire!*"

Francois smiled. "I need someone like you to travel with me," he said. "My friends need this too. We are too famous to pick up boys on the set. They are there and ready, but it would be career death to fuck with the movie publicist, or one of the grips."

The men began devouring their lasagna and pouring more wine. Derek, heady from the great sex, and slightly inebriated from the wine said, "Lately I've been thinking." He paused.

Francois listened as he continued to cut his food with his fork and to shovel his mouth full of pasta.

"There seems to be a need for someone to help poor, disenfran-chised celebrities to have more sex, don't you think?"

Francois nodded in complete agreement. "*Oui!* Yes! Heidi Fleiss! *Oui!*"

"No!" Derek countered. "Well, yes, in a way. I mean, there should be a service, completely secret of course, where gay movie stars—and name one who isn't at least bi—could have their sex needs taken care of."

"*Oui!* But I think you are naïve, my friend. There *are* such places for us to go. There are men who have contacts with other men for a very large price."

Derek chuckled. "I thought I was inventing something original. I should have known," Derek said. "So why don't you avail yourself of those places? And Brent too? Are they too expensive?"

"Sex is of course expensive. But not too, if you are rich and famous. You are *very* expensive. Mind you, I have never done what I am telling you, but my friend, who is nameless, said that the man in Beverly Hills who owns many boys is demonic. He attracts super-beautiful boys who are in skin movies, to service celebrities and movie executives. But there are many things wrong with the service."

Derek was intrigued. "What's wrong? Drugs? Police?"

"*Oui,* drugs. No police. Police are paid not to know about these things," Francois said, picking up his plate and taking it to the sink where he began rinsing off the tomato sauce. "My friend tells me that the man who has many boys for sale is a slime bucket—if that is the phrase. He was once a porn star himself. He is dangerous too. And he has been known to blackmail clients to keep them using his service. We want a friendly man. Like you. My friend thinks this, and I do too."

Derek smiled. "It's easy to be friendly to a friendly, sexy guy like you. So why does this person stay in business if he's not well regarded?"

"Many reasons," Francois continued. "For one, he is at least discreet. Nobody in the press has ever heard his name, or if they have, they got paid to stay mute. I only know that he and his boys exist because more than one man I know has been fucked by one of his helpers. Also," he continued, "some stars have no choice because this man has threatened to expose the star if he goes to solicit from someone else. It is like *The Sopranos.* Or a narcotic. Once you are addicted to this man's sex boys, you cannot go anyplace else. No, it is better to have word-of-mouth boys like you, I think."

Derek realized that it made perfect sense that there would be such a thing as a male madam in Hollywood. Although he had only known Brent and Rand and Pat and now Francois for a very brief time, there was an obvious need for healthy, honest, virile, and well-hung guys to serve as sex partners for those who could not so much as go to a grocery store without being noticed, let alone a gay bar, or to an online escort service for sex. He chuckled softly.

"It is a funny," Francois agreed with what he thought Derek was thinking. "The people think we have everything because we are on the movie and TV screens. We do have very much. But a reliable and safe fuck buddy is hard to find."

Derek slowly shook his head at the irony. "Maybe I should offer a service," he said. "I could start my own business. Brent could refer his horny friends to me." He laughed a little louder this time.

"But isn't that exactly what you do for him already?" Francois said, smiling.

Derek stopped laughing. He looked hard at Francois as his thoughts clicked by at about five hundred frames per second. "I guess," he said in a distant tone. "But not really." *Yes, really,* he thought. "I didn't consider it that way before. I'm fucking Brent . . . and you . . . and sort of Rand and Pat. But that's all. I think. For now at least. But, no, it's not the same thing because in my scenario, I have a stable of boys to farm out."

Francois made a quiet laugh. "Perhaps you are a one-horse stable. No?" He suddenly had the look of lust in his eyes as the wine went to his head, and the sight of Derek, shirtless and buff, went to his dick. "Come," he said, cocking his head toward the hallway. "I will pay you again. I will pay you with my dick stuffed up your ass. *Oui?*"

Derek had lost interest in sex with Francois. At least for the moment. However, he was already counting the money. And so, he pretended to be equally horny. He let the Frenchman lean in and kiss him, and then led him upstairs to the bedroom. It was nearly four in the morning, and they fucked until six. And then passed out.

TWENTY-ONE

The moment that Cathy Young discovered that Juan was walking the entire distance between West Hollywood and her home in Beverly Hills, she called her business manager and leased a Honda. "I admire your energy, Juan," she declared. "And God knows it keeps you fit, even Andrew has noticed. But you are totally insane!" When she handed him the car keys, Juan started to cry.

"Heck, when I got a car for Socorro, she cried too—because she wanted a BMW!" Cathy said.

Juan laughed through his tears. "I apologize," he said, sniffling. "It's just that I've never been treated so well. I can never thank you enough."

At that moment, Andrew Young walked into the kitchen and laid his briefcase on the center island counter. "Heya, Juan," he said before saying hello to his wife and giving her a peck to her cheek. "Your eyes are all red. Been smoking dope?" He laughed at his joke.

"No, sir," Juan said in complete earnestness.

"Andrew!" Cathy chided, knowing that her husband's attempt at levity was making Juan uncomfortable.

"I'm just happy to be in this house," Juan said.

"And we're happy that you're here too," Andrew said, taking in the view of Juan's dark skin showing through his white dress shirt. "So, I guess it's quittin' time. See you first thing in the A.M."

Juan thanked his employers and left the house through the back door. As he closed the side gate behind him, Juan saw his new car parked on the street, and ran to the driver's side. He opened the door, placed his shoe bag on the passenger seat and inhaled the scent of new car. He had never felt so rich, or so happy. During the drive home he thought only of how blessed he was, not just to be working again, but to have found the ideal people for whom to work. For the first time since starting the job at the Youngs, it would only take him thirty minutes to get home. His euphoria made him horny, and he decided to return to Macy's for another shopping spree and a blow job.

Juan parked his car on Fountain Avenue and happily walked into the garden courtyard of his apartment building. As he reached the door to his unit, he heard the telephone ringing. Quickly, he unlocked the door and rushed inside. The answering machine had already engaged, and when the sound of Derek's voice came over the speaker, Juan grabbed for the phone.

"Hang! One sec!" he begged. Juan turned off the answering machine and switched on a lamp. He flopped onto the bed and asked, "Boss?"

"Oh, man!" Derek said. "I am so sorry! I've been way too busy and haven't called. Brent's away, and we've got a houseguest, but how about coming up Friday night. He'll be gone by then. It'll just be the two of us. There's so much to tell you. This job is really kind of amazing. Nothing like what I thought it would be. And I'm raking in some serious coin."

Juan was perturbed that Derek had not asked how his own job hunt was progressing.

Instead, Derek boasted about his own financial gain, but didn't bother to inquire about whether or not Juan was even able to buy food.

"Sure," Juan finally said, coldly. "I'm available after eight o'clock on Friday."

"Available!" Derek chided. "You sound as though you have a schedule to keep or something." And then it clicked. "Oh, man, you've got a job? I'm such an idiot for not asking. Oh, God, I've become a self-absorbed asshole. I am so sorry!"

Juan smiled, immediately forgiving his friend. "You're right, we've got so much to talk about. I've got the best job, but I want to save the particulars until I see you. So, Friday night. Awesome, Boss. Just give me the address."

When Juan hung up the telephone, he noticed the answering machine had one message. "Is that ad still floating around out there?" he said to the otherwise quiet room as he pushed play and headed toward the bathroom and simultaneously unbuttoned his dress shirt. A familiar voice stopped him as he reached the toilet. "Heya, Juan." It was a man's voice. "You get sexier every day." *Click, buzz.* The answering machine cut off.

Juan shook his head in puzzlement and lifted the lid to the commode. He removed his shirt, unzipped his fly, and pulled out his cock. He released a strong, steady stream into the water. By the time he completed his duty, he had forgotten about the caller.

Juan slept straight through until four-thirty the next morning. He rose from bed, brushed his teeth, shaved his face, showered and dressed in his black slacks and a fresh white shirt, that he had picked up as part of his trade at Macy's. He was in his car by five-fifteen, and at the Youngs before six o'clock. There, he immediately prepared the coffee and laid out the newspapers.

At precisely six twenty-five, Andrew appeared in the kitchen. Both men smiled at one another

"Good morning, Andrew," Juan said, genuinely happy to see his employer. "Hope you slept well."

"I dreamed a lot," Andrew replied. "But good dreams. Men's dreams, if you get my drift."

Juan chuckled. "Those are always the best, aren't they?" He knew that most men could tell that he was gay, so he didn't feel the need to suddenly act like a macho stud and make some lewd reference to sex with women. He left the subject alone, hoping that Andrew would not pursue it further.

But Andrew tarried a moment longer than usual. "A stud like you must have those dreams all the time," he said, picking up his travel coffee mug with a shot of whisky in the mix, and the newspapers.

Juan simply smiled and nodded his head in a manner that suggested it was true. "Very natural," he said as he busied himself, hoping that Andrew would leave for the office, and wondering why Socorro was late.

"Natural," Andrew repeated, with a grin, staring Juan down. At that moment, Socorro finally came in. And in the same moment, Andrew departed.

"Fucking traffic!" Socorro said. "I would have warned Mr. Young not to take Coldwater Canyon, but the asshole pretends I don't exist. Ach! Let him idle in his fancy Rolls for an hour. That's about how far it's backed up. I pity the other drivers being on the same street with his road rage. Ha!" She laughed.

Although Juan had only known the maid for a week, he wondered how, with her negative attitude about practically every aspect of working at the Youngs, she managed to keep her job. He realized that Cathy would never terminate Socorro, even though there were times when it appeared that even Cathy Taylor's infinite patience wore thin around Socorro. "Do you think maybe it's your attitude that makes Andrew seem distant to you?" Juan said. "He treats me really well."

Socorro laughed again. "That's 'cause you've got something he wants," she said.

"And, I'd do anything for Mr. and Mrs. Young," Juan said in all earnestness.

"You may have to," Socorro said, under her breath.

"I'm not a moron," Juan said. "I know what he wants. And although it's none of your business, I know what hunger and unemployment is like too, and I'll be God damned if I'll ever let that happen to me again. I was out of work for a couple of months. I know how hard it is to find anything decent. I'm not afraid of the Andrew Youngs of the world. If I have to fuck the man's gringo ass to keep this job—" He stopped midthought. "I've got a ton to do today to prep for Cathy's Democratic fund-raising tea. So, if you'll excuse me." Juan wandered out of the kitchen to begin his household chores.

Friday arrived. Juan gratefully accepted his weekly paycheck, and looked forward to seeing Derek. He drove to the apartment, changed into his sexiest outfit of jeans and T-shirt and returned to the car with directions to the estate.

Beverly Hills was becoming more familiar to Juan and soon he was beside the call box outside the gates of Weybridge Cottage. Juan pushed the intercom button and Everett answered. He provided instructions for parking on the grounds. As Juan guided his car through the entrance and took in the sight of the two-story stone edifice of the Richardson mansion, Juan whispered, "Holy shit! And I thought the Youngs had money." He parked in the courtyard, next to the police car.

Derek opened the front door and waited outside under the vaulted front portico as Juan stepped out of his Honda. Derek's smile was warm and genuine. The two men embraced in a tight hug, and both exclaimed how well the other looked. "We've got a private gym!" Derek explained his appearance.

"I eat like a pig." Juan demonstrated by patting his stomach.

The men walked into the mansion and Juan tried not to give away his wonder at how anyone could live in such a lavish environment, while others, such as he, were sentenced to an overpriced one-room apartment.

Derek was delighted to play the role of the docent of the manse. "Allow me to introduce Everett," he said, acknowledging the butler who entered the room bearing a tray on which two flutes of champagne rested. Derek was comfortable in the character he presented, which was that of a man of leisure. "The tour tram is leaving the platform," he said, leading the way and pointing out various bibelots. Although none of the antiques and curios were his, he was content to act as if he was born to live among such extravagance.

Finally seated outside under heat lamps at the patio table by the pool, the two men faced each other and smiled contentedly. "So much has gone down in the past month." Derek beamed. "I never thought that I'd be living like this."

"Hell, you never thought you'd be hawking your *ass* to live like this," Juan joked.

Derek nodded his head, acknowledging that life had certainly turned out different than he planned. "One does what one has to do." He needed Juan to agree that his form of employment was acceptable. "Now, tell me about your job!" Derek said, raising his champagne flute to toast Juan's employment.

"You're not going to believe where I'm working," he began. "Cathy Young hired me. She liked the way I helped out at that cocktail crush and offered me a job." Juan didn't let on that he'd actually begged for the position. "She even leased a car for me."

Derek was stunned but happy for Juan. "She's the best!" He beamed. "But what's Andrew like to work for? I've heard horror stories."

Juan smiled. "I can handle his type. It's funny, the dude thinks he's being discreet when he hangs around me sniffing my ass like a dog in heat. He's obvious to everyone. I know that he'd like nothing better than to have me shove my nine inches of thick Latino tube steak down his throat. But I'm playing dumb. When the time comes, I'll fuck his skinny executive ass. But it's really awkward, because I don't want to hurt Cathy."

"Cathy's nobody's fool, my friend," Derek said. "It's not that she isn't every molecule the kind and gentle woman that everybody sees and adores. She's definitely all that. But not one thing slips unnoticed by that woman. I've worked enough parties in her home. I've socialized with her. I've seen how she is both the enchanted and the enchantress. She has ESP, or something mystical, and can tell you things about yourself that you didn't even know were true. Not to worry about her. Just always be honest, and she won't hold anything else against you."

Juan nodded his head. "Tell me about you, dude! Are they treating you okay? What's it like to fuck a movie star? Where is the old man anyway?"

For the next hour, Derek gave an overview of his new life, and the duties he performed as Brent's surrogate lover. "He's sexy as all hell, but I'm not keen on having to screw his friends, too."

"Are you like the community concubine?" Juan asked. "I hope you're getting combat pay for this."

"As a matter of fact, I'm making good money. And saving every penny. I'm doing this responsibly. When I'm through here, I won't have to work for a very long time."

Juan was concerned. "Boss, it sounds like you're one of those white slavery girls who have to save up to buy their freedom. Why do you have to service more than your master?"

"It's Tom's idea," Derek said. "When Brent's in town I only fuck him. I fuck his friends when he's away. It's not as disgusting as I once thought it would be. Most of his friends are well maintained. And their tips are generous. I can't afford not to do this. You remember what it was like those few months after Onyx closed. I vowed I would never, ever, be in that position again. Get me"—he smiled—"I sound like Scarlett O'Hara, for Christ's sake. But she knew what it was like to be hungry and broke. My only problem is that I'm getting way too busy. I used to be able to fuck more than twice a day, but now I'm exhausted."

"They can't force you to have sex, can they?"

"Nobody's forcing me to do anything," Derek said. "But I don't want to jeopardize this gig in any way."

"Do you realize how easily you could be replaced?" Juan suggested.

"There are a about a million other guys out there, some better-

looking than me," Derek agreed. "And if I won't do the job, they would
be more than happy to fill my pants. But I'm not going to give them
the opportunity."

"Sure, there may be a million other studs out there, but none of
them have what you have to sell," Juan said.

"It's only eight-and-a-half inches!" Derek joked.

"Seriously," Juan continued. "It's your uniqueness that got you the
job. Realize your value. You don't have to fuck everybody in Brent's address book. You're right about one thing. There are a million other
studs waiting in the wings. So why don't you outsource to a couple of
them."

Juan was joking, but it was the second time the idea had been presented to Derek. Francois had flippantly made that suggestion, and
now Juan was saying the same thing, if only for a laugh.

And Derek did laugh. "Yeah, I could open my own escort agency.
I'd call it, let's see, 'Shooting Stars.' " He laughed, drawing an arc in the
air above them as the fictitious and whimsical name occurred to him.
" 'Heavenly bodies,' " he added a tag line, as if he were advertising on
NPR. "I've actually been thinking about just such a business," he said,
with an earnest tone. "The more I get to know these guys who come
around for a fuck, the more they let down their hair, so to speak, and
tell me their fantasies. I can't fulfill them all. Plus, they're bound to become bored with me after a while. I have to diversify.

"One guy, a film composer, has a black fireman fantasy," he continued. "Another, the head of production over at General Entertainment,
has always wanted to be fucked by a gangbanger. Know any? And this
other dude . . . He won the Oscar for best costume design a few years
ago. His fantasy is to shower at the L.A. Men's Correctional Facility."

Derek stopped for a moment, stood up and walked over to the
Japanese bridge that arched over a koi pond. Fixing his gaze out across
the garden, he said, "There are so many men out there. They all want
sex. And a lot of them, I've learned, will pay a fortune to get what they
can't get at home."

Juan joined Derek on the bridge. "As a matter of fact, I do know a
couple of guys who at least look like gangbangers when they're
decked out in their street drag," Juan said. "But they're not dangerous.
Shaved heads. Tattoos and body piercing. Every gringo's worst dark
alley nightmare." He chuckled.

Derek turned to Juan. "That's exactly who I would want to introduce to this guy. He's a nice man, really. He couldn't handle anything that was legitimately rough. He wants fantasy, not reality. I would never get anybody involved in a situation that was really risky."

Juan shook his head. "What are you talking about, Boss? This is ridiculous. You're not a panderer."

Derek smiled. "Not yet. But think about it. I'm already connected with a big star. His friends trust me. I only do this when Brent's out of town. Who needs to know? Not Tom. Not Brent."

"His friends might tell. They'll find out eventually," Juan said.

Derek nodded. "It's ridiculous," he agreed. "And it could blow up and get Brent in deep trouble. Not to mention a jail sentence for me. I'd have to find incredibly discreet boys, preferably ones who don't go to the movies or watch television and would therefore not recognize the clients."

"The guys you fuck are of an age who wouldn't register on the radar screens of anybody under forty," Juan said. "Unless they're addicted to TV Land on cable," he added. "Just admit that you've sold your ass to the devil and now he's collecting his prize. You're a fucking slave whether you like it or not."

"Oh, I rather like it, all right." Derek laughed as the men turned to once again enjoy the garden.

As is usual in Los Angeles, regardless of the daytime temperatures, the night air became chilled. The brown skin on Juan's thick arms became cold, and he decided that it was time to return to West Hollywood. "Cathy and Andrew are having a thing tomorrow afternoon so I have to be at work early," he said. He opened his arms to take Derek in for a parting hug. They embraced for a long moment, each of them feeling the other's pants become tight with their cocks responding to the touch.

"I miss having sex with you," Derek whispered into Juan's ear.

"It was only a couple of times," Juan said. "And at least you get sex now. The only thing I have to look forward to is my hand." He omitted the fact that he had started exchanging his dick for Hugo Boss at Macy's.

"There's always Andrew Young," Derek teased. "What are you going to do when he makes his move?"

Juan shook his head. "He's getting closer every day. He's not hard to look at. And God knows, I've had to fuck worse scum than him."

Juan stepped off the bridge and Derek followed him. Together, the men walked across the backyard grass and around the side of the Olympic size swimming pool. "This is really an awesome job you've found," Juan said, admiring the way the blue light of the pool shimmered in the night. "The Youngs have a fantastic house. But this is a freakin' museum. Don't fuck it up by doing something you'll regret."

Derek picked up his champagne flute as he passed the patio table. "Trust me, I'm a big boy. I'll be here as long as I want to be here. Brent begs for my cock. He wouldn't give it up."

"And what's he do for sex while he's away," Juan asked, cattily. "Five finger exercise?"

"I suppose," Derek answered. "He says he can't have sex when he's on the road because it's too dangerous. If he were to sleep with the wrong guy he could end up as the headline story on *Access Hollywood*."

Juan gave him a dubious look. "You may be a big boy in the inseam, Boss, but don't be fooled by any man who says that he doesn't have sex."

With that idea hanging in the air, Juan walked through the house and out the front door. He slipped behind the wheel of his car and started the engine. As he backed out of his spot and slowly rolled toward the front gate, he tooted his horn and made his way off the estate.

Derek ambled back inside the mansion. He closed the door and set the security alarm. It was only ten P.M. and the place seemed overwhelming in its enormity of size and silence. Everett and Emma were long ago in their quarters and Derek decided he'd hit the sack too. He picked out some porn from the DVD collection and brought it to his bedroom in the tower. He pushed the remote for the drawer to the DVD player to slide open. He dropped the disc into the tray, slipped out of his T-shirt, and flopped down on his king-size bed. He was still hard from holding Juan and he reached into his pants to grope himself. Just as he grabbed hold of his python, his private telephone rang.

"No!" he said as he looked at the Caller ID box and his wristwatch. He could tell that it was Brent's publicist Gavin Sorrento. For the fraction of an instant that it takes to think that maybe a publicist calling so late at night might be important, he decided to pick up. "Hello?" he asked, and almost instantly wished that he had let the call go to voice mail. He listened for a moment. "I'm really tired, Gavin," he said. "I know it's a lot of money, but God, the time, it's . . . Yeah, he comes back late tomorrow. Yeah, I know, three weeks before he leaves again for London. Can you make it fast? Yeah, use your key and just hit the alarm pad. Okay. In a few."

Derek hung up the telephone and rolled his eyes. He went into the bathroom and gargled with mouthwash. "Juan thinks I'm having such a terrific time fucking everyone. What a load," he said with a deep sigh. "Farming out some of this work is beginning to sound like a great idea."

Per Gavin's specific instructions about how to present himself, Derek took off the rest of his clothes, turned the lights down to a soft glow, pulled down the bed comforter and top sheet, and laid spread-eagle on his stomach on the mattress. He closed his eyes, and soon he began to feel himself drifting off to sleep. However, before he had become completely unconscious and as the first dream sequence was about to be unreeled, he heard a stirring in the room, followed by the sensation of two hands that began to tenderly caress his ass. Derek slowly rolled over and looked into the sex-hungry eyes of Gavin Sorrento.

Without a smile or even a word of greeting, Gavin unbuttoned and removed his shirt, which revealed his smooth, middle-aged body. He unzipped his jeans. And as Derek watched, his sleepiness disappeared, and his cock swelled with anticipation. As often as Derek was having sex these days, it didn't take much for him to want more. The mere sight of a man's waxed or hair-covered chest or muscled and veined biceps made him instantly hard. Even shower scenes in shampoo commercials aroused him.

As Gavin eased himself onto the bed, he sighed with satisfaction when his bare skin touched Derek's. He tenderly caressed Derek's sculpted torso and reached down to hold his mammoth equipment before hastening down to draw the apparatus into his mouth. His tongue washed Derek's ball sack and then made the long ascent from the base of the tube up to its tender head. When he'd satisfied himself for the moment, Gavin seamlessly dragged his tongue up over Derek's stomach, sternum, chest, and throat, before laying his full body over the man who he saw as nothing more than a possession, something to be bought and used. They fused their lips in a bruising assault. Together they buried their tongues in the other's hot mouths before Gavin whispered, "Fuck me."

Christ, is every man in Hollywood a bottom? Derek asked himself, thinking that he would occasionally like having a another man's cock buried up his own ass. He reached into the bed stand drawer for his usual stash of condoms and lube.

In the meantime, Gavin adjusted himself on his back and dragged one hand over Derek's strong arm, while he simultaneously stroked his own dick.

In a moment, Derek was slowly easing himself into Brent's publicist's ass. *Imagine the* Daily Variety *headlines,* he said to himself. *Flack Fucked by Diesel Dick.*

Gavin perspired profusely, and writhed in ecstatic agony until Derek had buried himself as deeply as possible and began, slowly and rhythmically, to bring himself and Gavin to climax. It didn't take long for Gavin, who with one hand twisted Derek's nipples and with the other stroked himself into a frenzy. In time he ejaculated a load of thick, white cum, which landed only as far as his navel and oozed out more than it actually detonated.

It took Derek a little longer, but when he finally knew that he couldn't hang on a moment more, he retracted his dick from Gavin's ass, ripped off his condom and tossed it toward the floor as he cried out in tortured relief. He aimed his tool straight at a small patch of hair in the cleft between Gavin's pecs on his otherwise smooth chest. His load was copious, thick, and warm, and hit its target like a blast marking from a paintball gun.

Derek collapsed beside Gavin as both men relaxed and regained their composure.

Gavin wiped his own semen from his stomach and then dragged his hand over his chest to mix and blend his and Derek's fluids together.

Now, Derek was truly tired and wanted Gavin to leave. "Think I'll hit the shower," he said, getting out of bed, hoping to coax the publicist to depart.

"I'm the one with all the mess to wash off." Gavin chuckled. "I'll join you."

Fuck, Derek griped to himself as he padded into the adjoining bathroom with its institution-size shower. Gavin slipped out of bed and fell into lock step behind Derek who walked into the sunken, doorless shower. *I'll soap him up and he'll be out of here,* Derek said to himself as he set the temperature dial and turned on the multiple showerheads. "Let's get you clean," Derek said, encouraging Gavin to take care of business.

Both men stood under multiple showerheads and were gently bombarded on three sides by adjustable jets of soothing warm water pouring from the walls. A liquid soap and shampoo dispenser was affixed to the marble wall and Derek pressed the button for a strawberry-scented gel which he lathered over Gavin's body from his neck to his dick. As his hands glided over his shower mate's chest and stomach, Derek felt himself getting hard again and silently cursed his automatic reflex.

Gavin's boner had never abated and he leaned in to initiate a kiss from Derek. The moment their tongues met, both men became fully aroused again and it was a fait accompli that they would have to have sex in the shower. As they groped each other's wet bodies, each man took his turn at kneeling onto the hard tile to suck on the other's freshly washed dick.

Among the furnishings in the shower, which included a wall-mounted stereo unit, potted ferns hanging from the ceiling, and a Venetian statue of a male nude, was a long wooden redwood bench of the variety used in steam rooms. Gavin dragged it under the overhead showerheads. He guided Derek onto the hard slats and coaxed him onto his back. He splayed his own body over the stud as he continued kissing him deeply and as ardently as when he had first arrived at the bedroom.

Derek, too, was into the scene. He imagined himself making love under a tropical island waterfall. Gavin, he thought, was inventive, and now Derek was happy that he hadn't insisted that the publicity guru rush off immediately after their first orgasm.

"If you fuck me here, bareback, I'll double your price," Gavin said, practically hyperventilating with desire.

"That's not a good idea," Derek moaned between harsh kisses. "I fucked you once already. Let's just jerk off."

"Oh, God, fuck me!" Gavin begged.

Derek's hard-on was starting to deflate. He was being asked to do something that was against his principles, but the money was extraordinary. He wrestled with the dilemma. Although Gavin looked healthy, and Derek knew that he himself was HIV negative, he still didn't want to take the chance. "I said no," Derek affirmed and pushed Gavin away from him.

The sexual excitement was over. It had been washed down the drain. Both men sat on the bench for a moment before Derek rose and stepped up into the main part of the bathroom. He grabbed a large plush towel, then intentionally switched off the water to make Gavin either sit there and freeze, or dry off and leave.

Derek walked out of the room and back to where he had left his clothes on the chair by the bed. He stuffed himself into his jeans and padded barefoot and bare-chested through the hallway and down the grand staircase and into the kitchen.

From a cabinet that hung above the center island counter Derek withdrew a wineglass. He found a bottle of Merlot that Francois had not finished and emptied the contents into his glass. Derek took one long swallow, set the glass down and hunted in the refrigerator for the cellophane-wrapped platter of cheese, which Everett always had on hand. He found what he was after and set the cold plate on the granite countertop. As he removed the cling film, Gavin walked into the kitchen.

"You were right, man," Gavin said. "The logical part of my brain completely shuts down when my body says it has to be fucked. And then after a fuck, I realize it wasn't worth the risk."

Derek sliced a wedge of brie and fed it into Gavin's smiling mouth.

"Thanks, man," Gavin said. Not for the brie, but for Derek's common sense. He began to walk away but then stopped. "I left cash on the bathroom vanity," he said. "And, um, when Brent goes to London next month, I'd like to see you again."

TWENTY-TWO

Derek's reunion with Brent was a celebration. Brent was no sooner inside the mansion's foyer when he wrapped an eagerly waiting Derek in his arms and whispered, "Can we go to bed?" Without another word, the men raced each other up the grand staircase, practically tripping over themselves to reach the bed as quickly as possible.

They wasted no time with formalities. They shed their clothes and conjoined on the mattress, crushing one another with the strength of their limbs intertwining and their tongues buffeting together. Their hands roved across the plains and contours of the other's skin as they happily fell into ravaging the body both had missed during the past three weeks.

Three times during a marathon afternoon of sex, they sated themselves, then napped, then enjoyed sex once again.

When Derek finally awoke, he opened his eyes to the sight of Brent lying on his side, his head resting in the palm of his hand, and admiring Derek's body.

"You caught me," Brent said with smile.

Derek smiled too, and dragged Brent into his arms in a cuddle position without saying a word. Soon both men were aroused again but neither had the strength to carry out another orgasm. Finally, Brent suggested, "We should get something to eat. You must be starved."

Derek made a sound of agreement and then kissed Brent's chest and gnawed on his nipple. Playfully, Brent pushed Derek toward the edge of the bed. "Come on, sexy. Time to face reality."

After their showers, both men dressed in jeans and T-shirts and appeared together in the kitchen. "Staff's day off," Derek said, answering

Brent's unspoken question about why the house was so quiet. "You told me to take good care of them. Anyway, I didn't want anything to disturb our reunion. Yipes! It's later than I thought," he said, looking at the digital clock on the microwave. "I'll fix us something that's a cross between breakfast, lunch and dinner." He shushed Brent away and told him to take a seat out by the pool.

As Brent stepped out through the French doors, and into the wide backyard, he smiled at how peaceful and beautiful his home was. *It's always good to be back here,* he said to himself as he ambled over the freshly mowed grass and stopped to peer into the koi pond. The roses were in bloom, and the bougainvillea was so brilliant a color purple that it was a distraction against the mostly green backyard. Brent finally moved toward the pool and seated himself at the highly Windexed patio table.

Derek prepared one of Everett's brunch recipes for pigs in a blanket and in twenty minutes he was bringing the food outside on a tray. He poured coffee and mimosas and settled in for a blissful evening with Brent. "Enjoy," he said as Brent sipped his mimosa and proved that he was hungrier than he thought.

The two ate quietly, listening to the ambient sounds of traffic in the distance beyond the estate, and the sounds of swimming pool water being sucked through the filter. After devouring his meal, Brent sat back and smiled. He took a long look at Derek and said, "Seems that all my friends adore you."

Derek looked quizzical.

"My carrier pigeon brought me a few messages. You entertained Rand and Pat and even Francois. I forgot he was coming to town."

Derek was surprised that Brent knew so much of what occurred during his absence. Unsure of the extent of Brent's knowledge of his activities, or whether or not he was upset, he remained silent.

"Tom tells me that they were most satisfied for your company."

"You talked to Tom, but you didn't call me?" Derek asked, trying to sound less curious and more perturbed.

"He called *me,*" Brent said. "Every time I was available to phone here, the time difference made it too early or too late. But I'm delighted that everybody gets on with you so well," Brent continued. "I'm not surprised. They'd have to be morons not to be attracted to the sexiest dude I've ever been with."

Pushing back his chair, Brent rose and stood next to Derek. Then he pulled off his T-shirt and stood a moment longer. "I have to admit that I was incredibly envious when Tom mentioned that the guys were spending time with you. I wanted to be here instead. It's so unlike me to be comfortable with sex, but when I'm with you, I feel completely free."

Derek lost his anxiety of Brent's possible animosity. And, although he still wasn't sure if Brent knew the extent of how he had entertained, he focused on Brent's body and quickly became hard again. As Derek reached up and unbuttoned Brent's jeans, he said, "Everett showed me some of your movies on DVD."

Brent helped Derek by ripping at the rest of the buttons and producing his engorged cock.

"I'm impressed," Derek said. "Oh, with your acting, too," he joked as he wrapped his lips around Brent's beautiful piece of meat. "Is Angela Bassett as awesome as she seems to be? And tell me all about Christian Bale!"

"Don't try to talk with your mouth full," Brent teased. "Angela is my straight man fantasy. You'll agree when you meet her."

Derek nodded his head and sucked Brent dry.

"Juan, darling." Cathy smiled as she checked her lipstick and makeup in the foyer mirror. "I have to be in Washington for the next three days. Is there any chance you could work the weekend? Pretty please? I wouldn't ordinarily ask, but Andrew will be lost in this place unless he has someone to heat up the meals I've ordered from Spago. He specifically asked for you. He never liked Socorro. And she's made it clear that there's no love lost between them. Of course it's double time on Saturday and triple on Sunday."

"Absolutely. Of course I'll work during the weekend." Juan smiled, camouflaging his panic about being alone in the house with Andrew. "It'll give me an opportunity to rearrange the pantry," he said.

Cathy beamed. "Andrew is brilliant with his business, but utterly helpless when it comes to the slightest domestic situation," she said. "He is one of the most astute deal makers in Hollywood, and yet he can't make his own toast."

"And we couldn't do his job either." Juan was tactful as he busied himself polishing the stainless steel appliances, and debating whether or not he should voice his concerns to Cathy. *Of course not, you fool,* he berated himself. Instead, he simply said, "Have a terrific time in D.C. Sock it to the right."

Juan had long ago confessed to himself that he was actually attracted to Andrew Young. The man was handsome, well-groomed, and powerful. There was no doubting his sex appeal. When he entered a room, all eyes turned toward him. He had a vibration that automatically magnetized others. Juan knew that if his employer made a sexual pass at him, it would be impossible to refuse. But there was Cathy. Juan did not want to ever do anything that would hurt the woman who had rescued him from poverty. He felt a knot in his stomach as he considered the coming weekend.

When Juan returned to the apartment that night, he called Derek's private number. He reached the voice mail system and left a quick message asking for a return call ASAP. "Need your advice," he said, then hung up the phone.

The moment he placed the phone on its cradle, the telephone rang. Juan smiled widely as he picked up again, and seductively said, "You're fast! How's it hanging, sexy?"

"I was going to ask you the same question." It wasn't Derek on the other end of the line.

Juan was suddenly embarrassed. "Oh. Sorry, Andrew. I was expecting a call from someone else."

"I'm not sorry. I just wanted to tell you that I'm delighted that you'll be taking care of me this weekend."

Juan stammered. "I appreciate your confidence in me, Andrew, but are you sure you wouldn't rather have Socorro? She's a terrific cook."

"No cooking required. In the kitchen, that is." He gave a small lascivious laugh. "Cathy always arranges for food to be brought in when she's away. Anyway, Socorro and I have an unspoken rule. She doesn't speak to me, and I don't can her ass. Look, since it's the weekend you don't have to dress the way you usually do. Come in your bounce-around clothes. Whatever you usually wear when you're not working. Jeans. Tank. Shorts, if you like. Whatever. And if I'm not too busy with work-related stuff . . . maybe we can do something . . . together."

"Adventure Land?" It was unlike Juan to take a sarcastic tone.

"Hey, I'm going through the canyon, so the phone's cutting out," Andrew said. "I'll see you first thing in the A.M."

Juan hung up the phone and realized that he was hard. "What's this all about?" he asked himself, addressing the issue of his erection. "The guy's obviously a cheating creep. Sexy as hell, but a cheat nonetheless. Why am I attracted to him? This is the reason I desperately need a fuck buddy. So I'm not tempted by just any ole dick that passes under my nose. If I had sex on a regular basis, I probably wouldn't think twice about Andrew."

Almost immediately, the telephone rang again. Juan hesitated for a moment, thinking that perhaps Andrew had pushed redial. With uneasiness he answered on the third ring. It was Derek.

"I'm glad you called." Derek was practically hyperventilating. "I need some advice. I need your help with something."

"Me too, Boss," Juan said. "It's getting awfully hot and sticky over at Cathy and Andrew's. She's out of town this weekend, and asked me to look out for Andrew. I'll be alone in the house with him. What should I do?"

"Screw him."

"I would if it wasn't for Cathy," Juan said.

"No, I mean, to hell with him. As you always said to me, you don't have to do anything that's against your principles. You don't want to jeopardize your job."

"It's a lose/lose situation. If he comes on to me and I reject him, I'll end up like the last houseboys. If I agree to fuck him, I'm potentially hurting Cathy. This is a serious mess."

Derek sighed heavily. "I'm in a similar situation. I'm about to possibly fuck up my job with Brent. He's out of the country again and I'm going out to Rage tonight to look for a cute guy who can help service some of Brent's friends. This puts me in a really tough situation. Tom keeps sending guys to me but I can't handle the load by myself. And if Tom finds out that I'm sending a boy to do a man's job, so to speak, who knows what he'll do or what he'll tell Brent that I've been doing on the side. He suggested blackmailing me once when I didn't want to service some minor league studio executive from Sony!"

"It's not that hard to find a willing cock in a West Hollywood bar," Juan said. "They aren't there to simply kill time. If you find someone acceptable, send him to the guys you've never met. Tom's friends won't know that they're not being fucked by the legendary Derek Bracken," Juan explained.

"But what about the money? It's serious cash and I don't want some little cocksucker taking the entire amount."

"Most street boys will be happy with a hundred bucks," Juan advised. "Anything above hourly minimum wage will be a windfall." Juan tried to change the subject. "Boss, I know this is important to you, but my problem is just a bit bigger, at least to me. What the fuck should *I* do?"

Derek sighed. "Okay, first of all, relax. Maybe you're just imagining that Andrew wants your ass."

"He just called. Wants me to wear a tank to work tomorrow."

Derek was momentarily nonplussed. "Bold, isn't he?"

"He suggested that if he weren't too overworked we could do 'something.' I can usually take care of myself, but this is a quandary."

Derek thought for a moment. "Why," he wondered aloud, "do those with money think they can take advantage of those without money. They make us believe that we need them in order to survive. It's the same thing that's going on up here, Juan. Tom thinks that he has a noose around my neck. And he does. What would have happened if I had walked away from Brent that first night? Worst case scenario? I'd be homeless. What would happen if you simply didn't show up for work tomorrow?"

Juan was silent for a moment. "Worst case scenario? I might be fired. At least I've been able to save a couple weeks' salary. But I can't go back to where I came from, Boss. Doesn't everybody sell their soul for a paycheck? I mean, even if you're self-employed, you're at the mercy of clients. The only freedom is to be independently wealthy. What about you? What would be the worst that could happen if you set yourself up with a couple of hot studs who would be willing to work for a hundred bucks an hour?"

"Arrest for being a pimp. Suffer the wrath of Brent and his cronies; and I've seen how Tom can get angry. No more quick cash. Back to square one." Derek's voice trailed off.

"Honestly," Juan continued, "I'm not ready to give up what I've got. And neither are you. I would do just about anything to never be reduced to being penniless again. *Almost* anything."

Derek made a nonverbal sound of agreement. After a moment, he said, "I live in a freakin' palace. I drive one of half a dozen different cars. I have servants and the latest movies in the private screening room. This is Shangri-la. Peacocks roam the freakin' estate. The gym is free. The food is haute cuisine. The best wines and champagnes; all for the taking."

"You're definitely paying for all that luxury, Boss," Juan corrected. "I wouldn't say that you are exactly a guest."

"But three months ago, you and I were chugging beers with our last dollars wondering how we were going to survive another day. Now, look at us."

"We're still wondering how we're going to survive," Juan said. "Only the circumstances are different. We're still beholden to other people. Andrew and Tom and Brent represent the same thing that Jet represented at Onyx and Garson represented at the apartment. They hold the strings to our lives. Dance, Derek, dance! That's what Tom's doing to you, and you can't even go to Brent about it. And it's what Andrew is doing to me. Even Cathy, bless her soul, would have to fire me if she discovered that her husband was after my ass. I'd be out of that house and in the hands of INS in no time."

"So what do you want me to tell you to do about Andrew?" Derek asked. "I don't want to get you fired, and I don't want to hurt my friend Cathy."

Juan turned the tables. "Would you even listen if I told you what I thought you should do about your situation with Tom?"

"Yeah, I would," Derek said. "But tell me what I *want* to hear."

"That's right," Juan said. "Regardless of what either of us tells the other, we're going to do what we think is best. But I will offer you this. Take care of Derek first. This is Hollywood, my friend. The rules of engagement are different here than other places. Unless you make up your mind and do what you feel is right, regardless of the consequences, then you're screwed. And I don't mean what you feel is right in any moral way, necessarily. Do what is right to enable you to survive. If you left tonight, they'd miss you for a few hours. If you hang around and beat them at their own game by putting a few hot guys to work, they may be furious when the truth is revealed—if ever—but you'll have more money and less work."

Derek thought for a moment. "And right back at ya, Juan," he added. "You can run away from Andrew, or you can use this to your advantage. First of all, and, God, I hate to say this, but Cathy's out of town and chances are she'll never find out if you slip your shaft to her old man. It's a certainty that he'll never say a word. But you've got to get something that assures he won't just toss you out afterward."

"A contract, Boss?" Juan asked. "Something else to lord over him in case he pulls a fast one and tries to dismiss me?"

"If the man's as horny as I think he is, he'll do almost anything to get you in the sack," Derek said. "You shouldn't give it away. Just because he signs your checks doesn't mean you have to fuck him as a perk of employment. Make him pay in some other way. Tell him you're not cheap. As they say, 'You don't get what you deserve. You get what you negotiate!' This is a man who will understand that logic! He gets what he wants and doesn't mind paying for expensive things. If I were you, I'd start off with, oh, let's say, maybe a chunk of cash? Tell him that your mother in Mexico needs a liver transplant and you need a thousand bucks."

"My mother's dead," Juan said.

"It hardly matters whether he believes you or not," Derek said. "Tell him you'll have to fly down to your poor mother's side immediately if you can't send the check. Make him see that you will happily show your appreciation for his generosity. Wear that sexy tank, and keep adjusting your cock. He'll write you a check on the spot."

"What about you, Boss?" Juan asked. "Here's what I think you should do. Go to the bar at Mickey's tonight. I'll call ahead. Ask to speak to Sal. By the time you get there, he'll have half a dozen guys for you to look over. When's your next fuck appointment?"

"As a matter of fact, it's tonight after the premier of Disney's *Tricks of the Trade* at El Capitan. Some director I've never met. The guy who does all of those stupid so-called comedies, with those unfunny second-tiered has-beens from *Saturday Night Live.* He's expecting me at The Four Seasons."

"Bingo!" Juan yelled. "He doesn't know you personally. I'm calling Sal right now. It's too early for the best action, but head down to Santa Monica Boulevard at around nine. Tip Sal a hundred bucks and he'll set you up with as many guys as you want to choose from. Drive the kid to the hotel and wait in the car for him. Tell whomever you pick that you'll pay him two hundred. I guarantee that's more than any of them ever imagined they'd get for an hour of work."

"How can I be sure some young stud won't steal me blind?" Derek said.

"Call the director and tell him you want the cash in an envelope left with the concierge," Juan said. "Tell him it's for his benefit as well as yours, in case hotel security gets wise and decides to check you out. How much is he paying?"

"Five grand."

"Jesus!" Juan declared. "If security or the police found that kind of money in your pocket it would be a giveaway for prostitution or selling drugs."

Derek was suddenly emboldened. His adrenaline was rushing. "How the hell did you come up with a scheme like that?" he asked. "I would never have thought about using the concierge!"

"It just came to me." Juan laughed.

Even as Derek continued speaking to Juan, he was checking himself out in the mirror and preparing to hit the boulevard in search of someone with all the requisite assets he was told that the director was known for desiring in other men. "Okay, call your friend Sal," Derek said. "But in the meantime, I suggest that you do a gazillion push-ups, pick out your tightest jeans and your dirtiest wife beater. A pig like Andrew will fucking salivate when you show up in the morning."

Juan laughed. "I will, if you will," he said. "By this time tomorrow, we'll both either be starting new jobs as entrepreneurs, or living together again. You said it earlier, Boss. It's time we're no longer beholden to anyone else. From now on, we pull the strings!"

TWENTY-THREE

On this night, Mickey's Bar on Santa Monica Boulevard in West Hollywood was an overpopulated sea of mostly hot, young, self-possessed men in muscle shirts and shorts. A smattering of frozen-faced, gray-haired daddies were unabashedly delighted to be in the crush of youth surrounding them, and yet their hawk eyes did not miss even the most elusive prey. It was nine P.M., and the music was disco loud. Derek walked from the front sidewalk café into the dimly lit expanse of tables, dance floor and flesh. Dressed in the same manner that he had instructed Juan, Derek immediately became the center of attention. He loved that hundreds of pairs of eyes looked him up and down as he waded through the crowd to the bar. He leaned against the bar and the guys to his right and left both gave him the once-over.

"Buy you a drink?" the stud to his right said.

"Thanks, I'm not staying." Derek smiled at the guy who was wearing a leather vest over his pumped, hairy chest that was decorated with pierced nipples and a tattoo of a dragon on his left shoulder. He quickly caught the bartender's attention. "Looking for Sal," he said.

The bartender nodded his head and slipped out from behind his station. In a few moments he returned with a young stud with a wide smile. "You're Juan's friend?" the stud said. "I'm Sal." He reached out his hand in greeting. "How is my sweetie?" Sal asked.

"Juan's cool. He told you why I'm here?"

"Take your pick." Sal cocked his head toward the opposite wall of the bar.

As Derek's eyes followed the direction of Sal's gaze, he found four young men in what could have been a police lineup, each beautiful and each offering a different fantasy. "You've got good taste," Derek said above the din of the music and conversation. "Which is best?"

"Depends upon what you're looking for," Sal said. "Ya want a caption for this photo op? Left to right: Tim. Blond, six feet, nine cut, prefers to top, but will bottom for the right dick. Or the right price. Next to him is Ron. Variation on Tim, but he spends more time in the gym. Abs are rock solid. Next, David. Intellectual. So he says. Won five hundred dollars on *Jeopardy!* Too sensitive for sex work, but he's desperate to pay his rent. And Jamie. Busted his ass for that bizarro Marshall Topper guy for a while. Wants to work on his own but needs a computer to make it a career, and no dinero for an *Encounters* ad. It's hard to make money without advertising. Each is a walking case of self-loathing." Sal laughed. "They need the affirmation of some sex-obsessed pile of shit to validate their being. A prize, each of 'em. Got my money?"

Derek had not forgotten Juan's instructions to pay off Sal. He reached into his pocket and withdrew a crisp one hundred dollar bill. "Thanks for your help, Sal. I think I'll chat up the Jamie kid. We have Marshall Topper in common."

"He's done some porn too," Sal said absently, and walked away.

Derek returned to the bar and bought two bottles of Bud. Then he shouldered his way through the sea of men. When he reached the back wall he fixed his eyes on one boy and went right up to him.

Jamie smiled when he saw Derek in all of his gym-pumped glory.

"Have a beer with me?" Derek said, handing one of the bottles to the young man.

"I don't drink, but thanks," he said holding up a bottle of Calistoga. He tried to maintain eye contact with Derek but his focus kept slipping down to Derek's lips, shoulders, chest, arms and tight waist. He no sooner realized that he was being obvious and returned to look into Derek's eyes. Then he slipped again.

Derek wanted to make the meeting fast. "Wanna make an easy buck?"

Jamie reached out and touched Derek's chest. "All right," he said with a quick smile, his eyes sparkling.

Derek returned the smile. "A friend."

Jamie shook his head, disappointed that he wouldn't be flesh to flesh with Derek. "Nah. I don't do that anymore," he said. "Is he built like you?"

"Very good-looking." Derek nodded. "The Four Seasons. Easy money."

Jamie put his Calistoga down on a tabletop and picked up the bottle of Bud that Derek had offered. He took a long swig as he reconsidered his initial response. "Two hundred minimum. No more than an hour. I'm strictly a catcher."

"That's more than Marshall ever paid you," Derek guessed.

Jamie froze. "Marshall?" he asked tentatively. "Does he have anything to do with this?"

"I used to know him, that's all. Said great things about you," again Derek lied.

"Yeah, well he's still an asshole," Jamie said bitterly. "I'll dance the day I hear he's in jail and getting his filthy ass sodomized daily with a hot poker and a tazer gun. Or dead."

"And you were one of his favorites," Derek added to his fib.

After a long swallow of suds, Jamie followed Derek toward the front of the building and into the warm night air. A Santa Ana wind was passing through Southern California, and the air was filled with the scent of jasmine and lust. As the two walked to the car, Derek gave Jamie further instruction. "The dude is really horny. Very British. On the way over, I'll tell you exactly what he wants."

"What he wants? Christ." Jamie sighed. "He's not one of those who have to choreograph everything, is he?" Jamie began an imaginary dialogue. 'I want you to put your left leg here. It would be really hot if you raised your ass like this. Okay, you have to make this sort of sound while you're sucking my dick.' " Jamie look straight at Derek and said, "That's really irritating. The only kind of authority I like is the kind that's behind me, fucking me. Taking what he wants."

As Derek activated the automatic door lock release, he said, "He's not like that. He just lets things happen spontaneously. But he's paying for a certain kind of guy and you look about right."

Jamie looked at Derek's Jaguar and didn't let on that he was the least bit impressed. He simply slipped into the passenger seat, buckled up and thought of getting back to Mickey's to meet friends at midnight.

Derek continued his tutorial. "He's only in town for a few days and he wants to fuck someone until their head explodes."

"Bang me hard." Jamie nodded. "The best dicks are the ones with a lot of anger." Derek switched on the ignition, checked for opposing traffic, and eased the car out of its parking space. He made a turn around in the driveway of an apartment complex and slipped into Saturday night Santa Monica Boulevard traffic. As the vehicle crawled along at a military convoy pace, he opened the unused ashtray in the dashboard. "Here are a couple of condoms," he said, withdrawing two squares of foil-wrapped Trojans and handing them to Jamie. "When the pants come off, the condoms go on. Got it?"

Jamie made a snorting sound.

"No barebacking. It's stupid," he said.

Jamie laughed. "I go to bathhouses. Sometimes I stay there for two or three twelve-hour sessions. With a few lines of Tina, I can keep fucking for days. I keep reupping my room and just stay there, and have sex with thirty or forty or fifty people. I get fucked by a lot of guys and I'm here to tell you that eighty-five to ninety percent of these men are *not* into safe sex."

Derek stared ahead and was quiet for a long moment. "You're not serious."

"If I go to sex parties or go home from a bar with someone, nobody wants to use condoms. I've probably been fucked bareback about five hundred times. And that's no exaggeration."

Derek was unbelieving. "I know that some people have the attitude that they're eventually going to get the virus anyway, so they may as well get it over with," he said. "I don't look at it like that."

Jamie became pensive. "I am one of those people," he said. "I don't get tested either. Sex is too important to me to become worried about it. I know dudes who actually go out looking for someone who is positive to fuck them. To cum in them over and over until they test positive themselves. And then it's done. They're free. It's no longer an issue."

Only the sounds of Derek's blinking directional signal, and an occasional vehicle cruising past looking for a hustler or a parking space, intruded on the otherwise silent atmosphere in the car. Derek sighed. "There's a defect in people who think that sex is worth dying for."

Jamie nodded his head in agreement. "It's something I probably should have addressed in counseling," he joked. "But just so you know, it's not uncommon. In fact, it's the opposite. Why? Because people secretly want whatever is taboo and forbidden."

Jamie sniggered. "You're a smart guy. You know as well as I, that for any male alive—gay or straight—the penis is our diving rod. It leads us around. Somewhere during the fetal stage of development, a little tiny bit of our brain breaks loose and goes down the umbilical cord and gets lodged in our dicks. So we think with our dicks."

"Answer me this," Derek said. "How do you justify in your own mind the possibility of transmitting—or receiving—an STD?"

Jamie thought for a moment. "The way I look at it is that guys who are engaging in unsafe sex are adults. We're all responsible for ourselves. If you don't take personal responsibility for everything you do, then you're fucked, no matter what."

Derek looked at the condoms again, and then at Jamie. He decided that there wasn't time to find a substitute escort. "If you go on this call you must use these! I'll pay you an extra fifty."

"That's more like it." Jamie laughed.

Derek breathed a heavy sigh of relief. "You fuckin' little hustler." He grinned.

"Not that it would probably matter to your client, since bareback tops think they're immune," Jamie added. "They're usually into the whole machismo thing of just drilling a hole."

Derek drove down Doheney Boulevard, and hung a left into the semicircular drive of the hotel. A valet quickly approached the car. "Just dropping off," Derek waved the man away before the valet had an opportunity to open his door. Then to Jamie, he said, "He's in room seven-seventeen. I'll be around the corner. Make it as fast as possible, but let him give you all that he's got."

Forty-five minutes later, Jamie knocked on the passenger door window of the Jaguar. Derek had fallen asleep and was momentarily shaken by the stranger outside. Then he pushed the door lock release button and Jamie slipped into the front bucket seat.

"How'd it go?" he asked. "Any problems?"

Jamie shrugged his shoulders. "Got any Altoids?" he asked. "The dude was okay. Should have seen his room. Must be a rich guy. Anyway, he thought 'Derek' was 'a bit of all right,' to use his words. Never knew anyone so hungry to fuck! Thought we'd never get it over with because he didn't want to cum. Just wanted to bury his dick in my hole over and over."

Derek felt relief. If the director enjoyed himself, and was none the wiser about the true identity of the guy with whom he had sex, then Derek was free and clear. As he drove down Santa Monica Boulevard to return Jamie to the bar, he asked, "If you're interested in doing this again sometime, give me your number. I might be able to set it up so that you can make good money, if you want."

Jamie bobbed his head in interest. "Got a pen?"

Derek opened the glove compartment and withdrew a small spiral notepad and a pen. He handed the items to Jamie who scrawled his name and telephone number, then handed them back to Derek. "School takes up most of my time, but I'm around."

"School? How old are you?" Derek asked, suddenly circumspect.

"I'm legal."

Derek and Jamie rode together in silence until they reached Larrabee Street and stopped for a signal. When the light turned green, Derek turned left and slowly made his way across the pedestrian-crowded intersection. He double-parked next to the West Hollywood branch of the United States Post Office and reached into his pocket. He withdrew five fifty-dollar bills and handed them to Jamie. "Glad we met," he said. "And you're one of the hottest guys in West Hollywood," he said.

"Yeah, sure," Jamie responded with mock enthusiasm as he opened the car door. "If I'm so sexy, I'd be getting fucked by you, instead of some sissy Englishman. So call me sometime. Job or no job."

Derek smiled and nodded. "Count on it."

TWENTY-FOUR

A s Juan's Honda ascended Tower Grove Road he saw in the distance that Cathy was stepping into a black stretch limousine for her ride to LAX. He pulled his car to the curb until the black stretch passed by. He didn't want Cathy to see him, dressed as he was, wearing the clothes that Andrew had requested.

As the privacy windows of Cathy's limo hid her from view, there was no way of knowing whether or not she had spotted Juan. When her car was out of view, Juan slipped the transmission into drive and continued up the street and into the Youngs' driveway.

Juan parked in the spot reserved for the Youngs' household staff. Entering as he did each morning through the side gate, Juan let himself into the kitchen and pushed the keypad of the security alarm system. It was seven o'clock and he immediately busied himself preparing Andrew's carafe of Starbucks, as well as a light breakfast of croissants, yogurt, fresh pineapple and grapefruit juice. Although he had never worked at the house on Saturday, he was instructed that the weekend routine was only different by the extra hour that Andrew allowed himself to stay in bed. At seven twenty-five Andrew arrived in the kitchen.

Rather than his familiar suit and tie, this morning he wore only jogging pants with a white hand towel draped around his neck.

"Morning, Juan," Andrew offered as he picked up his mug of coffee and sat down to the breakfast that Juan had prepared.

"I guess I just missed Cathy," Juan said, making small talk.

"Hmm," Andrew said. He opened the *Los Angeles Times* and pulled out the "Calendar" entertainment section of the paper.

"Coffee all right?"

"Hmm." Andrew was absorbed in a review of a play at the Geffen Playhouse.

Juan was at first taken aback by Andrew's casual appearance and his lack of more than an indifferent greeting, and virtually no conversation. Juan found himself admiring Andrew's fit body. Although Andrew didn't work out with a trainer, he was muscled and toned from his disciplined gym exercise routine. But by the way his employer was acting, Juan thought that perhaps he had picked up the wrong vibrations from his boss. Perhaps, he thought, Andrew was just being friendly when he tarried longer than necessary in the kitchen each morning, or when he called last night to suggest casual attire for weekend work.

"If you need anything more, I'll be working around the house," Juan finally said. "Use the intercom if you need me," Juan said to the back of Andrew's head, which barely acknowledged having received the information. Juan left the kitchen and headed for the laundry room. He had promised Cathy he would jazz up the dreary room and stencil paint a border of funny-faced clothespins below the crown molding.

Having adjusted the ladder, poured the paint, and taped the precut stencils in place on each wall, Juan was ready to pursue a day of creative activity. With paintbrush in hand, he dipped the hairs into the paint tray, and began to methodically stroke the canvas of the laundry room wall. The work was laborious. His neck and back ached from the body position he was forced to hold while he reached up and out with the brush, aiming for the cutout center of each stencil.

Absorbed in the activity, time raced by. When Juan next looked at his wristwatch, it was nearly noon and he was hungry. He decided he could use a banana for energy. Gingerly descending the ladder, carefully making certain not to upend the paint tray, he left the laundry and entered the kitchen. He was vigilant about not accidentally leaving an errant paint smudge on the granite countertop, the floor, or any of the cabinetry.

Juan was impressed by how peaceful the large house was when Socorro wasn't around. There was no one with whom he had to make idle chatter. For once, he could simply perform his chores without having to divide his attention between Socorro's gossip and the work at hand. *And what of Andrew?* Juan thought. Was he in his home office or out running errands? Juan felt a mild release of anxiety. But he thought back to their morning encounter and how unlike Andrew it was not to have been giving off sexual vibrations. Juan thought about the way Andrew had appeared in his jogging togs. *A hot body for a hot-shot media executive,* he said to himself.

Juan peeled his banana and leaned forward against the center island with his elbows resting on the black granite. It felt good to relax for a moment. He stared out through the multipaned wall of windows to the backyard garden and pool. It was a pristine early Saturday afternoon. The sky was deep blue and the view reached as far as the ocean. His eyes darted from one brilliant floral color to another. Although he didn't know the names of the plants, he was impressed with the deep purples, vibrant greens, shocking reds and the profusion of lilac.

He loved the serenity of the house and the grounds. For a moment, he allowed himself to pretend that this was his own house. He imagined that his apartment was merely a place where he went for sex with a fuck buddy. The reverie caused Juan to feel himself growing hard. Rather than risk having to jack off in the guest bathroom, he decided to return to his project. He swallowed the last of the fruit, reached under the counter for the trash can and turned around directly into the face of Andrew Young.

So startled was Juan at the close proximity of his boss, that he actually recoiled in shock. Then he forced a laugh. "I didn't hear you come in," he said, panting and placing a hand over his chest.

Andrew had changed into blue jeans and a tight white T-shirt. He smiled. "I was attracted by the smell of paint," he said. "My favorite. Especially when it's mixed with the scent of sweat from hard labor." He slowly leaned in toward Juan and deeply inhaled the odor that emanated from his employee's clothes and skin. He and Juan stood face to face. Their eyes penetrated into the other's. The media mogul and his houseboy transmitted their precise thoughts to each other.

Andrew reached out and placed the flat of his hand onto the fabric covering Juan's chest. He leaned forward and tentatively pressed his lips to Juan's.

Automatically, Juan's heart rate increased and he gave in to his own desire. He closed his eyes and greedily received Andrew's lips and tongue. He placed his hands on Andrew's head and drew him in even closer. They were brutal with each other. And Juan sensed that Andrew wanted him to play the role of a tough, street-wise Hispanic. Juan gladly gave him what he wanted and pushed his employer against the kitchen wall. He peeled off his shirt and let Andrew stare at his half-naked body for a long moment. "You've wanted to suck my Mexican cock," he said. "Here's your chance, dude. And you better do it good." Juan laid the accent on thick. He slowly unbuttoned his jeans, slid his hands into his pants, and withdrew the nine inches of brown dick for which he knew Andrew was salivating.

Without further instruction, Andrew dropped to his knees and stared at Juan's engorged dick. He cautiously but deliberately placed his hands on Juan's stomach and slid them down to his waist before reaching behind and cupping his servant's ass. Juan's hard penis protruded like a steel pipe, and in measured moves, Andrew opened his mouth and gently surrounded the flange with his lips. He sighed in exquisite satisfaction as he tasted the skin, and his tongue felt the contours of Juan's helmet head endowment.

Andrew brought his hands to play with Juan's balls, which were the size of walnuts and hung like a pouch of gold nuggets. Andrew understood the possible consequences of sucking the dick of a relative stranger, and the possible repercussion if his wife or anyone in the industry were to ever find out about it. However, he would not alter the moment for anything. He thought, even if Cathy were to walk into the room this very moment, he wouldn't be able to stop himself from following through with his lust. There was nothing in the universe that could take him away from total immersion in this fantasy experience. He was completely intoxicated by the scent of Juan's pubic area, the taste and feel of Juan's dick in his mouth and the feeling of his own cock straining through the fabric of his jeans.

As horny as Juan was, he backed out of Andrew's mouth. He forced his boss to his feet and placed his strong hands on his T-shirt. In a quick burst of strength and unexpected demonstration of his authority, Juan tore the fabric of the shirt until Andrew's entire chest and stomach were exposed. He knew that Andrew was both taken aback and titillated by this display of aggression. "I'm gonna fuck your sorry ass, Andrew," Juan said. He then swiftly wrestled Andrew and caught his boss's neck in the vise of his arm. He slammed Andrew's body against the wall. Without another word, he turned Andrew around and pushed him toward the kitchen door.

Andrew was a quick study. He tripped out of the kitchen toward the outside stairway which led to the unused maid's quarters above the garage. He ascended with Juan behind him. They reached the small chamber. Then, Juan kicked off his shoes, and stepped out of his pants. Andrew did the same. Standing opposite each other, naked, with their respective cocks at full bloom, Juan again pushed Andrew, who fell back onto the queen-size bed.

From cleaning the room once a week, Juan knew where Andrew had hidden his stash of condoms. He pulled the drawer handle in the table beside the bed and opened a Bible—the pages of which had been hollowed out. He smiled wickedly as he withdrew a condom and a squeeze bottle of lube from their place of storage.

Andrew started to beg for mercy. Then: "Asshole. You think you can take me?" he snarled. "If you so much as touch me . . . Don't fuck with me, beaner!"

Juan didn't want the scene to get violent, but he sensed that Andrew could take a little roughhousing. He yelled with the force of a drill instructor. "Shut the fuck up! You're gonna take my fucking cock and you're gonna take it now! Do you hear me?"

Andrew nodded in agreement. He wanted Juan inside him, as he had never wanted anyone else. He ached to feel the penetration. Now he began to whimper. "Oh, God, fuck me! Fuck my hole."

It took very little time for Andrew to climax. And when he shot his load, his personality changed almost immediately. After only a few minutes of decompressing, he got off the bed and headed toward the bathroom. "Get your ass back to work," he said before he closed the door and turned on the shower.

Juan immediately knew he had made a mistake. Suspecting that the day would unfold into a sexual picnic, he should have either called in sick, or not agreed to the arrangement in the first place. Now he felt both used, and that he may have jeopardized his job. "Fuck," he said aloud as he ripped off his condom (he had not climaxed) and dropped it into the wastebasket next to the writing table. He picked up his pants and shoes and headed back down the stairs bare-assed.

Juan found his shirt, and redressed in the laundry room. He was desolate. With Derek, sex had been fun and safe. With Andrew, he knew that he was merely a conquest. He stood in the laundry room staring out the window at the garden, but not really seeing anything. He looked at his watch. It was two-thirty. He had promised to stay until six. After a while, he picked up his paintbrush. Slowly, he returned to his task. And in minute increments the sensation of fucking Andrew's ass began to fade.

At fifteen minutes to six, Juan stepped down off the ladder to admire his work. He nodded in agreement with himself that he'd done a reasonably good job. Picking up the painting implements, he washed the brushes under strong running water in the large porcelain sink. He folded the ladder, replaced the lid on the paint can, tamped it down with the butt of a screwdriver, and picked up the drop cloth. At six o'clock he stepped out of the room and into the kitchen. The house was silent. The only sound was the motor from the refrigerator.

Juan removed his car keys from the hook by the back door and left the house. As he departed, he dreaded the idea of returning the next day. "That is, if I still have a job," he said. He closed the back gate and walked to his car.

Entering the apartment, Juan heard the very end of a message from Derek. ". . . very adorable. So call me when you can."

Juan pulled off his clothes and went into his tiny bathroom. The first thing he did was to reach for the Listerine. He took a mouthful and rinsed and gargled thoroughly, all the while thinking of his tongue and Andrew's, fighting for dominance in each other's mouths. Juan then brushed his teeth for a longer than usual period of time. He stepped into the shower and washed himself to be rid of any trace of sex with Andrew. After towel-drying his body, Juan flopped onto the bed. He lay naked, staring at the ceiling as the room became darker. With only a small trace of light emanating through the bamboo shades, from the street lamp outside, Juan lethargically reached for the telephone. He pushed the star button and eight six on the keypad to dial the last number received. It connected with Derek.

"Boss," he said with what he knew was a slumberous tone. "Drilled a new one in the master today. All I got for it was a surly reminder from him that I was there to work."

As Juan began to describe the events of the day, the call-waiting beep announced that someone was trying to reach him. "Boss, can you hold a sec?"

Juan clicked over. "Yes," he asked curtly.

"Um, I just wanted to say you did a good job." It was Andrew.

Juan's heart jumped. He wanted to tell Andrew that he thought he was an asshole, but instead he listened.

"What happened today . . ." Andrew was at a loss for words. "You know, sometimes a man has certain . . . needs . . ." It seemed unusual for one who was responsible for overseeing a multibillion dollar media corporation to be tongue-tied. But that's the impression that he was giving to Juan. "You left before I had a chance . . ."

To have me fuck you again? Juan wanted to say, but kept the thought to himself.

". . . to ask if you wanted to have dinner with me. I'd like you to come back tonight."

Juan was dumbfounded. He stalled. "I'm on the other line. Let me get rid of the call."

Again Juan switched back to Derek. "I'll call you right back. It's him. Andrew. He's trying to get me to come back to the house. Tonight! I'll tell you about it in a few minutes."

Click. "I'm here," he spoke into the mouthpiece. "What were you saying? I don't think I heard you clearly. You're inviting me to come over for dinner? What's this all about?"

Andrew was suddenly testy. "Look," he said, "it's not a big deal. Either you want to have dinner with me, or you don't. A simple yes or no is all that's required."

Now, Juan was becoming incensed. In a fraction of a moment, he recalled Andrew's scorn after he had used Juan to sexually satisfy himself. The disdain was fresh in Juan's memory and in this instant of time he could only imagine that Andrew was horny again and wanted as much action as he could get before his wife's return the following afternoon. Juan was in a bind. What, he unconsciously asked himself, would be the consequences of rejecting Andrew now, after they'd already had sex once. Although Andrew had obviously enjoyed the sex play and wanted more of Juan, Juan was concerned that he was putting himself into a position of working for the Youngs and now being expected to provide sex as a condition of employment.

"What do I get out of it?" The question had not been formed in Juan's thoughts, when it reached the surface and pushed passed his lips.

"Excuse me?" Andrew said. He sounded irritated.

Juan was too shocked by verbalizing what should have remained unspoken.

And then Andrew's demeanor softened. "What do you want?" he asked.

Juan remained silent.

"Money?" Andrew continued. "Come over and we'll discuss it."

Juan took a deep breath and exhaled loudly. He looked at the clock. It was nearly nine P.M. "It's getting late."

"Bring your jammies," Andrew said, sarcastically. "Just get your Mexican ass over here."

After a long pause, Juan said, "I've got some stuff to do first. Give me an hour." And then he hung up the telephone. By the time Juan redialed Derek's number, the voice mail system picked up. "Boss. You're probably working your ass off, or someone's ass. Sorry I missed you. We need to talk. I'm going back to Andrew's. You can help me kick myself later."

TWENTY-FIVE

Within a week, Jamie was entered into Derek's speed dial. Derek flipped open his cell phone and pushed a button on the keypad. "Hey, it's me," he said, knowing that by now, his voice was instantly recognizable. "Wanna make another quick pile of cash? There's a dude at the Chateau. Only the best for you." Derek's smile faded as he listened to an excuse from Jamie. Derek's voice grew steely. "Just tell me the truth. Do you want to do this work or not? I can easily find someone else."

Jamie, lying in his bed, naked on top of the sheets in a post-climax daze with a butch, hairy-chested leather man he picked up at Mickey's said, "I'm cool, man. Just not feeling up to another pump 'n' dump tonight. Next time, for sure. Okay?"

Derek whined to Jamie. "The guy's really hot. It'll be an easy one for you."

David August, the star of the hit television medical drama series *Operation,* was ensconced in a suite at the famed and infamous Chateau Marmont on Sunset Boulevard. He was in town to do publicity for his show. Derek had seen the program a couple of times, and although he thought the actor was definitely worth spending time with, he, like Jamie, wasn't in the mood for sex. Jamie had a better excuse than Derek, who was simply not interested.

Jamie could not be persuaded to change his mind. However, he did make a suggestion. "Hey," he offered, "I've got a friend who might work."

Derek was skeptical. He didn't like the idea of sending someone to pose as himself without first having had a face-to-face meeting. His reputation was constantly on the line. "No. That won't work," he protested. "He may not measure up."

"This dude is awesome," Jamie boasted. "I can vouch for him myself."

"Nah," Derek continued. Then reconsidering, he said, "What're his stats?" The description sounded intriguing to Derek and he decided to meet with Jamie's friend. Derek wrote down the telephone number for a man named Vaughn. After one last plea to Jamie, Derek disconnected the line.

Jamie put down his telephone and turned to his man. He smiled devilishly and ran his fingers over his partner's pumped chest. He teased, "When I finally find a husband, he'll have to be hairy like you," he said.

The man smiled. "Guys who wax their chests are about as much of a turn-on as a woman's leg," he said.

Then, Jamie spread his own legs and the man rolled on top of him.

The moment that Derek's eyes adjusted to the dim lighting of The Rusty Spike, he decided that the man perched on a stack of beer cases, and wearing a black leather motorcycle cap and a leather vest over his muscled torso, was Vaughn.

Derek bought a bottle of beer at the bar and ambled up to the man. "I'm Jamie's friend," he said.

The man nodded absently as he looked first at Derek's tight jeans, and pumped chest and arms, and then into his eyes. "Got a client for me? I'm two hundred, minimum," he said.

Derek looked at Vaughn. He studied the way his body was cut and found himself getting hard. "This is a quick job. It pays one hundred. If you do well, and you're asked back, you might get a raise. Take it or leave it."

"Fraker pays me two hundred," Vaughn said. "I'm worth it."

Derek looked quizzical. "Fraker? Some guy who pays you to fuck him?" he said with a hint of derision.

The man was silent as his eyes bore into Derek's. "Forget it. I didn't say nothin'." He was demonstrably uncomfortable and mentally reconsidered his options: Take the money offered, and be able to eat for a few days; play hard to get and maybe never have another opportunity. "Where?" he said, agreeing to the assignation. "The Chateau, I suppose."

It was obvious that Derek was taken aback by the correct guess.

"Relax, man," Vaughn said. "That's where I usually go. Done it there enough for 'em to know who I am. They won't hassle me. Fraker used to . . ." He caught himself, speaking that name again, and stopped himself.

Derek was suddenly wise. "This dude, Fraker . . ." he started to say.

Vaughn held up the palms of his hands. He was self-conscious about what he had already revealed. "That name," he said. "It could land me in a ton of shit. Forget we had this conversation. Let's go. I'll do your little cock weasel job."

Derek nodded his head, indicating that Vaughn should follow him out of the bar. They left together and slipped into the car. Derek had borrowed the Honda Civic. He hadn't wanted to take one of Brent's expensive cars to this part of town, and he didn't want the trick to think he had any money.

"Shitty wheels," Vaughn commented on the condition of the car. "You must be new to the game. Send me out enough and pretty soon you can afford a Lamborghini."

Derek was surprised by Vaughn's obvious understanding of the business. En route to Sunset Boulevard, by way of Fountain Avenue and La Cienega Boulevard, he tried to give Vaughn instructions, but Vaughn was ahead of him. "Man, you need me to teach you Pimping 101," Vaughn scoffed. "Got any party favors? You know, Tina?"

"No drugs!" Derek said. "I don't use guys who do drugs!"

"Calm down," Vaughn said. "I'm substance-free. But what about the john? Sure he won't be expecting me to bring the party favors? So what's expected of me?" he said.

Derek didn't answer immediately. He debated whether or not to pull over and let Vaughn out of the car. He had been suspicious of him from the moment they met. It was not that he expected guys who sell themselves as sex slaves to hang out in the bar at the Peninsula Hotel in Beverly Hills, but he also hadn't expected such a remarkably sleazy saloon as The Rusty Spike. That dive had all the ambiance of a run-down machine factory, and the patrons were of the variety that made bank tellers hover over their silent alarms. Finally, Derek said, "The guy's a submissive bottom who wants to please. He's into the whole role-playing scene. 'Sir. Daddy. Boy.' Be an aggressive dominant top. But he doesn't want to be degraded. Can you handle it?"

Vaughn shrugged his shoulders. "What's a decent-looking dude like you doing fixing guys up, when you could be fucking for dollars yourself?" Vaughn asked the question with a smirk. He placed a hand on Derek's knee. "I could go for a piece of you myself," he said, giving Derek a squeeze. "What'dya say after I plow Mr. X, we get it on ourselves?"

Derek admitted to himself that he was physically attracted to Vaughn. But the attraction was perverse. He was intrigued by the rough nature of the man. He was getting tired of the men who simply wanted to worship him. Although the men he'd serviced had thus far been decently attractive, none of them had the smoldering bestial nature of Vaughn, who issued an aura of being slightly demented, which was both a turn-on and a red flag for Derek. He could only hope that Vaughn would treat the customer in the manner that Derek would. "That would be cool," he finally said in response to Vaughn's question. He rationalized that if he were to ever consider using Vaughn in the future, he'd have to know what he was like in bed. Just as Tom had tried him out.

"Gotta be wise about this guy," Derek said. "He only wants the *fantasy* of rough sex with a stud. You've gotta promise me to treat him well. He's a VIP and I don't want you to do anything that he doesn't ask for. Got it? The man's a friend of a friend, and if it gets back to me that he wasn't satisfied, you can forget about ever working this part of town again."

Vaughn removed his hand from Derek's knee. "You worry too much, man," he said. "I know what turns a guy on. The only thing you're gonna hear back is how much he begged for my dick."

"And use condoms!" Derek insisted, reaching into the glove compartment and pulling out a travel pack containing two condoms and a packet of lube.

Vaughn made a sound that meant, *Yes, Mother.*

An hour later, parked on the narrow street behind the hotel, Derek saw Vaughn in his rearview mirror, come around the corner. Derek honked the horn, giving the hustler his position. In a moment, Vaughn was seated beside Derek.

"And?" Derek asked, requesting a full report.

"Got your money, didn't you?" Vaughn retorted. "You're smart having the john leave an envelope for you with the concierge. He thought I was hitting him up for more when I asked for money."

"Fuck!" Derek exclaimed. "I forgot to tell you. You didn't make it an issue, did you?"

"Your precious client had his prostate massaged good and hard. That's all he cared about," Vaughn said.

Derek smiled and nodded his head. "More info," he said. "What happened?"

"What do you think happened? The little weasel was all over me. Not a bad cocksucker for a self-absorbed actor."

"Actor?" Derek queried innocently, concerned for his client's identity.

Vaughn harrumphed. "Don't fuck with my intelligence, dude. I read *People.* I recognized August the moment he opened the door. But don't worry, I wasn't impressed. I've fucked bigger names than his. Nobody dazzles me anymore. I might get a little charge of excitement if Senator Joe Biden answered the door. Now there's a piece of man meat. But otherwise, a dude would have to be somebody really important. Not an *actor,* for Christ's sake."

Derek was slightly offended. "What do you have against actors?" he said.

Again, Vaughn made a snorting sound as if he couldn't believe the question needed an answer. "What do actors actually do that is so important that they should be deified, make a shit load of money and expect to be treated different from everyone else? Every actor I've ever fucked has made me feel as though I was the lucky one to have the golden opportunity to put my cock up his famous ass."

"You're generalizing," Derek countered. "I know a few who are different."

"They're all needy little fucks," Vaughn denounced the profession across the board. "Insecurity is no excuse for their behavior. Not to worry," he concluded, "I've never let my disdain get in the way of work."

"That's a comfort." Derek smirked, still not sure how much to trust Vaughn. Silence filled the car for a few moments. And then Derek's curiosity got the better of him. "Can I ask a personal question?" he said. "I don't think you want to talk about it, but I'm really interested."

Vaughn turned his head and looked at Derek. "Yeah, I still want to fuck you."

"No," Derek said. "I mean, yeah, I want that too. But the question I have is about something else. You mentioned a guy named Fraker."

"Whoa, man." Vaughn held up his hands. "We're not going there."

"But why?" Derek begged. "If this guy is hooking for the stars, which is what I'm trying to do, I need to know what my competition is. I just want to know how the guy operates so that I can be successful. Who are some of his clients? What does he charge? How do people get in touch with him for his service? All that is important to me."

"He doesn't exist," Vaughn insisted.

"Someone like him exists," Derek demanded. "I'm not the first guy to come up with the idea of providing men to have sex with celebrities. A guy brought me into the scene; there have to be others like him."

"So ask that guy about Fraker. You're not getting a word out of me. I value my balls. I don't want my pretty face messed up, okay?" Vaughn was demonstrably upset. "Look, just hand over my money and let me out of the car. Forget that you ever met me."

Now Derek was disturbed. "Vaughn," he said, "forget that I said anything. I was just curious, that's all. I'll respect your wishes about not mentioning the guy's name. In fact, I appreciate your integrity. If you worked with me, I'd expect the same consideration. So, no more questions, I promise. Just say you'll let me call you again if there's another job."

Vaughn nodded his head in agreement. "That's cool. As long as we know where we stand with each other." He looked at Derek's right biceps stretching the fibers of his T-shirt. Vaughn placed his hand on Derek's arm and felt the muscle. "My apartment is over on Gardner," he said. "Hang a right."

Derek immediately felt himself grow hard. He shifted in his seat, adjusting himself as he divided his attention between driving, glancing at Vaughn's torso as it was revealed through his vest, and following directions. In a part of town notorious for limited parking, and parking by residential permit only, Derek found an available spot that wasn't governed by West Hollywood's innumerable laws.

After wending their way through a maze of units on the second floor of an apartment structure, which covered a city block, Vaughn finally came to a stop. "This is it," he said, using his key to unlock and open the door. Stepping into the room, Vaughn reached for a light switch on the wall and flipped it on.

Derek's eyes were met with an elegantly decorated, contemporary style living space. He looked at Vaughn again. "This is yours?" he said, looking at a grouping of modern leather and chrome furniture in the center of a sunken living room. Colored gels from track lighting cascaded in several directions and highlighted, among other objects, an enormous oil painting, which covered almost one entire wall. Smaller framed paintings accented additional wall space, and a large screen television dominated another wall. Two enormous ferns set on Corinthian column pedestals anchored either side of a sliding glass door that led to a terrace. Again Derek looked at Vaughn with surprise.

"I came to L.A. to become a set decorator," he explained Derek's unspoken question about his refined taste. "The film industry didn't want my creative talents. But a couple of movie stars wanted the raw talent between my legs," he said. "I've been smart with my body, and my money too," Vaughn said. "I'm almost able to get out of the sex trade. Then I can get out of this stinking town and settle down." He turned away from his achievement in interior design and cast his eyes on Derek. He confidently placed the palms of his hands on Derek's chest. "Let's see what you've got," he said and moved to pull Derek's tank over his head. He smiled at Derek's pumped chest and let the shirt drop to the floor. He nodded his head in approval of Derek's physique. Without another word, Vaughn removed his leather vest. Derek, too, nodded.

Vaughn's tanned, muscular chest was carpeted with just enough hair to give him an added dimension of masculinity. His biceps swelled between his forearms and shoulders. Derek determined that they would require two hands to encompass. The tattoo that Derek had partially observed in the half-light of The Rusty Spike was, in full view, a fire-breathing dragon whose scaled and gnarled body twisted around Vaughn's right arm and shoulder. Its fanged jaw snarled at Vaughn's ring-pierced right nipple. Derek gazed in dumbfounded excitement. He was speechless and hoped that Vaughn was a top.

"You better be a good kisser," Vaughn said and walked down a hallway, the walls of which were hung with more works of art. "I never let the guys I fuck for money kiss me. I miss getting kissed."

Derek followed Vaughn and in a moment they were in the bedroom, which was as well-appointed as the front living space. Without a word they undressed and joined each other on the king-size bed. The wall above the headboard was hung with a series of framed sketches of male nudes demonstrating various artistic poses.

Derek, lying on his back, his head resting on two pillows, and his cock fully loaded, took a long hungry look at Vaughn's impressive sex equipment.

Vaughn weighed his own cock in his hand. "This is why I get the big bucks," he sniggered his stock line at the common sight of a man awed by his physical endowment. He straddled Derek's waist. "You're not too small yourself," he joked as he grabbed hold of Derek's joint and gave it a few cursory strokes. Then he laid his body on top of his partner. "Now, kiss me. And make it good."

Derek was nothing if not a great kisser. He sucked face with an ardor that made every man whose mouth he bruised ride a wave of euphoria that made them desperately resist breaking the vacuum seal of their lips. Vaughn, too, happily surrendered to the mutual exploration of their tongues, swabbing the other's gluttonous orifice.

Skin to skin, muscle to muscle, the men instantly succumbed to their most base physical desires for sex. They became vicious with one another. Both were used to the priority of pleasuring other people. Tonight, they were selfishly pleasing themselves.

"You can't buy what I'm going to give to you," Vaughn said, without a trace of arrogance. "It's the limited edition, special reserve, one-hundred proof."

"I'm surprised that one of your clients hasn't adopted you."

"It takes an amazing stud like you to appreciate an amazing stud like me," Vaughn said. "Now shut the fuck up and give me your ass."

Derek grinned as precum oozed over the top of his dick.

TWENTY-SIX

During the following weeks, Derek realized that the amount of time he spent actually fucking had decreased dramatically, while the amount of cash he put away grew to tens of thousands of dollars. Jamie and Vaughn, and two newer studs, Stuart and Chris, were working out well.

And then it all began to unravel. Derek's cell phone rang one morning shortly after midnight. He looked at the display screen, and then answered cheerfully. "Vaughn. How'd the session go?"

"I'm out of here, man. You don't know where I am and if anyone asks, you've never heard of me. Got it?"

Derek was totally confused. "Are you in trouble? Did that prick do something to you?" he asked, genuinely concerned.

"Just listen to me," Vaughn whispered. "Do you even know the guy you turned me on to? He's trouble. I thought he looked familiar. It was that programming executive from Show-Line. I figured that out while he was having his little orgasm. Then, after I had fucked his brains out he said, 'Fraker must be nuts to have let you go.' Christ! Fraker. I told you that he was trouble. We're both dead if he catches either of us!"

Derek was concerned but tried not to reveal his feelings. "So what if he knows that I run an escort service. You sound as though he's Mafia or something."

"May as well be," Vaughn stuttered. "Look, Derek, the guy is crazy. He's been the only game in town for a long time. He's not about to share his clients, or their money, with anyone. You're infringing on his territory. I, for one, will not stick around to see what happens. I'm too close to retirement. Maybe I'll call you in a few months, after the heat dies down."

The telephone conversation was terminated and Derek sat in the Great Room at Weybridge Cottage wondering how serious the situation really was. *Is it possible that my little business is a threat to someone else in Hollywood?* he wondered. *And if someone else knows about my activities, then is it possible that Tom is aware too?* Derek decided to call Juan. Voice mail picked up, and then Derek went to bed.

By the time Juan returned Derek's call, it was late the next morning. "Boss, I didn't pick up my messages until just now," Juan said. "What's the problem?"

"I don't know if there is a problem," Derek said. "But one of my guys just quit because he's afraid that I'm too much competition for some asshole named Fraker."

Juan thought for a moment. "Have you been threatened?" Juan asked.

"No," Derek said.

"Then what's this dude's problem?"

"He thinks that this Fraker guy is going to go ballistic and do something harmful to him . . . and to me," Derek said. "I'm minding my own business, keeping a very low profile, and still, my guy thinks there's trouble ahead. I'm not sure what to do."

"What is there to do?" Juan said. "You've got every right to pursue your business. The dude who left you sounds paranoid. But to be safe, I think you should only be handling clients who Tom sends to you."

"Hell, if I did that, I'd only be getting a fraction of what I earn on my own."

"Two hundred an hour is far from shitty, Boss," Juan said. "Plus, you're on salary too," Juan reminded. "You don't have anything to spend your money on. No rent. No mortgage. Food is provided. Cars, too."

"I've got to make enough money to be independent," Derek said. "As long as I have to kowtow to anyone, I'm not free."

"Okay, listen," Juan said. "I'm not that well connected, but maybe I know someone who knows someone, who knows about this Fraker dude. Let me make a few calls and see what I can find out. I'll get back to you. In the meantime, I'd usually say don't sweat it, but when it comes to the sex trade, there's big money, and where there's big money, there are big people involved. Big people with big reasons to protect their territory. So be careful and lay low."

Derek was starting to feel funky. When he hung up the phone he got up and went to his quarters in the house. There, he put his clothes on. He wanted to call Brent, who was in Ireland, but realized the time difference would make it two A.M. in Dublin. He needed reassurance that Brent was none the wiser about his extracurricular activities. Instead, he dialed Tom's cell.

"Mr. Never Call, Never Write," Tom said when he heard Derek's voice. "To what do I owe this supreme pleasure? Need a fuck?"

Derek was evasive. He skirted the reason for his call and pretended that he was simply growing lonely of not having Brent around, and weary of fucking Tom's friends for a living. "Why don't we ever get together?" Derek said.

"Either I'm not keeping you busy enough, or you're the horniest bastard I've ever known." Tom chuckled. "I can come over now, if you're serious."

"Why wouldn't I be serious," Derek said. "You know you were always a big turn-on for me. If you're thinking about that time when I freaked 'cause you were in Brent's bed with me, I reacted that way because I thought you were taking advantage of a situation. But the way I see it now, you and Brent are taking advantage of me anyway, so why not have a little fun, too."

Tom said, "Derek, some might say you are the one taking advantage of *Brent*. You take his money. You live in his house. You drive his cars. All that you have to do in return is have a little sex now and then. Who wouldn't want a job like yours?"

"A *little* sex?" Derek responded, trying to control his anger. "A little sex would be pumping Brent three or four times a week. I'm nothing more than a fuck machine that you loan out to every visiting dignitary who comes to Hollywood. I'm not complaining, mind you."

"No?" Tom said. "The very act of you calling me for company is a clear indication that you're less than happy with the status quo. Are you ever going to understand that I'm able to see through you?"

Tom did have an uncanny ability to get to the root of a situation almost immediately. But it pissed Derek off that Tom thought that he was transparent. "Hell, I just wanted a little diversion, and you blow everything out of proportion," Derek said. "I don't care whether you come over or not." Then, not wanting to jeopardize cracking Tom for whatever information he may have about Fraker, Derek added, "I don't think Brent would mind if you and I did it. Do you?"

Tom sniggered. "It's early for me, but I'm horny. I'll be over in half an hour. But I'm *not* paying your fee."

Derek hung up the phone. "He thinks I'm so obvious. What an asshole," he mouthed to himself.

Derek was in the gym, supine on the bench press, when Tom arrived.

"Work that chest, boy!" Tom called out an order. "Gimme another rep!"

Derek, turned on by the commanding presence of Tom, completed his set, and stayed stretched out on the bench, panting. Wearing only workout pants, his body glistened with perspiration.

"Fuck, you're hot!" Tom said, as he straddled Derek and dragged his hands over Derek's slippery, perspiration-slick, pumped chest. "I think this home gym, and Everett's healthy cooking has made you even sexier than the last time I saw you naked." Tom laughed as he leaned his face down and lapped the sweat off Derek's abs with his tongue. Seated as he was on Derek's lap, he suddenly felt Derek's cock expanded to his full size. He grinned. "Hmm. Can Dickey come out and play?" he said, and then grabbed Derek's pants by the elastic waist and pulled them down to his ankles. "Who cares if beauty is only skin deep," Tom said, salivating at the sight of Derek's enormous cock. "I knew you'd be a huge success," he added before forcing as much of Derek's cock as would fit in his mouth.

After an exhausting workout of sex, the men laid out on the benches in the steam room. Tom's guttural sounds of lazy satisfaction turned to actual words. "Workin' tonight, right?" he asked. "Phillip, my freak from *Days of Our Lives?*"

Derek, equally indolent from the physical workout with weights, and hard-driving sex with Tom, could only muster a nonverbal "Mmm."

"I don't miss it," Tom said. "I could drive three or four studs a day when I started working my way through college. But after a while, it became such a chore. You'll see."

Derek didn't say so, but if he didn't have the extra help, he would have been burned out months ago. With Tom in the vulnerable position of being sated by sex, Derek decided that the time could never be better for interrogating his mentor. In a voice that sounded impromptu and lackadaisical, he asked, "Did you ever think of outsourcing? You know, hiring a couple of studs to handle the overload?"

For a long moment, Derek thought that perhaps Tom was asleep. Then Tom responded listlessly. "Yeah. I have a friend, Lonnie Penswebber—or Loony Pants Wetter, as I call him. A novelist. Crappy stuff. Sexy page-turners for summer beach reading. He thought his bod was hot shit. Other guys did too, I guess, 'cause they paid my price for him. But with that Fraker on the prowl, I didn't dare recruit anyone else."

Derek reacted. There was the name again. Fraker. And it sounded as though Tom was afraid of him. "What's a Fraker? Some new STD?" Derek asked innocently.

"Not a what. A who," Tom said, sounding half asleep. "Bad news. Thinks he owns the sex trade in Hollywood. Hates an independent like me."

"You mean he's like what, a male Heidi Fleiss?"

Tom coughed a small laugh. "Heidi was a classy businesswoman. Heidi was, and is, a very cool lady who was a victim of police entrapment. She was targeted by the LAPD. Fraker is an animal who treats his clients and his boys like shit."

"So why do the boys stay with him? Why does anyone use his services?" Derek asked.

"Answer number one: Drugs. Answer number two: Blackmail. Answer number three, although you didn't ask: Chances are he already knows who you are. But, as long as you're just fucking Brent and my pals, you're cool. He won't touch you."

Derek sat up, perspiration poured down his head, face and body. "What do you mean, won't touch me? Is this guy dangerous?"

"As I said, he doesn't accept competition. There have been a couple of guys who tried to make a go of providing studs for the stars. What can I say? They're not around anymore."

"Christ, Tom, what if one of Brent's friends knows someone who knows this Fraker dude and mentions me?"

"Relax," Tom said, trying to remain conscious. "This is the tightest circle possible. Only Brent and a few of my friends know about you. Trust me, they're not going to jeopardize not getting your ass on an as-needed basis. It's like alien abductees. The ones who have really had a close encounter would never talk about it."

Derek would not let the subject end. While Tom was trying desperately to let his body and mind drift off in a relaxing sleep in the sauna,

Derek continued questioning him. "If this guy is so dangerous, why didn't you warn me about him?"

" 'Cause he's a nonissue," Tom said, starting to become irritated. "Even if he knew who you were, you're not interfering with his business. Sure, Fraker would love to get his boys up here to take care of Brent, but it ain't gonna happen. Brent's too big a star to fall prey to any potential hassles from the likes of Fraker. That's why you're here, Derek. And you wouldn't be if we didn't think you were trustworthy. I don't count our fucking in the gym. As the man who discovered you, I'm entitled to a finder's fee every now and then."

Derek was silent as he stared into the steam and thought about the warning that Vaughn had given him. If indeed he was treading on Fraker's territory, then what Tom had said about being safe was moot. He thought about Jamie and Vaughn and Stuart and Chris. Each was a superior stud and each had previous experience turning tricks. From where, Derek wondered, had their experience come? When interviewed each had only said that they had been on call for a hotshot in the sex business, but had gotten out. However, without a job history, they were unable to land even a lowly position at McDonald's, and were forced back into prostitution. Derek decided he'd better pay a visit to each of these guys and find out what their backgrounds really were.

"That's enough rest for me," Derek said, standing up. "Got a job to do. But you enjoy yourself for as long as you want," he said to Tom as he picked up a towel and exited the steam room.

Stepping into a cold shower, Derek washed himself thoroughly. He dressed and picked up his cell phone. Exiting the mansion, he speed-dialed Jamie and insisted that they meet in Plummer Park. "This is not a request, it's an order," he said into the phone. "Be there in half an hour."

It was late afternoon as Derek drove the Jaguar along Fountain Avenue and pulled into a parking space next a picnic table. A few guys playing with their dogs occupied West Hollywood's poor excuse for a park. Derek left his car and wandered around. Finally, selecting a table close enough to the parking area to be seen by Jamie, he sat and waited. Soon, Jamie walked into sight. He cautiously approached Derek. Although he only knew Derek to be an easygoing, laid-back guy, the tone that Derek had used in their phone conversation had nearly paralyzed Jamie with fear. Too often, men who could be brutal and cruel had barked at him.

Derek smiled and tried to put Jamie at ease. "Hey, man, thanks for coming," he said.

"What'd I do?" Jamie said. He was defensive, thinking that word must have gotten back to Derek that he was tricking on the side.

Derek looked quizzical. "You tell me. Everybody seems to get a kick out of you. Haven't heard any complaints."

"So, like, why burn my ass on the phone and drag me way the hell over here?" Jamie said, taking on boldness. "I've got work to do for you tonight."

"Work," Derek said. "That's what I need to talk to you about. You're good at your job. I want to know who you worked for before me."

Jamie stared into Derek's eyes. "No one. I mean, there was this guy, but it didn't last long."

"What was the guy's name?" Derek pressed.

"Hey, I left him because he wasn't a good match for me."

"Who wasn't a good match? It's a simple question."

Jamie became flustered. He slammed his fists onto the metal picnic table. "What the fuck difference does it make? I hardly remember the guy. It's in the past, okay?"

Derek was now pissed off. He wanted a straight answer. He stared at Jamie and calmly said, "Fraker."

Jamie stood up from the bench and started to walk away. Derek was just as quick and caught up with him before he reached the street. "What the fuck is wrong?" Derek said. "What does this Fraker guy hold over you? Why is it so difficult to mention his name, let alone talk about him?"

"He's the devil, you asshole!" Jamie said. "I sold my soul to the fucking devil, then I changed my mind and wanted out. And he's coming after me. He's tracking me down. Is it you? Are you the one he sent to drag my ass back to his inferno?" Jamie was nearly apoplectic. He looked at Derek with new eyes. Frightened eyes. "Yeah, you're working for him, I should have known it!"

As Jamie began hyperventilating with fear, Derek wrapped his arms around him for comfort. In a calming voice he insisted that he did not work for Fraker. In fact, he did not even know who Fraker was. He steered Jamie back toward the park. "Get in the car," he suggested. "Let's get a drink somewhere. Your place?"

"Too dangerous," Jamie warned. "I think I'm being watched. Even just now, I think I was followed."

Suddenly Derek was filled with fear and trepidation. He looked around. Everyone he saw was a potential spy. "Oh, great. And if we go back to my place, chances are we'll be tailed." Derek thought for a moment, then opened his cell phone. He pushed Juan's speed dial number. "*Hola, Juan. Como esta?* Hey, I'm in the neighborhood and I need to use the apartment for a little while. Got someone with me. No! Just talk. We need someplace neutral. Maybe you can even help. Can we drop by? Okay. See you in a few."

Jamie was concerned. "The fewer people who know about this, the better."

"It's my pal, Juan. I trust him completely," Derek said.

In ten minutes the three men were seated on the bed and desk chair of the one-room apartment. Derek and Juan were listening to a horror story as told by Jamie.

"I was tweaked out on crystal. I nearly overdosed. He forced me to start using again, within a week of my near-OD. When I refused to fuck any more of his loathsome clients, Fraker personally came over to my apartment with drugs. He teased me with a needle. He said I could have as much as I wanted as long as I continued at least fucking that asshole director, Clarkson. The guy was incredibly hot for me, but I was disgusted by him. I said no. But I was jonesing for Tina, and desperate for money. I tried to barter. I begged for Fraker to fuck me in exchange for a hit. He agreed. And after he came, he intentionally shot me up with a massive amount of speed. Like ten times the normal amount. He wanted to kill me.

"He left me foaming at the mouth and naked, crawling out the door. I wound up convulsing on the lawn outside my building. I was naked and shaking and twitching because of the huge amount he injected. A neighbor called the paramedics who took me to the ER."

Derek held his breath as he listened to the details of Jamie's encounter with Fraker.

Juan, too, was staring with anguish as he thought of this handsome young man caught up in the world of sex and drug freaks.

"I don't understand why he would treat you this way," Derek finally said. "What could you possibly do to him?"

"He's a total control freak," Jamie said. "Plus, he doesn't trust anyone. He saw me as a potential danger to his business. As if I might turn him in, or sell gossip to the tabloids. I could name big names in the industry who play it straight but who pay huge prices for a big dick up their pansy asses. He made an example out of me. I was the poster boy for what would happen to anyone who ever tried to get out of the game, or cash in on their knowledge of what goes on behind the gates of some of the biggest estates in Beverly Hills or Bel Air. I could wreck careers with what I know."

Juan, who had been silent for the duration of Jamie's story, now asked, "Why didn't you tell Derek about this before? If this Fraker guy is as evil as you say then Derek's in trouble even associating with you. It could be seen by Fraker as though Derek recruited you because of your past experience with celebrities."

Jamie said, "I was desperate for work, but I didn't want to be one of those pathetic street hustlers. I wanted someone like Derek who had star clients. I've fucked around on the Internet, and trust me, the men who troll sites like LAM4MNOW, can be completely disgusting. I deserve a better class of man. And that's what I found with Derek."

Derek didn't speak for a long while. He was digesting the information. Then it dawned on him. "What about Stuart and Chris? What are their back stories? Fraker too?"

Jamie stared at Derek. His silence was the answer.

Derek's temper suddenly blew up. "Jesus Christ! It's like I'm infested with an insidious swarm of vermin! How the hell did this happen? One moment my life is peachy, and the next, it all falls apart. I let one pest in the door and it multiplies! Fuck!"

Derek turned to Jamie and his eyes smoldered. The man who was usually inordinately calm was now seething with anger. "I trusted you! And Stuart. And Chris. And Vaughn. You're all slugs! You're the ones who give this business its lousy reputation! But it's entirely my fault. I didn't do my homework. I didn't have you guys tested for drugs or STDs. I took you at your word, which was incredibly stupid of me. I was so naïve. Chalk it up to never having been in the whore business before."

Juan interjected. "Boss, just fix it. Quit the business and go back to being a waiter. You've got plenty of money to keep you going until you find something. And I heard that Onyx is reopening in a month. You can go back to being the best damn waiter in West Hollywood."

Suddenly, Derek saw himself back in his waiter apron, playing the destitute sycophant to table after table of ungrateful diners. He had a physical reaction that caused him to shudder. "Never," he said with resolution. "No way am I busting my ass for minimum wage and a few extra bucks that someone may or may not deign to leave me as a tip. Those days are over. For good."

Juan shook his head. "Boss, you've got to get out of this mess. The only way is to drop Brent. Drop Tom and his friends. Move back with me, and find something legit to do. You don't have to settle for minimum wage. Hell, Cathy and Andrew pay me more than that, plus all the perks."

Derek stood up and began pacing the room. He looked at Jamie and stared for a long moment. "You hated working for Fraker, right? How about the other boys?"

"Everybody hates him. But they have no place else to go. No other income. And Fraker provides drugs."

Derek continued. "Are all the guys on drugs? Are there any who are clean? What does Fraker hold over them?"

Jamie thought for a moment. He shrugged his shoulders. "Actually a good number of them are clean—of crystal, that is. I think we all use pot and alcohol to self-medicate. As for what he holds over them, some of the guys are in school, and don't have any other way of paying their tuition. A couple of others stay in Fraker's home—an incredible mansion in Benedict Canyon. They don't have any other place to go. Their luck—or misfortune—was to be physically appealing to other men. It's their stock in trade. They'd be on the street otherwise."

"But they're making a bundle," Derek said in their defense. "At what, two hundred per trick, surely they can afford their own place to live."

Jamie shook his head. "Fraker's smart. He sends the guys out just often enough to afford to pay for a few credits at Los Angeles City College, or to maintain the illusion of soon being able to afford a first and last month's deposit on a place of their own. He knows what he's doing. They never have quite enough, and therefore they have to continue working their asses off for him."

"Boss," Juan said, "cut your losses now. Don't go back to Brent's tonight. Stay here. Quit while you're ahead!"

Derek smiled. "What, and give up showbiz? No," he said. "That asshole Fraker doesn't own this town."

"The hell he doesn't!" Jamie interrupted. "He owns the sex trade."

"Screw Fraker," Derek said. "I'm not going away."

TWENTY-SEVEN

Derek walked into a second-floor bar called The Third Rail. Although at least twenty young men—all of whom were facsimiles of the others—populated the room, he intuitively recognized the one he arranged to meet. In the few months that Derek had been in the sex trade, he had become almost psychic about the intentions of other men he met. He could tell a hustler from just any ordinary dude looking for sex. And the man he was now approaching wore an aura of dollar signs like a green halo. It could only be Dow.

Dow was one of the men whom Fraker kept on a leash. Dow's wasn't as tight a ball and chain as some of the other studs because his particular physical look was relatively common in West Hollywood. Although he had all the right attributes: the gym-pumped body, blue eyes, straight black hair, ruddy complexion and five-o'clock shadow beard stubble, he lacked the exotic characteristics that made Blacks, Latinos, Asians and Middle Eastern boys the flavors of the month. In any other city, he could have been the most sought after man. But in West Hollywood, with its emphasis on the new, the original, and the cutting edge, he was literally just another pretty face. To pay for? Yes. To pay a thousand dollars a night for? Rarely. Fraker kept him on call, but treated him like a product that was slightly out of date and on back order.

Moving into the dimly lighted room, with its black walls and ceiling, black tables, black chairs and black leather-clad bartender, Derek locked eyes with a young man who was perched on a high bar stool of a tall table, knocking back a bottle of beer. As Derek approached, the young man stopped drinking mid-swallow and let the neck of the bottle linger at his lips.

The man watched with slight trepidation as Derek grabbed hold of another high stool and dragged it behind him. When he arrived at the table, Derek yanked the stool into position, and sat down looking directly at him.

For a long beat neither man spoke. Finally, Derek said, "Feel like moonlighting?"

Dow slowly shook his head. "Hazardous to my health."

Derek looked up and caught the bartender's attention. He silently indicated that he wanted to be served a bottle of beer. He reengaged Dow's blue eyes. "Overtime pay," Derek said.

Dow took another swig of his beer. "Jamie's already in trouble with Fraker. And Vaughn, too. I don't want the hassle."

Derek's beer arrived. He reached into his jeans pocket and withdrew a five-dollar bill. He waved away the change. He took a long swallow and placed the bottle firmly on the tabletop. "You've talked to Jamie, so you know what I want, and what I can offer."

"You're suicidal," Dow said. "I think you don't very much value your nuts, do you? I am perfectly satisfied with my employment arrangement."

Derek digested what Dow had to say. Then, after taking another long swallow of beer, he said, "The men I fuck are younger by a decade or more than the farts Fraker makes you service. They're wealthier, and healthier. Hell, last night I fucked a famous HBO star whose series is up for an Emmy. I know that you got sent to fuck that gnome who was famous way back in Vaudeville, for Christ's sake."

Although his face did not register surprise, Dow said, "Sucker was secretly videotaped too. Something Fraker will graciously offer to screen as entertainment at the guy's memorial service. That is, unless his widow discovers that Mr. X wanted to make a large bequest to the owner of the tape."

"That sucks," Derek said.

"Fraker sucks," Dow added.

"I don't like to see nice people ripped off and exploited."

"That's the way of the world."

In that moment, when Dow shifted slightly from insolent degenerate to compassionate guardian, Derek knew the potential to recruit him away from Fraker was possible. "At the One Night Stand Agency, as

I affectionately call my service, its one hundred percent guaranteed that the sex experience will be enjoyable for both client and stud," Derek said.

"No one has ever jeopardized Fraker's business by talking about it," Dow said, reluctant to continue the line of conversation.

"As it should be," Derek added.

Dow stared Derek down for a long time. "Don't try to sell me the horseshit that anyone actually likes this business," he said. "It's degrading, disgusting, and demoralizing. You may have some decent clients, and your guys could be cool, but it's still an obscene and detestable business."

Derek nodded his head as he poured another slug of beer into his mouth. "A year? Two years? How long do you figure until you can get out?"

Dow looked off into the blackness of the bar. He was seriously evaluating the question and considering the circumstances that would enable him to follow through with his plan. He did not respond to the question.

With a vague gesture to the bartender, Derek ordered another round of drinks. He silently watched the parade of sexy men wander through the room, each glancing a covetous eye toward him and Dow. Each envisioning fucking, or being fucked by, either or both men. After the bartender knocked the beers onto the table, and left with a ten-dollar bill, Derek and Dow sipped from their cold bottles. "Got a good business plan, do you?" Derek said.

Dow's facial expression was empty, but he was nevertheless amenable to listening to Derek. If Derek wanted to impart some wisdom that could help him achieve personal freedom, he was ready to listen.

"The guys and I have a financial advisor," Derek continued. He pretended to be momentarily distracted by the shirtless body of a man whose muscled chest was adorned with pierced nipples, and his head was shaved and tattooed on the back with Gothic symbols. "We all have individual plans too," Derek said. "Another year of this. Max. Then, like you want to be, we're outta here."

Dow made a face. "A year? For you, maybe. But not Jamie and the others. I know how the racket works. It's like any corporation. Labor is hired as cheaply as possible but with the maximum amount of work required. The boss gets rich, the rest of us dumb shits drag our asses from one bed to another and still can't meet the rent. I don't even own a decent car, let alone a prayer of getting out and on my own in the foreseeable future. And I know I've pulled in at least a hundred thou for the boss."

Derek scoffed. "So you think there are no alternatives," he said. "Shit, man, you're more than a walking dildo. Ask Jamie what he's been making in just one night since he started giving it up for you know who from *The West Wing*. In fact, I don't know why I'm bothering to waste my time sitting here with you. I guess you're satisfied with Fraker."

Derek drained his bottle of beer and stood up. "Catch you later, man," he said, and turned to leave. He started to walk toward the exit but then suddenly changed direction.

Dow watched as Derek headed for the men's room. He also saw that as Derek wended his way through a sea of tables, every head that he passed turned and tried to make eye contact.

With a deep intake of breath, Dow too, pushed back his chair and stood. He followed the same path, elbowing his way through the crowded room, and knowing that the horny studs who peppered the bar were giving him the same eye that they used in their attempt to reel in Derek.

When Dow pushed open the bathroom door, he saw Derek slightly leaning into the room's one urinal. Derek turned to check out the new arrival, and Dow sidled up directly behind him. They did not exchange words.

Dow inspected Derek's butt, which seemed stuffed into his jeans. He heard the hard steady stream of Derek pissing into the shallow water in the bottom of the trough, and he moved slightly to the right to get a better view of Derek's cock.

Dow involuntarily raised an appreciative eyebrow when he saw how Derek's large prick laid across the palm of his hand, with his thumb on the head and fingers supporting the shaft. Dow felt a stirring in his pants, and a sudden urge to suck a big piece of dick.

As the sound of Derek's heavy stream dissipated to a trickle, Dow put his hand on Derek's shoulder. "Don't shake it, man," he said as he lightly turned Derek around and backed him up against the wall. In one simultaneous move, Dow fell to his knees, placed his hands on Derek's hips and drew his long, thick, flaccid penis into his mouth. As Dow slathered the shank with his wet tongue, he tasted the last drops of piss, and inhaled the intoxicating scent of the surrounding pubic bush. He went to work feasting like a starved animal. He was desperate to be sated with a full load of Derek's hot load.

As Derek became stone hard, Dow could taste the first sour drops of precum, which made his own dick harder, and his resolve all the more urgent to have Derek shoot his thick cream down his throat.

Working with one purpose, and so completely engrossed in his activity, Dow paid little attention to the sound of the bathroom door opening followed by the echo of boots scraping the floor and the releasing of a beer-filled bladder.

Derek, leaning against the cold tile wall, opened his eyes for a moment when the man came in, but then went back to concentrating on being serviced by Dow. He opened his eyes once again and saw the tattooed skinhead he previously cruised, dividing his attention between watching the sex scene and his aim for the porcelain. The idea of having an audience, and this muscled man in particular, brought Derek to the brink of climax. He grabbed at two tufts of hair on Dow's head and began to rapidly force himself deep into his mouth and throat. Focusing on the perfectly packed chest, arms and abs of the voyeur, Derek could not hold back for another moment. With a sudden shudder, an expression of pain on his face and a glassy-eyed stare, he ejaculated into the eager hole of Dow's slobbering mouth.

"Shit, man," the onlooker moaned and stepped forward. He kneeled down beside Dow and put his face up to Derek's cock, effectively nudging Dow to the side. For a moment he cleaned up Derek's dick with his tongue. Then, as Derek became flaccid, the man turned to face Dow and instantly began kissing him and tasting Derek's cum on his tongue, lips and chin.

Derek stepped away from the wall and buttoned up his pants. He looked at Dow who was completely absorbed in being molested by the new arrival. When the two crawled into the room's one stall and closed the door, Derek walked toward the bathroom door. "Bend over!" he heard a voice demand. He was sure it was not Dow's voice. Then Derek walked into the bar.

Derek slipped into the Jaguar and turned the ignition. He fed a disc of The Dave Matthew's Band into the tight, thin mouth of the CD player, looked at the clock on the dashboard, then sat watching the door that led in and out of The Third Rail. Fifteen minutes later, Dow emerged, alone.

Shifting the transmission into drive, Derek cautiously rolled toward Dow who was walking to his ancient Chrysler LeBaron. When Derek's vehicle was beside Dow, he rolled down the electric window. "Best blow job I've had in a while," he said, as the car continued rolling slowly.

Dow continued walking and facing straight ahead. "A whore gets a ton of practice. Nothing's free."

"You expect me to pay for something I get every night, and didn't even ask for in the first place?" Derek said.

Dow didn't respond right away. He continued walking. Finally, he said, "It was an audition. And I better get a call back. Here's my pager number." He reached into the front pocket of his jeans and produced a paper napkin with a telephone number hand-printed in blue ink. He offered it to Derek through the open window.

Dow jangled his car keys as he arrived at his vehicle. "How are you going to protect me?" he asked as he unlocked the driver's side door. "Word is bound to filter up to Fraker. He'll send his flying monkeys, then we're both dead."

"I don't let my guys or my clients down," Derek said as he stepped on the brake and shifted into reverse. "Back to you later, man," he said as he retreated and then shifted once again into drive. He turned the volume up on Dave Matthews as he slowly ventured out onto Highland Avenue and waited for oncoming traffic to allow an opening through which to drive off. When the way was clear, he hung a right and then another right onto Melrose Avenue. Looking at the clock he thought, *Shit, my ball sack is so drained, I'm not interested in fucking tonight.* Although the costar of the latest Cameron Diaz–produced film was in town for a press junket and had made arrangements with Tom to be serviced, Derek was not in the mood.

Derek pulled the car over to the curb. He picked up the cocktail napkin that Dow had given him, and glanced at the number. Then he reached for his cell phone. He dialed the numbers, punched in his own and sat back and waited. Within two minutes the telephone rang. Derek didn't bother to say hello. Instead he said, "The Bel Age. Room seven three nine. This one needs a nasty dick, so stop at Gelson's Market and buy a small wedge of Limburger cheese and massage it into your cock and crotch. Call me afterward."

TWENTY-EIGHT

In the weeks that followed, as Brent flew from one film location in New Zealand to another in South America, there was seldom a day or night in which Derek felt obliged to have sex with anyone. He now had his retinue of six studs, all of whom were kept busy in their apartments, or in hotel rooms around the city. Word-of-mouth advertising had provided more than enough work. And the money began to pile up. Derek was satisfied. His clients were satisfied. And his boys were satisfied and well paid. And then, on a Saturday morning, his cell phone rang. The call changed everything.

It was Marshall Topper. He had somehow obtained Derek's private cell phone number.

"Told you I could smell talent a mile away," Topper bragged. "Took one look at you and knew that a lot of men would have their dreams come true if you'd nail their asses. And I hear that your piece is even more impressive than even I gave you credit for. This I've gotta see. So how 'bout a meeting? For old times' sake?"

Derek took a deep breath. "As a matter of fact, Marshall, I'm taking a break from that work. But I've got a pal who I know you'd love. When do you want to book him?"

"Book him?" Topper said snidely. "You sound like the maitre d' at Soledad's. You don't pencil me in like someone making an appointment for a perm and color. And you don't come into my territory and start competing with me. I know what you're up to. It's old news. I've been watching you. And waiting. Thought I'd see where you were going with your little scheme. I'm giving you a friendly warning. I wouldn't do this for just anyone. But since we go back a ways, this is me being a good sport. What I'm saying is, take your little business to another town, preferably another state, 'cause you're cutting into my profits. Understand me?"

Derek was confused and angry. "How am I bothering you, Marshall?" he asked. "I'm nobody. I'm not doing anything that could possibly interfere in your life."

"As I said, you've ventured into my territory, stud. Either you pay a franchise fee, or get out your passport and take a trip to San Bernardino."

"Why do I matter to you?" Derek said. "And why are you so hostile? I thought we were friends."

"Friends? I don't have friends. At least you and your pal Juan—yeah, I remember Juan—didn't tolerate all those guys who used to make fun of me. Too little hair on my head, too much on my back and belly, they said. You and I had some good talks, at least you didn't snub me. Which is why I'm sort of returning the favor now. Trust me, I haven't been so decent to other guys who've tried your bullshit."

Derek listened to Marshall's adenoidal voice over the cell phone. He reminded Derek of a school yard bully. Marshall alternated between benevolent old friend, and acrimonious business rival.

"Which is why I'm personally delivering this message," Marshall replied. "I could have sent someone else to do the job. I wanted to make this more personal."

"I'm touched," Derek snorted. "I hope you don't mind if I take time to consider our discussion."

"There's nothing to consider," Marshall said. "Pretend I'm a customer at Onyx. I've placed an order and you damn well better deliver—with a smile. The only difference is that I've given you a tip in advance. I'd hate to see you become impotent at such a young age."

And then the line disconnected.

Derek was stunned. The world of sex for sale was apparently a small one in Hollywood. If Marshall, whom Derek considered a small-time panderer, knew what he was up to, then it wasn't a stretch to believe that Fraker, too, was wise to the fact that he had branched out. Derek took a moment to consider his options. Quitting was not one of them.

It was midday, and although Juan was working, he needed to speak to him right away. He dialed Cathy's number and hoped that she didn't answer.

"Please record at the tone. Thank you."

The outgoing message was succinct, if not unceremonious. Derek stalled for a moment, then hung up. He didn't want a lot of questions raised by Cathy, should she be the one to pick up the messages. Derek then dialed Juan's apartment and left a message there. "This is really important, so please call the moment you hear this. Thanks, bud."

Derek was in a daze. The idea that Marshall Topper was trying to call the shots in his life made no sense to Derek. Who the hell was Marshall to make any demands with regard to whatever endeavor Derek pursued? Why should he be the least bit concerned about the relatively little business enterprise that Derek was quickly building? And where had he heard about One Night Stand? This was supposed to be the most discreet boutique escort service in Hollywood. As Derek further considered the unsettling conversation, it occurred to him that it was probably one of the new boys who had flapped his lips.

But more frightening than someone suspecting that Derek was illegally procuring sex partners for the rich and famous, was the obvious conclusion that if he was known, then his celebrity clients, too, were known to be involved. "Holy shit!" Derek said quietly, as he considered the repercussions of what he had done with the trust that Tom and Brent and his friends had bestowed upon him. If it were true that someone had a list of his clients, and if that list was divulged to the district attorney—or Mary Hart—half of Hollywood could implode on itself. And by association, Derek could quite literally wind up dead.

Derek left the estate and drove the Jaguar toward Malibu. He had to get away and think about what to do. He thought about calling Tom for advice, but decided it was too soon, he needed time to think through the possible consequences of admitting his racket. Derek considered each of his hired men. Jamie was too frightened of his former employer to ever consider blabbing that he had joined Derek's team. The same for Vaughn and Stuart. They were all exceptionally horny guys who couldn't get enough sex and who were grateful for the way they were treated by Derek and the clients.

In a very short period of time, One Night Stand had become the service of choice for the six degrees of separation groupings who knew someone, who knew someone, who knew another someone who had been serviced by Derek. And Derek was able to arrange the hottest sex of their lives. He was almost certain that his full-time stable of boys were loyal and discreet. He trusted them completely. But then he thought of the latest addition to the family.

Three weeks ago, Jamie came down with food poisoning, and was unable to work. During that time, Derek had visited him and asked if he knew anyone who could do one out call job. Drowsy and weak from the loss of fluid in his body, Jamie mentioned that he had received a call from one of Fraker's ex-boys: Tag Tempkin. Jamie said that Tag had called, desperate to get away from Fraker. He had once been a celebrated figure skater and had made his way to Hollywood with the expectation of becoming a star. Jamie, in his weakened state muttered, "I hardly know the guy. But he's got a killer bod. Maybe you can use him."

Derek was in a bind, and rather than meet the boy, he called Tag's pager, introduced himself and offered him a job. Tag eagerly accepted the assignment, and, from Derek's conversation the next morning with the client—a CNN anchor who was on assignment in Los Angeles, covering a story about, of all things, male prostitution—he had been more than satisfied with Tag. Derek began giving Tag more work, and he still had never met the man.

As Derek drove north along Pacific Coast Highway, with the ocean on his left and the Malibu hills on his right, he thought about Tag, and Fraker, and Marshall.

After passing Las Flores Mesa, and a short way past the Malibu Inn restaurant, Derek signaled a right turn. He found a parking space along the stretch of highway and pulled up behind a Ford Explorer SUV. From the back hatch of the SUV, a surfboard extended beyond the cab, and a classically beautiful Asian man with the taut, compact body of a gymnast was changing into a wet suit. Derek pretended to be absorbed in an animated conversation on his cell phone. In reality, he was taking in the sight of this perfectly built man with smooth skin and a packed body. Derek was sexually attracted to the man, whose face was exotically beautiful. His shoulders were round, his arms and pecs pumped, and his stomach flat. From the distance, the man's hairless body looked as if he would be silk to the touch. Derek had been looking for an Asian to satisfy a particular client, and the man in front of him was everything he had been led to believe his client wanted.

Just then, the wind came up and blew the man's tank top, which he'd laid over his shoulder, onto the busy highway. The Asian man responded automatically and lunged for his shirt. A car swerved and the driver laid on his horn as the Asian jumped back. Derek checked his rearview mirror for oncoming traffic and gingerly opened his car door.

"Hang tight," he shouted to the man above the din of traffic and the roaring ocean just a few hundred yards away. When Derek saw an opportunity to quickly retrieve the shirt, he dashed into the road, snatched the black mesh tank and sprinted back to the safety of the sidewalk, as a car horn joined the roar of "Motherfucker!" from a passing car.

"Gotta be careful," Derek said to the Asian stud. "Kinda dangerous here."

"It was only a shirt," the man said, thankful for Derek's efforts, but making it clear that the act of heroism was unnecessary. "Not worth risking your life!"

Up close, Derek was even more impressed with the man's physique and overall appearance. His teeth were bright, and his smile made Derek's naval ache. His eyes actually twinkled, and dimples anchored both sides of his cheeks. His nose was so perfect that it was nondescript. And his black, windblown hair fell halfway to his collarbone. "Thought it was a good way to get to know you." Derek smiled, wondering if the man was going to suddenly kick the shit out of him with some form of martial arts maneuver.

The Asian was definitely taken aback for a moment. Then, as he took a more deliberate review of Derek, who was pumped and tanned, he smiled. He offered his hand and said, "My name's Hiro. And thanks for grabbing my shirt."

Derek smiled too, and accepted Hiro's hand. "Derek," he said, introducing himself. They looked into each other's eyes until Derek broke the spell by asking about surfing. "Never tried it." He shrugged a regret.

"If you ever want a lesson . . ."

A cool wind came up from the water and Hiro's smooth skin was suddenly a blanket of goose pimples. "Better get my suit on," he said, reaching for his gear. "What brings you to the beach, aside from rescuing strangers from a life without their clothing?"

"Just out for a drive," Derek said. "Thought I'd clear my head with a walk along the shore. Mind if I watch you for a while?"

Hiro shrugged. He finished dressing in his wet suit, dragged out his surfboard, and locked the car. He cocked his head toward the beach.

"Let's dodge the traffic together." When the volume of cars on the road abated, they raced to the opposite side of the four-lane highway and made their way down toward the water.

The surf was relatively mild, the waves no more than three or four feet high. But the water was filled with other surfers. Hiro entered the ocean and straddled his board. As he began to paddle out beyond the breakers, he turned to Derek and waved. Derek waved back and watched as Hiro reached a waiting place, where he floated on his surfboard until just the right wave came along. Suddenly, he was lying on his board, paddling furiously, going after an incoming swell. Derek watched as Hiro sat up and kneeled onto his board as the wave bore down on him. Keeping just ahead of the rushing water he suddenly jumped to his feet and struggled to maintain his balance as he rode the wave—larger than the others that had been breaking—to where it tumbled onto the sand.

"Whoa-hoo!" Derek enthusiastically yelped and raised both arms to the sky. "Awesome!" he cheered into the wind.

Hiro smiled broadly. "I'm going out for a few more," he yelled to Derek on the shore. "Take your walk and meet me at the car in an hour."

Derek nodded his head. "An hour. Very cool," he called. "Have fun." His eyes made an obvious tour of Hiro's smiling, wet face and the dark hair, which was plastered over his head. Even in his wet suit Hiro was stunning to observe, and Derek wanted to reach out and take the man's face in his hands and taste his mouth and tongue. Derek nodded again. "One hour. Make it fly by," he said, then turned and began walking down the stretch of sand.

The sky was overcast. Gulls overhead squawked as they caught an updraft of air. They appeared to hover in place for a while. Then they spiraled toward the water's surface and plunged headfirst into a specific spot where food was waiting. Derek watched as one by one the birds repeated their routine, some of them floating for long stretches of time on the water's surface. The wind whipped off the water and tousled Derek's hair. Soon, Derek's thoughts of Hiro and the craving he had to make love to his body, were pushed away by his concerns about Marshall's warning, and the possibility that he had endangered the reputations and careers of his clients.

As Derek slowly walked the length of the beach, he reflected on all that had occurred to him since the moment that Jet had addressed her staff at Onyx that early Sunday morning, when she announced their dismissal. He thought about his attempts to find another job as a waiter. He remembered Marshall's early encouragement that he could sell sex to make money. He balanced his memory of advertising as a massage therapist with the retrospection of his first offensive clients, and then the man who literally altered his life forever: Tom. "I never knew whether to hate you, or to love you," he heard himself say aloud about Tom.

Derek knew that Juan would tell him not to think about all the possibilities of what might have occurred in his life had he not met Tom and accepted Brent's offer to serve as his on-call sex toy. The fact that he traveled the particular path that he was on, was the only thing worth thinking about. It was useless to imagine any other scenario. "What's done is done," he said, wondering if he should simply go home, collect all the cash from the safe, and disappear. "There's enough money to start a whole new life."

But again he thought of Juan. And he thought of Cathy, whose friendship he missed. He also considered Brent, who he actually liked a lot, and the guys who had joined his team and expected him to help take care of them. "Why don't I just say, screw 'em all and simply look out for number one? Yeah, I should go back and find Hiro, let him fuck my brains out, then drive back to Beverly Hills, and skip town."

Another voice chimed in and replaced those thoughts. *What are you going to do for wheels? You can't take the Jag or any of the other cars. It's called grand theft auto. Yeah, you can afford to buy a new car, but anything decent is going to take a chunk of change, and paying with cash is bound to raise suspicions about you. What's your contingency plan? You idiot, you haven't even thought that far ahead. Where will you go? A big city where you can get lost in the crowd, or a small town where Marshall and the police would never think to look for you? Shit, what have you gotten yourself into?*

Derek was used to questioning himself on the subject of his business operation. Some days, when he wondered why he wasn't in a socially acceptable business, he told himself that he was smarter than Joe Average. He associated with some of the most important people on the planet, and he got paid a large amount of money for doing what most people do for free—reveling in pig sex.

On other days, he wondered why he hadn't achieved the career goals he had set for himself. Sure, he was making substantially more money than someone with an advanced academic degree, but he never imagined that his work would take him to the most base of all animal urgings. Still, on other days, he convinced himself that although he was breaking the law, he was actually providing a badly needed "service." The overprivileged were entitled to sex, as was everybody else in the universe. Stars had to get laid, and Derek determined he might as well be paid to help them.

But today was different. After the call from Marshall he was suddenly faced with the politics of the sex trade. Was he too successful, and therefore a threat to his competitors? Like a CEO with his company stock climbing, there were resentful wolves nipping at his heels, plotting a hostile takeover and desperate to run him out of business. As Derek continued to walk along the sand, he was conflicted between genuinely wanting to quit working as an escort/panderer, and being embittered by anyone who would attempt to impose their will against him. Marshall, he thought, might be protecting his own interests, but he had no right to try to push Derek around. He determined that if Marshall wanted a fight, he better be prepared to lose. With that resolve, Derek turned around and walked back toward Hiro and the car. "I'll get a well-deserved fuck and then take care of business," he said.

Derek reconnected with Hiro. Driving in tandem, they ended up at a small beach house on the grounds of a large estate in the Malibu colony. There they had sex for the rest of the afternoon.

TWENTY-NINE

It was evening, and Derek was exhausted. Not only had he been emo-tionally drained from his altercation with Marshall earlier in the day, he was physically depleted of energy from being fucked by Hiro—three times. Although he enjoyed every sheet-soaking moment of sex with the amazing Asian, he left the beach house feeling numb. It was time to face reality and take an unflinching evaluation of where he stood.

Behind the wheel of the Jag, Derek turned the key in the ignition and then checked his phone for messages. "Two new messages have been added to your mailbox," the familiar feminine voice stated. He listened. The first was Juan, who was anxious about the tone in Derek's voice on his own answering machine. "I'm home after seven. Come over when you can," Juan said.

"Message two." This one was from Tag, telling him that something had gone wrong with his client at the Wilshire Regency Hotel. "The dude was hostile. Then he and I got into it. Before I knew it, Security was breaking in and dragging me out with hardly a stitch on," Tag said. "You're supposed to protect us from these assholes. Come and get me. I'm at the Beverly Hills police station. Hurry."

Derek angrily beat the palm of his right hand against the steering wheel. "What the Christ happened?" he asked aloud. "That was my big country star! He's never been any problem!"

Suddenly Derek's rotten day was turning in to a full-fledged night-mare. He pushed speed dial for Juan's number. "Thank God, the voice of sanity," he said to Juan. "Depending on traffic, I'm about an hour out. I've gotta bail a friend out of jail, but I'll be over as soon as possible. I'm in deep shit."

Although Juan was deeply concerned about Derek, Andrew had called just moments before. He had sneaked back into town and was going to stay the night at the condo. He told Juan to join him. "Boss, there's something I can't get out of. An emergency. You know I'd be here for you if I could. Look, go to the apartment, and I'll try to get away as soon as possible."

Derek was incredulous. The one friend he thought he could count on was suddenly preoccupied with a mysterious crisis. "Dude, I'm in huge trouble," Derek said into the phone. "I'm going to the police station, then home. I'm reachable, so call when you can. And good luck with your urgent business. Hope 'he's' worth it."

Derek shifted his car's transmission into drive and slowly rolled up to the Colony guard kiosk. When the gate arm lifted, he floored the engine and raced out to the Pacific Coast Highway. As he drove the long stretch of road, bordered on the left by tall cliffs, and on the right by the ocean, he drove well over the speed limit and thought about who else he could run to for help and advice. Would Tom be of any use? he wondered. Derek hated the idea of running to Tom for anything, but he couldn't think of where else to turn. He picked up the phone and dialed Tom's number.

"Doesn't anybody pick up their telephones anymore?" Derek bellowed as he heard Tom's recorded outgoing message. "Tom. It's Derek. Need to talk, ASAP. Call me. Please."

Derek tossed his cell phone onto the front passenger seat and sighed. "Screw everybody!" He drove in silence and when he reached Sunset Boulevard, he waited an inordinately long period of time at the signal. Finally able to turn left, he sped up the hill through the Palisades, Bel Air and Beverly Hills. He ended up at the police station. There, he discovered that Tag was no longer in custody. No charges had been pressed by either the hotel or the hotel guest. Now Derek had to find Tag and get some answers.

Tag didn't answer Derek's page. A half hour went by and Derek tried again. Still there was no response.

Finally ensconced in Weybridge Cottage, Derek's phone rang. Hoping that it was Tag, or Juan, or even Tom, he looked at the Caller ID. It was unfamiliar. However, he immediately recognized the voice. "Hey, pussy boy." It was Marshall.

"I've got something that used to belong to you. Hold the line for a sec." The next voice that Derek heard was also familiar. It was Tag.

"Thanks, asshole. Because of you, I spent the whole fucking afternoon and evening in a holding tank in the fucking Beverly Hills Police Station," Tag said. "Do you have any idea how it feels to be treated like a criminal, for Christ's sake? If it wasn't for my *real* friends, like Fraker here, I'd probably still be there!"

Derek was as confused as he was furious. "Fraker? You mean Marshall," he said. "What happened at the hotel? Laird has never been a problem before."

"You calling *me* the problem?" Tag accused.

"According to the Beverly Hills police you were high! My boys *never* use drugs! Second," Derek continued, "don't tell me anybody bailed you out, because I spoke to the desk sergeant and he told me that all charges against you were dropped, per Laird and the hotel management. Just tell me what's going on. And what's this about Fraker? Are you and Marshall connected with him?"

Derek heard Marshall's voice muffled as if a hand was covering the mouthpiece. Still he could make out shouting, and Marshall calling Tag stupid. Then Marshall came back on the line. "Man, I told you this morning to get the fuck out of Dodge. I didn't mean at your convenience. I meant now. Pronto. Like yesterday. I don't want you or any of your boys to be fucking anyone in this town ever again. Wait, I take that back." Marshall was silent for a moment. "I'm thinking."

Derek wasn't interested in what idiot thoughts ran though Marshall's head. Still, he listened.

"You seem to like whoring around so much, I've decided to offer you and Jamie and Stuart, and who's the other one? Never mind. I'm prepared to offer you guys all the sex you want. But on my terms. You've got a decent client base and you've got a good reputation. Well, at least you did until that drama at the Wilshire Regency this afternoon. We'd make a good team. Tag here, has already come back to me . . . I mean, he's accepted my terms."

Derek could not believe what he was hearing. What did Marshall mean when he said that Tag had "come back"? And what did Tag mean when he said he had a friend like Fraker? He paused for a very long moment, trying to collect his thoughts and to say the right words. Rather than jump to the obvious conclusion—that Marshall and Fraker were one and the same—Derek tried to buy more time. "I didn't want to work with you the first million times you offered, and I sure as hell don't want to now." He spoke as calmly as his anger would allow. "Listen, just get off my back. You can take your fucking cock and stick it up someone else's ass. I'm not leaving town, and I'm not giving up my business and I'm not fucking for you!"

Marshall laughed. "I told Tag you'd say that. You're one of those gamblers who just has to let it all ride until the wheel of fortune skips past your number and you lose everything. Because that's what's happening. You've more than lost, man."

"Why are you doing this to me?" Derek finally said.

Marshall made a sound that meant he thought Derek was a loser. "I don't have a century to run down the entire list," he said. "Just try to go to sleep tonight thinking about Diane Sawyer's morning news scoop as she looks into the television camera and solemnly lists Brent, Ray, Jim, Martin, Dickie, Paul, to name just a few, and tells America how much their movie and television idols love taking it up the ass. If you think the Bible Belt was shocked by Janet Jackson's Super Bowl tit, wait'll they hear about these guys.

"Tonight, as you say your 'Now I lay me down to sleep's, imagine your picture gracing CNN, The Drudge Report, and the front pages of every respected newspaper on the planet as well as *Time* and *Newsweek,* and the tabloids. Before I'm through with you, the world will recognize your picture as that of the man who single-handedly destroyed Hollywood." Marshall laughed devilishly. "Sleep well, my pretty friend." And then the line went dead.

Derek was practically catatonic. He sat on the sofa in his living quarters and stared out the window at the shimmering blue light from the pool reflecting off the walls of the cabaña. Anger, fear, resentment, and guilt all vied for attention. His thoughts bounced from fury at Marshall and Tag to his personal liability to Brent and his friends. He panicked with the prospect of being arrested and jailed for pandering. He felt bitterness that the nearly destitute life he had experienced prior to being inducted into the elevated world of the rich and famous, was a place to which he might have to return.

Derek remembered how frightened he had been when he was unemployed. He recalled having only enough money in his pocket to buy a six-pack of beer. The realization came that for the past six months he had been on an extended vacation from the real world. *Yeah, sex can be messy,* he thought, *but most of the guys Tom turned me on to were cool. And God knows I'd never have gotten a taste of what it's like to live in Brent's world on my own.*

And then the telephone rang. He answered with a melancholy voice.

"Boss!" It was Juan. "I'm just leaving Century City."

"Hmm," Derek said, flatly.

"So, are you home? Tell me where you want to meet. If you're home, I'm closer to you than if you drove to the apartment."

Derek sighed. "Yeah. Home."

"Boss, you don't sound well. Leave the gate open."

They simultaneously disconnected their telephone lines.

THIRTY

"You smell like sex," Derek said absently.

Juan, seeing a look of despair in Derek's eyes, put his hand on the small of Derek's back and guided him into the study. He led him to the sofa and suggested they open a bottle of wine. "Just sit," Juan said as he worked his way over to the bar. "Talk to me," he said, with a corkscrew in hand. "Anything I can do to change your terrible disposition?"

"Cyanide might help," Derek quipped. "I'll settle for a lung full of carbon monoxide."

"Where's the big quake when you need it? Right?" Juan said as he returned with two glasses of red wine. He handed one to Derek. "Here's to the ladies who lunch. Oh, and to that Fraker jerk you used to talk about."

Derek was abruptly shaken from his personal thoughts. His quick movement caused him to slosh some of his wine onto the floor. "What?" he said. "What made you say that name?"

"'Cause he's the one person in Hollywood who has more troubles than you."

Derek was dazed. "I don't follow."

"The news. It was on NPR on the way over. You did say there was a male Heidi Fleiss and that his name was Fraker, right? He's in deep shit. LAPD sting. Grand Jury indictment. Buncha stars are sweating it. They've already named practically the entire cast of *Man to Man,* and those two mimes on *The Alice Paris Show.* All clients. *Alleged* clients. Report said that literally dozens of other celebrities are being investigated. So cheer up. Your life can't be half as ugly as his."

Derek was dumbfounded. He thought back to his conversation with Marshall and Tag, which had been a relatively short while ago—a few hours at most. Therefore, his theory that Marshall and Fraker were one and the same could not be correct. Derek picked up the television remote control and pushed "power." *Queer Eye for the Straight Guy* was on with an episode he'd seen at least a dozen times. He channel surfed until he found CNN. A video clip of someone with a leather jacket over his head and covering his face, standing beside an arrogant-looking Tag Tempkin dissolved into an image of hip-hop star L M N O P.

"There's . . . Tag!" Derek stuttered loudly.

". . . more arrests are expected," the news anchor ended his report in a disinterested tone. "Also in the news at this hour, scientists in England claim to have unraveled the mystery of Jennifer Aniston's success."

"Holy fuck!" Derek said matter-of-factly, as he again pushed the power button on the remote control. The screen instantly went to black. "I spoke to Tag just a few hours ago."

"Who?"

"One of the guys I hired to work for me," Derek exclaimed. "A real shit. Almost ruined a relationship I had with a good client. But then I find he also works for that creep Marshall Topper."

"He used to tell me how much money I could bring in if I let him send me out to a guy who he said was hard-up for me. Someone who apparently came to the restaurant a lot," Juan said. "Wanted to pay me five hundred just to let him suck my dick. I never told you this," he continued, "but after we all got canned from the restaurant, Marshall called me. Offered to send me out. I would have gone, I was so desperate. But that was the day you came to my apartment and brought me back to yours. You saved me from that scumbag."

Derek stared at Juan, stunned by another surprise and a bit miffed. "He never called me. That is, not until today," Derek said.

"Did you tell him you were already gainfully employed, that he can take his money and stick it?"

"He knows that I'm working, all right. The problem is, I'm working in his territory."

"How the hell did he find out?" Juan was anxious. He knew Marshall's bad-ass reputation. "Is this why you're in a mood? Is Marshall trouble for you?"

Derek was pensive. "I thought so a little while ago. But on the news, the guy in the picture with Tag . . . the guy with him had a leather jacket over his head so I couldn't tell but . . . Marshall wore leather . . . Maybe that was him being hauled away, and not Fraker."

"Boss, I'm confused," Juan said, sipping his glass of wine and yawning because of the late hour. "What's Marshall got to do with Fraker, or vice versa?"

Derek took a sip of wine and plopped himself down on the sofa. He looked at Juan and began chronicling the events of the day, from the bitter telephone confrontation with Tag to the argument he had with Marshall to meeting and being fucked by Hiro to Tag's incarceration and ultimate release.

"And I thought I had it tough, working all day for Cathy, and screwing her husband all evening."

Derek was serious. "This whole day has been horrible. I've gotta find out if that really was Marshall being hauled into jail. But how? Who do I know who might be able to find out? Christ, I'm at a loss."

Juan sat in contemplation, looking around the room and admiring the objets d'art. "One of your new boys is bound to know the score," he finally said. "Call 'em up. If they don't know, they're bound to know someone on the street who does."

Derek nodded his head in agreement. "Absolutely," he said. "These guys have been around. A couple of them even worked for Fraker."

Juan chugged down the remaining wine from his glass, stood up and said, "On that note, I've got to get my ass to bed. I'm completely exhausted and have to be at work in five hours. If you don't need me for anything else, I'm heading back to West Hollywood."

Derek apologized for the drama, and assured Juan that he'd be fine, especially now that he had a mission to accomplish this very night. "Drive carefully, and I'll call tomorrow with an update," he said. The two men embraced, and Derek walked Juan to the front door. They hugged again and repeated their good nights as Juan stepped into the chilly early morning. "Wash Andrew's cum off you before you sleep." Derek smiled.

Juan simply waved good-bye as he opened the car door and slipped into the vehicle. When the car had safely crossed through the open gateway, Derek closed the front door to the mansion and pressed the series of numbers on the security system's keypad. He realized that he was feeling particularly vulnerable and was grateful for the extra protection.

As Derek passed through the foyer and into the Great Room, he turned out lights along the way. He was anxious to get to his quarters and begin the process of checking on his boys, and finding out the status of the man arrested for pandering for the rich and famous. When he arrived in his room, Derek stripped off his T-shirt and tossed it onto a leather wingback chair. He fell onto the king-size bed and propped himself up against pillows and the headboard. He picked up his cell phone and pushed auto-dial for Jamie. After a dozen rings, and no voice mail, Derek made a face and pushed the disconnect button.

He made another selection on the speed dial menu and pushed send. After three rings he whispered in frustration, "Pick up, goddamn it!" Six rings later, he again pushed disconnect. This was not only unusual, it was against the policy that he had established. All parties had to be reachable 24/7, unless they were in the middle of a job. As far as Derek could recall, the last client was scheduled for seven o'clock. It was now nearly one A.M.

Frantic to learn more about the fate of Fraker and or Marshall, and apprehensive about the trouble that was going on in the world of Hollywood escorts, Derek decided to call Tom. He pushed the speed dial. On the third ring he heard a fully alert voice ask, "What?"

"Did I wake you?" Derek said.

"Christ, who can sleep with the phone ringing," Tom said testily.

Derek apologized, and Tom dismissed the contrition.

"I guess you're calling about the big news," Tom said with a smile in his voice.

"You sound stable," Derek said, relieved.

"The guy is completely loco," Tom continued. "If anybody deserves to get their ass whipped by the district attorney, it's him. He's threatening to take the whole freakin' town down with him, and God knows he has the means to do it. All I can say is that I am relieved that I had the foresight to find someone like you, for Brent. I don't even want to think about the trouble his career could be in, if he had to worry about being in Fraker's black book. Brent can read about this in the trades and know that his secret is still safe because he surrounded himself with me and you."

As Derek listened to Tom lavish praise on him for his discretion and trust, he could feel the blood drain from his face. He was suddenly feeling light-headed, and he closed his eyes.

Tom continued speaking about Fraker and the rat whores that were more than likely already jumping from his burning ship. "I wouldn't be surprised if one of his boys was a mole for the DA," Tom said. "They hate him, but they don't have anyplace else to go. Fraker was their meal ticket. He was the only game in town, except for the private guys like me."

Derek interrupted. "What about Marshall Topper?" he asked. A moment of silence filled the earpiece of Derek's cell phone. "Marshall was always trying to get me to pull out my dick for his customers."

"But you never did, right?" Tom asked, suddenly more serious than he seemed before.

Derek was now feeling queasy. "Why?"

"Just tell me that you never had anything to do with him, especially after you moved in with Brent," Tom said.

"No. I mean, I totally lost touch with the asshole after Onyx closed . . ."

Tom breathed a deep sigh of relief into the telephone. "He's evil incarnate."

". . . until today," Derek continued his sentence. "He called me this morning."

"Fuck!" Tom screamed into the phone. Now he was very agitated. "Did you talk? I mean, was it a phone message or did you actually have a conversation? What did he say? Why did he call?" The questions tumbled out of Tom's brain as he tried to assess the situation. "Well, talk to me!" he yelled. "What did he say, for Christ's sake?"

Derek was taken aback by the sudden burst of anger. Although he had experienced firsthand Tom's mercurial nature, this was unexpected, coming as it did on the heels of praise. "He, um, he warned me . . ."

"About what?" Tom asked, distraught. "Why was he calling you with a warning about anything? You guys don't have anything in common. You don't hang out with any of the same people. So? What? And how did he get your private number? Oh shit, he did call your cell and not Brent's home! Tell me it was your cell!"

Derek was suddenly frightened. "Yeah, my cell." Derek suspected that anything he said from this moment on would have far-reaching consequences. If he lied and claimed that Marshall had simply wanted to say hello, Tom wouldn't buy the pretext of a purely social call. If he admitted that Marshall was giving him one final opportunity to stop putting a dollar price on his cock, Tom would interrogate him about how the hell Marshall could ever have discovered that he was a working boy. Derek was a mouse in a corner facing a hungry cat. "I met someone who used to work for Fraker," he partially explained with a tentative voice.

"Who? Where? That still doesn't answer my question about why he was warning you! And what was he taunting you about?" Tom bellowed. "I mean, so what that you met someone who used to work for Fraker. Big deal. It's bound to happen in this town. But he would have no idea that you service Brent and his friends. So why any kind of warning? What?"

When confronted with the embarrassment of making a mistake, it's human nature to try to pass the buck and blame a disaster on another individual or unavoidable circumstances. Derek decided to try to place the accountability on one of Brent's friends. "I think maybe he felt that I was intruding on his territory. In fact, he actually said that. And maybe . . . you know how short the grapevine is in this town . . . maybe one of the guys that you and Brent sent to me told someone else, and that person told another, and before you know it, it's common knowledge. Maybe?"

"No!" Tom screamed. "That would never happen in a million years! My friends stay friends because wild horses couldn't drag the smallest amount of personal information about Brent or me out of them. I wouldn't ever believe the possibility of your scenario. Not ever! Never!"

Derek suddenly became defensive. "Then, I don't know why he assumed I was competition. Or, for that matter, who might have tipped him off. You think of something. Come up with a logical explanation. And why the hell does it matter anyway? Marshall's just a small-time businessman. He doesn't matter dick."

More silence filled the other end of the line. Tom was collecting his thoughts and emotions. Finally, in a calm and quiet voice he said, "Are you as dumb as you sound right now?"

"I'm not an idiot," Derek spat. "I know Marshall. He's a prick. A small-time, ugly, fat, balding prick without a conscience. He's a smart businessman. I'll give him that. But I don't know why you're all over me about this. I'm not frightened of him. After all, he's no Fraker!"

"Yes, he is. I'm coming over."

THIRTY-ONE

D erek hung up the phone and returned to the Great Room of the house. He switched on the lights, punched the security system keypad to disengage the alarm, and poured himself another glass of wine. While he waited for Tom, he tried once again to reach Jamie and Stuart by cell phone. Neither man answered. Slowly he was coming to the conclusion that he was about to be fucked. He sat in detached silence, listening to the house creak and the sounds from the central air-conditioning running.

After a long while of contemplation, Derek speed-dialed one last number. "Juan?" he begged. "I know it's late. I'm in deep shit. Tom's coming over. He's hostile. I can't call the cops . . ." Suddenly Derek froze. "Fuck, I hear someone at the door. Gotta go."

From the distance, Derek heard the front door slam. He knew it was Tom.

As Tom entered the Great Room, Derek was seated on the over-stuffed sofa, holding his glass of wine and pretending to stare out into the lighted garden and pool.

Then with a swift and unexpectedly startling gesture Tom back-handed the wineglass out of Derek's limp hand, sending it crashing into a million shards in every direction of the room. Red wine splattered everywhere.

As large and imposing a man as Derek was, he became frightened and meek in the presence of Tom's violence. With no time to recover from the shock of the assault, Derek was suddenly seized off the sofa by Tom, who dragged him by his hair and his shirt and ejected him across the Great Room, sending him crashing into a Mies van der Rohe chair. He upended the furniture, along with a potted ficus tree. Blood ran from his nose, and from gashes in his arms as his body met shards of the wineglass along the way.

Neither man said a word during the struggle. As Derek's body continued to collide with lamps, potted plants and the loud crash of a Remington sculpture, he was unable to retaliate. He considered that he was probably about to die. But just as suddenly as the brawl had begun, it ended. Tom stood at one end of the room, depleted of energy and breathing heavily. He fell back into an overstuffed love seat, staring with contempt at Derek who was crumpled on the floor.

Tom left Derek where he had landed, and headed to the bar. There he grabbed a dish towel and soaked it under the tap. Wringing it out, he staggered back to Derek. Standing over the battered body, he dropped the wet towel onto Derek's chest.

Still mute from shock, anger and fear, Derek accepted the wet rag to blot the blood from his left arm and shoulder. He sniffled and tasted his own blood. He knew that his nose was bleeding and held the cloth to his nostrils for a moment. Still, he did not move from his place of refuge on the floor. He kept an eye on Tom, who was now at the bar pouring himself a glass of bourbon. He settled himself onto one of the sofas and took a long pull of his drink. Now, looking over at Derek he said, "Get your ass out of this house."

Derek was weak, but he managed a "Fuck you."

Tom snorted. "You're the little ass wipe fucker who's fucked," he said. "What did you think you were getting away with, cocksucker? Did you think you were so clever that I wouldn't find out about your dating game scheme? Did you think those little twinkies you hired were somehow loyal to you? They're whores, for Christ's sake. And most of them are hooked on speed. They'll do anything for a couple a hundred bucks—including spilling their faggot guts about your stable of clients and escorts."

Derek tried to regain his equilibrium. He stood up unsteadily and lumbered to the sofa opposite Tom. He folded himself into the plush cushions, wincing at the pain in his head and ribs, and assumed a fetal position. Rivulets of blood oozed from gashes in his shoulder and arm, and stained the fabric. "You hurt me," he managed to say.

Tom knocked back the remainder of the bourbon, took a deep

breath and then looked over at Derek. "Would it be a huge imposition for you to explain why you not only fucked me and Brent, but yourself as well," Tom said.

Derek, lying on his side, considered the question but did not respond.

"I know I sound like your father when I say this but, we gave your ungrateful ass everything anyone could want." Tom's eyes roamed the room. "You got to live in this magnificent house. You earned more money—and for doing next to nothing—than you ever dreamed of making. This was Shangri-la, with servants to wait on you and expensive cars to drive. And sex. Don't forget that you got all the sex you wanted. What did we ask in return? Discretion. Honesty. And this is how you repay us. You sell us out. I guess gratitude sounds simpler than it actually is. You may as well have called Cindy Adams with an exclusive interview."

"What did I do?" Derek managed.

Tom sighed in frustration. "Derek, if I didn't know you better, I'd think you were an idiot," he said. It was the second time that evening that Tom had used the phrase to belittle Derek. "Christ, maybe you are a moron and I was blinded by your beautiful face and fuckable body. I misjudged you."

Lying on the sofa, Derek physically ached from the beating he'd received from Tom. His ego was badly pounded, too, by Tom's droning on about being disappointed in him. He began to shed tears as he was reminded that as a result of his carelessness the pot of gold into which he had fallen was all but gone. Equaling the pain from the cuts and bruises, Derek was in agony over his fate of being thrown back into a common life, like Eliza Doolittle. "I didn't fuck you," Derek said in a feeble voice, trying hard to make a case for his salvation. "I never, ever jeopardized Brent. Nobody knows that I fuck him."

Tom leaned forward on the sofa, and rested his elbows on his knees. "Jamie knew. Stuart knew. Tag knew. They certainly didn't read about it in Liz Smith."

Derek found the strength to raise himself up to a sitting position. He looked warily at Tom, as though he might be struck at any moment. "Small world. You didn't mention before that we have friends in common."

Tom leaned back in his seat. "New friends. Ordinarily I don't mingle with assorted whores and crack heads. I'm an elitist. I don't have anything in common with such lowlifes. But when the news broke about Fraker and after our brief conversation, I made it my business to know if and how any of it might impact me and Brent and his friends."

"Why, if you trusted me, would you have thought twice about Brent's reputation being secure?" Derek asked.

"I'm just glad that I did, that's all," Tom snapped. "Needless to say I was surprised by what my moles revealed. You can't imagine how stunned I was to find that you were the head of an elite escort service. . . . Double-dipping the dollars right under my nose."

Derek corrected his posture and slowly got to his feet. The pain was subsiding, and his blood coagulating. Timidly, he made his way to the bar. He picked up a wineglass and pulled the cork from the bottle that Juan had opened earlier. He poured a drink while keeping his eyes on Tom, who was keeping his eyes on Derek.

After downing his drink, Derek breathed a heavy sigh. "What's my punishment for outsourcing the workload around here?" he asked in a newly steady voice. "Am I banned from having to fuck another opera tenor's cottage cheese butt? Do I have to give up the slobbering lips of that Broadway composer who acted as though sucking dick was akin to slurping up a fucking Popsicle? Maybe I'll have to pass on the jack-off sessions with that old congressman, the one whose pecs have turned to tits. I'll be so shattered if you deprive me of such physical pleasures."

Tom switched his position on the sofa in order to face Derek at the bar. He cocked his head to one side, then to the other, considering his response. "What did Marshall threaten? Something about impotence?"

"How the hell do you know what Marshall told me this morning?" Derek said, his voice once again weak and clearly confused. Suddenly he was feeling dizzy. "Tom, what's going on here? If you know the specifics of my conversation with Marshall, then you know I never intentionally compromised Brent's security. Why are you really here? What do you want from me?"

Tom stared at Derek, looking perturbed, but without saying a word.

"A cut of the money I've made? Is that what you want, Tom?" Derek said with defiance in his voice. "Or, now that Marshall and Fraker— who it appears, are one and the same—are out of the way, you want to take over my business and control the sex-for-sale trade in this town? Or—" Derek stopped for a moment, considering other scenarios.

"Who is the biggest star of the moment?" He waited a beat. "Brent Richardson," he answered himself. "Who has, for years, been rumored to be gay, but there's no proof?" Again he waited a beat and then answered, "Brent Richardson."

Derek poured another glass of wine for himself, and moved out from behind the bar into the center of the room. "Brent, Brent, Brent. It's a nice name, isn't it? A rich-sounding name. A masculine name. But it's a vulnerable name—at least where fame and fortune are concerned." Derek took his eyes off Tom for a moment and looked around the room. "You made a mess. Brent's going to be pissed." He swiped at a particularly large shard of glass with the side of his shoe.

"Again, laying blame elsewhere," Tom said. "The damage here is entirely your fault. You're a thieving, double-crossing, cum-sucking whore," Tom growled. "Your greed could have ruined the career of Hollywood's biggest star, if I hadn't stepped in to save him," Tom said.

"Yes, you're always saving Brent from one disaster or another, aren't you? I always thought it was curious the way you seem to control him. You even tell him who to screw. He's basically a doormat to your boots. The brilliant actor, singer, dancer, pianist that he may be, he doesn't think that he deserves his bloody success and fortune. Mostly, I think, because you've convinced him that he just got lucky, and that there are younger and more dazzling actors nipping at his heels, ready at any moment to pounce and topple him as the number one box office draw. The man is adorable, in every conceivable way, and if you think I would betray him, you're out of your mind."

Tom leaned back into the sofa and crossed one leg over the other. Holding out his rocks glass he said, "Fill 'er up, will you?"

"Fucking get up and make your own drink," Derek lashed out.

"You didn't have that kind of mouth when we first met," Tom said. "You didn't pick up such language from Brent, Mr. Goody-Goody. Must have been those trash boys you hired. By the way, did you bother to audition them before you sent them out to do your dirty work?"

"You're the man with all of my answers," Derek said, distinguishing between what he could say as fact, and what Tom would imply was presupposed certainty.

"You should have. Tag is especially hot. Even with his clothes on. He may be a tad short, but when he's wearing a tight black T-shirt and jeans, I literally have to take a deep breath. Of course, without his clothes . . . He's got a fucking gorgeous vein that travels from his left biceps all the way up to his pec. Jesus. And that skater's ass! God, what a fucking package deal. Jamie and Stuart were cool, too. Jamie always shot the biggest load. Stuart could cum at will. Amazing. But none of them compared to you, Derek. You were the prize. USDA Prime. Brent couldn't thank me enough for bringing you into the family. Poor bastard will be devastated that you're gone."

"Why are you doing this to me?" Derek asked. "You made a ton of money off of my ass. Oh, I know Brent paid me a weekly retainer, but then his so-called friends—guys *you* personally arranged for me to fuck—coughed up tens of thousands of dollars to spend an hour with me. You collected the big loot, while I got a pay envelope with a fraction of what you earned. Does it really surprise you that I'd get wise enough to start making money off other guys' asses. I pleased a lot of men—your men. Then I figured I could make some real cash on my own. But I swear I *never* did anything to jeopardize Brent's career. Not ever!"

Derek studied Tom who appeared to be contemplating what to say next and possibly a change of plan. Derek's major concern was not that he was being forced out of the escort trade, or that he would be portrayed to Brent as an untrustworthy whore, but rather, that he would be forced out of Weybridge Cottage. That would prevent him from collecting his hidden money, which as he now mentally calculated, ran upwards of a hundred thousand dollars.

Tom heaved a heavy sigh. "What the fuck am I going to do about you?" he said. "You're too beautiful to waste, and I do mean that in the gangsta vernacular. Trust me, it can happen. But there's no way I can let you fuck up my interests."

Derek was silent for a long time. "I don't know how things got so out of hand. One day I'm a waiter, then the next I'm destitute and willing to sell my soul for enough money to pay the rent. Then another day follows and I'm living on an estate in Beverly Hills with Brent Fucking Richardson. What's next? I don't have a clue. Since I never anticipated any of my life's big changes, I can't make any predictions about tomorrow."

Tom flopped down into one of the large plush chairs and swung a leg over the arm. "That's life, isn't it? I mean, one day you're nothing, then you're soaring, and you make a wrong turn and you're plummeting back to earth. And that's what this is, really, you've been in a golden balloon, but the air is rapidly leaking out and you're going to crash."

The room was once again tense with anticipation. Now, instead of fearing what Tom would physically do to harm him, Derek was on alert for an edict that would determine his fate. He suspected that simply being banished from the aristocracy he had always admired, and which he had come to enjoy, was getting off too easily. There would have to be some penalty for his tampering with the standards and practices of a live-in whore. Derek's thoughts conjured up one scenario after another, and with each mental illustration that came to mind, he simultaneously considered ways to get even with Tom. Stalling for time he said, "I'm tired. I'm sure that you are too. What do you say we have a farewell fuck and then we can pick up this conversation in the morning."

Tom made a face that said, *Oh, no. I'm not putting myself in a vulnerable position.* "I'll just keep my memories, thank you. But you're right, I am tired. It's been a harrowing day. I want to get this thing over with."

"Thing?" Derek said, aware that Tom was threatening more than just expulsion from the world of Hollywood's elite escorts. "Haven't you hurt me enough? I could, and should, get up and kick the shit out of you. So don't sit there and try to intimidate me. Yeah, I'm tired too. I'm tired of playing a spineless wimp."

Derek stood up and took a deep breath. He shook his head. "Oh, Tom," he said, "my smart and sexy Tom. I want you out of my house."

Tom made a small laugh.

"I'm fucking serious," Derek said. "Go. Now. Resist only if you want twice as much as what you gave me earlier."

"Sorry." Tom smiled. "You're the one who's leaving. In fact, the reason I let our time together draw out as long as it has, is because Tag has been busy throwing your clothes into a plastic bag." Tom saw the look of confusion on Derek's face. "Yeah. If you would have greeted me at the door like a proper host, you would have seen him. But then we probably wouldn't have had this scintillating conversation."

Tom took a stance in front of Derek. "No more stalling. Get up. Some old friends of yours are waiting outside ready to help take you away."

Derek sat a moment longer.

Tom reached into his pocket and retrieved his cell phone and pushed speed dial on the keypad.

"He needs some motivation," Tom said into the mouthpiece.

In the distance, beyond the kitchen and foyer, came the vague sound of voices, which grew louder by the second. In a moment, four men—Tag, Jamie, Stuart and Dow—were standing in the entrance to the Great Room.

Tom cocked his head toward Derek and the men immediately but tentatively gathered around him.

Jamie looked down at the floor and sheepishly whispered to Derek, "I'm sorry. It's not personal."

Derek looked at Tom. "You're serious. I can't believe that you think I'm a threat to you. And I can't believe that you turned these guys against me. What did you do, promise them a life outside of prostitution? That's what every whore wants. It's their common denominator."

He turned to the group, all of whom, with the exception of Tag, appeared uncomfortable in their roles as thugs or kidnappers. "Why are you going along with this?" he asked the group. "We were making decent money together. It was only getting better. I tried to make the work a little better than anyone else would. So why are you doing this?"

"We didn't have a choice," Dow said. "He's got our balls in a vise."

Tom was suddenly impatient. "Stop with the questions!" he bellowed. "Get him out of here!" Tom yelled at Tag and the others.

As the men grabbed hold of his arms, Derek struggled. He twisted in an effort to extricate himself from their firm grip. "Can I at least take a piss!" he demanded.

Tag looked to Tom for guidance. With an expression of boredom, Tom nodded his head. "Make it fast."

The men released Derek, who straightened himself up, and tried to walk with an air of dignity toward the bathroom.

"Stay with him," Tom commanded of Tag.

At the door, Derek said, "I think I can handle it myself, thank you." He opened the door, stepped into the guest bathroom and closed the door behind him. Although he locked it, he knew it would only take but a moment for one of the men to bust in, if they wanted to. He immediately turned on the taps at the sink and pulled out his cell phone. Pushing speed dial, he was frustrated by the automaton voice of a woman who stated, "To leave a message, press one." Derek was caught off guard by the absence of a real person but quickly pushed one on the keypad and said, "Juan! I need your help! Please!" He then pushed the button to exit the voice mail system and put the phone back into his pocket. Derek stalled for as long as possible.

Tag became impatient and called for him through the door.

"Shut up!" Derek yelled back. "You can't hurry nature!"

Presently, there was a loud banging on the door, and Tom's voice called, "Time's up! Get out here now, or we're coming in!"

Derek flushed the toilet and then ran his hands under the tap at the sink. When Derek emerged from the bathroom he flicked a spray of water from his fingers at Tag, who flinched and ducked. Then Derek looked at each of the men to estimate the amount of resistance he could expect to face if he attempted to fight his way out of the situation. He decided it would be futile. But he was determined not to be taken away; not without a ferocious battle, if necessary. He suspected that they would simply follow orders from Tom and carry out whatever punishment he deemed appropriate. Derek looked at Tom. "I told you to get out of this house. And take your boyfriends."

Tom looked at Derek with disgust. He cocked his head in a signal for the boys to do their job. They turned toward Derek and simultaneously reached out to take him by the limbs and wrestled him into a half nelson. But Derek ducked the second before the attack and ran toward the foyer and front entrance. Tom and his crew immediately followed and caught up with Derek just before he opened the front door. With several swift punches and a foot that tripped him to the ground, Derek was quickly subdued. He cried out in pain as the men punched him into complete submission. They yanked him by his hair until he was back on his feet. "Get him out of here!" Tom commanded and reached for the doorknob.

Upon pulling open the heavy door, Tom and his boys were stopped in their tracks. Taken by surprise, they faced a Maginot Line of six Latino men who looked every bit the stereotypical gangbanger. Positioned on the front portico, these were tough-looking guys. Dressed in wife beaters, and displaying a variety of tattoos, shaved heads, diamond ear studs, and scarred faces, they counted on their archetype to disguise the fact that they hardly spoke any Spanish. And in combination they were a film school instructor, a policeman, a Disney Studios marketing executive, grocery store manager, male model, and airline flight attendant. They looked to be imported from East Los Angeles, and an Anglo's worst nightmare. Derek managed a smile when he saw that Juan was at the center of the group.

Tag and his associates were immediately unstrung. Not only were they not used to fighting, they were outnumbered. They feared that this posse of Latinos would mess up their handsome faces or break bones.

Tom stared at Juan. "It's a little early to start the gardening, boys," he said with disdain. "Why don't you beaners run along and look for a vision of the Virgin Mary in a taco salad," he said.

"We're not staying long enough to clean up your shit, man," Juan spat in his best south of the border accent. He reached out to retrieve Derek from the custody of the four Caucasians.

However, Tag, the self-appointed leader of the pack, stepped forward and placed himself between his charge and the Hispanic intruders. He didn't allow his fear to show. Still, Juan knew that white boys, when faced with the menacing demeanors of any other race, were easily intimidated. The two glared at one another for a long moment, each trying to anticipate the other's next move.

In the meantime, as the standoff continued, Tom surreptitiously leaned against the inside wall and blindly felt with his hand for the security system keypad. Without looking, he pressed a button, then just as furtively took a few steps forward again.

In a split second, Juan pushed Tag aside, grabbed hold of Derek's arm, and pulled him forward as the Latinos and Caucasians simultaneously rushed one another. As Juan and Derek reentered the melee against Tag and Jamie and Stuart and Dow, Tom slammed the heavy door closed and locked himself in behind it. And then just as suddenly, the parking court was awash with the bright ultra high beams and pulsing red and blue lights of half a dozen Beverly Hills private security patrol cars. The whoop of a siren and a platoon of armed officers shouted for everyone to drop to the ground.

Soon, a helicopter was overhead, shining its spotlight over Weybridge Cottage, as police officers arrived en masse and began handcuffing the eleven men who still lay on the mansion's cobbled parking court.

Presently, Tom appeared at the door. In a voice that embodied controlled hysteria, he explained to the officers that just as his guests were departing the house from a dinner party, a gang of trespassers had attacked them. "We all could have been robbed and killed, but I managed to get to the security system," he said in his most convincing voice of horror. "Thank God you guys came so quickly!"

As two officers began taking Tom's official statement, and the other policemen roughly dragged Juan and his friends up off of the ground, they automatically assumed that the Latinos were guilty of a crime, while the Caucasians were all victims. With Tom's attention diverted, and the officers' arrogant supposition of who was criminal and who was innocent, Juan whispered to Derek to get away.

"I'll be cool," Juan murmured. "You get out of here."

With the blood on his nose still wet from his earlier fight with Tom, Derek easily convinced the police that he was the victim of an assault. "No, I'm not hurt enough for the hospital," he said. "I just want to go home." And with that, he was released. He slipped into the Jaguar, used the spare key that he kept in his wallet, and drove off the estate grounds.

THIRTY-TWO

"Where the fuck's my coffee!" Andrew bellowed at Socorro as she arrived at the house entering through the kitchen door. "And where the hell's Juan?"

Socorro shrugged. "I just got here."

"Late as usual," Andrew bitched at the maid. At that moment, the house telephone rang. Neither Andrew nor Socorro made a move to answer it. If it were important, the caller would have dialed Andrew's cell phone. Anybody else could leave a message.

"Christ. No newspapers either." Andrew threw up his hands and grabbed his briefcase. Without another word to the maid, Andrew turned on his heels and began to leave the room.

Cathy came in just as he was trying to get out. She was holding the cordless phone.

"It's Juan," she said. "He's in jail! He wants to speak to you."

"What did he do, steal a car?"

Cathy tried to hand the telephone to her husband, who waved it away and said, "I'm late for a meeting."

Cathy insisted that Andrew take the call. She pushed the telephone into Andrew's hand as Socorro watched in silent curiosity.

With a sigh of reluctance, Andrew took the phone. "Who did you rape?" he asked without so much as a "hello." He listened with disinterest to what was being said. Finally, he said, "The LAPD doesn't go around arresting people for doing nothing, Juan. Listen, you'll have to find someone else to help you. And I can't have a felon working in my home either. Gotta go. I'm late."

Andrew handed the telephone back to Cathy. He departed the

house, in an angrier mood than when he first discovered that his Starbucks wasn't available. His rage was directed equally at Juan and at himself as he realized that he had just cut himself off from his fuck buddy.

Cathy immediately spoke. "Juan, what's going on? Why were you arrested? Yes, of course it's a mistake. How much is bail? Will they take a check? Okay, just sit tight and I'll be there right after the bank opens. Oh, which station are you being held at? Stay calm, Juan."

By noon, Juan and Cathy were back at the Youngs' home. Cathy had cancelled a luncheon and given Socorro the rest of the day off. She wanted to be alone with Juan, who was still wearing his now filthy shirt, an earring and a temporary tattoo that was fading on his left biceps. As Cathy prepared lunch for both of them, Juan was too ashamed of himself to do more than sit in silence on the kitchen bar stool with his eyes cast downward.

"Lemonade?" Cathy asked, even as she poured from a pitcher into a tumbler filled with half-moon–shaped ice cubes.

"Thank you," Juan whispered.

The drive home from jail had been deathly silent. Juan was mortified and confused. Cathy had not pushed for details. However, now that they were seated together in the safety of familiar surroundings and Juan was ravenously consuming a tuna melt on rye, both were calmer.

After finishing the first half of his sandwich, Juan said, "I can't keep you, of all people, out of the loop. First of all, I didn't break the law. At least I didn't plan to."

"Let's take the rest of our lunch into my office," Cathy suggested. "We'll both be more comfortable."

In a moment, Juan was seated on a long, black leather sofa, opposite Cathy who found a comfortable position in a plush chair with its back to her writing desk. She placed her feet up on the matching ottoman and held her lemonade glass on a napkin in her hand. She sat waiting for Juan to speak first.

After what appeared to be a difficult moment of introspection, Juan sighed and said, "I was trying to help a mutual friend. He's still in danger."

Cathy leaned forward and placed her glass and napkin on the coffee table that occupied the space between her and Juan. "Derek?" she asked.

Juan nodded.

Cathy automatically brought her hands to her lips and wrinkled her eyebrows. "He and I used to chat all the time. But since Onyx closed . . ." Her remarks trailed off. "It's not drugs, is it?" she asked, silently begging that the answer was no. "I suspected that he was too embarrassed to tell me that he hadn't found a job. Oh, Christ, that's nothing to hide. Not with the whole ugly unemployment rate in this county." She reeled herself back to the moment.

Juan too, placed his sandwich plate and glass on the low table between them. "As a matter of fact, he has been working," Juan began. "But not in a restaurant. And not as a major domo or in any place that you would guess in a million years." He sat back. "I'm breaking a confidence by telling you this," he continued. "But if we don't help, he's going to end up dead or messed up in some way."

Cathy stared at Juan, anxious to discover the fate of her friend. "If it's that serious, it must be drugs. Or prostitution."

The surprised expression on Juan's face made Cathy's widen. "Drugs?" she asked.

Juan slowly shook his head, and Cathy stared at him in shock. He tried to create a foundation for her to understand the situation. "When we worked together at Onyx, he was constantly being hit on by customers, and harassed by a guy who insisted he could make a bundle by . . ."

"It's easy to fall in love with a face and body like his," Cathy said. "I can fully appreciate men actually paying to be naked with him."

Juan continued. "When Onyx closed, even Derek couldn't find another wait job. And if *he* couldn't, there was no hope for me. But he saved me just in the nick of time from giving in and accepting what he's ultimately ended up doing. I was literally hanging out at my apartment waiting for a knock on the door from a guy that this freak at Onyx had set up for me. Then Derek called and spent practically his last dime on the bus fare to bring me to his place."

Cathy silently agreed that what Juan was saying sounded like something that Derek would do for a friend. "So what happened to make him fall so low?" she asked.

"Not so low, really. He met Brent Richardson."

Cathy gave made a loud sound of incredulity. "Here! At that cocktail evening!"

"Before that," Juan said to avert any feeling Cathy might have of possible culpability.

Cathy stared through Juan. "Brent. Derek. Why didn't either of them say anything to me?" She answered her own questions. "Brent can't come out. Hollywood would crumble. A shame. All that fame and money, and he has to hide behind a façade of what the world expects him to be."

Cathy shrugged. "But I still don't understand. If he was Brent's lover . . ."

"Brent hired Derek to live in at the mansion, to be on booty call."

"Brent doesn't need to pay for sex!" she said. "There are millions of men who would gladly offer their bodies and souls to be with him."

"You of all people should understand that a man of Brent's status in Hollywood would practically be forced to pay for it," Juan said. "The man is a hero to hundreds of millions of moviegoers around the planet. The rumor that he's queer can't become a matter of fact. That's why Derek was ideal for the job. He's the best-looking thing around, and he's discreet."

Juan offered another theory. "Brent Richardson is so busy with movie star commitments that he has someone essentially telling him what to do all the time. That someone's name is Tom Dixon."

"He's one of Brent's attorneys. They're also best friends," Cathy said, remembering numerous times they had met.

"He's the man who had me arrested last night," Juan confirmed.

"Tom?" Cathy said again. "Why? He's a lovely man. Well educated. Handsome as hell. I always thought perhaps he and Brent were sharing a bed."

"They were. But he's not the decent guy you seem to think that he is. In fact, Derek was actually afraid of him. You know Derek isn't scared of anyone. He can handle himself. But this guy has a mean streak and Derek considered him dangerous. I know from experience that he is."

"So you broke into his house?" Cathy asked.

"I don't even know where he lives. We were arrested at Brent's. I was rescuing Derek."

Cathy was perplexed. The ideas that she had about Derek's and Tom's private lives were being obliterated and she trusted Juan enough to believe that he was telling the truth. "You were arrested for crashing a party and for assault," Cathy said. "That's absolutely impossible for me to believe. But you're also telling me things about Brent and Tom that I would have found impossible to believe even yesterday. Why were you at Weybridge Cottage?"

"Derek lives there."

"Then he invited you over."

"He called me for help," Juan said. "Look, we talked earlier in the evening, and after the arrest of Charles Fraker . . ."

"Yeah, I saw on the news," Cathy said. "Half of my friends are panicked that their names are in his little black book."

". . . Derek's life was suddenly at stake."

"I don't follow," Cathy said. "What did Derek have to do with that lowlife Fraker?" A light seemed to dawn on her. "Derek was working for Fraker?"

"No!" Juan was becoming impatient. "He was actually a rival of Fraker's." Juan waited a beat. "There so much more to this whole story, Cathy."

Cathy scrunched up her face in total bewilderment.

Juan took a deep breath. "Derek was tired of being blackmailed into servicing Tom's friends. Yeah, that was part of the job. Since he was so trusted, whenever Brent was out of town, it fell to Derek to take care of the sex needs of others in Tom's circle. Derek got tired of that and started hiring other guys to take care of the clients. Then he started eliminating the middleman, Tom."

Cathy pondered the news for a moment. "Do you think that Tom is a panderer, like that Fraker?"

"Yeah, he is," Juan said.

Cathy stared at Juan.

Juan continued. "Derek didn't talk much about this, but from the little he did say, it seemed like this was all Tom's doing. Then Derek started farming out his work, and not being very wise about the choices he made with regard to the quality and background of the guys he hired. Things got messed up. Tom got wise, and . . . well you know what a small town this is. Maybe Tom was trying to protect Brent by getting rid of Derek before the news broke."

"Oh, this belongs on Andrew's network," Cathy said. "It's so . . . *Jerry Springer!*"

Juan added, "What I really think happened between Derek and Tom is that Tom was pissed that Derek was competition for his own business. Tom's a smart guy. And so is Derek. They know there's a fortune to be made in the escort business from all of those closeted gay stars and studio executives. Millions of dollars, in fact."

Cathy interrupted. "But Tom's already rich. He doesn't need more."

"He made his money procuring boys from The Rawhide to have sex with the A-List. But I'll tell you this, he had four guys beating up on Derek when I arrived at the house last night. There was blood to prove it. When the cops came, they presumed, from the color of my skin, that my friends and I were responsible. That's why we were locked up, and the real thugs, who were loyal to Tom, were let go. Derek escaped because they thought that, being Caucasian and at the fabled Weybridge Cottage, he was a victim."

Cathy was stunned by what she had just heard. After a moment of taking it all in she announced, "We've got to find Derek!"

"Where? He wouldn't risk being at his old apartment. Tom knows where he lives."

"What can we do?" Cathy asked anxiously.

"He used to have tons of friends, but they were mostly the people he worked with at Onyx," Juan said. "After the place closed, people went their own way." Juan thought for a long moment. "This is really a long shot, but there was a guy and his wife . . . They seemed to like Derek, and Derek said they were friends of Brent's. Marty and his ancient wife. They apparently showed up at Brent's occasionally."

"Marty and Felicia Riggs?" Cathy said. "Oh, I know those two. Sort of." Cathy thought back to various events which they all attended. "They throw a ton of cash to my Africa famine relief charity. I actually like them. And he's not the idiot stud he pretends to be."

"Call them. See if they know anything?" Juan said.

Cathy stood up and walked behind her desk. Picking up her Palm Pilot, she touched the screen with the stylus to retrieve her phone book. She found the number and dialed the telephone.

After reintroducing herself to Felicia and reminding her of where they had previously met, Cathy got to the point of the call. When she smiled broadly and nodded her head, Juan knew that his hunch had paid off. "May I speak to him?" Cathy asked. She waited for over two minutes, but then she heard Derek's weak voice.

"Hello?" he asked.

"Honey, it's Cathy. Don't say another word. Juan and I are on our way over to pick you up. And don't say no. We're coming now." *Click. Buzz.*

Cathy came out from behind her desk and Juan was already halfway down the hall. As they reached the door in the kitchen that led to the garage, it suddenly opened, and Andrew walked in.

Cathy immediately took control of the situation. "Before you say anything, I wasn't about to let Juan stay in that jail cell. Anyway, he's completely innocent of the charges."

Andrew said, "Halfway through my meeting with Keanu I realized that I shouldn't have jumped the gun like that. I got rid of Mr. Matrix, and I called the Beverly Hills Police Department. The desk sergeant said that Juan had been taken downtown, but someone had bailed his ass out. I had a feeling it was you."

Cathy picked up her car keys. "They've accused Juan of breaking and entering into three homes last night! But he has an alibi."

Andrew froze. "Alibi?" he said. His eyes expressed obvious anxiety and desperation as they darted from Cathy to Juan. It was usually Andrew who enjoyed control over other people. Now, in a rare upending of his authority, Andrew was loath to realize that Juan was in the potentially powerful position to manipulate him.

"About my alibi," Juan started to explain, looking at Andrew, whom he knew was holding his breath. "I worked here as usual, until six," Juan said. "Then we um, I, went . . ."

Cathy interrupted. "Anyway, there's absolutely no evidence that places you at any of the other crime scenes. Once the police put two and two together, you'll be in the clear. Just make sure you can account for those five hours between work and showing up at Brent's."

Andrew uncharacteristically stammered. "Um, how tight is your alibi? Can anyone corroborate your whereabouts?" He looked at Juan's outfit, remembering that it was what he had worn when he left the Century City condo. He found himself growing hard thinking of the feel of Juan's brick-hard body against his, and the pleasure of being fucked by him.

Juan answered cryptically, "You never know how friends will respond when the police are involved," he said.

Cathy picked up her purse and her key ring. "We're your friends," she said. "Andrew," she said, "we'll fill you in later. We've got to run and rescue Derek Bracken. Unless you want to come along?"

Andrew rolled his eyes. "Are we suddenly a halfway house for ex-cons?" he said and immediately realized that he was insulting Juan and Cathy's friend Derek. "No, I'm late. I just popped back in to pick up my prescription. That fucking new programming director Shari Draper has got me shaking with rage."

Cathy gave Andrew a peck on the cheek and as she reached for the doorknob to the garage said, "Oh, hon, don't let that little whore bother you anymore. A friend of Joe Ezsterhaus tells me that Shari's about to get her little fake candy striper ass kicked all the way back to the mail room at Sterling Studios."

THIRTY-THREE

Hancock Park is one of the oldest and most fashionable neighborhoods of Los Angeles. An island of old mansions and older money, the district is surrounded by a moat of seedier areas. It was exactly where Juan presumed that someone like Felicia would live. When Cathy rang the doorbell at the mansion on June Street, Marty opened the door. "It's like the old days," he said in greeting, looking first at Juan, and then Cathy. "Got the two sexiest men from Onyx in the same place! Heya," he addressed Cathy. "We met at Mr. Geffen's last year."

Cathy smiled warmly. "Yes, you were wearing that exquisite . . . oh, there it is!" she said, admiring Marty's diamond and sapphire wedding band. "Who could forget a man with such an impressive piece?

"Come." Marty beckoned. "Mr. Heidi Fleiss is in the trophy room."

The house was overwhelming in its enormous size. Marble floors, marble walls, and a marble staircase to the left of the entrance made the place seem like an austere exhibition hall in an art museum. And like a museum, frayed and threadbare tapestries hung against the cold walls from the eighteen-foot ceiling. The furniture—only a few delicate pieces—were grouped in front of an immense fireplace. A grand piano in a far corner seemed almost miniature in the vast room. The ticking of a massive grandfather clock echoed throughout the expansive first floor room.

"I'm pouring margaritas. You'll have one?"

Cathy looked at her wristwatch, then shrugged.

"I need fortification," Marty said. "The stud's telling a whopper of a story. Jeez, the deviant things that go on in this town! Whodathunk? I mean, I know that movie stars are different from you and me, what with all their plastic surgery and such. But who knew their sex lives were so far out there? The kid's creeping me out!"

Marty smiled as he led Cathy and Juan down a long corridor that opened up into a cavernous room. There, under a vaulted ceiling and surrounded by wall-to-wall French doors with a colorful overgrown garden just beyond the multipaned glass, sat Derek on an overstuffed sofa. He was talking to Felicia. The old woman's attention was completely focused on Derek.

In unison, Juan called out, "Heya, Boss," as Cathy simply said, "Derek."

Derek and Felicia both turned to the new arrivals.

Cathy walked first to Felicia and extended her hand in greeting toward the old woman. Felicia's thin, bird-like limbs were covered with nearly transparent skin. "We met at the Eisners a few months ago," Cathy said. "And, we have the same subscription night at the Phil? Thank you for taking such good care of my Derek."

"He's always been *my* Derek," Felicia said, sounding territorial. "But he said nice things about you, so I'm willing to share."

Turning to Derek, Cathy's eyes gave away her surprise at how poor he looked. His right eye was blackened, his swollen nose still had flecks of dried blood, he was unshaven, and his head of hair was a bird's nest of tangles.

"The body'll heal." Derek smiled. He hung his head in embarrassment. "How did you guys know where to find me?" he asked.

"No offense," Juan said to Felicia, "but I thought of the last people on earth anyone would think you might hang out with."

Just then, Marty reentered the room with a tray of margaritas. "Yeah, but you can't say that Felicia and I aren't progressive and cool." He smiled. "Oh, I know we look like an unlikely couple. And we've heard more than our share about the May-December thing."

"'The archeologist and his fossil,' is what they say." Felicia laughed. "From what Derek's been telling us, we're not the deviant aberrations in this town. We've been trumped by practically everybody else."

Marty laughed as he held out the tray of drinks for Cathy and Juan, and then handed a salt rimmed glass to Felicia and one to Derek. "For instance, some of those folks on the Link Media news team—that's your husband's network, isn't it—wouldn't want a report about their peccadilloes!" Again he laughed.

Cathy, knowing to whom Marty was referring, joined in. "Do you keep count too?" She smiled. "The last time I tuned in I swear at least six of those anchor boys and girls were what you might call *embedded.* With each other. Ha! Yes. It's Andrew's station, all right. Time and again he proves that he's got a sweet tooth."

Cathy gave Juan a look that he had never seen from her before. It was a wry smile combined with an arched eyebrow, and it left Juan wondering whether she was addressing the issue of Andrew's sexuality, or if she was simply making a joke about having an insider's knowledge of the aberrant lives of news media stars. Then, turning to smile at Marty and Felicia she said, "I've always thought you were both adorable. And God knows you're generous with your donations to my annual Diamonds and Orchids gala benefit. Now you've taken such good care of Derek."

All eyes shifted to where Derek was seated. Still unable to make eye contact with anyone, he sat staring out at the garden. Among the thoughts racing through his head were reflections on the times that Cathy and her socialite friends had come to Onyx specifically to be waited on by him. He had been a man in charge, making certain that his customers' every wish was fulfilled, even before it was spoken. Remembering those bygone days, he recalled that sex had been playtime, not a job. He realized that less than a year ago he had had a sense of purpose and self-value. His posture had illustrated his inner strength and character. The other waitstaff and the restaurant management looked up to him. He was appreciated. He was courted by some of the most beautiful men in West Hollywood.

Now, as those thoughts and images melted away, they were replaced by flashbacks of the night before when Tom had beaten him. He cringed when he thought of the narrow escape from God-only-knew-what fate he may have had at the hands of Tom's thugs. He felt his eyes begin to burn and his throat constrict, as he desperately tried to hold back tears.

The others in the room, seeing their friend beginning to crumble, were speechless. Finally, Juan moved to Derek's side. "Boss?" he said.

Derek, glassy-eyed with unshed tears, turned to Juan. Involuntarily they both leaned in to each other and embraced in a tight hug. As Juan patted Derek's back and rocked him gently in his arms, Cathy, Marty and Felicia all took long, self-conscious sips of their drinks, allowing the two men what little privacy they could offer.

Eventually, aware that the others in the room were politely waiting for him to compose himself, Derek took a deep breath and gave Juan an extra firm hug. Wiping his eyes and nose with the bottom of his tank top, Derek tried to manage a smile. "God, I've really fucked up, haven't I?" he said. "I thought I was being so clever. Easy money has an expensive price tag. And when did sex become such a fucking chore?" He picked up his margarita glass and took a swallow. "Here's to another chapter in the definitely not tedious life of Derek Bracken," he practically whispered.

Felicia took a swallow of her drink, coughed as the tequila burned her throat, and said, "What are your plans for fighting that bastard?"

Derek thought for a moment. "I'm not a fighter," he said. "I'm so out of the business. If I can just keep Tom away from me, I'll be happy."

"You're going to let a candy ass like Tom force you out of such a profitable business?" Felicia said in her strained but authoritarian voice. "If my first husband had let competition get in his way, we wouldn't have been able to afford a double-wide in Florida, let alone this fancy mausoleum."

Derek leaned forward. "It's not just Tom," he said. "That Fraker is the king of the sex business in this town."

"And he's out of the game," Felicia interrupted. "Arrested. History. He won't be around to bother you for a very long time."

Marty weighed in. "You know what your mistake was?" he asked. "Greed and ego," he answered himself. "You wanted to be noticed. It's the actor in you. Instead of simply doing the work and collecting a more than decent wage, you not only talked about your services, you hired other people to do your job. That's just plain stupid, if you don't mind me saying so."

Felicia noticed that Derek took an uncomfortable swallow. "You've heard the phrase, 'There's no such thing as a perfect murder,' " she said. "Well, of course there is such a thing. But you've never heard of it because it's perfect. The killer kept his trap shut. Same with the best sex services in this town. You never hear of them because their people don't talk."

Marty sat back and placed his hands in his lap. "On the other hand," he said, "every day I read that someone's been arrested because they confided their crimes to a so-called friend. Idiots! If you tell just one person something private, it's no longer a secret. Do you follow me?"

Derek, Juan and Cathy nodded their heads in collective agreement with Marty and Felicia's observations, but still not understanding where the line of reasoning was going. "Not everyone has to brag about their crimes in order to get caught," Derek countered. "Look at O.J., for instance. Or the Menendez Brothers."

"Those are pure sociopaths," Felicia said. "We personally knew those two spoiled rich dorks. Both were spineless sissies who told their psychiatrists about blowing away their parents, for crying out loud. What did Marty just say about loose lips?"

"What about Fraker?" Derek asked. "If he was so good at keeping a secret how did he get caught?"

"Disgruntled employee," Marty said with authority. "Yapped to undercover vice. Wanted revenge. Always be nice to subordinates."

Derek took another long pull of his drink, which had become room temperature. "You guys look like the sort of people who wouldn't even believe that Richard Chamberlain was gay although he wrote a whole autobiography about himself that said so," he said.

"Richard and I go way back," Felicia said with an air of boredom. "His father came to me and asked that I talk his son out of wanting to become an actor. I took one look at that kid and fainted. After regaining consciousness my first words were, 'Honey, get your beautiful ass to Hollywood!' Who do you think instigated Brent Richardson's meeting with you?"

The room fell into silence, save for the sound of the gear mechanism in the grandfather clock down the hall.

Marty coughed and all eyes shifted to him. He turned to Derek. "We've had our eye on you ever since the first time we came in to Onyx. You don't think that someone like Tom would troll the bars or answer an ad like the one you placed in *Encounters,* do you?" Marty chuckled.

Felicia cackled. "Finding the right man for our dear Brent was a long and arduous project on our part." She grinned at her young husband and said, "Marty, remember when you tried to take Derek for a test drive, but he wasn't interested?" Felicia looked at her husband and smiled with genuine love. "Handsome thing, isn't he?" she said to the room, and touched Marty's arm in adoration. Slipping back to the point at hand she said, "Tom had to be the go-between. He gave you high marks and that was good enough for us."

Derek and Juan both thought back to the umpteen times that Marty and Felicia had been patrons at Onyx. Derek had always been reluctant to wait on them, but still treated them as cordially as he did all of his customers.

After a moment, when billions of bits of visual and intuitive information had bombarded their brains, they connected the dots of Marty's pats on their butts, his cryptic winks, obscure double entendres, and sexual innuendo. It dawned first on Derek and then almost simultaneously Juan. They were both pawns in an obviously elaborate and highly clandestine sex-for-trade business—Hollywood style.

THIRTY-FOUR

Cathy placed her empty glass on the coffee table. She lifted her head slightly, nervous about meeting anyone's eyes. "I'm not supposed to hear any of this, am I?" she said nervously. She began to panic. "Marty," she said, "you're a regular Tony Soprano." Cathy tried to make a joke of her uneasiness, then realized that her comparison was probably appropriate.

"I'm really just a little ol' pussycat when it comes to business," Marty said. "Especially this business. Felicia's the one with the brains in the family."

Derek heaved a heavy sigh. "I still don't understand what the hell you two have been saying." He forced a small laugh. "Must be my confused mental state, and the fact that I've been drinking on an empty stomach. It sounds as though the entire experience of me being an escort was instigated by both of you." He chuckled. "For all intents and purposes, you created a discreet sex slave out of me."

Derek made a dry chuckle and then tried to put the pieces of their conversation together. "Let me try to figure this out," he said. "You guys scoped me out at Onyx for Tom to pass along to Brent?"

"You give us way too much credit," Marty said.

"Farfetched as I know that is, it could make sense," Derek said. "But I wasn't just servicing Brent. There were a whole lot of Tom's friends, too."

"And that wasn't supposed to happen," Felicia chimed in. "We hired you for one purpose . . ."

"Tom screwed us, and Brent, by making money off of you," Marty added.

"Excuse me," Cathy said tentatively, addressing Marty and Felicia. "Call me naïve but what did you two get out of this? I mean, did you make lots of money from Derek having sex with clients?"

Felicia said, "From Brent. A finder's fee. I like to think of us as job recruitment specialists," she said. "You need a job done well, you go out and scout for experienced experts. So, we found experts."

"Plural?" Cathy said.

Felicia nodded vaguely. "Look," she said, "you probably get a ton of business cards in your mailbox, advertising everything from landscaping services to piano lessons. But would one hire such people? I suppose some would. Just as someone might hire boys out of *Encounters*. But when you want the best, you don't find them in the classifieds. Especially if they misspell Juilliard in their ad offering piano lessons. And, don't forget, Derek was unemployed and nearly starving to death."

"I did place an ad in *Encounters*," Derek reminded.

"By then we had made up our minds about you, dear," Felicia said, giving him her seal of approval. "We just needed a sample of your work. You provided that to Tom."

"Casting yourselves as the good Samaritans, eh?" Juan said.

"We just felt that Brent and Derek would be a perfect combination," Marty said. "Felicia has a talent for matchmaking," he noted proudly. "I think you're all overreacting."

Derek found a stronger voice. "How are we reacting?" he said. "Should I be sitting here thanking you for all the pairs of lips that have sucked on my dick? Am I supposed to be genuflecting in supplication for all the hairy asses I've been privileged to mount? If so, then thank you, Marty. Thank you, Felicia. What can I do in return? Maybe I should suck your dick as an expression of appreciation."

Felicia spoke up. "What you can do is sit back and listen to what we have to tell you. I promise that when we're through if you want to walk out of here, it will be fine and dandy. But just listen up for a little while." She picked up Marty's drink glass and poured what remained into her own glass. She then took a long gulp and finished it off. Her old tongue darted out and lasciviously scooped up the salt around the rim, then she licked her lips. "News flash," she finally announced.

Marty cleared his throat, straightened his posture and completed Felicia's thought. "We're moving," he declared. "Yup. It's time. Los Angeles is an SUV-congested swill hole. We've had enough. Bought a castle in the Loire and we're taking French lessons. *Bonjour, Madame Young. Comment allez-vouz?*"

"You're trying to keep one step ahead of the law?" Derek said.

Marty chuckled. "Nah. Nobody would believe this philanthropic little lady would even know what a male escort was, unless he was like someone hired to drive the elderly to their cardiologist. And me? I'm just her half-wit gold-digging toy boy husband. I don't know nothin' 'bout birthin' babies, let alone hiring homosexuals to fuck each other. We're simply ready to move on."

Juan said, "What will your star clients do? I mean, won't it be tough for your pals to find fresh flesh?"

Marty looked at Juan, then he shifted his gaze to Derek. Then he looked at Felicia, who nodded her head in agreement with her husband's unspoken thoughts. "Here's what we have in mind," Marty began. "We've decided that Derek should take over our humble business."

Marty ignored an outburst of incredulous gasps from Derek, Juan and Cathy. "During the past hour we've made it perfectly clear that this venture is operated in the strictest secrecy. The few clients that we have are household names. They trust us completely. And there is no way in hell we would ever betray that trust. To whomever we hand the reins of our business they will be of equal discretion."

Derek, stunned by what he was hearing from Marty, interrupted. "I've already shown that I can't be trusted. I told you that I made money going behind Tom's back."

"You didn't know what the real arrangement was," Felicia countered. "And you were tired of Tom using you for his own purposes."

Derek shrugged his shoulders. He looked at Marty, who was now holding Felicia's scrawny hand. "You guys operated a boutique sex-for-hire business, very mom and pop. You had a couple of clients, and you solicited Tom to service one or more of them. Then he started working on his own. Then I come along and although I'm your discovery for Brent, Tom covertly engaged me to service his clients. The trickle down continued because I started farming out my work to other guys."

"Smart man," Felicia said.

For the next few minutes, Derek and Juan, and Cathy sat in stunned silence, not daring to utter a word as they listened to Marty and Felicia banter back and forth about their business and their plans.

Felicia said, "With Fraker in jail, and Tom about to be indicted by the grand jury—for income tax evasion—his sex business will remain a secret—you'll have the playing field pretty much to yourselves. The right clients will find you. Oh, and Derek, you should consider staying with Brent. He E-mails me about you all the time."

Derek took a deep breath. On the one hand he saw dollar signs that added up to a potential fortune. On the other hand, he was dubious about a career that, when he first began working as an escort he thought was for a finite period of time. "What about the probability that Tom will implicate you, and me too?" Derek asked one of a million questions that began to enter his thoughts.

Marty answered. "You haven't been paying attention. Tom doesn't know that we've done anything more than find a friend for Brent— you. He doesn't realize how we fit into the whole equation. Plus the IRS is getting him. Not vice."

Marty looked at his wristwatch. "It's time for Felicia's nap," he said. "Let's convene back here at cocktail time. Shall we? We'll discuss this further."

"Wait a minute," Derek said as Marty helped Felicia to her feet, and Cathy, too, rose from her chair. Derek waited until he was acknowl- edged as having the floor. "You guys have talked the whole afternoon about yourselves, and about me." He waited a beat. "You haven't said one word about Juan. What about this man and his friends who risked their lives yesterday to get my ass out of trouble? They were arrested, basically because of you? Cathy's the one who bailed Juan out, not ei- ther of you. And where does he stand now? He's going to have an ar- rest record. He could go to jail again. What about that? What are you going to do for Juan?"

"Thanks, Boss," Juan said, turning to his friend. "I've never been in trouble with the police." His eyes focused on his memory of the past twenty-four hours. "It was really, really scary."

Juan sat down and put his face into his hands. When he had com- posed himself he said in a quiet voice, "It was a horror. As a gay person I was supposed to be placed in PC—protective custody. The general jail population is looking for reasons to fuck with anyone they think they can jump or steal from. I was supposed to be separated from all that."

"What happened, Juan?" Derek said, easing an arm around his friend's shoulder.

"Jail in Los Angeles is like a third world country," Juan said. "If you're gay you're supposed to go to what's called the K-11 ward for protection. I was denied that. God, you wouldn't believe the conditions down there. People were lying on dirty, cold, concrete floors with only little foam mats that were falling apart and eaten away. It was freezing.

"I was kept in the bathroom cell," Juan said as tears began to form in his eyes. "Oh, my God. Imagine having forty or fifty guys pissing and shitting right by your head all day! A bedsheet was hung by the toilet to make a curtain, but the bottom foot of it was crusted with feces and pee. And pieces of newspaper were stuck to it. Wads of toilet paper were on the ground. People would just throw it there to be an ass about it. There was an unbelievable stench.

"Finally, I was moved to another cell. I was given the top bunk. I looked down once and there were rats going through a sleeping prisoner's lunch bag. When he woke up I told the dude not to eat the bologna and apple because rats had gone through it. He totally didn't care. He was hungry and it was the only meal he was going to get. So he ate what the rats left."

The room was silent. Each envisioned Juan's incarceration and was mute with shock and disgust for what they were hearing. Derek reached out and hugged Juan who was now wiping his tears with his dirty shirt.

"There's a lot of pent-up animosity and rage and macho pride in jail and prisoners are just looking for any reason to uncork it," Juan continued. "It's not just the other prisoners, but the peacock sheriffs too. Everyone's looking for attention to prove who's the bigger big shot. They're all a pack of animals, and if you're gay, you're like a wounded animal and you're going to get eaten by them. I was kicked and spit on by sheriff's deputies. I was called a brown hole-poker. A mama's girl. A butt fucker. A dick licker. A pole smoker.

"I tried to ask a question and they yelled, 'Shut up, faggot!' and then they kicked me. This one officer, who was chewing tabacco, spit on the ground. And when I tried to ask another question he made me sit in it. These conditions are the norm, according to another prisoner I talked to. I thought this was like just a bad cell. He said it's the same all the time."

Juan's words trailed off. He was depleted of energy. "And Andrew fired me, so I'm out of work again," he added.

Cathy reached out and touched Juan's arm. "You're not fired. In fact, Andrew can be Derek's newest client. He can finally pay for what you've been giving him for free."

Juan simply stared at Cathy.

"If you think I'm the least bit interested in who or what Andrew plays with, you're wrong," Cathy said. "Andrew's a brilliant man. He's often difficult to live with, and God knows how his staff can stand his bombastic ass, but the man is a certifiable genius, and he's got sexual needs. I'm not about to judge. But I refuse to keep losing my own household staff just because he wants their dicks. I almost didn't hire you because you're so darned handsome. And God knows Andrew has a weakness for long black eyelashes." Cathy almost laughed. "But that would have been discrimination, and I won't have that."

"What about Juan's criminal record?" Derek demanded of Marty and Felicia.

Marty nodded his head in understanding. "No record," he said. "The DA and Felicia are tight. False arrest is the name of the game. But he'll probably make you and your friends sign something saying that you won't sue the city."

"It's you who Juan should sue!" Derek said, lashing out at Marty. "A class action suit. We should round up all the men you've turned into sex slaves and bring your ass to justice."

Marty looked at Felicia. "No nappy today, hon," he said. He returned his attention to Derek. "Sex slaves?" he said. "And who are these 'people' you're speaking about? There's Tom, but he's going away for bad behavior with the government's money. And I wouldn't exactly call you a sex slave." Marty sighed.

Felicia looked up at Derek and crooked a finger for him to come to her. Derek seated himself on the sofa next to her. She put a gentle hand on his knee, and looked lovingly into his eyes. "When Marty and I began patronizing Onyx, the first thing we agreed on was that we liked you. You seemed to have confidence and courage. You were helped by natural resources—physical beauty and above-average intelligence. But we recognized more. It didn't take a mind reader for us to know that you were not content to simply exist or survive. You wanted more. You wanted to experience a larger and deeper life. We knew that you would succeed at anything you really and truly wanted. You obviously didn't really want the acting thing."

Derek nodded his head in reluctant agreement. "Who doesn't want more from life? And the acting thing was just a means to get to where I've already been for the past six months."

"You'd be surprised at the people who really don't want more than what they already have, because they don't feel they deserve more," Felicia said. "You moved yourself forward. With your imagination and your energy you transformed an ordinary life into something extraordinary. You allowed yourself to be brought into an unfamiliar world. As you found out, it is a world that welcomed you with open arms. I don't believe for one moment that you can look back and seriously consider returning to the smaller world you once knew."

Again, Derek nodded his head as he thought to himself how mundane his former existence had been compared to what he had grown accustomed to. *Who among my friends ever met the likes of Brent Richardson, let alone slept with him?* he asked himself. The answer was, not one. He silently agreed that in many ways, as difficult as his current experiences appeared to be, at least they were unique. He had always wished for a life in which he moved among the social elite. And for the past six months that's exactly what he had been doing, although not in any way he'd ever anticipated. *Barbra Streisand might not know my name, but she smiles at me at parties,* he thought to himself. *Jennifer Garner, and David Hyde Pierce know me by name, and Tom Cruise, and Clint Eastwood, and Tom Hanks, and Tyne Daly, too.*

"Life is a curious series of experiences," Felicia said wistfully. "I don't mean to sound all woo-woo, California psychedelic weird, but I do believe that we're all connected, and that Marty and I were attracted to you for a reason, and that likewise you were attracted to us."

Derek reluctantly agreed. But he had always used this theory to explain the lovers he attracted. What Felicia was offering was another point of view: that Derek's upward movement—which he knew some people would see as a *downward* spiral—was also the result of unseen forces moving him into a position to experience all that he thought he wanted out of life. *I wanted to be with the rich and famous, but I should have been more precise about what I meant by "with,"* he said sardonically to himself. "I'm afraid I still don't know what you guys want from me," Derek said aloud. "Or, rather, why you selected me to be the one to take over the family practice."

"Who better?" Felicia asked. "Do you know anyone more qualified? Anyone with a better set of pecs?" Felicia chuckled as she caressed

Derek's shirt and felt his chest. "And like it or not, your wee-wee is famous."

Derek took a long silent look at Felicia, and then at Marty. He thought, *My instincts are usually right. I thought that they were a strange pair when I waited on them at Onyx.* "How did you two become sexual leeches?" he asked. "I mean, at what point in your lives did you think, 'Gee, everybody wants sex, let's get us some studs and sell 'em to our rich and famous friends. It's win/win for everybody."

Derek did not wait for either Marty or Felicia to respond. He stood up and ran his fingers through his hair. "I'm outta here. I just want to get a clean life again. But don't worry about your precious secret, Felicia," he said. "I can't speak for Juan and Cathy, but I won't tell a soul. As long as you take care of Juan's arrest situation, and you leave me alone. But if you fuck around, so help me God, I'll personally take you and this town down. So you better get your butts over to Europe, pronto."

Juan and Cathy rose to their feet and looked down with pitiable stares at the two eccentric hosts. Without a word, they followed behind Derek and together they walked out of the vast room. They retraced their path to the foyer. At the heavy oak door, Derek turned the knob and the three of them exited into the weak late afternoon sun. Cathy pushed a button on her car key chain and unlocked the doors of her Mercedes from twenty-five feet away. The group slipped into the vehicle and, after turning the ignition and checking for traffic, Cathy pulled away from curb and headed toward 6th street. She turned right and asked where Derek wanted to be dropped.

THIRTY-FIVE

Entering the tiny one-room apartment on Fountain Avenue with Juan, Derek was as morose as he ever remembered being. He looked around at the dirty stucco walls. He glanced up at the familiar dark stains on the ceiling. He looked down and grimaced at the dingy and deteriorating shag carpet.

The contrast to Brent's home, with its floors of polished hardwood, marble, sandstone, and Oriental rugs, and walls adorned with priceless art, pummeled Derek's self-worth.

Here, the movie poster reprints were still taped above the table that served as a desk. At Brent's home Andrew Wyeth was prominent under pin spots of track lighting. Always there was classical music wafting through surround sound speakers. Here, the CD stereo boom box had been reduced to mono after being dropped. The dominant sounds in this space came from the traffic along the streets, and the heavy footfalls from the neighbors upstairs.

After half a year surrounded by the luxury of a seemingly boundless estate, the interior of which was decorated by Colin Cowie, Derek was slammed with the reality of an ordinary life.

He stared at the thin mattress on the bed, then flashed on a mental image of the king-size bed in which he had become accustomed to sleeping at Brent's. His eyes drifted to the ironing board, which seemed permanently anchored to the floor and perennially piled with clothes. His eyes found the bathroom door frame, the molding of which was thick with years of being carelessly painted over and over until the coats were so thick that the door had to be pushed or pulled with extra effort to open and close. The sink in the kitchenette had ceased to look anything like porcelain. It was more a big rust stain from a perpetual trickle from the ancient faucet protruding out from the grimy green, ceramic backsplash.

Derek flashed on Brent's gleaming, pounded copper sink in his kitchen. He instantly saw the wide pink granite countertops, and the two center islands with their futuristic cooking ranges that were activated only when a pot or pan was placed on top of it. Brent's cabinetries were custom made, as were the appliances. Indeed, the kitchen was larger than the apartment to which he was now relegated. Here, on Fountain Avenue, doorless shelves served as storage space for Derek's three dinner plates and four drinking glasses.

The room suddenly seemed so tiny that Derek became claustrophobic. *I'm so fucking noble,* he said to himself, nearly catatonic with the realization of all that he had given up. *How can I live this way?* he thought, as a tear began to form in his eye and his nose started to run. "Juan," he called out quietly. "I can't do this. I can't start over."

"Boss, you deserve a better life than what you were doing."

"There was nothing wrong with the life," Derek said. "I wasn't ashamed of it. I actually enjoyed the work. And the money. I lived at the top of the world." Derek gestured for Juan to take a look at their accommodations. "Does living in a shit hole apartment and having zero money in my pocket give me any more self-value than plugging my cock into a bunch of strangers' asses in exchange for living like a star?"

Juan faced his friend and placed a hand on his thick biceps. "Things won't be like this forever," he said. "You're young and smart. You can do whatever you want to do with your life. And you don't have to be beholden to anybody."

"It was a fair exchange," Derek said, shrugging off Juan's hand. "I earned my place there. I did the work. I deserved the rewards." Derek was quiet for a long moment as he stared at the blinking answering machine. Finally he said, "I don't know what I'm going to miss the most—laughing with Brent, fucking Brent, or living in Brent's world."

Juan sat down on the bed's mattress and scratched his head. "You weren't in love with Brent, so what's it really matter?"

"What the fuck is love, anyway?" Derek said.

Juan cocked an eyebrow, contemplating an answer. "In your case, love is confused with admiration. And envy. Brent has accomplished what you couldn't."

Derek grunted in cynicism.

Juan exhaled loudly. "Look, who wouldn't love to live at Brent's estate and have sex with the man? He's not unattractive. A lot of guys would love to fuck him. But is sex the same as love? Of course not. But I think there's a lot involved in loving someone, and we've just mentioned a bunch of the ingredients that should be in the mix. So maybe you are in love. But you have to question whether you're in love with the man, or with his lifestyle."

"Hardly matters now," Derek said. "Something fundamental has been yanked away from me. I just can't lead an ordinary life. I've been to the other side, and now I'm back where I started. I feel trapped because I know what else is out there."

Juan arranged himself on the bed and leaned his back against the wall. "Everybody wants something better," he said. "When Felicia said she knew that you weren't content to simply exist or survive, she was merely parroting every wannabe Dr. Phil self-help guru on the planet. Of course you want a larger and deeper life. Everybody who ever lived would say that's what they're seeking. Felicia was speaking as much to me as she was to you, Boss. You're not so special when it comes to daydreams. Do you think I like coming back here after spending the day at Cathy's or after fucking Andrew at his luxury condo? I want what they have. And, I'm fucking lonely here."

Derek said ruefully, "Things don't really change all that much, do they?" he said. "Old wine in new bottles. We're on a never-ending cycle of getting our asses fucked by the universe."

Both men fell into silence. All either man could think about was that they were worse off now than six months prior. And then their reverie was shattered by a knock at the door.

Derek and Juan exchanged looks. "Hold a sec," Juan called out. He got off the bed and walked the few paces to the door.

"Just me," Garson said. "Rent day," the apartment manager practically sang.

Juan turned to Derek with a look of panic. "Fuck, it's the first already?" he whispered. "I didn't get my weekly check from Cathy!"

"Want me to come back?" Garson asked politely. "I can wait until tomorrow if it's more convenient."

"Thanks, Garson," Juan called through the door. "I'm in the middle of something and can't get to the checkbook. I'll catch you in the A.M."

"Cool," Garson said, before Juan and Derek heard the apartment manager's footsteps retreating down the walkway.

"Déjà vu?" Juan said, looking at Derek. "Haven't we experienced this same scenario before? Christ, I hope you can help me out with rent 'cause I pretty much live hand to mouth."

Derek gave a weak laugh. "I have a fortune."

"Thank God." Juan smiled.

"But it's locked in Brent's safe," Derek said. "By now, Tom has probably cleaned me out. I didn't put all that cash in the bank because of IRS issues. Anyway, I couldn't get back on the estate if I tried. So I'm just as broke as the day I left here."

The wailing sound of a police siren penetrated the walls of the apartment, as Juan and Derek blankly looked at each other. Derek, feeling enslaved by his lack of money, saw himself in a large crystal ball surrounded by a haze of green smoke, and the Wicked Witch of the West cackling happily at the misery of her prisoner.

Juan visualized the jail cell he had recently occupied. He saw himself returning to the cage in shackles, serving a sentence for breaking and entering. Without Marty and Felicia's help getting his arrest record cleared up, and without Andrew as his alibi, he would certainly be tried, convicted, and sentenced for the multiple burglaries the Beverly Hills cops were eager to hang on him.

Suddenly, Juan began shaking. His teeth clattered and he rolled himself into the fetal position on the bed. Tears drained from his eyes, and between hot sobs he said, "Ya know what, Boss? You're an egomaniacal son of a bitch!"

The statement astounded Derek, and shook him out of his reverie. "What?" he asked, as if he had not heard Juan correctly.

"Self-absorbed. Self-serving. A pitiable piece of crap," Juan stated matter-of-factly. "You complain that you can't go back to the life you had before you started fucking Brent Richardson and all his rich and famous friends. You're pathetic."

Derek's jaw dropped as he looked at his friend and listened to his tirade. "Look, man, I'm going through hell right now, so cut me some slack, will ya?" Derek said.

"You're going through hell? That's a laugh," Juan said. "I feel so sorry for you. It's such a fucking tragedy that you have to start over and find another free ride to the good life. All I hear are complaints.

Poor Derek, he's unemployed and broke. You relied on your good looks and charm to get you into the inner circles of fucked-up Hollywood, and now your stock analyst tells you the bottom has fallen out of fuck futures. Shit, man, it's as bad as Martha Stewart's life, isn't it."

Derek stood up from the floor and kicked the boom box. The CD stopped for a moment and then began again at the first selection. A chunk of plastic separated from the right speaker. "What the fuck brought this on?" he demanded of Juan. "I'm not complaining. I'm merely stating facts. I'm fucked. We're both fucked."

"Some more than others," Juan said between intermittent sniffling. "The way I see it, you're not physically or mentally handicapped. You've got a perfectly good pair of eyes, arms and legs. You're not shuffling around with your head cocked to one side and drooling like a baby. Tons of other guys would kill to have your face and body. You've got it made, man."

"If that's your criteria for a perfect life, then we're equal," Derek said, recognizing that what Juan was saying about him was in fact true. "You're a hot dude with all your limbs, and a brain too."

Juan was silent as he half listened to Derek, and half thought about the legal and financial predicament he was facing.

"You blame me for this miserable turn of events, don't you?" Derek said. "I'm the root of all *your* problems." He thought for a moment. "Maybe I am," he continued. "If you hadn't come to my rescue last night you wouldn't have an arrest record. I'm really sorry, but I can't change the past."

Juan sniffled again and swallowed hard. "Never mind, Boss," he said. "I just don't know where to begin to rebuild my life. Hell, I may not even have much of a life once the police get through with my ass. So many people I used to hang out with went to prison for one crime or another. I never thought I'd find myself facing that possibility. Forget what I said about you being pathetic. You're not. It's me."

Derek walked to the bed and sat down. He put a hand on Juan's head and began stroking his thick black hair. He looked at the beautiful features of Juan's face; his long black eyelashes, the perfectly shaped nose, and his full lips. A pang of lust washed over Derek as the remembered the feeling of cradling Juan's bare body in his arms and stroking his dark velvet smooth skin. He began to grow hard as he inhaled his friend's unwashed scent, wafting through his warm skin. Derek's memory jumped to one of the nights when they had been entwined, and he had spent hours slathering his tongue over every inch of Juan's body. The memory of tasting his friend immediately played back and made him wish that the time were right to have sex with Juan again.

Derek petted Juan's head once more. Then he leaned down and pressed his lips to Juan's temple and gave it a long tender kiss. "Get some sleep, babe. I'll be back in a while," he said. He stood up and walked to the door.

"What are you doing?" Juan asked. "Your date nights are over, remember?"

"Have a beer. It'll help you sleep," Derek said as he placed his hand on the doorknob and pulled open the door. "I'll be back soon. Don't latch the chain."

"Don't leave me," Juan moaned.

"I won't be long."

THIRTY-SIX

"I know it's late, but I need to see you," Derek spoke into his cell phone. "I'll be there in twenty minutes." He pushed the disconnect button, and continued driving down Highland Avenue. He passed Santa Monica Boulevard and Melrose Avenue. At Beverly he turned left and made another left at June Street. He slowed the car down to a crawl as he tried to remember what the house looked like. All of the homes on this street were mammoth, but he recalled that the one for which he was searching, was perhaps the most impressive. And then he recognized it.

Derek pulled into the driveway, doused the headlights and switched off the ignition. He slipped out of the car and walked along a flagstone path leading to the front door.

Marty answered the door wearing Levi's and an open shirt that revealed a better body than Derek had imagined. Marty's stomach wasn't as toned it could have been, but it wasn't paunchy or spilling over the waist of his pants. He had pecs where Derek had expected tits. With a cock of his head he invited Derek to enter the house. "At Felicia's age, she needs her sleep," he said. "So it's just you and me. Come."

The men moved in tandem down the long marble corridor and through a twelve-foot archway and into the Great Room where they had met earlier in the day. Marty motioned for Derek to take a seat on the sofa. The men sat down opposite each other.

Derek folded his arms over his chest and stared at Marty. After a moment of silence between the men, Derek said, "I have to confess something. When I was at Onyx, I only pretended to like you."

Marty gave a dismissive shrug.

"I always thought that your marriage was weird," Derek said. "I didn't get it."

"She's been real good to me, okay?" Marty said, marking an invisible line of loyalty over which Derek was nonverbally cautioned not to step. "You make yours pay," he said with a loose jerk-off gesture of his right hand. "What's the diff?"

Derek's silence was his concession to the truth of what Marty said. Sex was a commodity and he and Marty were both skin traffickers in their own way. Sex had an adjustable sliding scale value. It all depended on the terms and conditions set forth between two or more parties. For the young and beautiful, and exotic and unique, it was always a seller's market. The relative scarcity of superior stock made the going rate for services rendered as fluid as the caprice of the vendor. In the sex trade, no line could be finer than that which exists between what one man considers a priceless treasure and another sees as a worthless bauble. "What I wanted to say was, that I think that I was wrong about you," Derek said.

Marty smiled and nodded in understanding.

"But why me?" Derek asked. "Why did you and Felicia want me to be the next whore to the stars, so to speak?"

Again, Marty shrugged. "Felicia's better at explaining these things," he said. "She thought you were special."

"I'm not the pandering type," Derek countered.

"You've been doing the job for the past six months," Marty retorted.

"I fell into that role. That's not who I want to be," Derek pleaded. "I'm a nice guy. I work hard. I'm compassionate. I fall in love too easily. I . . ." Derek was suddenly lost in thoughts of how much he had enjoyed Brent's companionship, as well as his feelings for Juan.

Marty nodded his head. "Continue. You're doing well."

"I'm a fake," Derek said as tears began to well in his eyes, the stress and sadness of the past few days finally catching up with him. "I pretend to be a strong self-assured man, and I'm not. I'm weak. I liked the work I did but I hate the way my life has turned out."

Marty scratched the hair on his chest. "At twenty-three your life has hardly 'turned out' yet," he said. "And trust me, from personal experience I know that life is crammed with options. All you have to do is say yes once in a while. I'm here, in this house, with Felicia, because I once answered, 'why not?' to an important question. I didn't know what I was getting myself into, but thank God I accepted the opportunity. It was the best decision I ever made. And now you have a decision to make. Although I think you've already made up your mind."

Derek was silent for a long moment. Finally, he looked up at Marty and said, "Things aren't the way they seem to be. I don't think this is only true in Hollywood. It's just more obvious here. I mean, look at Brent Richardson, for example. His fans around the world would never guess that when he's horny, he's only satisfied if he's got a stiff cock pumping and grinding away inside his famous ass. And look at Felicia. No disrespect intended, but on the surface, she's Angela Lansbury. She's the type to bake cherry pies for orphans. She's a thin Barbara Bush—minus the creepy kids. But in reality, Felicia is Heidi Fleiss.

"Then there's my friend Juan," Derek continued. "He's fucking Andrew Taylor, who pretends to be straight. Andrew's wife, Cathy, keeps a photo-ready smile plastered on her face and pretends to be understanding of her husband. She's even rumored to have a girl-friend. And you . . ."

Marty casually draped an arm over the back of the sofa. His shirt further parted from his body and revealed more of his shape.

"Look at you," Derek said. "I would never have suspected that you'd have a hot bod."

Marty smiled with embarrassment. He wasn't exactly certain where Derek was headed with his thoughts.

"You're another contradiction," Derek said. "I used to think you were scummy. But on the other hand, I used to think the world of Dr. Dillon, the guy who was everyone's family physician where I grew up. Then when I was fourteen my mom took me in for a tetanus shot after I stepped on a nail during football practice. I was filthy and sweaty. He gave me an examination I'll never forget. He had me strip naked, even though it was my foot he was supposed to be treating. Then he lifted my balls with a tongue depressor. He made a big deal about weighting them on the flat stick. Said he'd never seen such large testicles on a boy my age. I think I sort of chuckled, 'cause I knew from showering with the other guys in gym class that he was right. He instructed me to lay back on the table. Then he blew me. My first blow job.

"He said that if I told anyone, he'd make certain that I had an oper-ation. He didn't say what sort of operation, but the thought of being in a hospital, and with Dr. Dillon behind a surgical mask, holding a scalpel over me, was enough to keep the secret. I hated him. Not for the blow job, which I actually liked. I hated Dr. Dillon for his power over me. You just can't tell anything about people from their surface attributes. And you can't trust the ones who you think are holier than thou."

Marty said, "Not everybody has an ulterior motive," he said. "You just have to trust your instincts, and maybe trust everybody until they give you a reason not to be trusted. That's what Felicia has taught me. Hell, I didn't trust anybody before I met her. Even after her husband died and I started taking her to Onyx, I didn't trust you. But she did. And I came around to her way of thinking."

Derek made a face. "Why didn't you trust me? And what changed your mind?" he asked. "I always treated you guys well."

"Yeah, to our faces," Marty said. "But I have a sixth sense. I knew you didn't approve of me. And quite honestly, I thought you were pretty two-faced. I noticed how you put on that killer smile for every customer."

"It's my nature to be friendly," Derek defended himself. "Plus, the bigger the smile, the bigger the tip."

"Well, Felicia liked the way you treated her, and she saw something in you that I didn't get right away."

Derek smiled. "That's funny. Felicia liked you, and saw something in you that I didn't get either. At least not until this afternoon. I liked the way you treated her. You didn't talk down to her because of her age, and you were concerned about her nap. The way you helped her up from the sofa was, to me, a telling moment. Who knows why people get together, and it's nobody's business but yours. All that matters is how you treat each other and the happiness that you each bring to the other."

Both men stopped talking. They looked at each other with less circumspection than either had before. Finally, Derek cleared his throat and spoke. "I've decided . . . I'm not going to judge this business, or the people in the business, or the men who patronize this business. Nothing is all good or all bad. Nobody is always right or always wrong."

"What changed your mind?" Marty asked.

"Felicia, I guess. And you, too," Derek said. "And Brent, and Tom, and all of Tom's boys, and the men I've met in the past six months. Everyone has contributed. Brent is still someone to whom one can look as a role model. He's classy and deserves to have sex just as much as anybody else, even if he believes he has to pay for it. And Tom is still a disgusting, mean-spirited son of a bitch, but I don't have to run a business the way he or Fraker did. And I don't have to hire detestable guys to do the job, the way they did. Most of the men I serviced were very decent guys and they appreciated me. And for the amount of money they paid, they deserved a good time."

"Are you accepting our offer so that you'll be worshipped?" Marty asked.

"It's not hard to have the following of horny men," Derek said. "Not to sound immodest, but that's never been a problem. I may as well make some money too."

Marty snorted. "So this is only about the money?"

For a moment Derek didn't know if he should try to sound philosophical and spew some sort of Miss America bullshit about wanting to make the world of sex-for-hire a better and safer place. Instead he blurted out his true feelings. "Hell, yeah, it's about the money. If I could make this kind of bread doing almost anything else, I would. But, I was born to fuck."

Marty smiled. "Smart answer. Felicia will be happy to hear that she was right, as always. She said you'd come back after you gave the offer some careful consideration. In fact, she wouldn't have wanted you to make a snap decision. It's too important." Marty stood up. "So, wanna spend the night and suck my cock for starters?"

Derek did a double take.

"Kidding!" Marty said. "Well, sort of. You should get back to Juan. Tell him Felicia's already talked to the DA. He and his pals won't have any problems. And Felicia would like to have you back here tomorrow for a meeting. She wants to introduce you to our clients."

"Except Brent," Derek said. "He's still in Ireland doing that film."

"No, he's back. He's already been invited. And, he knows you're going to be here," Derek said.

"He already knows that I'm taking over your business?"

"Felica explained everything to him. He was livid at first, but he doesn't want to lose you. He figures that this way you can devote yourself to him sexually, when you're not helping the overprivileged get laid by a core staff of guys of your choosing."

THIRTY-SEVEN

Evening settled over Beverly Hills. The scent of night-blooming jasmine perfumed the air surrounding Weybridge Cottage. Brent sat on the poolside settee and stared at the softly rippling water. He sipped champagne from a crystal flute as a collage of memories whirled through his mind; all reminders that his life was more unsettled than ever before.

"You look pensive."

Brent turned abruptly toward the unexpected voice.

"You should have changed the security code," Derek said, answering Brent's unspoken question. He leaned against the handrail of the wooden bridge that arched over the koi pond and hooked his thumbs into the pockets of his jeans.

Brent felt the prickle of hairs on his ball sack as he absorbed the sight of Derek's familiar face and the smooth, muscled skin exposed around his white tank top.

"Felicia talked to you about . . . things?" Derek asked, as he moved toward Brent.

"Yup." Brent nodded. "Want some champagne?" He leaned forward and withdrew the bottle of Dom from the ice bucket. He filled his flute, replaced the bottle, and then took a sip from the glass. He reached out and held the vessel toward Derek who accepted it with caution, thinking that in the next instant Brent might throw the contents into his face.

"What I want is for you to try to be understanding," Derek answered, then consumed the champagne in one uninterrupted swallow.

Brent shrugged his shoulders. "Not a problem," he said, taking back the empty glass. "We're all opportunists, in one way or another."

"That sounds lousy," Derek said.

"I didn't mean it as a pejorative," Brent said. "Just a fact. I include myself."

"Nothing has to change between you and me," Derek said. "I still want to have sex with you."

"Sex." Brent harrumphed and dismissed Derek's attempt to maintain the status quo of their arrangement. "Sex is the common denominator in this whole disaster," he said. "Sex and money. Thanks to avarice, in one fell swoop I lost my best friend who, I had to learn from a very old straight woman, was my attorney by day and every queer star's pimp by night."

"Only a select few," Derek said. "Not like that Fraker dude who's in jail."

Brent continued to run down the list of his life's recent calamities. "Even my home was Command Central for an escort service, operated by my very own personal whore."

"Please don't call me that," Derek said, and took a deep breath to control his embarrassment. "You guys pursued me. And I wasn't with you just for the fat paycheck. Tom was the greedy one."

"You and I had an agreement that you would be my on-call"—Brent searched for a less offensive word—"partner. I never expected you to parlay that into a celebrity sex club."

"It was your idea that I fuck your friends," Derek countered.

"That was Tom's ludicrous inspiration," Brent said. "He insisted it was the best way to keep your sack drained so you wouldn't get bored out of your skin and trick around town when I wasn't home."

"That was stupid," Derek said. "I would have agreed to parameters. You could have trusted me."

"Trust," Brent said wistfully. "Again, I've been screwed by those I believed in. Christ. Will I ever learn?"

"Tom insisted that the men he sent to me were part of a package deal with you," Derek said.

"Are you blaming me for all this?" Brent asked. He reached for the bottle again, found it empty, and looked around, perplexed.

"I accept the blame for thinking I could get away with farming out the stud work," Derek said. "But let's not bother with blame for the moment. I'm here because I wanted to talk to you face to face."

"Marty said you'd eventually drop by with a portfolio of hot men to replace you in my bed. I'm not interested," Brent said.

"Neither am I," Derek said. After a moment he became aware that the evening air temperature had dropped, and that his tank top was not adequate cover against the chill. "How cold does it have to get before these switch on?" he asked, nodding at the half dozen automatic heaters scattered about the vast patio. He rubbed his arms for the warmth of the friction.

"We need another bottle anyway," Brent said, raising himself up from the settee. "Let's go inside."

Derek stood and followed Brent across the lawn. They entered the house through French doors that led into the kitchen. All at once Derek was rooted by memories. A faint and obscure odor, like a school lunchbox, instantly triggered within him a sensation of unfathomable loss and regret. He remembered how awed by the mansion he had been—and still was. And how safe from landlords and the pressures of unemployment he had felt when he and Brent were together in this house. The good life had been handed to him, literally on a silver platter. Just as swiftly it had been wrenched away. Now, on his first return to Beverly Hills since being evicted, he was overcome by the realization that his once-upon-a-time fairytale dream had vanished.

Brent opened the refrigerated wine chest and removed another bottle of champagne. He easily read Derek's thoughts and body language. "Now who's looking pensive," he said.

After a long moment, Derek spoke in a near whisper. "It's true what they say."

"What do they say?"

"That we don't know what we have 'til it's gone."

"I know what I have, and how close I came to losing it because of you and Tom," Brent said. He unwrapped the foil that surrounded the wire and cork at the bottle's neck. "But things have a way of working out."

Derek fell into silence. *Brent's attitude is amazing,* he thought as he watched the star pour champagne and place a wedge of Brie on a round granite platter. He sensed that if he tried to speak, he would cry—from a combination of his affection for Brent, and knowing that life could never go back to the good times they had shared.

"Let's take this into the Great Room and talk," Brent said.

* * *

There was no debate that Brent was one of the world's most prominent celebrities. He knew this as a fact of his life, as simple and true as
that his eyes were blue. There was no ego or judgment about his position. Things were what they were. Thus, when in the privacy of his
home it was Brent's nature to draw attention away from himself, and
to make friends and guests feel as comfortable as possible. To jump-
start his conversation with Derek he made an innocuous observation:
"You're still working out."

For the first time since returning to Weybridge Cottage, Derek smiled.
"Not often enough," he said. "Only every other day. What about you?"

"When I can. Hardly ever," Brent confessed. "You know I hate
weight training."

Derek chuckled. "Your natural build was always a turn on for me,"
he said.

Brent lowered his eyes. "I don't think of myself as a turn on for any
man." He changed the subject. "Do you ever see your old friend Juan?"
he asked.

"Of course. We're doing this business thing together," Derek said.
"Didn't Marty or Felicia tell you?"

"Probably," Brent said. "Those two chattered a lot. But after filling
me in on Tom's IRS grief, which of my friends might be in Fraker's
black book, and that you were taking over their business, mostly all I
heard was 'Wah, wah, wah, wah, wah.' Like when Charlie Brown is day-
dreaming in class and not paying attention to the teacher."

Derek smiled again. "I've missed your sense of humor," he said,
meeting Brent's eyes. A moment passed. Then he asked, "Speaking of
Tom, what's the latest?"

"His assets are frozen and he's waiting for a court date," Brent said.
"We don't talk. His decision, not mine. But it's for the best. He's pretty
much in seclusion. By the by, have you and Juan started?"

Derek shrugged. "It's a slow process, but we're interviewing guys.
Finding the right combination of talent and integrity isn't easy. I thank
God that Juan's with me on this. I couldn't do it alone."

Brent sat quietly for a moment. He wanted to know everything
about Derek and Juan, but was cautious. Finally he asked, "Are you
guys living together?"

Derek's smile evaporated as he looked at Brent. "What's it to you?"
He hoped for a Hollywood movie twist where Brent would promise to
forget about the past if they could just start their lives over together.

"What I meant to ask is, are you guys happy?" Brent modified his query. "Juan's my best friend. We've been through a lot together," Derek said. "He's a smart man. Sexy, too. I should marry him. But . . ." Derek left the door open to accept a hoped-for affirmation of devotion from Brent.

Brent stared at Derek for a long moment. When he became aware that he was Superman with x-ray vision, and looking through Derek's clothes, he caught himself. But it was too late. He knew that Derek was aware that his body was being coveted. "I've always thought that people should marry their best friend," Brent said to direct his thoughts back to the subject of the conversation. "We should be with people we like to talk to. Sex isn't the be all and end all."

Derek grinned. "My new clients better not feel that way," he said and immediately regretted continuing the discussion of his job. The opportunity to reel in Brent had slipped by. After another beat, Derek said, "There's a reason why I'm here, Brent. Can I just tell you a few things? From my heart?"

With the tilt of his head and a raised eyebrow, Brent gave his non-verbal permission.

"I have nothing to lose by getting all of this off my chest. So here goes," Derek said. "Yeah, I'm now sort of a panderer."

"Sort of?" Brent interrupted.

"Let me finish," Derek said. "I'm really just a matchmaker. That's all. No whoring around. Been there done that. I have no need or interest. I simply want to settle down with someone. In truth, I want to settle down with you. I know that's never going to happen. As great a guy as you are, you'd never be able to put aside thoughts of where the money I earn is coming from. That's cool. I understand. Still, I want you to know how I feel."

Brent placed his elbows onto his knees and leaned forward. "Derek," he whined, and placed his face into the palms of his hands. "Don't do this to me. I'm still upset by the fallout from everything that's happened. I can't think straight. For the first time in my life, I don't know what to do. I'm never confused. But now..."

The unspoken message was that Brent needed more time to think about what place Derek could hold in his life. As he ran his fingers through his hair, he felt Derek's hand on his shoulder. Brent held his breath and turned to look at his former sex partner. He saw tears in Derek's eyes.

"I'd better go," Derek whispered. "If and when you ever want to see me again, even if it's just to share a bottle of champagne, I've got the same cell number. Call me."

Brent reached up and placed his hand on the one still resting on his shoulder. He gave it a squeeze and realized that his own eyes were beginning to sting with tears. He nodded his head and gave Derek's hand one last strong squeeze.

The men simultaneously stood. Derek followed Brent through the Great Room and down the hallway to the front entrance hall. There, Brent slowly opened the door, and the two stood between the cool night air and the sanctuary of the mansion. Brent initiated an embrace, and the two were flooded with memories of holding each other's naked bodies. In the instant before they separated, Brent said, "I won't change the security code."

And then Derek stepped out under the portico and down the steps. As Derek walked to his car, Brent languidly closed the door. He leaned his back against the strong wooden surface and shut his eyes. The silence of the big empty house enveloped him and he thought, *Where's that stupid Greta when I need companionship the most?*

THIRTY-EIGHT

As the next few weeks passed, Derek and Juan finalized their collection of a small group of the most seductive men on the planet. Each man was unique in appearance and endowment, but they all had one thing in common: they loved sex and wanted it as often as possible. Finally, Derek and Juan settled on an official date to receive transfer of Marty and Felicia's operation. When the day arrived they called an assembly of their cadre of studs for one final group meeting.

"There's a lot of dogma and crap in both the hetero and homo communities against the idea of using our God-given physical endowments to sexually please men in exchange for money," Derek said to a group of twelve young men. They were gathered together for a meeting with him and Juan in Juan's Silverlake apartment. The accomodations were new to Juan, and his home was decorated to "Queer Eye" perfection by Vaughn, as a last creative gesture before moving back to his hometown in Indiana.

"But personally, I'm proud of what I bring to the table," Derek continued. "And I know that all of you are too. Otherwise we wouldn't have selected you to be on our team. What's your job?" he asked. "To provide the overprivileged with something they can't find elsewhere," he answered his own question. "A safe playground for great gay sex!"

Everybody in the room chuckled.

"Does the fact that we don't have any emotional blocks on sex make us whores?" Juan interjected.

"No!" was the resounding answer among the men. They could have been a squad of self-satisfied cheerleaders.

Derek looked at the assembly before him. Twelve men, each someone's sexual fantasy, sat listening to him offer what was essentially a first-day-on-the-job orientation lecture and pep rally. Derek was a capable motivational speaker. He was an all-in-one Dr. Phil, Deepak Chopra, and Dr. Ruth. And the men in the room hung on his every word and became enthusiastic about their careers as elite Hollywood escorts.

As Derek discussed the responsibility of each man—which was to sexually satisfy a distinguished clientele—he cautioned against bringing judgment about a client to any sex encounter. "You would probably have sex with most of these men for free anyway," he said. "You may have even fantasized about some of them. But remember, this is not dating," he said. "This is sex. You *will* kiss. You *will* fondle and caress. You *will* hold and cuddle a client, if that is what they wish. Regardless of their weight issues or anything else you might find unappealing."

A hand was raised by one of the men. "I don't have the best body in the world," the young escort-in-training said to Derek. "Stars could pay for lots better."

For a long moment Derek looked at the young man who was twenty-one, five feet, seven inches tall, and weighed one hundred forty pounds. His build was slight, with a naturally defined musculature. He wore his blond hair in a shoulder-length shag, which was reminiscent of seventies rock stars. One front tooth was slightly crooked. It was his combination of boyishness mixed with a sexual mystique, and an eight-inch dick that made Derek select him for the group. Derek had a list of several stars of daytime dramas who he knew would salivate at the sight of this young man.

"Are there way better-looking escorts out there?" Derek answered the boy, and included the group. "Sure. Tons are hotter than any of us. But we absolutely can hold our own in the looks department," he said. "It's sort of an axiom of the business that the better-looking an escort is, the more vacant the sex experience for the client. The most classically attractive escorts are not usually all that hot in bed. Many of these guys seem to feel they are there to be looked at and admired, cherished and worshipped. Your job is to become totally involved with our clients. At least for the time they're paying for you."

As the meeting progressed, Derek reiterated everything his private consultations with these men had made clear: that each of them would be providing a service that, although not unique in Hollywood, was going to be the best that could be offered. They were told to throw away the memories of their previous sex-for-sale experiences, or any preconceived ugly ideas of what the sex trade was like. The One Night Stand Agency, as Derek had settled on as a name for his coterie of boys, was going to be a lucrative escort service because it offered more than any other agency in town. Specifically, they were guaranteeing a friendly, fun, safe, discreet, mind-scorching hour of hot man-to-man sex, with no attitude.

Derek explained that their clients were not just getting a quick fuck. He insisted that the boys were not to simply be an unanimated hole that would lie on a bed for someone plow away at. "Sex is the most interactive experience you can have with another human being," Derek said. "You will talk and listen to our clients. You will touch them in ways that they would never get from a street prostitute or even a spouse. And they will be begging to see you again. You'll make certain that nobody will be unhappy with you. I won't charge a client unless he's one hundred percent satisfied."

The boys all looked at each other, telegraphing the same thought, which was that they couldn't possibly ensure a perfect experience for each man with whom they had sex. Derek decoded their facial and body expressions. He, too, knew that one can't please all of the people all of the time. However, he had learned from Marty and Felicia, as well as his own experience as an escort, that as long as the customers were fulfilled, there would never be any trouble.

"The same goes for your enjoyment," Derek said. "I want you to have as equally satisfying an experience as the client, if possible. I won't send you back to someone you didn't feel compatible with. And if one of our clients finds you lacking, I won't withhold your pay as long as you've tried your best to please him. I won't be happy unless you and the client are both pleased," he said. "Now, Juan wants to say a few words."

The men all turned toward the seductive Hispanic wearing a white T-shirt tucked into the waist of his blue jeans. Juan smiled. "Although Derek and I are not playing 'good cop, bad cop'—we're both *good* cops—I have to insist on something important. You have to have a hard-on for your job, or you can get out now. It's one thing to be doing this just for the money. It's another thing to be an escort because you have a boner for genuinely enjoying sex and making clients feel good about themselves and about gay sex."

"That's a good point," Derek interrupted. "This is not about you cumming 24/7, and getting off each and every time. You can take care of your own business in the bathroom."

"You've heard the saying, 'It's about the journey, not the destination,' " Juan said. "Well, putting it bluntly, cumming is of course the destination. You're going to get there eventually, so it's no big fucking deal. This is all about what happens in between. It's important for your clients to cum, and if they want you to also, that's cool. But make it happen for them. They're paying for it."

Derek reentered the discussion. "Sometimes it's important to clients that you get off too," he said. "They might think you haven't enjoyed yourself and that they're not sexually exciting if you don't get off. One of my best clients always insists that before he cums I jerk off until I shoot my load in his mouth. He wants me to straddle his chest, jerk off, then go back to finishing him off. I'm always exhausted by the time I'm done making that man happy!" Derek laughed and the others laughed too.

Another young man raised his hand. Derek nodded his head toward the black kid with the bright white teeth and shaved head. This boy was gym pumped and nipple pierced. His audition had left Derek's ass sore for days. A scar from a knife slashing decorated his chest and gave him an extra aura of danger that would suit a certain William Morris Agency talent rep to perfection. Derek had in fact already made an appointment for the two to have sex this very night. "What if a client wants us to do something that doesn't turn us on?" he asked.

Derek said, "This isn't about what you want. You're not out at a bar cruising for Mr. Right. You're providing a service." To further illustrate his point, Derek said, "When I worked in a restaurant and someone ordered chicken or veal, I didn't react by telling the customer how chickens are wedged into overstuffed cages for shipping. I didn't explain that at the processing centers, while the birds are still alive they're put through machines that simultaneously chop off their beaks and feet. Same with baby calves and the conditions in which they're raised to make veal. In other words, *you* don't decide what to serve your customer based on your personal tastes and principles. In this case, you're serving sex. Raw or medium rare. Whichever way they want it, is how you deliver it."

Juan added, "There are a lot of things that may not turn you on, but may not necessarily turn you off," he said. "You have to make the distinction. For instance, I'm not really turned on by guys who wax their chests, or guys who use those little ball stretcher things that crush your nuts. That stuff doesn't turn me on, necessarily. But it doesn't turn me off either."

Derek added, "There are a lot of things that guys have asked me if I'm *into*. I may not necessarily be into it, but I may be *open* to it. Know what I mean?" he said. "So *open* and *into* are two separate things. And then there's definitely *not* into it. So there has to be three ways of looking at this, otherwise it can really fuck you up. Remember, this is a service business. It's based on making another man happy, and making yourself worth the price they're paying. Be open."

For a moment, the twelve escorts sat in silent contemplation. They thought about sexual fetishes that, from personal experience, they knew they would not be into performing for any amount of money. Then there were the sex acts in which they wouldn't necessarily choose to participate, but to which they would not be opposed should the situation present itself.

"Questions?" Derek said. He looked at each man individually and mentally recalled what their skin had felt like next to his, when he auditioned them for work. He remembered the taste of their tongues on his, and the scent that emanated from their bodies as they perspired during an exhausting workout of sex. He knew that any gay or bisexual man—star or otherwise—who was lucky enough to have one of these boys in his bed, would not be disappointed. They were erotically exciting and as eager to fuck or be fucked, as they were for the money that came with selling their bodies to satisfy the hunger of men.

Another hand was raised. Derek smiled at Hiro. "Um, I know that escort services are targeted by the police," Hiro said. "Was I safer doing this on my own?"

Derek recalled the afternoon that Hiro had fucked him repeatedly in the Malibu Colony. At the time, Derek had thought that Hiro was so hot that he should be selling his Asian dick to the highest bidder. For Derek to later discover that Hiro was amenable to supplementing the income he received as a houseboy to the owner of one of the biggest Ferrari dealerships in the country, was to confirm his gaydar and his sixth sense about what a man will do for sex and money.

Derek took a deep breath. The last thing he wanted was for any of these men to believe that they would be better off escorting over the

Internet or through an ad in *Encounters* or *Frontiers.* "We all want to be our own boss, and not have to be answerable to anyone else," Derek said. "But this is truly the best way for us to all get what we want, which is money and sex. It's doubtful that the police will ever discover that we exist. We're a small outfit, and we won't get any bigger. And, our customers are celebrities who have to be discreet," he said. "No one's going to mess with us. It's a win/win all the way around.

"Also, being with One Night Stand, you're a lot safer than if you fucked around with strangers," Derek said. "There won't be any flakes to deal with who'll waste your time. You'll only get a call when there's an actual job to do. And you won't be harassed by bargain hunters who dick you around to cut your rate. The men who come to us are willing to pay the price, and they don't care how much it costs. And speaking of costs," Derek continued, "working with us, you won't have to spend a dime for Web sites or photos or ads."

Hiro nodded his head, satisfied with the answer. "How about perks, like fucking the boss again," he joked. The other men, including Juan, chuckled.

"My door is always open." Derek smiled, letting Hiro and the others know that they could come to him at any time if there was a problem with a sex client, or if they simply had something they wanted to talk about.

Juan spoke out. "I think everyone should know our policy about webcams," he said, looking at Derek. "They'll never be used, in any way."

Derek said, "Our client base is definitely aware of webcams and the potential they pose to disastrously ruin their careers if a tape of them were ever to get out and be circulated. To make certain that they're completely comfortable with us, you will always meet a client in their own space. Usually their home or a hotel room. Regardless of how well they know and trust me, I will never send them to your space. They might think it's a turn-on to go slumming, but I never want them to look back and have the slightest paranoia. If they want to tape the scene themselves, that's up to them. From my point of view, I would not care if the whole wide world were watching while I fucked. But I know it would be important to our clients."

Derek looked around at the men. He gave a glance toward Juan and raised an eyebrow to silently ask, *What else?*

Juan shrugged his shoulders.

"All right, then," Derek said, "that's it for now. John, you're at the Chateau at seven. Eric, you're at Crescent Drive at midnight. Stevie, you're expected at The Four Seasons for dinner in room twelve thirty-three. Hiro, I've got you set up with You-Know-Who from *Access Hollywood* at eight o'clock. Everybody report in to me within a half hour of completing your assignments. Git! Go take a nap, or work out at the gym, or use your expense account at Macy's, whatever you do to prep for work. And give yourselves time to clean yourselves out, whether you're planning on catching or pitching tonight. We'll talk later. And good luck!"

As the men gathered together in a small knot and headed to the apartment's front door, they talked amongst each other. Derek and Juan overheard bits of conversation, in which each man seemed filled with excitement for their career and for the night's work ahead. "Mine starred with Denzel Washington!" one man bragged to the group about his intended client for the night.

"Mine was bare-assed in one of the touring companies of *The Full Monty*," crowed another.

"I get to fuck in Sean's actual bed tonight!" said another. "I've been hard ever since Derek told me he was the one who I was fucking!"

And then they were gone. Derek and Juan looked at each other and smiled. "We're off and running," Derek said, as he picked up water glasses from the glass-topped coffee table and used a cocktail napkin to wipe away water rings.

"Speaking of 'off and running,'" Juan said, "what are you wearing this evening to Marty and Felicia's going away dinner at Brent's?"

"My new black cashmere turtleneck and a sport coat," Derek said. "Oh, and come over a little early. I've gotta show you the awesome new computer Brent bought me."

"The only thing hard that man's giving you is a disk drive," Juan joked as he took off his shirt *en route* to the shower. "But I'm glad you two are tight again," he called over his shoulder. "Still, are you ever going to get around to his Oscar-winning ass?"

"There'll be a news conference," Derek smiled. "For now, I'm just glad that Brent and I are living together again."

"While you two are cruising the chat rooms on the new computer, and pretending that you don't know that you're both dying for a fuck, I've got to figure out how to get some myself," Juan complained. "I'm practically forced back into the closet because of this new gig. We have to be so covert. That's the part that sucks."

Derek caught up with Juan who was now unbuttoning his jeans as he moved through the hallway. "All this talk about sex, and my not getting any, and Brent teasing me with his game of chastity, is making me nuts," he said. "Everyone, including Felicia—and I suspect Marty too—gets dick, except us." He placed his hands on Juan's chest.

"Whose fault is that," Juan smiled and reached out to clutch Derek's crotch. "Mmm, you really do need it." Juan said, feeling the full load in Derek's pants.

Derek tentatively placed his lips on Juan's and their tongues automatically met.

"Whoa, man," Juan said playfully, and leaned away. "You're not in my appointment book. Anyway, how would you manage to pay for it?"

"Huh?" Derek asked, smiling, but taken aback.

"You said it yourself, 'No freebees, no matter how hot our clients are.' Gotta set a good example for the boys."

Derek grinned, mischievously. "I'll show you a freebee," he said as he pushed Juan down the hall and into the bedroom.

In a moment, Derek and Juan were stripped of their clothes and naked in each other's arms on the bed. "Will this be cash or charge, sir?" Juan asked as he began exploring Derek's chest with his tongue.

"I'll give you a charge," Derek said, blindly reaching for Juan's cock. "Now shut up and give me a demonstration of your product."

For the next hour, Derek and Juan forgot about Brent and Andrew, and their clients and rent boys. All that mattered was that they were horny for each other, and that they were on a fast moving train hurtling toward the destination of an intense climax for both.